Evil Tide
The Five Kingdoms Book VI

by
Toby Neighbors

Evil Tide
© 2013 Toby Neighbors

Published by Mythic Adventure Publishing
Post Falls, Idaho

Copy Editor: Sharon LaValley

Books by Toby Neighbors:

The Five Kingdoms
Wizard Rising
Magic Awakening
Hidden Fire
Crying Havoc
Fierce Loyalty
Evil Tide
Wizard Falling

The Lorik Trilogy
Lorik
Lorik The Protector
Lorik The Defender

The Avondale Series
Avondale
Draggah
Balestone
Arcanius

Other Books
Zompocalypse
Third Prince
Royal Destiny
The New World
The Other Side

Dedication
To my mom, Peggy Lunsford,
For always giving me money for the book fair,
And all the trips to the library,
And letting me browse the book stores,
And for buying me my first word processor,
But most of all for loving me no matter what.

And to Camille, my fellow adventurer in the quest for our dreams
I savor every minute with you.

And to Myles Howard, just because he asked.

Prologue

Willam could see the castle in the distance. It was his boyhood home, the place where he'd grown up and become a man, but he'd never seen it from the air. It looked strong, but ancient, and Willam felt both excitement and fear. The Five Kingdoms were in chaos and after being enchanted by a witch and tortured by a king, Willam, first Prince of Yelsia, was finally coming home. He only hoped that his home would accept him and his news of the events in the south.

An image flashed into his mind; Gyia the graceful purple dragon he was riding on was speaking to him. They had been moving north for a week, covering the distance that would normally have taken two months. Gyia was long and slender, with large wings and a narrow head. She could fly with Willam on her back for nearly an hour before needing to stop and rest. Willam didn't push the dragon. He was no more her master than she was his, but they had bonded, first when they had met on the battlefield near the Grand City in Osla, then on the long trip home. Gyia was intelligent and resourceful; now she was suggesting a suitable place to land.

"That looks good," he said loudly over the whistling wind that raced past them as Gyia glided down toward Orrock with Willam on her back.

The image had been of Gyia landing on the roof of the castle. Willam knew the strong stonework would hold her weight easily enough. They dropped lower and lower, gliding over the sprawling city as they flew toward the castle. Willam couldn't hear the voices below, but he could see the people looking up and pointing at them. He was making a grand entrance, only fitting a future king, but Willam had no desire to impress his subjects. He had considered leaving Gyia a good distance from the city where the dragon could hunt and rest without being subjected to the King's scrutiny, and the circus he was sure Gyia's presence would create with the nobles at court. Still, the young dragon's keen mind and calm demeanor made Willam change his mind. He wanted Gyia with him when he spoke to his father.

They dropped low over the castle now, circling once and then landing gracefully on one of the tall lookout towers. Willam had no idea that only a month before Zollin had fought the massive black dragon Bartoom from that same tower. Gyia settled down on the tower, coiling its long neck and tail around the slender body. The long wings folded neatly and lay flat against the dragon's back. Willam patted the purple neck affectionately and slid down onto his feet. Walking always felt slow and sluggish after flying through the air with Gyia, so Willam flexed his knees and stretched his back once he got his feet on the smooth stones of the tower.

He only had to wait for a moment, then the wooden trap door was flung open and a contingent of the King's Guard scrambled up onto the tower. They stood with weapons ready, their short swords and round shields were as familiar to Willam as the back of his own hand.

"Hail, men," Willam said loudly. "We come in peace. It is I, Prince Willam."

Another head rose up from the wood stairs that led to the top of the tower. Commander Corlis was now a general and in charge of the King's Army in Orrock. He looked around, his eyes wide at the sight of the dragon, but seeing Prince Willam between his men and the beast calmed his nerves somewhat.

"Prince Willam," Corlis said in a haughty tone. "Explain yourself."

"I've returned from Osla," Willam said, "With news. I must see my father at once."

"Of course," Corlis said. "But what of your..." he let the sentence trail off.

"Gyia," Willam explained, "A dragon yes, but one that is loyal to me and who bears no animosity toward us. Gyia is here to help."

"Help with what?"

"There is treacherous news I'm afraid. I must see the King. Should I come down or would it be better if he came here?"

"Under the circumstances I think the King will want to come up. Are you certain your dragon is no threat?" Corlis asked uncertainly, his hand gripping the hilt of his sword.

"Positive, but you can leave your men. I assure you that all is safe for the moment."

Corlis grunted; frowning then disappeared back down into the tower.

"He fears me," hissed Gyia. The dragon could form words, although it was difficult with her long mouth and forked tongue.

"Yes," Willam said. "Give them time. Most of my people have never seen a dragon."

The men on the tower were soldiers, each a veteran, their resolve hardened by dangerous encounters and pitched battles. Still, they were visibly afraid of Gyia. To Prince Willam, the long, serpentine dragon with glistening purple scales was beautiful. Their friendship had grown as they traveled together. Gyia was smart, and although their conversations took the Prince time to get used to, he recognized that the dragon was more than just a powerful beast.

When King Felix hurried onto the roof of the tall castle tower, he was not alone. A group of advisors came with him. They stared wide-eyed at Gyia, even the King, who seemed not to notice his son at all.

"Father," Willam said after a long moment.

"What?" Felix said irritably. "Oh, you're back. Of course I was told that you had come. Forgive me, but seeing you here with a dragon has come as a bit of a shock."

"May I introduce Gyia," Willam said in a flat tone.

"Highness," the dragon hissed.

Gyia's voice was raspy, but soft. Still, King Felix and the other officials with him flinched back at the sound of it.

"Your dragon talks?" Felix said in awe.

"Gyia is not *my* dragon," Willam said. "We are friends."

"I don't understand," King Felix said.

"It's a long story and one that you need to hear. Yelsia is in danger."

"That much we already knew," Felix said. "We were attacked by Osla and Falxis while you were gone."

"Yes, I heard that, but the kings of the south are not the threat I speak of. Gwendolyn the witch is building an army. I know, I was under her spell for a long while and helped her build it."

"I care not what happens in the south. Those traitorous bastards broke the treaty. May their kingdoms fall to ruins for their folly."

"Father," Prince Willam said. "I killed King Oveer. I was captured and tortured by King Zorlan. If not for the Wizard Zollin, I would be dead or a cripple. We cannot ignore the war brewing in the southern kingdoms."

"So, you've come home to lead our people into war, is that it?"

"I've come to help. I've come to protect our people."

"So be it, but you still haven't explained why there is a dragon on my castle."

"Gyia was in a group of dragons with Zollin and the lady Brianna."

"A pride," Gyia hissed.

"Yes, a pride of dragons," Willam corrected himself. "Gyia wants to help us rebuild Yelsia, to make our great kingdom strong again."

"Our kingdom is strong," King Felix said, anger leeching into his voice. "If anyone has said otherwise they were mistaken. We have pushed back the armies of the south. If what you say is true, then King Oveer is no longer a threat. Ricard to the east will not attack us without good cause."

"We must find out what has happened in Osla," Willam argued. "The fate of the Five Kingdoms lies there."

"You give Osla too much credit. We've heard rumors that King Belphan is dead."

"He is, but King Zorlan has taken control of his army. It won't be long before he has either conquered the Grand City or fallen under the witch's spell."

Felix paced across the roof top. His face was pinched in thought as he considered what his son was telling him. Willam thought he looked old, his face more lined, his hair turning dull and gray around the gleaming band of gold that sat snuggly on his head.

"We've heard rumors about a witch," he said after a few moments. "She has power over men."

"Yes," Willam said.

"And if King Zorlan takes the Grand City, he'll be in a position to take over Ortis as well."

"Almost certainly."

"I must think on these events," Felix said. "Your dragon is welcome here as long as she doesn't do any damage."

"Gyia isn't a she," Willam said. "Dragons aren't male or female."

"Fine, the beast can stay but only under your care."

"Of course," Willam said. "I had no doubt of that."

Gyia hissed quietly, not liking the way King Felix seemed to think he could say where the dragon went or what it did. Willam gave the beast an understanding look.

"You're probably hungry," Felix said after another moment of thought.

"We both are," Willam agreed.

"Fine, go and eat. Homan will see that something is brought up for your dragon. Clean yourself up and then come to my quarters. I wish to hear your tale."

"Yes, father," Willam said.

Felix turned and left the tower. His advisors and guards, most still wide-eyed and staring at Gyia, followed the King. Willam waited until he was alone with Gyia, then he approached the massive dragon.

"I'm afraid my father still doesn't have faith in my abilities," he said, trying to hide his shame.

"He is foolish," Gyia hissed. Then she sent a mental image of Willam wearing the crown.

"Yes, some day," Willam said. "Until then I am little more than a servant in my own kingdom, I'm afraid."

"We will have to change that," Gyia said.

* * *

King Felix walked swiftly back down to his domicile, which consisted of a large outer room and several smaller rooms. He threw open the large wooden doors with the images of rearing horses carved in relief. Warmth from the blazing fire washed over him. The nights were growing colder, and the castle's long passageways often grew chilly. He was grateful for the warmth of the fireplace; he hadn't been able to stay warm since he was wounded on the battlefield. His body felt old and tired, but his ambition was stronger than ever.

"This changes things," King Felix said.

"How so, my lord?" General Tolis asked.

"We now have a dragon," the King said happily. "Perhaps we won't have to rely on subterfuge after all."

"My lord, can we really trust the beast?" Tolis asked. "It seemed tame enough, but I wouldn't pin my hopes on a dragon."

"The dragon won't even have to fight," the newly promoted General Corlis said. He was now head of the King's army, second only to King Felix, a fact the other generals bristled at. The brash young commander enjoyed bullying the older men. Corlis had risen fast in the King's Service, and the invasion by the southern kings had sped his career along even faster. King Felix liked the young commander's ambition and his daring ways. The new military strategy they were discussing had been as much Corlis' as it was the King's.

"A dragon flying over our forces," Corlis continued, "will strike fear into every enemy we face. Even if the beast won't fight, it will be the sign of our victory and dominance over the Five Kingdoms."

"There will be only one Kingdom when we are through, gentlemen," King Felix stated. "And one King... Willam's dragon will aid us in any way we see fit."

"My Lord, I hardly think we can command a dragon," General Yennis said. Yennis was an older man, a cautious man, and King Felix despised him.

"We will find a way," King Felix said. "The southern kings somehow convinced the black dragon to attack us."

"They had a wizard," Yennis said.

"They had their asses handed to them," Corlis snarled. "Don't you dare sully the King's plan with you sniveling, sir, or I'll have you removed."

"My Lord," General Tolis said in a placating tone. "It's not that we don't think using the beast is a good idea, we just aren't sure how to do it."

"That's right, my liege," Yennis said, avoiding eye contact with Corlis. "Of course I think it's a good idea."

"We need to find a way to bring the beast under our control," King Felix said, "To ensure that there are no surprises."

"How does one control a dragon?" Yennis inquired. "There hasn't been one in Yelsia in centuries."

"Now there have been two," King Felix said. "And if the rumors are to be believed, there have been more."

"My lord," said Commander Hausey, a stiff, highly disciplined officer from the King's Light Calvary in Felson. "I don't know if there is anything to be learned or not, but we did uncover a trove of ancient scrolls in the Ruins of Arnak. They were sent to Ebbson Keep to be translated and studied."

"Were there writings about dragons?" King Felix asked.

"I'm not certain, my liege, but I do believe so. The scholars at Ebbson were translating the scrolls; I know that much. It might be worth our while to send word to the Keep and have the translations sent back to us."

"That is an excellent idea, Commander. Send someone immediately. I want to know everything that was discovered about dragons in those scrolls."

"Yes, my lord," said Hausey.

He bowed before swiveling on his heel and walking from the room. Hausey was happy to be away from the King and the constant plotting. He was a warrior and would fight whoever his King commanded him to fight, whenever the orders came, but it took all his self-discipline to hide the disgust he felt over the current situation. It was true that Osla and Falxis had attacked the kingdom of Yelsia first, but now King Felix was plotting to do the same and it felt wrong to Hausey. He couldn't help but wonder just how much the arrogant young General Corlis had to do with the whole plan. Corlis had wormed his way into the King's inner circle and had found a way to alienate every other advisor who disagreed with him. Commander Hausey couldn't change the King's mind and didn't want to trade his command for a place in the royal court's inner circle, but he didn't like seeing the king manipulated either.

Back in the King's domicile, King Felix was pacing the floor. He felt an excitement he hadn't experienced in years. He had an opportunity none of his forebears had possessed. The Five Kingdoms were in chaos, and Yelsia was growing stronger by the day.

"We'll need to bolster the army," King Felix said. "How is our conscription faring?"

"Things are improving, my Lord," said General Yennis, who was in charge of pressing men into the King's Army. "We've focused mostly on the displaced farmers and villagers. Most are all too happy to have a position and bit of coin to pass on to their families."

"We'll need more than farmers and shopkeepers," Corlis said.

"We're instituting a training regimen," Yennis hurriedly added. "They'll be armed and battle ready."

"We'll be the judge of that," Corlis snorted. "We must strike while the iron is hot, my lord. The southern kingdoms are weak. We cannot let them rebuild their strength."

"Yes," King Felix said. "That is true. Prince Willam will tell us more, but I don't want him to know our plans. Not until we have the dragon under our control."

"I agree, my lord," said Corlis. "If the beast were to fly away and alert our enemies, there is little we could do to stop it."

"My thoughts exactly," King Felix said. "For now, no more discussion of our plans are to take place outside of this room, is that understood?" The generals and advisors nodded. "Also, I want the training ground moved immediately. Take the new conscripts south. You can recruit as you go, General Yennis. Form your base of command north of the Twin Cities. From there, we can go by sea and bypass the Rejee Desert and the Walheta mountains. If what Prince Willam has said is true, then Falxis is undefended. We can move around the Sea of Kings and take control of Ortis as well."

"King Ricard will join us," General Corlis said. "Once he sees our strength he cannot resist."

"And our dragon," General Tolis said, trying to sound confident but failing.

"The time for change is upon us, my lords," said King Felix cheerfully. "It is time for Yelsia to rise up and take its rightful place among the Five Kingdoms."

The other men in the room all cheered. Then wine was poured and most of the advisors and generals fell into their cups. They enjoyed the plotting and scheming, but very few were keen to start the work involved with a full scale invasion. General Corlis was the lone exception. He sipped his wine slowly, his face hiding the plans that were forming in the back of his mind. King Felix had a vision for a new era in the Five Kingdoms, but Corlis had a vision for a new position for himself.

Chapter 1

The sea was bright blue and reflecting the sunshine. The briny wind filled the ship's sails and blew through Mansel's thick mane of shaggy hair. He and Nycoll had booked passage on a ship sailing north, but the trip had not gone as expected. The Fisherman's Daughter was an older ship and although the captain, a large man named Sorlyn, had seemed honest and decent on shore, once they were at sea, he showed his true colors. The sailors were lazy and barely competent to sail the ship. The captain had taken passengers aboard with lofty promises, but once the ship left the harbor he began to act like a tyrant. He beat his men and cursed them regularly. One of the younger girls on board with her aging merchant father had been lured to Sorlyn's cabin and not seen again. Nycoll and the other passengers on board hid in their cabins. Only Mansel braved the deck and faced down the murderous looks from the sailors.

Captain Sorlyn watched Mansel, who stood on the deck with his sword in hand, guarding the entrance to the passenger cabins. Mansel had no doubt that the Captain and his villainous crew meant to kill him, but he gave them no opportunity. He stood ready each day, and at night he barricaded Nycoll and himself inside their small cabin.

Strong winds pushed the Fisherman's Daughter north quickly; the shoreline of Falxis seemed to fairly fly past them. Mansel was reminded of sailing south with Quinn on their mission to rescue Prince Willam. That had been a difficult trip. This time Mansel had fought his sea sickness with quiet resolve. He wasn't sure if he was growing more accustomed to sailing, or if his worry for Nycoll's safety had somehow strengthened him. Fortunately, he didn't get as sick as he had on previous sea voyages.

Nycoll, for her part, didn't mind staying in the little cabin. She was accustomed to solitude and although she seemed happy with Mansel, she still needed time to adjust to the changes around her. She had lost her home and nearly drowned hiding from the soldiers who were pillaging along the coast of Falxis. Mansel and Zollin had rescued her, but then Brianna appearing with a pride of dragons had been almost too much for her fragile psyche. When Zollin suggested that Mansel take her north, he had reluctantly agreed. He was happy to be with her, but he still felt guilty leaving Zollin alone.

Mansel swung his sword a few times and then rested the cold steel on his shoulder. The sword had been a gift from Zollin. His friend had crafted it with magic and even set a glossy, black stone into the pommel just above the leather wrapped handle. Mansel wasn't sure what the stone was or what Zollin had done to the weapon, but he knew that when he held it, he felt invincible. The sword wasn't light, even though Mansel was strong and accustomed to using a hefty weapon; still, he never seemed to grow tired when working with the long sword. He had named it Death's Eye.

Six days had passed from the time they set sail. The Fisherman's Daughter was making excellent time, despite the poor handling of the crew. Mansel didn't know much about how ships were handled, but he could tell that the sailors on board were average at best. He had watched them at their work, or more accurately he watched them avoid their work. That was how he knew when something was about to happen. The crew, which normally milled about, almost aimlessly seemed tense and more focused on their tasks. Mansel did his best not to let his concern show, but he stayed vigilant for what he knew was going to happen. He had known that the Captain would send men to attack the passengers at some point, which meant they would have to go through him.

It was almost noon when a group of men led by the captain came out from the crew's quarters. They carried weapons, mostly clubs but there were a few rusty cutlasses and a dagger or two. Mansel could tell by how the sailors carried their weapons that they were not fighters, but their numbers made them dangerous.

"We have come to see the passengers," Captain Sorlyn said gruffly. "We've no quarrel with you or your woman, so step aside."

"Tell me what happened to the girl," Mansel replied. "Her father says she's missing?"

"Is that so? Well, I happen to know she's very happy down in the hold with the men. She's providing a very important service."

The sailors chuckled but Mansel felt bile rise in his throat. He'd spent his fair share of time with tavern maids and wenches.

He had no problem with women selling their bodies freely, but a young girl forced into prostitution was wrong.

"I'll make a deal with you," Mansel said. "You lay down your weapons and bring the girl back to her father, and I won't kill you all."

A few of the sailors laughed nervously, but most looked worried.

"You have worn out your welcome on my ship," said Sorlyn. "I think it is time you disembarked."

"We'll have a go at your woman too," said one of the other sailors, a fat man with blackened teeth and ragged clothes.

Mansel didn't reply he just raised his sword and smiled.

"Take him!" the captain ordered.

Two men rushed at Mansel, both had cutlasses, but neither was skilled with a blade. Mansel stepped backward so that the open stairway that led down to the passenger cabins was to his left. One of his attackers had a straight path to Mansel, but the other had to circle around the stairwell.

The first man raised his rusty blade, but Mansel thrust his own sword, which was easily twice as long as the cutlass, straight into the sailor's throat. The sailor tried to scream, but all that came out was a wet, gurgling sob.

Mansel jerked his sword free from where it had lodged in the sailor's neck and with one fluid movement spun around, slashing his sword at the second attacker. The sailor raised his cutlass, but the rusty metal snapped under the blow and the man scurried backward. Mansel turned back toward the group in time to see one of the more vicious looking sailors darting forward with a dagger. Mansel drove his sword tip into the wooden planking and then used the weapon to steady his balance, while he lashed out with a side kick that connected with the attacker's stomach. The dagger was lost as the sailor collapsed onto the deck.

Then, Mansel took the fight to the sailors. He pulled his sword free and spun forward, waving his sword in a wide arc that sent the sailors reeling back. Mansel then targeted the slower men. One stumbled and Mansel brought his sword around in a powerful overhead chop that was aimed at the sailor's head. The desperate man threw his arm up to ward off the blow, but Mansel's sword cleaved the sailor's arm in two, then glanced off his skull, slicing open the side of the man's face and severing his ear.

The man's screams sent most of the attackers running for their lives. Captain Sorlyn turned to escape as well, but Mansel chased him down. With one vicious thrust, he ran his sword through the evil captain's back. The long blade sliced through muscle, organ and bone, to come sticking out the captain's stomach. He wailed and writhed, his bellows echoing off the water around the ship.

"Sailors!" Mansel bellowed. "Sailors, hear me now. Your captain is dying and unless you want to join him you will bring the girl you are holding below decks back to her father and gather here before me now."

The sailors on deck looked at each other, but Mansel merely twisted his sword causing the ship's captain to scream in pain.

"The alternative is death!" Mansel shouted.

The sailors dropped their makeshift weapons and hurried forward. Two went down below the main deck, and after a few moments came hurrying back up into the bright sunlight with the girl. She was bruised, and her clothing was torn. Blood and tears streaked her face. The girl's father had been watching and came hurrying from the passenger cabins. He took his daughter in his arms, picking her up as she wrapped her arms around his neck and sobbed into his shoulder. The merchant gave Mansel an appreciative look and then hurried back down to his cabin.

"I want us put to shore," Mansel told the group of sailors. "I don't care who leads the ship, or what you do once we've been safely landed, but if you try anything, I'll kill you all and take my chances. Do I make myself clear?"

The men nodded.

"Good, no more shirking your tasks; do your work. We should find a place to go to shore before sunset."

The sailors stood looking wide-eyed, first at their dying captain and then Mansel. He put his boot on the captain's back and pulled his blade free. Sorlyn collapsed onto the deck.

"Throw him overboard and the others as well. Then, scrub everything down."

The sailors knuckled their foreheads and fell to work. Mansel waited on deck to ensure that his orders were being carried out. Then, he went down to the cabin he shared with Nycoll. He knocked and waited for her to unlock the door from the inside.

"Who is it?" she asked.

"It's me, Mansel," he said.

He heard the wood scraping as she lifted the heavy cross beam that held the door closed.

"Is everything alright?" she asked; worry plain to see on her face.

"Yes, we'll be landing sometime today and getting off this wretched ship."

"Landing where?" she asked.

"I'm not sure, but I can see the Walheta Mountains, so we must be close to the border. Perhaps we can find a quiet place to make a new home."

Talk of making a new home always seemed to cheer Nycoll. Mansel had always enjoyed being free to wander from town to town, but since Nycoll's home had been destroyed, finding a new one was all she seemed to think about.

"Come up on deck with me."

"I don't want to," she said. "The captain makes me nervous."

"The captain is dead. Please come up and get some fresh air."

She followed him as he climbed back up the stairs to the open deck. The sailors were busy trimming the sails or scrubbing the deck where the blood had stained it. The wind was blowing and Mansel thought the sunshine on Nycoll's delicate skin would do her good.

It was late in the afternoon when the ship finally approached a small harbor. There was several fishing boats in harbor and one rowed out to the ship. Mansel and most of the other passengers chose to leave the Fisherman's Daughter. Mansel watched as the fishing boat rowed them toward the shore. There was a small village on the other side of the rounded, sandy dunes along the beach. He could see the rooftops and softly curling chimney smoke rising into the air.

He smiled at Nycoll and was rewarded with a smile in return. She was a stoic woman, passionate in her own way, but never frivolous. Life had been difficult for her and she found little to amuse her, but she felt hopeful for the first time in weeks. They climbed out of the fishing boat, Mansel carrying their meager possessions in a bag over one shoulder with his long sword in a scabbard that hung from his belt. They followed a path between the dunes and found a small inn with room for them. Soon, they were settled, and Mansel enjoyed a pint of ale with his supper.

The next day, they began to ask about land and finding a place to make a life for themselves. Mansel had apprenticed with Quinn as a carpenter before he had fled Tranaugh Shire, and he could earn a living as a carpenter. He didn't know much about building or repairing boats, but he could learn.

They found an abandoned house on the edge of town.

"This could work," Mansel said, after inspecting the house. "I'll have to repair it, but I think I could make it livable in a day or two."

"We could plant a garden," Nycoll said.

"There's work in the village," Mansel added. "Would you be happy here?"

"The mountains *are* beautiful."

"And we're close to the sea."

"Will it get cold here, you think?"

"Not too bad," Mansel said.

"Okay, let's do it," she said with a smile.

"I like to see you smile," Mansel said, drawing her close. "I'll make you happy; I promise you that."

"You already make me happy," she said. "Promise instead that you won't march off to war."

"I promise," he said, but deep down he hoped that he wouldn't have to break that promise.

Chapter 2

Zollin jumped from Ferno's back just before the dragon belched fire in a devastating attack on the horde of creatures below. The creatures, part horse, part human, with massive scorpion tails, and oval-shaped wings that looked like dragonfly wings, scattered in different directions to avoid the flames.

Zollin used magic to levitate himself slowly toward the ground. His magic swirled inside him, like the current from a hot spring. Lifting himself into the air, or in this case, lowering himself down, was not difficult, even though he was tired. Zollin and the massive green dragon, Ferno, had been traveling steadily north, swinging wide to the east to avoid the Great Sea of Kings. They could have made better time if they didn't stop to fight the monsters released from the Abyss in Osla, but Zollin felt at least partially responsible for the creatures. They had come pouring from the Abyss, which had begun in the Great City and stretched as far as Zollin could see, even when Ferno had flown high up into the air. The creatures attacked humans, impaling them on their stingers and then carrying them back to the Abyss where Gwendolyn the witch waited.

The images of Zollin's fight with Gwendolyn haunted the brief snatches of rest he'd managed to get. Zollin had gone south to fight the Torr, but Gwendolyn had gained a mastery of dark magic in the absence of her former master, and after slaying

Offendorl, she had released her evil hordes on the Five Kingdoms. In some ways, Zollin felt like he was trapped in a bad dream.

His feet had just touched the ground when three of the monstrous beasts came charging straight toward him. Their faces, human with long, flowing hair that streamed out behind them as they ran, were contorted with rage. Zollin let his magic flow out toward the creatures. He had to keep his fear and anger in check to ensure that he didn't over tax himself. He didn't need to use a great amount of magic to kill the creatures. He let his magic flow around the creatures, and then he slammed them together in a bone shattering crash. Two of the creatures survived, but they were injured so badly they couldn't rise from the ground.

Zollin jumped and let his magic propel his body up into the air in a huge, arcing bound. He landed on the strip of scorched earth that Ferno had just engulfed in the dragon's fiery breath. When two more creatures charged toward him, Zollin let two streams of crackling, blue, magical energy shoot out. The energy hit the creatures and burned through to their black hearts, killing them.

Zollin felt his waning strength begin to flag. He used his magic to drive another small group of the beasts into the ground. He could feel their bodies smash under his wave of magic. It reminded him of crushing a bug under a leaf as a child, feeling the shell crunch and the flesh split apart under his fingers. Inside, he felt his magic flaring up like the fire in a smithy's forge. The more magical power he tapped into, the hotter the flames of magic became. He had built a magical containment field around the inner reservoir of magic which allowed him to do great feats of wizardry without it weakening him physically, but the longer he exerted his power, the weaker that containment became. His magic threatened to engulf him if he wasn't careful. The temptation to let his magic take control of him was like water to a man dying of thirst. His magic was fueled by his emotions; it swirled and danced inside him, surging against his containment field like a raging river threatening to spill over its banks.

He tamped down on the magic, calming his raging power and his emotions at the same time. There were more of the centaur like creatures, but they were scattered and it was easier to let Ferno mop them up. The great green dragon was a sight to behold. Its long neck was lined with small horns, and the end of its tail was a thick, bony knob it could use to batter an enemy to a bloody pulp. Ferno was much faster in the air than the creatures from the Abyss. Ferno rose high in the air and then dove, sometimes engulfing his prey in fire or swatting them its massive tail. The creatures lashed out with their scorpion like tails, thrusting their stingers at Ferno whenever the dragon came close. Zollin doubted that the stingers could penetrate the dragon's scales, but Ferno didn't take the chance. Instead, the dragon stayed just out of reach while destroying the wicked creatures.

Once Ferno had taken care of the stragglers, the green dragon turned back toward Zollin. A mental image of a flowing river popped into Zollin's mind. In return, he sent back the image of himself and Ferno drinking from the river. Then, as Ferno swooped toward him, Zollin used his magic to lift himself up into the air and down on Ferno's back.

Zollin settled in with his legs stretched across the dragon's massive shoulders, just in front of the huge, leathery wings. Zollin could reach out and hold onto the short horns that started at the base of Ferno's neck, to hold himself steady as the dragon flew. They rose back up, high in the air and began searching for a place to stop and rest. They soon found a small stream that danced across the countryside. Ferno circled as they came closer to the ground, finally landing gracefully near the ribbon of water. Zollin hopped off Ferno's back, using his magic to steady himself. His leg was still deeply bruised and stiff. He'd been wounded by one of the creatures as he fought them in the Grand City, but he hadn't had the time or the energy to heal himself properly.

He limped over to the stream and dropped onto his knees. The water was cold. He wasn't sure where he was but he guessed he was at somewhere north of Ort City, which was the capital of Ortis. Autumn was now in full swing and the days were growing colder, more so the farther north they traveled. Still, despite the falling temperatures, the cold water was refreshing. He cupped his hands in the water and raised it to his lips, slurping the water into his mouth. Ferno dropped down, sinking its massive maw into the water to drink. Zollin splashed the cold water into his face and ran his wet hands through his hair. He wanted nothing more than a hot meal and soft bed, but he had no time to rest. His mission was too important, and he hated being separated from Brianna. He wanted to finish his task and turn south as soon as possible.

Night was falling when they took to the air again. Zollin had slept briefly while Ferno hunted. The big dragon needed substantial food at least every other day to keep flying with Zollin on its back. Zollin was content to eat the dried meat and stale bread in his pack. His mind was always on the danger that he felt was coming. It was as if someone or something was watching him with evil intent. He had to get to the Northern Highlands and recruit the magical peoples he had encountered on his journeys there. Whatever the vile witch Gwendolyn was up to, he knew it would be deadly unless they were prepared.

They flew through the night and saw no more bands of the centaur-like creatures. The next morning, Zollin was groggy. He had dozed fitfully on Ferno's back, but it was not a restful sleep. It took him several minutes to recognize the feeling that seemed to pulse toward him. At first he thought it was just dizziness from lack of sleep, but soon the repeated waves of magic took shape. They were unlike anything Zollin had experienced before, and they coaxed Ferno toward the source of the magical power.

Soon, they were passing over ruined villages and burned farms. Zollin could see the destruction, and Ferno sent regular mental images of what the dragon could see with its superior vision. The land seemed deserted, almost as if war had already reached the Kingdom of Ortis.

Zollin grew more curious as they approached what looked to be a massive battle and beyond that lay an incredible forest. Ferno circled high in the sky and below them they could see a huge camp. There were tents and fire rings, wagons and what appeared to a throng of captives. There was also a tall, stone watch tower, which was surrounded by warriors with the intent on knocking the ancient structure down.

"Why on earth are they tearing down the tower?" Zollin wondered aloud.

Immediately, the image of a man popped into Zollin's mind. The man looked like a living statue with muscles bulging under his sweat slick skin. The man had two swords and was brimming with a strange magic that was unfamiliar to Zollin, but obviously the source of magic he had been sensing all morning.

"Get us closer," Zollin said.

Ferno dove down in a tight spiral. As they flew closer, Zollin could sense the danger. The watch tower was starting to lean. It would collapse soon; he knew that. He let his magic flow out toward the battle. It was a strange sensation. Hundreds of men were focused on the destruction of the tower, and there were no other combatants. The man on top of the watch tower had taken on the entire army camped below.

Then, the final support beam shattered, and the tower started to fall.

"Save him!" Zollin shouted, but Ferno was already swooping low.

Just as the man on the tower jumped in a vain effort to escape the wreckage of the tower, Ferno's dive leveled and the massive dragon caught the man in its powerful talons. Zollin felt the thrill of terror, and then the man's body sagged as he passed out.

Ferno landed between the army who had destroyed the watch tower and the massive forest. Zollin roused the man.

"Hell of a fight," Zollin said. "I hope we saved the right person."

"Who are you?" the man asked.

"I'm Zollin, Wizard of Yelsia. And this is Ferno," he said, waving to the dragon, who roared so loudly that it shook the ground. Zollin grinned as the man instinctively covered his ears.

"And you are?" Zollin asked.

"I'm Lorik."

"You from Ortis, Lorik?"

"I'm from Hassell Point in the south; on the coast, past the Marshlands. I just volunteered to help guard the border when the king's troops went south."

"So, those are Norsik you were fighting?" Zollin asked.

The army had followed Zollin and Ferno, coming into the clearing between their camp and the forest before they hesitated. They were staring at Ferno in awe, too afraid to continue the attack and too mesmerized to flee.

"Yes, they've invaded and taken a lot of captives. My friends and I rescued a group of nearly a hundred women and children."

"They've got five times that many in chains on the far side of their camp," Zollin said.

"I've got to save them," Lorik said.

"By yourself?"

"If I have to."

"Well..." Zollin said, smiling, "don't make me ask twice."

"Would you help us?" Lorik asked, the doubt evident in his voice.

"I think we could," Zollin said. "Go ahead; show em' what you're made of, Ferno."

The dragon roared again and jumped high in the air. Then, the great green beast's mighty wings flapped hard and propelled the dragon even higher. Zollin watched Lorik, who in turn, watched in awe as the dragon dove and bellowed flame. It took only one pass to scatter the Norsik. Most fled toward the huge forest and some came close enough that Zollin felt compelled to act. He let his magic flow out and sent invisible walls of magical power smashing into several small groups. Most of the Norsik warriors fell and didn't rise.

"Are you doing that?" Lorik asked.

"Yes," Zollin said, focusing on the fleeing raiders.

Zollin had to fight down the feeling of anger that kept creeping into his subconscious. With every warrior that he battered down, he felt the sharp tang of disappointment. He was supposed to be recruiting help to stop Gwendolyn's hordes, not killing Norsik warriors. Still, the groups of captives gave him all the cause he needed to join Lorik's fight. He had heard of the Norsik; they were slavers who raided across the North Sea into Baskla and Ortis, sacking villages and taking captives to sell to the Borian people farther east. He couldn't stand by and let the Norsik take innocent people as slaves from the Five Kingdoms. Neither could he recruit such an army to fight against the witch's forces.

It took less than five minutes to clear the plain of raiders. Ferno turned the field between the camp and the forest into a charred plain, but the fierce dragon didn't fly too close to the massive trees of the forest. It was almost as if Ferno feared something in the dark woods.

The Norsik broke and fled; there was no sign of any resistance. They abandoned everything; all they had pillaged and all the slaves they had captured. Lorik looked at Zollin.

"I can't thank you enough," he said.

"I have news, and most of it isn't good," Zollin said. "Why don't you rest here while I go see about freeing those captives?"

"All right," Lorik agreed.

Zollin turned and then began to rise up into the air. He could sense the surprise from Lorik, but he ignored it. Ferno swooped down underneath Zollin and they flew back across the wide camp toward the captives, who were mostly women and children.

"Better not get too close," Zollin said. "We don't want to frighten them."

An image of Ferno circling overhead while Zollin floated down came into his mind.

"Good idea. Make sure there isn't anyone else who might try to hurt these people nearby."

Zollin gathered his legs under him and then Ferno turned, tiling the massive, scaly body so that Zollin could jump away from the dragon. For a second, Zollin felt the terror of falling, and then his magic formed an invisible bubble around him and slowed his descent. He landed gracefully on the ground near the captives who were obviously in shock. He let his magic flow out until he could feel the ropes and chains that held the women in place. It took a massive effort to affect the bonds of all the captives at once, but he succeeded in shattering them.

"You are free," Zollin shouted. "You are free and safe. The Norsik have fled. Find yourselves food, water, and shelter."

There were nods and few of the women managed to say thank you, but Zollin was already rising back up in the air. The women and children watched in awe as Ferno swooped under Zollin again. They flew back toward the forest and Zollin sensed there was more in the massive trees than just birds. He couldn't see anything and he was tempted to let his magic flow toward the forest, but then he remembered what had happened when he let his magic into the ocean and decided not to take the chance.

He soothed Ferno who wasn't anxious to get any closer to the massive forest. At first, Zollin thought the size of the trees to be so intimidating. The trees were huge, both is in girth and in height. Zollin had never seen such massive trees, and he couldn't help but wonder what his father could make with wood milled from the huge forest. They came back to where Lorik stood and found that there was another man and woman with him. Zollin studied Lorik, taking in the light-colored clothing and the strange swords. Lorik had the beginnings of a beard and shaggy hair, but he also had kindness in his eyes. Zollin could tell that Lorik would do anything to protect the people around him, and a large group of wide-eyed women and children were emerging from the forest behind Lorik. They watched as Ferno landed. The dragon growled and then curled itself up, resting on the ground behind Zollin. The women and children behind Lorik were fearful at first, but slowly they came out of the trees to get a better look.

Zollin walked slowly, favoring one leg as he moved over to where Lorik waited with the other man and woman. The man was smaller than Lorik, not short but thin and wiry, much like Zollin's father, Quinn. He wore twin sheaths slung low on his hips, although there was only one knife visible. Zollin could feel the pain radiating from the man's knee, although he showed no outward sign of injury.

The woman had an air of confidence and pride. She was pretty in a way, with knowing eyes that seemed to see deep inside of Zollin. She had an open, friendly look, but there were traces of pain and fear in her face too. Her clothes were tattered, and there were marks on her wrists from where ropes had worn the skin raw.

"Zollin, meet Vera and Stone, my very best friends," Lorik said.

"It's nice to meet you both," Zollin said. "I wish I were here under more pleasant circumstances."

"You're a wizard, huh?" Stone said, his voice cynical.

"Liam!" Vera said.

Zollin just smiled and raised his hand, letting his magic flow out and engulf the smaller man. Stone rose slowly into the air and began thrashing and shouting.

"Hey!" he roared. "Let me down! Put me down!"

The children watching from the trees laughed as Zollin lowered Stone gently to the ground. Stone hobbled to keep his balance on his injured leg. Zollin focused his magic on the injured knee. He could tell at once that the ligaments in the knee were severed, although enough time had passed that they were beginning to grow into the surrounding tissue. Zollin knew that if he didn't do something, the smaller man would be crippled for life. He began to repair the damage, melting the scar tissue and reconnecting the tendons and ligaments.

Stone grabbed onto Lorik's shoulder, obviously expecting the pain in his knee to intensify, but instead it dulled and after a moment, it disappeared altogether. It was a relatively quick fix for the young wizard, but one that took all his concentration. When he was finished, Zollin took a deep breath, as if he were coming up out deep water.

"Believe me now?" Zollin said with a smile.

"I never doubted you," Stone said, trying to smooth his clothes, but there was a look of excitement and relief on his face. "What did you do to my knee?"

"Try it out?" Zollin said.

Stone put his weight on the leg, but instead of pain it felt strong. He bent the knee and then lowered his body down into a squat and straightened back up.

"It's fine," he said. "I can't believe it. You did something to my knee."

Zollin just smiled.

"We are very pleased to meet you," Vera said. "And it is a great honor to see your dragon, no matter what the circumstances."

"Oh, that's Ferno, but he isn't mine. I'm more of *his* pet project. It's a long story, but one for another time. Right now, I need to tell you what has happened in Osla."

"Osla?" Lorik said. "How does that concern us?"

"Well, for one, your King and most of his army were destroyed there. I'm afraid King Oveer came under the power of a very evil witch. She led your King away and forced him to bring along all his troops, which is why your border was left unprotected, I suspect."

"Why?" Vera asked. "What is going on?"

"When King Belphan and King Zorlan attacked Yelsia, Osla was left undefended," Zollin explained. "Your King Oveer was supposed to lead his army north, join with the Basklan army and attack Yelsia from the east. Along the way he fell under the witch's spell. I went south to confront the Master of the Torr, and we were both attacked by the witch. She has delved into some very dark magic, and I'm afraid she's unleashed a terrible horde of monsters on the Five Kingdoms. I'm looking for people to fight this evil and help those who need it. The Yelsian army and what's left of the army from Falxis are going to make a stand at the Walheta mountain range. I'm going to try to convince King Ricard to bring his troops south and hopefully stand with you here, along the border."

"What about the people in the southern part of the kingdom?" Lorik asked.

"I'm afraid many of them are already lost," Zollin said. "The creatures that the witch unleashed are capturing people and carrying them back to Osla, where she is building an army."

"And you think that army will come here?" Vera asked.

"I fear so," Zollin said. "I can't be sure of who or what exactly is coming this way, but I am certain the witch intends to rule all of the Five Kingdoms. I've got to stop her, but I can't do it alone. Can you help?"

"Of course," Lorik said. "You saved us today. The whole of northern Ortis owes you a debt we cannot repay."

"No," Zollin said. "I think you could handle the Norsik. I'm hoping that with a little help you can fight whatever the witch sends against you. But you don't owe me anything. I would stay and help you, but I have to move on. I have to warn King Ricard, and then I'm going to the Northern Highlands to find more help."

"I'm not sure what we can do, but we will spread the word," Lorik said. "If King Ricard will join us, we'll make a stand here at the Wilderlands."

"That's good enough for me," Zollin said. "If I get a chance, I'll come back this way."

"We would like that," Lorik said.

"Very much," Vera added.

"Consider it done," Zollin said.

He walked over to where Ferno was waiting and rose up in the air in one smooth, effortless motion and then descended gracefully onto the dragon's back. He waved and then they were in the air, Ferno flapping its leather wings in powerful strokes that carried them high up into the sky just as the sun cast orange light across the massive forest. Zollin looked and in the distance saw a tree that rose above the others in the massive forest. It was a mountain of a tree, and Zollin felt magic radiating out from it like a bonfire shining in the night. The magic was different than his own, more protective, more secret. He could tell right away that it was the same power that filled Lorik, but it wasn't welcoming to him, so he decided to fly around the forest.

"Why don't we go around these woods," Zollin suggested.

Ferno growled a reply that Zollin recognized as affirmation. Then they sped away from the scene of the battle toward the setting sun.

Chapter 3

Brianna fought to keep the frustration she felt from the dragons that still remained with her. She was glad that Ferno had gone with Zollin, but she felt as if the pride of dragons was vulnerable split up as they were. She worried about the reception Gyia would have in Orrock as well. She didn't know Prince Willam well, although refusing to allow Gyia to go with the crown prince never entered Brianna's mind. She didn't control the dragons and would never dictate what they could or couldn't do, but she couldn't help but worry about them the way a mother worries about her children. The pride wasn't the only issue on her mind; she was concerned about Mansel. She knew her old friend could take care of himself in most instances, but with the creatures from the abyss spreading across Falxis like a wildfire, she worried that he would get overwhelmed.

She had searched for Mansel as she traveled north, but even with her Dragon vision she didn't see him. She knew Mansel was taking Nycoll somewhere to start a new life, and she had hoped that she would run across them so she could warn them. However, once she crossed the Walheta Mountains, she knew she had missed him.

Selix, the huge golden dragon she was riding on as they flew toward Felson, shook slightly and then let orange and yellow flames roll back over both dragon and rider. The heat felt good to Brianna, even though it singed her clothes. It would have burned anyone else, but Brianna was dragon kind; she could produce fire at will and was impervious to the heat. Unfortunately, her clothes were not, but Tig, the much smaller blue dragon carried a pack that contained food and extra clothing for Brianna. They flew together, swooping back and forth playfully. Selix could carry Brianna throughout the day, but they stopped occasionally in isolated areas, so the dragons could hunt and rest.

It was nearly ten days since she had left Zollin, and Brianna missed him more each day. Her heart still pounded when she thought of him, just as it had done the day he revealed his powers to her in their small village. She wondered what he was doing, as she urged the dragons to fly higher into the sky. In the distance, Brianna could just make out the watch tower in Felson, and she didn't want anyone to see the dragons as they flew.

Felson was a major city on Weaver's Road with the King's Calvary stationed just outside the city where they could easily be deployed in any direction. Brianna wasn't worried about the army or the people of the city, for that matter. They weren't a danger to her dragons, but she didn't want to alarm them for no reason. She didn't have time to explain her powers or the nature of the dragons, but she did need to stop. She wanted to speak to Zollin's father, Quinn.

The dragons circled high the air, letting Brianna watch the small home and barns where Miriam, the animal healer that Quinn had fallen in love with, worked. She could see animals in the corral and people moving about the yard. With her enhanced eyesight she could make out tiny details far below, but she couldn't see Quinn. They waited, flying around and around for nearly an hour. It was almost twilight when he finally arrived. Brianna and the dragons watched as he came walking toward the house. He led a horse which was pulling a small, two wheeled cart. Quinn led the horse into the barn, and it was dark when he finally came back out. He had just started back across the yard toward the house when Brianna slipped off Selix's back and glided toward the ground far below.

Brianna couldn't fly per se, but she flipped and twirled on the invisible currents of air, gliding lower and lower, until finally, she landed gracefully in the yard behind the house. She looked around, her eyes seeing well in the darkness. No one was around, and it appeared that no one had seen her descend. She went to the door of the house and knocked gently. There was movement inside and a moment later, the door swung open. Quinn raised his lamp high to see out into the dark yard.

"Oh my god," he declared. "Brianna! What a surprise to see you girl. Get in here!"

He pulled her into a one armed embrace, his other hand still holding the light over his head.

"You're not alone, are you? Where's Zollin?"

"It's just me."

"You didn't find him?" Quinn asked, his voice tight with worry.

"I did find him and Mansel too. It's a long story."

"Well, come in, come in," he said, pulling her into the house and closing the door behind her. "We're just about to sit down to dinner. I'll open a bottle of wine."

They walked past the bedrooms and into the open kitchen. A young girl was stirring a pan of vegetables that were sizzling and popping. Miriam was pouring ale over a skewer with two plump chickens that were roasting over the open fire.

"Oh my," she said when she saw Brianna.

"Hello Miriam," Brianna said.

"Well met, Brianna; it's wonderful to see you. What a surprise!"

Brianna could tell that the greeting was forced. There was a tension between Miriam and Quinn that Brianna hadn't expected.

"Yes, it is wonderful to see you too."

"Are your dragons here as well?" Miriam asked.

"No," Brianna said with a smile. "The pride is divided. Those that remain with me are waiting overhead."

"Won't they grow tired?" Miriam said with a frown. "I'm sure they could find a place in the yard."

"They would probably just eat your patients," Brianna said with a giggle. "They won't grow tired. They can coast on the currents of air the way a duck floats on water."

"But a duck's legs are always moving," Quinn said lightheartedly. "You can't see them, but they're always paddling away below."

"The pride is fine for now. They will let me know if they need rest."

"That is truly astonishing," Miriam said. "My work would be so much easier if I could communicate with the animals."

"You can in a way, ma'am," said the girl, who was lifting the pan off the small stove. "The animals always seem to tell you what's ailing them."

"She's right," Quinn said. "You're a gifted healer."

"Thank you," Miriam said, turning back to the chickens.

Brianna caught a note of bitterness in the older woman's voice but couldn't understand why. She and Quinn had seemed as happy as infatuated teenagers when she had last seen them and that had been just under a month before. Still, it seemed their passion for one another was growing cold just like the autumn weather.

"Here, have a seat and I'll fix some wine," Quinn said, suddenly anxious to find something to do. "Tell us your story."

"It isn't a pleasant story," Brianna said. "Evil is spreading across the Five Kingdoms."

"Cora," Miriam said to the young girl. "Fix your plate and go to your room. There's no need to burden yourself with our business."

"Yes, ma'am," said the girl.

Brianna thought the young woman had a sweetness that reminded her of the sisters Brianna had left in Tranaugh Shire. She watched the young girl go, while trying to guess her age. She waited until Cora had left the room to speak again.

"She's sweet," Brianna said.

"Aye," Quinn said, "sweet but prickly. You don't want to get on her bad side."

"She's had a hard life, Quinn," Miriam scolded. "We can't imagine what it must be like to be orphaned."

"No," Quinn agreed. "And I think she's an amazing young woman."

"You took her in?" Brianna asked.

"We've had a bevy of orphans rotating through," Quinn said. "It seems Miriam has a soft spot for the broken, be it man or beast."

"Forgive me for having a heart," Miriam said coldly.

"No one would blame you for helping orphans," Quinn said. "But that's not the only way to help people."

"I don't want to fight with you again," Miriam said.

"Nor, do I," Quinn agreed turning to Brianna. "Tell us what has happened in the south."

"I found Zollin and Mansel. They were tracking King Zorlan, who was leading an army south to Osla."

"We heard that King Belphan was killed," Quinn said.

"Yes, well, Zorlan thought to take the throne in the Grand City, but the witch beat him to it."

"Damn!" Quinn said.

"She had Prince Willam under her spell as well as the King of Ortis. Willam led the Ortisian army against Zorlan but was defeated. We found him just north of the Grand City. Zorlan had him tortured for information."

"The crown prince of Yelsia?" Miriam asked in shock. "Tortured?"

"That's right," Brianna continued. "Zollin healed him and Gyia insisted on flying back to Orrock with him. Zollin and I continued south."

"What about Mansel?" Quinn asked.

"He and Nycoll turned north. I was hoping to find him when I returned, but I was unsuccessful."

"But he's alright, isn't he?"

"I don't know," Brianna said. "Zollin and I found the Grand City under siege. We attacked the witch in the tower of the Torr, but she escaped and used powerful dark magic. It opened a great crevasse and released hoards of creatures from the underworld."

"It's like a nightmare," Miriam said.

"Yes, it really is. The witch is raising a wicked army and our only hope of survival is to make a stand, south of the Walheta. I am going to Orrock now to convince the King."

"What of Zollin?" Quinn asked.

"He is going around the Great Sea to recruit King Ricard to our cause. Then he will go back into the Northern Highlands to try and convince the magical creatures there to come and fight with us."

"Good god, is it really that bad?" Quinn asked.

"Three of the Five Kingdoms are lost," Brianna said solemnly. "Our only hope is to come together and fight whatever army the witch raises. I'm afraid we can do little more than protect Yelsia for now."

"And you?" Quinn quizzed. "What are you going to do?"

"I'll fight alongside my pride," Brianna said.

He nodded.

"What of the wizard who attacked Orrock with the black dragon?"

"He was slain by the witch. Bartoom fled south; I don't know where exactly."

Quinn sat twisting the bottle of wine he had brought to the small, wooden table. He had completely forgotten to open it. His face was a frown of worry.

"So an army marches north," he said.

"It will soon," Brianna said. "The witch released retched creatures that are capturing people and returning them to her. She will transform those innocents into something awful to serve as her foot soldiers. When she has enough people, she'll move north."

"What kind of creatures could capture enough people to make an army?" Miriam asked.

"I don't know what they are," Brianna explained. "They have the body of a horse, four legs, hooves, and even wings along their back, but where the horse's neck should be, there is instead, the body and head of a man. They have long hair and pointed teeth. Their fingers are like eagle talons. For a tail, they have huge scorpion tails with stingers."

Miriam shuttered.

"They impale their victims," Brianna continued, "with their stingers and then carry them back to Gwendolyn. I don't know if the people they attack are dead or alive, but it wouldn't surprise me if the witch can transform the dead into a hideous army."

"So there will be a war," Quinn said, standing and beginning to pace.

"I'm afraid so."

"And Mansel was caught by these beasts, you think?"

"I don't know," Brianna said. "I know he and Nycoll planned to head north, and we left them in a village by the sea. If they booked passage on a ship, they may have been spared."

Quinn grunted but didn't speak.

"What can we do?" Miriam asked.

"Whatever you can to prepare for war," Brianna said. "That's not why I came here though."

"Why did you come?" Miriam asked.

"She wants me to find Mansel," Quinn said sternly.

"What? That's absurd," Miriam said angrily. "If she couldn't find Mansel, how do you hope to find him?"

"I don't know," Quinn said.

"Surely you're mistaken," Miriam said as she turned to Brianna. "Tell him he's lost his mind. Tell him why you've really come."

"He's right," Brianna said. "I've no right to ask it and there's no guarantee that Mansel is even still alive, but there's a chance."

"Well, why don't you go look for him?" Miriam stated, her voice loud now and angry. "There's nothing we can do."

"I would if I could," Brianna said. "But I must see that King Felix raises the army and marches south."

"This is outrageous," Miriam said. "You can't seriously be considering this, Quinn. I know we've had our differences but if what she is saying is true, you'll be riding to your death."

"I can't turn my back on Mansel," Quinn said.

"Mansel made his choice," Miriam said so loudly she was almost shouting. "You are needed here."

"We've had this discussion, Miriam. I'm not a healer, I'm a fighter."

"You can't go," she said. "You'll be lost. Zollin would never forgive you."

"Zollin knows the risks," Quinn said. "He's out risking his life everyday while I sit here getting fat and lazy."

"Don't, please," Miriam said.

"I'm sorry," Brianna said. "I didn't mean to drive a wedge between you. I'm sure Mansel can look after himself."

"But he doesn't know what's coming, does he?" Quinn said.

"No," Brianna affirmed.

Miriam burst into tears. Her face was still comely despite her age, but now it was a mask of lines and tears. She folded her arms on the table and laid her head down, sobbing.

"I can't stay," Quinn said softly. "I thought I could. I wanted to, but I can't. It simply isn't in my heart to stay."

"You'll be killed," Miriam managed to say.

"Aye, you're probably right. But I have to go, just the same."

Chapter 4

Baskla was a kingdom of steep hills and thick foliage. Wildlife was abundant and while there were farms here and there, most of the people hunted or fished to provide for their families. Zollin had never traveled to Baskla, but he felt a certain kinship to the people there. Yelsia and Baskla were the northern kingdoms and close allies. Zollin only hoped King Ricard would believe his story and commit his resources to the fight.

Forxam was the capital; Zollin and Ferno glided above the city which was built partially into the side of one of the steep hills. The gray stones and red tiled roofs seemed out of place surrounded by what looked like overgrown forest. Zollin could see the people watching him as he circled. He would have liked for Ferno to be able to land so they could greet King Ricard together, but Ferno needed to hunt and Zollin knew that landing in the middle of the city on a dragon would be more trouble than it was worth.

"Hunt," he shouted to Ferno. "I'll call for you once things are settled."

The green dragon shuttered and a low growl rumbled from the beast's thick chest causing smoke to pour from between the razor sharp teeth.

"No, I'll be fine," Zollin reassured the dragon. "You go on."

Ferno swooped downward until Zollin and the dragon were only a few hundred feet above the castle. Then, Zollin lifted himself magically. It was much like holding a heavy object at arm's length. Zollin's power was strong and his mental concentration was improving each day, so levitating himself or another object wasn't difficult, but it did tax his strength. He could feel the heat of his magic washing through him as he drifted down.

He looked up to see Ferno flying away. The green dragon was a magnificent creature. Zollin had always enjoyed seeing horses run; their graceful strides and rolling muscles were a sight to behold. But compared to Ferno, horses seemed as puny and insignificant as small dogs. Ferno's tail lashed as the great leathery wings propelled the dragon's huge body higher and higher.

Zollin looked down to see soldiers forming a circle around where he would land. He thought of moving himself around just to watch the soldiers scramble to keep up with him, but he didn't want to antagonize anyone. The soldiers had ornate looking pikes, each on a staff that was nearly twice as long as a tall man. The blades were thick and polished to a high gleam, and the spike, which was curved slightly, looked honed to needle sharpness.

"Who goes there?" asked a man with a high-pitched voice.

It was one of the soldiers, obviously frightened. Zollin let a sense of calmness, trust, and peace flow out with his magic.

"I mean you no harm," Zollin said. "My name is Zollin, Wizard of Yelsia. I've come to speak to King Ricard."

The soldiers looked at each other nervously, but they soon relaxed visibly. Then the man with the high pitched voice spoke again. Zollin guessed he was the senior officer of the group.

"Drusy, run and tell the King's steward that a... a wizard is here to see the King."

"Aye, sir," said the man named Drusy. Zollin watched as the soldier turned and hurried into the castle.

Zollin looked around. He had landed on what he thought of as courtyard, but it was actually the roof of a large, square structure. Not far away, rising from the craggy hillside was a round tower. There were covered walkways carved into the side of the hill that reminded Zollin of the dwarf cities he'd seen under the mountains of the Northern Highlands. Below them, more buildings were fixed to the rocky side of the hill and below that, sprawling into the valley, were houses, shops, barns, and taverns. People walked up the steep streets, many leading donkeys or mules laden with goods. Zollin could see a market that was laid out along three tiers, like broad steps, that divided the mountain fortress from the sprawling city below.

"How did you know the King was here?" asked the officer with the high pitched voice.

"Lucky guess," Zollin said.

"Or some dark sorcery, I'd imagine."

"No," Zollin said, suppressing a smile, "nothing that nefarious; I assure you."

"Wizards and sorcerers are demon lovers, my old mother used to say. She told the most frightening stories when I was a boy."

"I'm sorry," Zollin said.

"Do you steal souls?"

"No," Zollin said.

"But you commune with demon spirits, don't you?"

"No," Zollin said. "I do not. I'm just a man, like you."

"Not like us," the officer said. "We don't ride dragons and fly, do we?"

"Perhaps not," Zollin said. "And under normal circumstances neither do I, but unfortunately these are not normal times."

"Indeed, they're not," the soldier said.

Just then a group of people came out of the tower, led by the soldier named Drusy. Zollin recognized King Ricard, although he had never seen the man before. Ricard was a barrel-chested man, with only a ring of silver hair around his ears and the back of his head. He had a neatly groomed beard and a large, round nose. He wore woolen pants tucked into tall boots that were polished to a high shine. A fur-lined cap draped over his shoulders and hung down to his calves.

The men around King Ricard looked nervous. They were all armed, but Zollin could tell that the weapons were merely ceremonial. He guessed they were the King's advisors. Zollin bowed as the group approached.

"King Ricard, I come with news from the south."

"So, the rumors of a dragon are true?" he asked. "My men say it was green, not black."

"Ah, yes, Ferno is a green dragon and my companion on this endeavor. Is there a place where we can talk?"

"I don't normally meet with men I don't know and certainly never alone," the King said.

"Of course, I merely meant that my story is long, and I thought we might find a more comfortable place than standing in the sunshine."

"The sun is warm and welcome," the King said. "You better start your story before I decide if I want to hear more."

"Alright," Zollin said, having to work at staying calm. "As you must know, the armies from Osla and Falxis invaded Yelsia."

"Yes," King Ricard said, his eyes narrowing.

"As I understand it, King Oveer was to bring his troops north and join you in an invasion from the east."

King Ricard looked at Zollin with a withering gaze that would have cowed most men. Zollin just kept talking.

"Oveer did not make his rendezvous because he came under the power of a sorceress named Gwendolyn. She bewitched King Oveer and led his armies south, into Osla!"

"What? Why?"

"Gwendolyn was part of the Torr. She knew that Offendorl had gone north with the armies from Osla and Falxis. I suspect she wanted to overthrow her master and gain his power."

"Alright, you've convinced me," Ricard said. "Jorvin, take our guest inside and see that he has refreshment. I'll join you both very soon."

"Aye, my lord," said one of the men nearby.

Zollin bowed again and followed the man into the tower. He was taken to a well-appointed room and given warm towels, a large basin, and a pitcher of hot water. There was a full length mirror in the room and a folding shade that blocked the corner of the room from view. Zollin took the water and towels into the corner where he found a table. He stripped out of his grimy clothes and bathed himself with the hot water.

"My lord, I have clean clothes if you would like them," said Jorvin, who was obviously a servant.

"Thank you, I would like them."

"Shall I send your clothes down to be washed, my lord?"

"I'm not a lord," said Zollin. "And no, you can throw them into the fire; there's no need to clean them."

"As you wish."

When Zollin came out from behind the screen, he found that fruit, bread, and cheese had been laid out on the low table between the room's comfortable chairs. There was also wine. Zollin helped himself, pouring a large goblet of wine and devouring the food. He knew he wouldn't have time to eat once the King arrived. He would be riddled with questions, and he didn't want to waste time.

He had finished most of the light fare and had drunk half of the wine when the King entered, along with his retinue of advisors.

"I hope you feel we have treated you well," King Ricard said.

"You are too kind," Zollin said. "Thank for the clothes and the food. It is a welcome change."

"Are you refreshed enough to continue your story?"

"I am, but I promise you this more than just a story; it's an accurate report."

"Alright," said the King. "Tell us more."

Zollin told how King Zorlan marched south to overthrow Osla and of the great battle in the Grand City. He told of Gwendolyn's dark magic and of the creatures that had come pouring out of the great crevasse that now divided the kingdom of Osla.

"This story is becoming a little too fantastic to believe," King Ricard said, holding up his hand.

"Please believe me, my lord," Zollin said. "I only want to help."

"And how do you plan to help?"

"Gwendolyn is raising an army. Her monsters are carrying innocent people back to her refuge deep underground. She is using dark magic to transform those people into her soldiers. They will march north soon. I am going to gather what help I can from the Northern Highlands. King Felix will take his forces south and join with the remnants of King Zorlan's army on the southern side of Walheta Mountains. If you could take your army south and join with the volunteers from Ortis, you may be able to hold your border."

King Ricard laughed. Zollin looked surprised, but the men with King Ricard joined him in laughter. After a few moments, the King wiped his eyes and spoke.

"You really expect me to just take your word and march south? What kind of fool do you take me for?"

"My lord, I come only to warn you of what is coming. What you do with that information is for you to decide. Evil is spreading across the Five Kingdoms, and my only hope is to turn back that tide of darkness."

"You are a grand story teller, I'll not deny it."

"My lord, I implore you, send scouts to the south; they will confirm my story. You must not allow the witch to overrun your borders."

"I was in the Grand City when the wizard of the Torr told me a similar story about a dragon and wizard from Yelsia. He said you were the one who was out of control."

"It's true; I resisted the Torr," Zollin said. "They sent wizards and mercenaries to my village when I was just discovering my power. Those same wizards tried to kill me when I wouldn't surrender to them. They killed people close to me and chased me into the mountains. They sent assassins and even convinced Prince Simmeron to send a legion of the King's soldiers to capture me. There was a dragon, a great black beast bent on destroying everyone in its path. But my only aim throughout all these events has been to protect the people I love."

"Spoken like an honest man," King Ricard said. "So I will be honest with you. I don't trust wizards. If what you say about the Torr is true, perhaps we're better off. I'm a simple king with only one aim, to protect the people of Baskla."

"Then send your armies south," Zollin said.

"How do I know you haven't been sent by King Felix to trick me into leaving our border undefended?"

"Why would King Felix want to invade Baskla?"

"You said yourself we were prepared to invade Yelsia."

"That may be true, but you did not invade. I cannot speak for King Felix, but I know that Prince Willam is on our side."

"Prince Willam, the spy master? It was his folly that allowed this idiocy to start in the first place."

"No, it was Offendorl's greed for my power," Zollin argued.

"Even if you're telling the truth, how can I know that Yelsia won't swoop in and gobble up the other kingdoms once this witch is defeated? You call yourself the Wizard of Yelsia, but as I recall, the peace of the Five Kingdoms was based on the principle that no kingdom would have a wizard."

"King Felix doesn't control me," Zollin said.

"Perhaps, but I doubt a loyal subject could turn his back on his own country."

"No," Zollin said. "I could not, nor could I use my powers to further a king's vain pursuits, not even my own."

"Well said," King Ricard stated. "I find your story difficult to believe, but I agree with you. If you are telling the truth, your plan is sound. I can promise you no more than to say I will investigate your story."

"That is all I ask, my lord."

"Then it is settled. Now, for more pleasant matters. You will stay for dinner, won't you?"

"I can, if it pleases you, my liege, but I must leave tonight."

"And will your dragon pay us a visit?"

"Ferno isn't *my* dragon. They are intelligent creatures. They can communicate and reason much like we do."

"Fascinating," the King said. "I would like to meet this Ferno."

"I shall arrange it, my lord."

Good, I'll let you rest. My counselors and I have much to discuss, as you might imagine."

"Thank you, King Ricard."

Zollin stood stiffly as he watched the King's retinue follow him out of the room. There were still a few hours before nightfall. He sent his magic out, like a fisherman flinging a net. He soon felt Ferno, swooping gleefully toward an opening in the trees. An image of a fat boar trotting into the open space, its snout almost down to the ground, oblivious to the danger above, popped into Zollin's head. He closed his eyes and saw almost as though he were the dragon as Ferno swooped down and snatched up the boar with its talons. The dragon's wings flapped, and Ferno shot up into the air above the tree line. Ferno flicked its talons, and the boar flipped up in front of the dragon. The beast's head shot out like a viper striking its prey. The razor sharp teeth sank deep into the boar's flesh, and Zollin was filled with a sense of joy that was both overwhelming and unpretentious.

Zollin drew his power back in and moved to a thickly padded lounge chair. He stretched himself across the bench and closed his eyes. He saw Brianna's face rise up in his mind; her delicate features contrasting with her fierce determination. He savored every detail until he drifted off to sleep.

Chapter 5

Dinner was a spectacle; there were singers and acrobats, artists painted on huge canvases, and dancers twirled around the room. The feasting hall was a large, open room with a raised platform on one end where a long table was set up with chairs along the back side. King Ricard had six daughters, and he made sure their meals were as entertaining as possible. There were nobles and advisors at the dinner too, but Zollin noticed that very little work was being done by the diners. Everyone seemed to huddle in small groups in order to be heard over the noise. Zollin was seated next to King Ricard; their chairs were very close and servants brought food, ale, and wine from the behind the guests, pouring drinks over their shoulders.

Zollin was never comfortable being the center of attention, and he had been afraid that he would be forced to entertain the dinner guests with stories of his adventures. Thankfully, in Zollin's opinion, no one seemed to even notice he was there other than King Ricard.

"My wife died during childbirth with our last daughter," Ricard explained. "We don't hold a very formal court here in Baskla, I'm afraid."

"That's quite alright," Zollin confessed. "I prefer less formality."

"King Felix likes a little pomp and circumstance when he entertains guests, as I recall. It has been a while since I was in his Orrock."

"Much has changed, I'm afraid."

"What do you mean?"

"Prince Simmeron has been removed from court for poisoning his father," Zollin said. "King Felix is a difficult man to understand."

"Rulers have many burdens to bear," King Ricard said. "Most people cannot fathom the weight of it all."

"I'm sure you're right. I should learn to hold my tongue."

"I hope you do not. I have need for news from beyond my borders. I was not in favor of the attack on Yelsia, and I confess that I was relieved when King Oveer failed to show up in Black Bay. I had hoped that since Felix had beaten back King Belphan and King Zorlan, there would be no more bloodshed."

"I wish that were the case," Zollin said.

"Tell me what happens, supposing you are correct about this witch and her army, if King Felix refuses to send his troops south."

"Why would he refuse?" Zollin asked. "I hadn't considered it, to be honest."

"Only a fool would leave his kingdom undefended," Ricard said. "There are raiders in the Highlands and at least rumors of a disloyal ally to the east. And don't forget the fear of another invasion from the sea will make him weary to commit troops south of the Rejee desert. It would take weeks to move his forces north again, especially through the mountains."

"I hadn't thought of that," Zollin confessed. "I'm sure it must be hard to take my word, but for those of us who have seen the devastation in Osla and fought the wicked creatures that have risen up from the abyss, there is simply no alternative. We must fight and we must give that fight every resource. To fail means to lose all we know and hold dear. The Five Kingdoms is on the brink of falling into darkness."

"And you mean to hold back that wicked tide?" Ricard asked.

"I mean to do everything in my power to help," Zollin said. "I don't know why I have magical powers, my liege, but I am certain that I was given these gifts to help others."

"Your generosity is refreshing," Ricard said, holding up a goblet of wine for his servant to refill. "But you must also be aware that your magic makes others nervous."

"I am aware of it," Zollin said. "In fact, I've discovered that I have to keep my guard up. Most of the people I've met are anxious to bring me under their influence."

"I've no doubt that's true," Ricard said. "You are both a threat and a temptation to people in power. I know that I, for one, covet your abilities if the war comes that you are speaking of."

"I can't stay and help, although I would gladly do so under other circumstances," Zollin said. "But there is another who may be of great service to your cause."

"Another wizard?" Ricard said, worriedly pinching his face.

"No, not a wizard, but a man full of magic just the same. He is from Ortis and has been fighting the Norsik."

"We have all been fighting the Norsik," Ricard said.

"This man's name is Lorik and I don't know much about him, but I could sense his power from a distance. I saw him fight and slay over a hundred Norsik warriors singlehandedly."

"I am beginning to think that you are given to exaggeration, my friend."

"I swear to you, I'm not," Zollin said. "This man, Lorik, has a type of magic I don't recognize, but I can sense it woven into the very fibers of his body. It is strength unlike anything I've ever seen."

"Are you saying I should seek this man's help, or fear him?"

"Magic, by itself is neither good nor bad, but it magnifies the nature of the person it inhabits. I believe Lorik is a good man, a protector of his people. What you do and how you defend your kingdom is entirely up to you; I would never suppose I know better than you how to care for your own people, but if you meet Lorik, remember that he has my trust."

"Well, that's something, isn't it?" King Ricard said. "Trust is something we are in sore need of these days."

"I agree."

"I have sent scouts to see if your story is true, and I will send word to King Felix once I know what we are facing and how we will defend ourselves. If what you have told me is truth, perhaps my letter will help your King understand the wisdom of your plan."

"I am grateful, King Ricard. You have been kind and generous, but I'm afraid I must be going. If you would like to meet Ferno, now would be the time."

"The dragon is here?" King Ricard inquired, the excitement in his voice was tinged slightly with fear.

"Ferno has been circling over the city since nightfall."

"Yes," Ricard said. "I would meet this dragon. Let us go."

They left the feasting hall and were led by a small group of soldiers up onto the same rooftop courtyard that Zollin had landed on. Jorvin appeared with a large pack filled with food, water, wine, and a change of clothes.

"I took the liberty of supplying you with a few necessities," Jorvin said. "I hope your lordship doesn't mind," he said, handing the pack to Zollin.

"I'm honored," Zollin said. "But please, call me Zollin, I'm not a lord. Here, take this for your trouble."

Zollin pulled two gold coins from a small pouch inside his shirt.

"Oh no, sir, I couldn't take payment. All I've given you was the King's to give and at his orders."

"Well, here then," Zollin said, holding the coins in his open hand where everyone could see it. "Perhaps this is more appropriate."

The gold began to shimmer, as if it were trembling in Zollin's hand. King Ricard, the soldiers, and Jorvin all leaned close to watch the coins. The metal seemed to blur and then melt together. After another moment, the metal reformed into a small sculpture of a dragon that looked very much like Ferno.

"Consider it a keepsake to remember me by," Zollin said, again offering it to Jorvin.

The servant looked to his master, and King Ricard nodded approvingly.

"Thank you, my lord."

"You can tell a lot about a man by the way he treats others," Ricard said. "You are an interesting man, Zollin, Wizard of Yelsia. You are welcome here in Baskla anytime."

"Thank you, sire."

"Although, perhaps you should refrain from calling yourself the Wizard of Yelsia. If what you have told me is true, I would say you are the Wizard of the Five Kingdoms."

"I would like that," Zollin said.

Just then there was a whooshing sound overhead and as everyone looked up, the stars were blotted out by a huge, reptilian creature. Ferno's massive wings caused a downdraft that battered the men below. The beast had massive hind legs that stretched toward the ground as the dragon descended into the circle of torchlight. The powerful talons gripped the stone rooftop and the magnificent tail stood out straight. Ferno folded its wings and laid them flat against its body. The long neck was thick with bunched muscles, and the ferocious head swung toward them as smoke puffed from between the barred teeth.

Zollin's mind was filled with an image of the two of them flying away into the night and he smiled.

"We will be off in a moment, but this is King Ricard," Zollin said, indicating the King. "He was anxious to meet you."

"How do you know what he's saying?" Ricard asked.

"Dragons communicate mostly through mental images," Zollin said. "But they understand words, don't you Ferno?"

The dragon roared. It was a soft cry and Ferno lifted his head so that the heat of its breath wouldn't scorch the king or the soldiers, but still it sent the party scuttling back. Zollin had to choke back a laugh.

Then Ferno dropped its massive head and looked intently at the king. The mouth opened revealing rows of razor sharp teeth. The forked tongue flickered out for an instant, tasting the air that was full of King Ricard's scent.

"My liege," Ferno hissed in a rumbling voice.

King Ricard's complexion faded a little, but he bravely stepped forward, straightening his shirt and trying to smile.

"I'm not sure how to address a lord of the sky," King Ricard said.

"Ferrrnnnnooooo," hissed the dragon.

"It is a great honor to meet you. I'm afraid you are the first of your kind to be seen in Baskla in many generations."

Ferno's head bobbed.

"May I touch your scales?"

Again the great, horned head bobbed up and down. King Ricard walked to the dragon's shoulder and ran his hand over the rough scales. They felt like metal plate armor. Then he touched the wing, which was like leather stretched over a frame, only it was covered in very short, soft fur.

"Remarkable," King Ricard said. "Does he breathe fire?"

The question was directed to Zollin, but in reply Ferno lifted its massive head and spewed a massive pillar of fire high into the air. Everyone on the rooftop felt the heat as they were illuminated by the bright, orange glow.

"Ferno is one of a pride of dragons. They are young and just getting a taste of the world, but they have been invaluable in the fight with the Torr and with the witch Gwendolyn. In fact, Ferno saved my life in the Grand City."

"If they are all like Ferno, then they are grand, majestic creatures," King Ricard said. "I say the Five Kingdoms are richer to have you and your pride in them."

Ferno nodded again and Zollin bowed.

"I'm afraid we must be going," he said. "Thank you again for your hospitality."

"Thank you for the warning," King Ricard stated. "We shall be ready if the war comes our way. We won't be found wanting."

"I believe you," Zollin said. "I'll come back if I have the chance."

"As I have said, you are always welcome here."

70

Zollin bowed again, and then he rose magically up in the air and settled on Ferno's back, taking hold of the dragon's short horns at the base of the beast's long neck. Ferno roared again, smoke billowing out of its mouth and then jumped into the air, wings beating swiftly and lifting the huge dragon up and away from the castle. Zollin leaned over, looking down at the small circle of light on the rooftop. The city of Forxam was dark, but lights twinkled here and there from windows and small fires in courtyards. The torches along the wall behind the King and his retinue shone brightly, casting long, dark shadows as the men watched them fly away.

The wind was cold and the land below them was dark, as they made their way north through the night. It was an hour before dawn when the attack came. The moon had set and clouds were scuttling across the sky above them, blotting out the light from the stars. Zollin had been dozing, as his body hunched low over Ferno's back when the great dragon was hit hard and flipped. Zollin was thrown clear of the dragon and woke to find himself falling into the darkness below.

Chapter 6

Brianna was nervous. She had met King Felix before and even lived in the castle at Orrock for a time, but now she needed to convince the king of the threat coming north from Osla. The prospect of petitioning the king made her feel like a little girl begging her father to let her have something she wanted from the sweet shop. She knew if Zollin were with her she wouldn't be afraid, but he wasn't there. In fact, she had to convince King Felix to move his troops now, so that when Zollin returned from the north he wouldn't have to wait on her.

It had only taken a day to travel from Felson to Orrock, and then she had made camp rather going straight into the city. Brianna knew that Bartoom had attacked Orrock, and she wasn't anxious to place her pride in harm's way if the army had installed some type of dragon defenses. Instead, she rested, letting Selix and Tig hunt through the night. The next morning, she tried to contact Gyia. It took a little effort to push her mental inquiries far enough for the purple dragon to respond, but as she had hoped, Gyia was in Orrock. It took less than a minute to convince Gyia to come to her.

Brianna was camped near a stream and had already bathed herself in the cold water. She let flames wash over her, warming her up and drying her off at the same time. Then, she pulled fresh clothes from the pack that Tig had carried. It wouldn't do to meet the King in tattered clothes. Her father always said that a person's clothes made the loudest first impression.

It only took a few minutes for Gyia to find Brianna and come swooping into the small camp. Selix and Tig roared happily as Gyia approached. Brianna came to the slender, purple dragon smiling. She held her hands up and Gyia bowed. Brianna stroked the dragon's narrow head.

"It's good to see you, Gyia," she said. "How was your journey north?"

"Pleasant," Gyia hissed.

"Good," Brianna said. "It sounds like you've been practicing your speaking skills."

"Prince Willam says that communicating with words builds trust."

"He is probably right," Brianna said. "Humans are often slow to accept anything new or different. We bring news."

Brianna found it easier to share the news about the battle in the Grand City and the creatures from the Abyss by using the dragon's natural mental communication. Brianna could send images of the battle and of the monsters they had fought, so that Gyia saw for herself what they were facing.

"I must convince King Felix to send troops south to join King Zorlan, south of the Walheta Mountains."

"That will be difficult," Gyia said. "Your King is not a reasonable man."

"What do you mean?" Brianna asked.

"You will see. I will inform the castle of your arrival. Come at midday."

"We will. And thank you for your help."

Gyia bowed, and then flapped purple wings, gliding up in the air and looking like a snake swimming across a stream.

"Gyia flies effortlessly," Brianna said aloud.

She saw a mental image of the pride flying altogether.

"Yes, I wish we were all together too," Brianna said, "back in the mountains with no concerns except our next meal."

Tig let out a lonely wail and the image of Torc, the small blue dragon that had been Tig's twin until it was killed by Bartoom, flashed into Brianna's mind. She sent feelings of sympathy and love toward the small dragon.

They spent the rest of the morning lounging. The day was bright, but the temperatures were colder than the dragons or Brianna liked. They spent most of their time curled around one another for warmth and comfort. Brianna's nervousness was shared with the pride through their mental link. By midday, none of them could stay still. Tig had been flying for the last hour and a constant cloud of dark smoke rose with every breath Selix took. Brianna paced back and forth near the stream, trying to decide how she would make her case to the King.

When an image of the sun flashed into her mind, Brianna knew it was time to go.

"Well, better to get it over with than keep worrying about it," Brianna said.

She jumped into the air, rising higher than any normal person could dream of jumping. She summersaulted and then landed lightly on Selix's back.

"Now!" she cried.

The huge golden dragon jumped into the air, its wings beating furiously as it rose higher and higher. After only a moment, the capitol city of Yelsia came into view. Orrock was a sprawling city, built more for productivity than for show like many of the other royal cities among the Five Kingdoms. The outer wall was thick and tall, the buildings within were sturdy stone constructs, outside the wall were sprawling ghettos of wooden shacks and mud huts. The castle near the riverside of the city was easily the tallest and most massive structure. Soon, Brianna could see the castle's walls rising above the congested space around it. The castle itself was a simple structure, wide and sturdy, with tall watch towers rising over the city and giving unobstructed views of the countryside all around Orrock.

The two dragons glided along on thermal updrafts, sliding from side to side playfully. They circled the city once and then came to land beside Gyia in the courtyard in front of the castle. There were soldiers standing at stiff attention on either side of the castle's wide, wooden doors. Brianna sprang off of Selix's back, and after flipping head over heels, landed gracefully beside the big golden dragon. A moment later, the doors swung open and Prince Willam came striding out of the castle.

"Brianna," he called cheerfully. "It's so good to see you."

"And you, Prince Willam."

"Welcome to Orrock. Come inside, my father is waiting for you. I've given instructions for the dragons to be given a place outside the castle. They'll be fed and given fresh water."

Brianna smiled and sent a mental image of the three dragons lounging together. Then, she turned to Selix and patted the big dragon's neck.

"I'll see the King and then come check on you."

The dragon growled in response. Brianna walked forward and climbed the wide stairs that led to the castle doors where Prince Willam waited. He flashed a smile at her and then led the way inside. They went to the main hall and were seated at a long table where food and wine was being served. People from army commanders to visiting merchants were waiting patiently, many enjoying their midday meal. Willam poured Brianna a goblet of wine and then one for himself.

"My father is extremely busy," Willam said, his cheerful demeanor not quite covering his embarrassment for making Brianna wait. "There is much to be done repairing the damage from the invasion and the black dragon."

"Bartoom," Brianna said. "The black dragon's name is Bartoom. I don't think we'll have to worry about it coming back, at least not while my pride is around."

"That's welcome news. What of the invasion of Osla? Did King Zorlan succeed?"

"No," Brianna said, "Although the news from Osla is not good. It's a long story, and I better wait to share it with your father."

"Of course," Willam said, sounding a little petulant, like a child who has just been rebuked.

"Oh, I didn't mean to offend you, my lord. I'm just not sure I'm up to telling the tale more than once."

"I understand. Here, have some food. We may be waiting a while. It seems my father is going out of his way to make sure I understand my place."

"What do you mean?"

"You should understand better than most. Perhaps it is paranoia, but my father has been poisoned by my brother and invaded by the southern kingdoms. He seems intent on teaching me that I have no place in ruling Yelsia; at least, not yet."

"That seems silly," Brianna said. "I doubt you are as foolish and power hungry as your brother."

"Power is a temptation to us all. I dare say that Simmeron was only doing what I may have done under similar circumstances. I've never not had a duty to keep me busy before. I was shipped off to serve in the King's army when I was fourteen, and then I was sent to the Grand City to serve as ambassador. But, the last week I've been here with nothing to do. I almost feel like an outsider."

"But you would never turn against your father," Brianna said.

"No, you are right. I wouldn't do that. But, I've never been a patient person. I'm afraid my civility is running thin."

They ate a light meal, mostly fruit and bread, with a little cheese. Brianna enjoyed the wine, but she was too nervous to drink much. The afternoon slowly passed, and Brianna watched the King's steward, Homan, call in other visitors to see the King while she sat waiting.

It was almost nightfall when she was finally called in to the see the King. She did her best to remain calm. She knew that the King didn't understand her concerns or the danger they all faced. It was up to her to convince him to act and getting angry at having to wait would only make that job harder.

She wasn't taken up to the private room the King occupied on the upper level of the castle, as he had expected. She and Zollin had been put up in the castle just down the hall from the royal quarters and had met with King Felix in his private rooms, but now she was led into a grand audience chamber. The room was long and the ceiling was very high. There were marble pillars lining each side of the protracted room, and huge paintings in gilded frames filled the spaces between the pillars; their dark textured surface offering a stark contrast to the highly polished white pillars.

At the end of the room was a grand throne, high backed and decorated with gold leaf. It was padded with red velvet cushions with gold tassels and was set on a round dais that was six steps up. There was a thick, red carpet running the length of the hall and up the steps to the throne. King Felix sat waiting while servants hurried behind the grand chair and advisors whispered near the dais on either side of the room.

Prince Willam escorted Brianna down to the throne and announced her.

"Lady Brianna," he said in a loud voice that filled the room, "Dragon master of Yelsia."

Brianna bowed, a little embarrassed by the title. No one had mentioned her being a noble lady, much less a dragon master. The dwarves had called her a fire spirit, and she considered herself dragon kind, but the title of dragon master seemed wrong to her somehow. Still, she didn't think it was wise to bring that point up in front of the King.

"Lady Brianna," said King Felix, "you are looking well. It has been a long time since you were a guest here with us in Orrock. You are welcome."

"Thank you, my lord, but I'm afraid I come with bad tidings."

"All tidings are bad these days," King Felix said. "We heard that you were lost in the mountains, taken by the black dragon. And now here you are, as beautiful as ever, and with two magnificent dragons in tow. I would say that alone was reason enough to celebrate."

"Again, I thank you, O' King, but there are more pressing concerns that I must inform you of. Osla has fallen, and the Grand City is lost. King Oveer of Ortis is dead, and the armies of Falxis decimated."

"Again, I hear nothing to lament over," King Felix said, his contempt for the other kingdoms that had plotted against him dripped from his voice. His advisors laughed.

"But my Lord, please hear me. There is evil sweeping across the Five Kingdoms. An evil sorceress, the same witch

Gwendolyn who entranced your own son, Prince Willam, has awakened a very dark magic. In an effort to overthrow Offendorl, master of the Torr, she has called on the powers of the underworld and destroyed the Grand City. She opened a portal to the underworld, a great abyss that stretches east and west from the Grand City across Osla. She has unleashed horrid beasts that are capturing innocents from all over the Five Kingdoms and taking them back to her subterranean lair where she is transforming them into a massive army. They will be marching north soon and laying waste to the Five Kingdoms. Zollin and my Pride stood against this witch and her dark powers, but help is needed. King Zorlan has fallen back, gathering his people at the southern foothills of the Walheta and he urgently awaits your help there. We must make a stand, my King. We cannot allow the wicked tide to sweep into Yelsia."

For a moment there was silence and then King Felix began to laugh. His advisors laughed with him, thinking that the King was laughing at Brianna, but he held his hand up to silence the room.

"Why should I care about Osla or Falxis?" he said. "Why should I help stop a war I did not start? Why should the strength of our army and the prosperity of our kingdom suffer? I do not doubt your sincerity, Lady Brianna, but I think you are naive. First, do you bring any proof of this threat you speak of?"

"Only my word, your highness, and that of my Pride."

"And do your dragons talk like Prince Willam's?" the King asked.

"In a fashion, all dragons talk," Brianna said. "They are as intelligent as you or I, although they use projected mental images in place of words in most cases. Their mouths and tongues are ill-suited for forming words."

"Yes, I've seen the purple dragon communicate with Prince Willam in this fashion, although it is hard to believe that a beast can talk."

"Gyia speaks, Father," Prince Willam said.

"Yes, indeed," King Felix said. "But, back to the point. I cannot send armies south without further proof of your claims. It would leave Yelsia painfully exposed. As you might guess, our forces took heavy casualties during the invasion. The royal army must be reserved for our kingdom's defense."

"But it is our kingdom's defense that I am petitioning for," Brianna said. "Surely you would agree that it is to our benefit to fight the coming war on foreign soil."

There was a murmur around the room in response to Brianna's words. She didn't know if it was affirmation of her claims or derision, but at least she was getting a response, she thought.

"Your plan would be sound in the event of a crisis, but I am not yet convinced that we face a crisis."

"Father, the witch is powerful. I've seen her entrance whole armies. If she is moving north, we must prepare ourselves," Prince Willam said.

"I will take your news under consideration," King Felix said. "For tonight, you are welcome to dine with us. We will speak again tomorrow."

Brianna felt frustration building up inside her, but she held it in check. The King was reluctant to act, but he was not completely opposed, and she still had a chance to convince him.

"Thank you, my lord," she said, bowing.

"Homan will show you to your room, my lady, and I will see you at dinner, I'm sure."

Brianna bowed again and followed Homan from the room with Prince Willam tagging along as well. Homan led Brianna down stairs into a small room with no windows. Unlike the room she had shared with Zollin, her new chamber was tiny with only a narrow bed and table with a basin and pitcher of water.

"It is austere," said Homan, "but not uncomfortable."

"It is fine," said Brianna, at once reminded of the cave she had shared with her Pride in the Northern Highlands and also mourning the wide open spaces she had grown accustomed to over the last few weeks.

"If you need anything, let one of the servants know," Homan said. He seemed in a hurry to get back upstairs.

"Thank you," Brianna said.

Homan left and Prince Willam looked around frowning.

"It seems we're both being put in our places," he said. "This is no way to treat the woman who saved his life."

"I didn't save him," Brianna said. "Zollin did."

"It is still a calculated move," Willam said. "One meant to intimidate you. Don't let it."

Brianna smiled.

"It would take much more than this to frighten me," she said. "Once you have seen what I have, even the power of kings isn't frightening."

A servant poked his head into the room.

"My lord," the servant said, holding out a note.

"Thank you," Willam said. He held open the note and read it. "I must go," he said. "But I will look for you at dinner. Will you sit with me?"

"I would be honored, my Prince."

"Good, I will see you soon."

He bowed gallantly and then hurried away. Brianna sat on the small bed and wondered what Zollin was doing.

Chapter 7

It took a moment for Zollin to register what was happening. Then Ferno roared, unleashing a wave of massive flame that lit up the sky. Zollin felt his heart thundering away in his chest as he realized he was falling. His magic erupted, pouring out of him in a blistering rush. He was suddenly floating and once he caught his breath, he was able to regain control of his magic.

It was too dark to see what was attacking Ferno, but the massive dragon was striking out in every direction. Zollin quickly lowered himself to the ground. The exertion of getting his magic under control left his head spinning, and it took another moment for Zollin to compose himself before he could help Ferno. Finally, he sent his magic out toward the battling dragon who was unfortunately moving further and further away from Zollin. In the darkness, he couldn't see the creatures that were attacking Ferno, but he could feel them. They were smaller than the dragon, but thick, heavy creatures with distorted human bodies.

"Ferno!" Zollin shouted. "Ferno!"

He sent out the cry magically and mentally, trying to draw the green dragon back. He then reached out with his magic and pulled two of the gruesome beasts off of Ferno. The dragon dove instantly, soaring down at breakneck speed until Zollin couldn't see Ferno at all. He was surrounded by trees which blocked his view, so Zollin levitated himself up into the top of one of the trees. The branches swayed under his weight and although there were still limbs above him, Zollin had a clear view over the forest around him.

Ferno pulled up, right above the tree line. It could feel the creatures swooping down right behind it, so the powerful green dragon let flames spew out of its mouth and flow back over its body. It wasn't meant to harm the creatures attacking it, but Ferno hoped it would keep them off its back until a better way to attack the beasts became clear.

Zollin sent a mental image of Ferno flying past the tree where Zollin was waiting. He could attack from a distance, but because he didn't know what they were dealing with yet, he wanted to bring the creatures close. Ferno turned and flew hard toward Zollin, who let his magic flow out toward the dragon and its attackers. There were six of the nightmarish beasts; two were already wounded and falling behind the others, but four seemed eager to destroy Ferno. They weren't quite as fast as the dragon, but they were lighter and could keep their pace longer.

"Blast!" Zollin shouted, sending two thick beams of lightning-like, blue energy shooting toward the four creatures in the lead.

There was a crackle as the energy shot out. It hit two of the creatures and shocked their bodies into a rigid paralysis. They fell and were smoking into the forest with such momentum that they knocked down trees and crushed their bodies in the process.

The two untouched beasts continued their pursuit of Ferno, but the two wounded creatures slowed and dropped into cover behind the trees. Zollin knew he couldn't stay in his perch high in the tree. He wasn't mobile enough and the creatures knew exactly where he was. He climbed down as quickly as he could; using his magic to levitate himself down once he was clear of the wide spreading branches.

His feet had just touched the ground when one of the creatures came rushing toward him, bellowing a frightening scream as it came. Zollin's blood ran cold. It was even darker on the ground than above the treetops, and all he could see was a dark shadow hurdling toward him. The creature was flying, swooping down toward him at speed. In the second he knew he was being attacked, Zollin's only discovery was that the creature had a wounded wing and seemed to be flying with a hitch that made it jerk to the left each time its wings flapped. He knew hitting the creature with a blast of magic would be difficult, so he simply raised an invisible wall of magic like a shield. To his horror, the creature seemed to sense the invisible barrier and pulled up to avoid it.

Zollin felt a tingle just between his shoulder blades and was filled with the horrifying feeling that something was behind him. He instinctively fell to the ground, but he was a faction of a second too late. The other wounded creature was charging and managed to inflict a bloody gash along Zollin's back as he fell. The creature looped past Zollin, who screamed in agony from the wound. Still, Zollin rolled to his side as he fell and sent a blast of magic after the creature that had hurt him. Blue energy shot from Zollin's hand and engulfed the creature, which burst into flames as it fell. The creature crashed to the ground and lay in a burning heap. The light from the fire lit up the ground in the small clearing around Zollin, but it made the treetops where the other creature was readying to attack even more dark. Zollin knew he wouldn't see the creature before it was too late. He considered extinguishing the flames that were still burning up the carcass of the dead creature, but he knew his night vision was already ruined. It would take several minutes to be able to see in the darkness with even the slightest detail, and he simply didn't have the time.

Zollin let his magic flow out in an expanding bubble all around him. He felt the creature circling around to attack from behind. There was a foulness and demented nature to the creatures. Zollin knew he could kill the wretched beast, but he needed to know why they were being attacked and by whom.

Ferno had climbed high up into the air. The massive dragon was bleeding from several minor wounds. The creatures had attacked out of nowhere, first crashing into the dragon and then digging into Ferno's iron-like scales with long claws and sharp teeth. Ferno was angry and ready to finish the fight, but the threat of being dragged down by the creatures was too great. Ferno knew that its only chance was to get high enough that it could face the creatures and defeat them during a long fall. The air was cold and thin, so much so that Ferno was having difficulty breathing, when finally it turned and faced its attackers. There were only two of the creatures now, both struggling to fly high enough to reach Ferno. The dragon belched fire, a huge billowing pillar that struck the oncoming creatures head on, but to Ferno's consternation, the fire didn't even slow the wicked looking beasts.

Ferno could see them clearly in the flames. They had round heads, like humans, but without hair and they had pointed ears. Their mouths were open, and their pointed teeth seemed to fill the darkness inside. Their wings were like Ferno's, only thicker, the skin stretched over bone and some sort of flexible tissue. Their bodies were small and fat, their hind legs raised up so that it looked like they were squatting. Their arms were tiny, atrophied limbs, but each hand had long, curled claws. Their feet were a cross between human feet and eagle talons. Each toe ended in a claw, and the heel was more of a bony stump.

Ferno arched its back in midair, bringing its tail forward in an arc as it swung from low to high. It caught the creature on the right, smashing its leg and sending the beast tumbling away. The second creature was untouched and was speeding toward the softer scales on Ferno's belly. The dragon waited until it was almost too late, then Ferno struck. Ferno's neck was not as long as Gyia's or Selix, and it was much thicker with muscle, but Ferno still had the flexibility to strike like a serpent at anything that got too close to the dragon's underside. Ferno caught the creature's head in its mouth. Normally, the dragon's sharp teeth and powerful jaws could crush anything, but the creature's head was like a stone. The beast's thick skin was almost as impervious to Ferno's teeth as it had been to the dragon's flames. Instead of severing the flesh, it gave beneath Ferno's teeth like a tough piece of overcooked meat.

Ferno felt the creature clawing the dragon's neck and thickly muscled jaws. Unlike Ferno, the creature's scrabbling counter attack, even while its head was caught in the vice of the dragon's bite, scored long, shallow gashes. Ferno swung its head, shaking the creature from side to side like a dog, but the beast was still unfazed. When Ferno realized the attacks weren't working, it released its bite and the creature was hurled away.

Ferno dropped back toward the ground, folding in the huge, leathery wings and pointing its body straight down so that it fell with blinding speed. Both of the wretched creatures were still alive and still able to attack. Ferno wasn't sure what to do next, but it knew that Zollin had somehow attacked the group of hideous beasts. So, the dragon returned to the young wizard in hopes that Zollin could fend off the creatures that seemed impervious to its attacks.

Zollin felt the last of his assailants recoil at his magical touch, although the beast could do nothing to stop him. Zollin focused on the creature, using his magic to drag it down to the ground. It reminded Zollin of seeing farmers pulling sheep toward the shearing pin. The sheep would always resist, digging their cloven hooves into the ground and pulling against the ropes the farmers had tied around their necks. The creature screamed as Zollin drew it in, the high-pitched wail made Zollin's flesh crawl. He wanted to kill the creature, but he needed answers. Where did the creatures come from? What were they, and who had sent them to attack Ferno?

After a minute of futile resistance, the creature changed tactics, opting to stop resisting and dive toward Zollin. The attack caught Zollin off-guard and in his panic he slammed the creature into the ground. It was a knee jerk reaction to the attack, and his fear made his response much more powerful than he had wanted it to be. The creature was crushed against the ground, its back broken as Zollin's magic smashed it down.

"Damn!" Zollin cursed.

He was frustrated with himself and started toward the creature, which was partially buried in the ground from his magical blow. He had only taken a few steps when he heard Ferno's roar and a mental image of the two creatures flashed into Zollin's mind. He was a little surprised that Ferno hadn't made quick work of the two beasts, but Zollin sensed Ferno's fear and frustration. Something had kept the dragon from destroying the two creatures still chasing it. Zollin sent a wave of magic high up into the air. He found the two creatures still high above Ferno and spread apart. They were trying to close the distance back to the dragon, although Zollin got the impression that both of the beasts were now much more cautious. They barked as they flew, communicating in a guttural language of snarls and yelps that sounded completely bestial to Zollin. He waited as they continued their attack, drawing nearer to one another as they closed the distance toward Ferno. When they were only a few yards apart, Zollin used his magic to smash them together. Their bodies collided in a tangle of limbs and wings, both falling into the trees where the limbs smashed and raked them into a bloody heap. Zollin ran toward where he could feel the fallen creatures. Both were still alive, but wounded and frightened. He used his magic to pin them to the ground, although with wings broken and bones shattered, they had little chance of escape anyway.

Zollin sent a mental image to Ferno, showing the two creatures on the ground. Ferno circled over Zollin, keeping watch for further attacks and also keeping its distance from the wicked beasts that seemed intent on harming the green dragon.

It took Zollin a few minutes to reach the creatures. They were yelping like dogs from the pain of their wounds. Zollin found that one of the creatures was dying; its back was broken and blood was bubbling from its mouth. Zollin had no idea about the anatomy of the creatures, but he guessed that some broken bone had punctured its lung. The dying creature lay still, except for its head, which turned back and forth on the ground as it gurgled its pitiful death cry.

The other creature was wounded; its wings ruined and one leg obviously broken with the bone sticking out of the leathery skin. It growled menacingly as Zollin approached. His adrenaline was still high, blocking the pain in his back from the gash, although he could feel the blood running down his back and soaking into his pants. It was quickly obvious that the creature couldn't communicate with Zollin vocally. It was disappointing to realize that there was little he could learn about the beasts from them directly, but he had been around magical creatures enough to know that he couldn't base what he could learn from traditional methods. He let his magic flow into the creature. There was a weak resistance and the beast writhed, as if the touch of Zollin's magic was painful.

What Zollin discovered mystified him. The creature felt like a puzzle piece. Physically it was autonomous, but its mind was connected to something or someone else. Zollin examined the dying creature and sensed the connection to the first, but alone the beasts were less mentally aware than any animal Zollin had ever encountered. He sensed their need to ward off magic, although he could also detect a form of magic connecting each of the creatures. As Zollin looked at the creature he suddenly recognized, either from his mind recalling the stories he had treasured as a child or because his magic was giving him some supernatural insight; he couldn't tell, but he knew he was looking at a gargoyle.

Zollin was partly fascinated and more than a little terrified. Gargoyles were mythic creatures created to ward off evil, yet he had never seen one or heard of one in real life. The stories he remembered described gargoyles as creatures carved of stone that served as decoration on ancient castles until evil awoke them. Zollin guessed the creatures could be something else, but the sense that he was right about them was so strong he had trouble shaking the feeling that something ominous was afoot. The question was: where did the gargoyles come from? Were they already here, perhaps hidden in some overgrown castle ruin, or were they created recently?

Zollin let his magic flow more heavily into the creatures, trying to trace their tenuous threads of magical connection to one another, but he failed. The connections were like spider webs, barely perceivable and fragile. His blundering efforts severed the connections. The gargoyle with the punctured lung shuttered and died. The gargoyle with the broken leg, moaned, and then slowly turned to stone before Zollin's eyes.

There wasn't much that surprised Zollin as far as magic went, but seeing the gargoyles turn to stone took his breath away. The broken leg was now just a deep crack in the stone of the creature's spindly legs that were curled up close to the bulbous body. The wings, which should have been stretched from the gargoyle's back, were now shattered across the ground behind him.

Zollin bent down and ran his hand across the stone. It was old and rough, pitted by long exposure to the elements. There were even traces of lichen and stains from bird droppings. The hideous face stared up at him in a blank, lifeless expression of menace with its mouth open and fangs bared. There was nothing more to learn from the gargoyles at the moment, so Zollin looked up, hoping to catch sight of Ferno circling above. He was just about call out to the dragon when a wave of panic washed over him, and he saw a mental image of trees rising toward him. Zollin understood in that instant that Ferno was crashing down somewhere, although he had no idea why or where the dragon was. He listened, but all he could hear was the sing-song chirping of nocturnal insects.

He let his magic flow out in all directions. His back began to burn and ache. He knew he needed to see about the gash, but first he wanted to find Ferno. He couldn't imagine what had caused the ferocious dragon to fall from the sky, and he wasn't going to wait around to find out. He sensed animals all around him, mostly small burrowing animals and those that lived in the thick trees. It took several moments, but he finally found Ferno nearly a mile away. There were two more gargoyles flying low over the treetops, but they were moving away from Ferno. Zollin's first thought was to follow the gargoyles back to their home, or wherever they came from, but he quickly dismissed that idea. Ferno was hurt, and he hurried to try and help.

Running under any circumstances with his leg still stiff from his fight in the Grand City was not an easy task. He silently cursed himself for not taking the time to mend the wound properly. When he'd initially been hurt, he hadn't had time to do more than stop the bleeding. Then, they were busy fighting Gwendolyn's monsters, and Zollin had been too tired to worry about his leg. When he finally had the time, as he and Ferno flew north, he had simply been too tired. By that time his leg was healing on his own, and to fix it properly he would have to reopen the wound. He wasn't keen on enduring the agony healing himself would require, even if he could block almost all the pain. Now, getting through the woods with his wounded leg was even more difficult.

The pain in his back from the gash the gargoyle had inflicted began to ache with each step. He let his mind focus on the wound as he made his way between the trees and around the clumps of underbrush in his path. It was extremely dark in the woods, so he kindled a small flame that danced over the palm of one upturned hand. The flame cast enough light around him that he could see where he was going.

The gash was long, running from just below his neck, down, between his shoulder blades, almost to the small of his back. It wasn't a deep cut, but it was painful. He let his magic, hot and powerful, bind the wound. He could feel the fibers of the muscle matching up, and then his skin stretched over the gash and sealed together. The pain eased and then slowly disappeared altogether. By the time he came into view of Ferno, his back was completely healed.

The dragon was another story. Ferno was a proud, strong creature, but now the dragon was laid low. Zollin increased the power of his flame so that he could see the dragon better. There were broken tree limbs all around Ferno, but the crash through the trees didn't seem to have hurt the dragon at all. There were scratches and bite marks on Ferno's back and underbelly, although none seemed deep or serious. Blood was flowing, but hardly enough to be concerned about and nothing Zollin could see should have resulted in Ferno being so seriously affected.

"I'm going to help," Zollin said, running one hand over Ferno's jaw.

Ferno growled miserably. The dragon's bright eyes were glazed, and its forked tongue lolled out between the sharp teeth.

Zollin was tired. His adrenaline was no longer in his system, and the lack of sleep combined with his physical and magical exertion was wearing on him. His body felt weak and his magic was growing painfully hot. He needed rest and sustenance, but first he had to help Ferno. He let his magic flow into the green dragon and immediately his connection with Ferno, which had been like a close friendship, expanded with a snap that took Zollin's breath away. Ferno was a fusion of fire, magic, and living stone. Zollin couldn't describe it exactly, but there were components of all three substances inside the dragon. Ferno had organs, a heart, lungs, and digestive system, all of which were straight forward and easily identifiable, but the dragon was infused with a magic that was different from Zollin's.

Zollin's magic was overtly powerful; the way a sword is made to be sharp, created to cut and slash. The magic wasn't good or bad, but it was willful, wanting to exert its nature, which was to create or destroy. Ferno's magic was more like the radiant heat of the sun; it existed to shine, to live, to simply be. It was strong, like a powerful muscle, but it had its limits as well. The magic in Ferno couldn't be exerted outside the dragon, even though it was drawn to the magic inside of Zollin. It reminded the young wizard of the staff he carried for a long time. The staff had been infused with magic after lightning had struck the tree it had come from. Zollin had sensed the magic in the wood, but when he touched it, the magic of the staff had combined with his own, mingling like the juice of a fine wine. There were times when the magic of the staff overflowed, effecting Zollin physically, and there were times when the pull of the connection between his own magic and that of the staff was intensely powerful, almost intoxicating.

Zollin felt his magic flow into Ferno and the dragon's own magic leapt into Zollin. He felt the strength and solidarity of the dragon magic fill him. Then he concentrated on Ferno's wounds. Zollin guessed that healing the scratches and gashes would be easy enough, but more concerning was the foreign matter he felt spreading through the dragon. Zollin knew at once it was poison, but it was in Ferno's blood stream and had already spread across the dragon's whole body.

"This isn't going to be easy, my friend," Zollin said quietly.

The sun was just peeking over the horizon as Zollin sat down on the ground next to Ferno. His eyes were closed and his hands rested on the dragon's stomach, to either side of the nasty cuts in the softer scales. Immediately, a green substance began to ooze out of the dragon, but Zollin feared he might be too late. Removing the poison would be extremely difficult, and he wasn't sure he had the strength to save Ferno, before the poison snuffed out the young dragon's life.

Chapter 8

It was another hour before the first rays of sunshine appeared over the small village of Barnacle Bay, but Mansel was already up and working. He did his best to spend the first part of each day working in the village. There wasn't much money in the small port. Most of the trading vessels only stopped in Barnacle Bay due to emergencies. There were plenty of fishermen, so food was abundant, and a few craftsmen had made the small, seaside village their home. Mansel traded labor for materials, food, and even ale. In the afternoons, he worked on the small cottage he and Nycoll occupied. It had only taken a few days to get the roof in good shape. Lumber was in short supply, but there were a few other abandoned buildings that Mansel could salvage from. Pitch was plentiful in the village and Mansel traded for a barrel of the tarry substance and after pulling down the wooden shingles, he coated the sub roof in pitch to make sure it was waterproof. Then he shingled the roof, using the shingles he had pulled off the roof and some from other buildings that were abandoned.

The cottage's fireplace was well built and still in good shape; Mansel only had to clean out the chimney. The doors were reinforced and new locking beams set. The floor was patched, and Nycoll set about making the little, one-room home livable. She used soft grasses that grew near the shore to stuff a mattress. It wasn't as soft as a down mattress, but it was better than sleeping on the floor. She repaired an old table and chairs. The locals gave her some cookware, and Mansel traded labor for blankets and quilts. At night they sat near the fire, cozy and warm. The days were cool, the nights chilly, but the views of the ocean and the mountains were unparalleled.

While Zollin was healing a dragon in the wooded hills of Baskla, Mansel was repairing a shop near the harbor. Most of the shops consisted of workspace with a large open window that faced the sea. The shutter on the windows could be raised and propped open with wooden dowels, and customers could do business with shop owners without going into the cluttered workspace. Unfortunately, most of the shutters were warped from the salty air, which allowed rain to get into the shops. Most of the buildings had at least some need of repair, either from lack of maintenance or from rot caused by the moist conditions.

By the time the sun rose, Mansel had his tools, which he had used the last of Zollin's gold to buy, and his materials arranged and ready. He started his day and worked hard. When he had been an apprentice with Quinn and Zollin, he had found carpentry to be onerous. Now, he was grateful to have learned a trade, and to be honest, he was happy to be out of his father's tannery and in the sunshine on most days. Still, the work hadn't been satisfying then, but now he found the work enjoyable. It wasn't as much fun as riding a horse into battle, but it was still satisfying, especially when he was able to trade his labor for some little thing that Nycoll wanted. He loved coming home with a little nicety and seeing her eyes light up. Nycoll had been on her own for a long time and had become very self-sufficient. There was very little that she couldn't make or trade for on her own. She took care of their cottage, fixed their meals, and mended Mansel's clothes. When he came home with a little lace or a particular spice that Nycoll couldn't find on her own, it gave Mansel a sense of joy he had never known before.

It was almost midday before Mansel took a break. He was almost finished repairing the frame around the baker's window. The wood around the window had begun to rot, and the heavy shutter had been tilting further and further out of place. Mansel had cut away the rotten wood and replaced it; now all he had to do was reattach the hinges and rehang the heavy shutter. He sat down with a sweet roll the baker had given him. He still had some ale from the night before. He had been careful not to over indulge in strong drink, but water that wasn't tainted with salt was sometimes hard to find in the village. So he drank ale, but he kept a tight rein on his self-control and thus far he had been successful.

He was lounging in the shade when he heard a commotion. He looked up and saw a group of people running toward the harbor. He got to his feet.

"What is going on?" he asked loudly.

"Monsters!" one man shouted, pointing back over his shoulder.

Mansel looked back to the south and he could see movement, but he couldn't make out what was coming.

"Run!" screamed another woman.

The shopkeepers were coming out of their businesses and looking to the south. Then Mansel heard a deep thrum. That sound mixed with the shouts and screams sent a chill down his back. He had his tools with him, but not his sword. The cottage he shared with Nycoll was slightly more than a mile to the north. The winding path that leads toward the mountains was a pleasant stroll in the mornings. He could walk the distance in about 15 minutes, but now he felt like he was too far from Nycoll. He started running, leaving his tools and half eaten lunch behind. The shouts and cries behind him turned from surprise to terror, but Mansel didn't turn back. Whatever was coming, he knew he needed to face it armed and with the knowledge that Nycoll was safe. Until then, he had only one thought, to get back home as fast as he could.

It was times like these when he really missed having a horse. He hadn't minded walking, or even carrying his tools, but he missed the sense of strength and freedom riding on horseback gave him. And now of course, all he cared about was speed, although if he had to fight whatever was behind him, he would probably be better off fighting mounted. But that was just wishful thinking. He didn't have a horse, not since they had sold their mounts in Osla and booked passage on the Fisherman's Daughter going north. Mansel had even saved some of their money in hopes of buying a horse, but the opportunity hadn't presented itself.

He topped a small hill and saw the cottage in the distance. It looked peaceful, and the sounds of carnage in the village behind him had faded away. Mansel hoped that whatever danger had come to the little town wouldn't follow him home, but he knew he couldn't bank on that hope. He looked around the house for Nycoll as he ran. They had cut back the weeds and wild grass that grew around the cottage. Nycoll had planted a garden. The cottage had a wide porch where they could sit and watch the waves crashing against the rocky shore or see the sunset turning the sky above the mountains pink and gold before twilight set in.

Nycoll was nowhere to be seen. Mansel hoped with all his heart that she hadn't wandered far from the cottage. He was out of breath, but he still managed to bellow her name.

"Nycoll!" he shouted. "Nycoll, where are you?"

The door to the cabin swung open and Nycoll stepped out, her eyes wide with fear.

"What is it?" she shouted.

"I'm not sure," he panted as he finally came running into their small, sandy yard. "Get my sword. Then bolt the door."

"Aren't you coming inside?"

"No," Mansel said. "Find a place to hide, and stay there until I come for you."

"Mansel, you're scaring me," she said, her voice rising in pitch and volume.

"Good," he bellowed. "Now do as I say!"

Mansel kept the sword Zollin had fashioned for him just inside the door. It was still in the scabbard, although it wasn't hung to a belt anymore. Nycoll grabbed it with two hands and flung it out to Mansel. It flipped in the air, but he caught it deftly, slinging the scabbard aside with one fluid motion.

Mansel was a big man, young enough that his beard was still soft and patchy on his square jaw, but thick through the chest and shoulders, his waist narrow, but his legs strong. He turned back to the south, watching the path that led to the village. He didn't have to wait long. The thrumming sound he'd heard in the village was the first sign that the monsters he'd been warned of were coming. The sound grew louder until he saw the first of five beasts fly over the low hill. Mansel's mind rejected what he saw. The creatures had a horse's body, but with the torso, arms, and head of a man. The wings looked like dragonfly wings, flapping so fast they were hard to make out, but obviously the cause of the thrumming he'd heard. Still, as frightening as the head and body of the creatures seemed, it was their huge, scorpion-like tails curling over the body and head of the beasts, the stingers dripping venom, that made Mansel's blood run cold.

He swung his sword to loosen the muscles in his arms and shoulders. The heft of the weapon calmed his nerves a little. He didn't want to die and seeing the creatures made it hard to think of anything else but death. Still, he comforted himself. If he did die, at least it would be with a sword in his hand.

The creatures didn't slow; they flew on down the path toward Mansel, unfazed by the sight of the big man and his long sword. Mansel didn't wait either; he bellowed his war cry and dashed forward. The temptation to look back and make sure that Nycoll was ok was strong, but he knew looking back would only confirm that someone was in the cottage. Mansel could only hope that Nycoll had barred the doors and found a place to hide.

Mansel anticipated the first creature's attack. They had massive arms, their hands ending in talon like claws, their mouths filled with pointed teeth, but it was the tail was the true danger.

Mansel was fully expecting the tail to strike down as he approached. He watched the tail, swaying back and forth in a serpentine pattern as he rushed forward. As soon as the tail twitched back, he dove to the side. The tail struck out, like a viper, but Mansel was no longer in front of the creature. He swung his sword in a massive overhanded strike, like a woodsmen chopping lumber. The blade hacked the massive stinger clean off the segmented tail. Blood and venom poured out, and the creature reared, then pulled backward, screaming in pain.

Mansel didn't take the time to admire his handiwork. He spun around, dropped to one knee, extending his sword in a level, one-handed slash that caught the next creature just below the knee. The beasts were flying; their horse legs didn't even touch the ground, yet when Mansel's sword nearly severed the creature's leg just below the knee, it reared back, hissing.

A third creature closed on Mansel, but the other two circled around him and continued toward the cottage.

"No!" Mansel screamed.

He was forced to bring his sword up defensively to block the strike of the third scorpion's tail. The stinger hit the metal and drove Mansel backward with the force of the blow. Both Mansel and the creature recovered at the same time, and both dove forward. Mansel ducked as he came, thrusting his sword out in front of him. The creature's tail struck again, but this time it missed high, meanwhile Mansel's sword punched through the beast's chest. The clawed hands reached for Mansel, but he dodged back, yanking his sword free.

Black blood poured from the wound and the wings faltered, causing the beast to crash to the ground with its horse's legs giving way beneath it. Then Mansel spun around and with one vicious slash he severed the beast's head, which flew to the side and went bouncing into the weeds. The slain creature's body twitched, the tail flailing, the arms and legs convulsing, but Mansel didn't stay to watch. He used the momentum of his spinning strike to turn away from the creature and chase after the two that were closing in on the little cottage.

Mansel sprinted as fast as he could and then vaulted onto a large stone before launching himself at the nearest of the two monsters. Time seemed to slow as he flew through the air with his bloody sword raised with two hands in an underhand grip. Then he was falling, using all his weight and momentum to stab the sword down. The thick blade struck in the thick part of the tail, stabbing through the shell-like exoskeleton segments of the tail and into the horse's exposed back. The creature dropped to the ground, it's human side screaming in pain and rage, the rear of the horse, including the tail, dropping suddenly limp.

Mansel landed on his knees, barely able to hang onto his sword. He got back on his feet quickly, using one foot to hold the beast in place, while he arched his back to pull his sword free. The other creature was rising up in the air, almost as if it was going to fly over the house, but at the last minute, and to Mansel's horror, it dove down, smashing through the roof.

"Bastard!" Mansel shouted, drawing out the word in one long battle yell.

Then he was dashing around the fallen beast in front of him and up onto the wide porch. Lumber and stonework were falling all around. The roof caved in and the creature moved forward, casting debris to either side in a frenzy-like a child digging through a haystack in search of lost treasure.

"Nycoll!" Mansel screamed.

Then, he saw her head and shoulders as she tried to pull herself through the window on the porch side of the cottage. Mansel sprinted toward her, ignoring the dust and falling debris. The monster dug into the house, casting around for any humans inside. Mansel got to Nycoll just as she was falling out of the window. He grabbed her body and with his sword in one hand and Nycoll holding firmly under his other arm, he sprinted from the house toward the ocean.

"If it gets past me, go to the water," Mansel said. "Zollin says the magical creatures don't like water."

That wasn't precisely true, but it was all Mansel could think of to keep them safe. They stood watching the little cottage being torn apart for a few moments. They were both thinking of the hard work and hours of effort it had taken to clean up the abandoned structure and get it habitable again. Now it was being destroyed in seconds, right before their eyes, and they were helpless to stop it.

Mansel stood panting. There was thick blood dripping from his sword and spattered across his wide chest, neck, and face. His face had taken on a look of intense fury that scared Nycoll.

"Are you hurt?" she asked.

"No," Mansel answered, "You?"

"I'm okay," Nycoll said, but the tremor in her voice made it obvious that she wasn't.

"We need to get out of here," Mansel said.

"And go where?"

"To the mountains," Mansel said. "They came from the south, so we keep moving north."

"But we don't have anything, no food and no clothes."

"We have what's on our backs and we have a sword, I'd say that's more than most. We have to move."

Just then, the last creature rose up out of the destroyed cottage and spun around. As soon as it saw Mansel and Nycoll on the beach, it moved toward them.

"Get in the water!" Mansel shouted.

He had no idea just how cold the water was or how dangerous it would have been for Nycoll to swim out into the frigid ocean. She took several steps back, until the surf was foaming around her feet, but there she stopped.

Mansel raised his sword to one side, while waiting for the attack he knew was coming. The other creatures hadn't been terribly bright, but it was as if they didn't expect to be resisted at all. The last creature looked more intelligent, although that was just a thought in Mansel's head. He knew that it was probably just fear distorting his thinking.

"Stay back!" he shouted, as the creature drew close to him.

Nycoll had a plan of her own. She stooped down and picked up a handful of rocks. When she looked up she was horrified to see the creature's tail striking like a snake at Mansel. He dodged to the side, but stumbled and fell in the shifting pebbles that lined the beach. The creature hissed, and moved to finish Mansel off, but Nycoll hurled a rock at the beast. It struck the creature square in the chest, causing it to scream in rage. The scream was so terrifying that Nycoll dropped her rocks and covered her ears. The beast was moving toward her now, and she was too afraid to flee. But Mansel was back on his feet in a flash, driving his sword into the creature's side, just behind the foreleg. The beast fell, thrashing and dying on the rocks.

Mansel held out his hand to Nycoll and she ran to him, jumping into his arms.

"We have to move," he said. "There might be more."

Nycoll was sobbing uncontrollably, but she could run. He stepped toward the beast and grabbed his sword, pulling it free with a mighty heave and then they were off. Mansel ran, holding tight to Nycoll's hand and pulling her along after him.

Chapter 9

The day passed swiftly for Zollin. Removing the poison from Ferno took all of his strength and concentration. He felt the stability of Ferno's magic buoying his internal containment, but the magic inside was so hot it was difficult at times for Zollin to keep working. Whenever he stopped to rest, the poison seemed to spread, so Zollin was forced to work through his exhaustion. He had tried to heal the scratches and bites but for some reason his magic simply didn't work on Ferno's body. He could draw out the poison, but he couldn't mend the wounds.

To add to their troubles, Zollin's pack with all their supplies had been lost during the fight with the gargoyles. By the time Zollin had healed Ferno of the poison, his head was spinning and he was nauseous with fatigue. The dragon, on the other hand, was sleeping soundly. The flesh wounds weren't healed but were no longer dangerous. Still, the poison had caused Ferno intense pain throughout the day. So Zollin collapsed beside Ferno, and they both slept through the night. The next morning, Zollin felt like a dried husk. His tongue was swollen, and his eyes felt gummy.

"We need water," Zollin said.

Ferno grumbled, but they both got to their feet. Ferno's keen sense of smell led them quickly to a small stream. The big dragon's bulk was difficult to move through the dense forest, but once they had drunk their fill, they both felt better. They rested by the stream until midday, when both of their stomach's began to growl with hunger. Ferno was sore, but well enough to fly and hunt. The green dragon took to the air and was soon back with a small deer. Zollin cut a small portion from the deer's flank, which he then cooked with magical fire. Ferno gobbled the deer down, eating everything, including the short antlers.

Then they slept again, sipping water from the stream and resting. Zollin felt guilty for taking the day to rest and recover, but he knew he couldn't push himself too hard. For dinner, Zollin caught a few small fish by levitating them out of the water. He built a fire and cooked the fish on flat stones he nestled in the coals. It felt good to do something without magic for a change. It took much longer, but it reminded him of cooking for his father when they lived in Tranaugh Shire. Zollin had always prepared the meals. It was simple fare; he wasn't much of a cook, but it was something he could do for his father and that always left him feeling happy. There were so many things that his father could do that Zollin had no aptitude for, but cooking wasn't one of them.

Zollin sat back against Ferno's giant form, which was curled around the small clearing they were camped in. He watched the fire burn low and thought about Brianna. He missed her so intensely he wanted to cry. He could stay busy and the ache of being apart didn't affect him as much, but healing Ferno and being exhausted himself, left Zollin longing for Brianna's bright smile and gentle touch.

The next morning, they left at dawn. Zollin stayed alert, but there was no more sign of the gargoyles. Zollin hoped that at some point he could come back and search the countryside for the source of the magic he had felt, but he had no time for such a mission now.

It took two more days to reach Mountain Wind, which was one of the larger cities just outside of the Northern Highlands on the border of Yelsia and Baskla. Ferno went hunting while Zollin walked the last few miles into the town. It was late afternoon when he arrived and the market was mostly closed down, but he had planned to spend the night at an inn, have a hot supper, maybe even a bath and sleep in a bed. It felt lavish, but he didn't care. The next morning he could get supplies and push on.

There was a large inn near the White River. The White was a swiftly flowing river that bounced around large boulders which churned the water into a white froth. The roar of the rushing water was soothing to Zollin. He could smell the food from the inn long before he arrived. The inn was a large structure, built of stone with thick, timber accents. The common room was large and there were two fireplaces, both burning brightly and warming the room nicely. The inn was crowded, and Zollin was met at the door by a young serving maid who showed him to a table. The inn keeper arrived after only a moment.

"Welcome traveler," the man said. "Can we get you a room for the night?"

"Yes," Zollin said. "And a hot bath if that is possible."

He slid a small gold coin across the table.

"Anything is possible. Would you need someone to keep you warm through the night as well?"

"No," Zollin said, trying not to blush.

"Well, if you change your mind, let me know. We don't often get gold here in Mountain Wind."

He snatched up the coin and hurried away. The serving girl returned with a mug of ale and loaf of bread. By the time Zollin had slaked his thirst and cut a chunk from the loaf, the serving girl was back. She had a bowl of steaming soup and a pitcher of wine.

"Ernst said to give you the best," she said with a smile.

"Thank you," Zollin said, as the girl poured him a goblet of wine.

"I'll bring you a platter of smoked pork and vegetables too," the girl said. "But we're famous for our fish soup."

"It smells wonderful," Zollin said.

"I'll show you to your room when you're ready. Abbatha is heating a tub of water for your bath now. It should be ready by the time you finish eating."

"Great," Zollin said around a mouthful of bread.

The girl smiled and then hurried away. Soon the locals were singing bawdy songs. A few played instruments, a flute and a fiddle; the rest banged the rhythm on the wooden tables with their hands. *It was a fine night*, Zollin thought. He forced himself not to think of the monsters far to the south that were attacking places just like the River Walk. He felt helpless whenever he considered the fact that he couldn't stem the tide of Gwendolyn's evil by himself. And fear placed a gloomy hand on his heart whenever he thought of the witch. He wasn't afraid of fighting her, but her dark transformation was the stuff of his nightmares. He feared what he could become if he wasn't careful.

The smoked pork was tender and flavorful. Zollin ate his fill and then ate some more. The wine made him feel warm and mellow. When he had finished his meal, he was shown upstairs to a large room. The bed was big enough for two, with a thickly stuffed mattress. There was a round wooden table and a full length mirror. A washtub was set up in the corner. The water was steaming, and Zollin found a thick towel folded neatly near the tub. He stripped off his grimy clothes. His shirt was rudely mended and stained with blood from the gash on his back. He realized he would need to purchase new clothes from the market, hopefully thick winter gear since they would be going into the mountains. The first snows of the season were only a few weeks away Zollin guessed, but the mountains would be cold, wet, and full of snow already.

He dipped one foot into the tub. The water was very hot, but he found that if he moved slowly, he could bear the heat. Once he lowered himself all the way down into the water, he marveled at the warmth that seemed to soak into his bones. He wished he could sleep in the steaming water, but the water wouldn't stay hot and the tub was much too small to relax in.

After a few moments of rest, his eyes grew heavy, so he quickly washed using the block of soap and scrub brush that had been provided. Then he stood up and toweled the water off his body. He was cold as he crawled between the sheets of the thick bed, and he fell asleep almost instantly.

An hour later there was a soft knock at the door. The young girl who had brought Zollin his food, peeked her head into the room. Zollin opened his eyes lazily.

"Yes?" he asked.

"I was wondering if you needed anything," she said, flashing him a self-conscious smile.

"No, just sleep," he said, stretching under the covers.

Zollin felt more than a little self-conscious himself. He hadn't bothered putting on any clothes after his bath. The thick quilt on the bed covered him up, but he still felt exposed. The young girl stepped into the room and closed the door.

"I could stay, if you like," she said.

"No," Zollin said quickly. "That's kind of you, but I'm promised to another."

"That doesn't stop most men," she said moving closer.

It was dark in the room, but Zollin could make out the robe the girl was wrapped in and how it was pulled down to reveal her shoulders. He realized the inn keeper must have sent her up, but she was young; Zollin guessed she was maybe fourteen-years-old. The thought of the young girl selling herself for any amount of money was repugnant to Zollin.

"Did the inn keeper send you here?" he asked.

"No," the girl said. "I wanted to come."

"I doubt that," Zollin said, raising himself on one elbow.

"I did," the girl said. "I like you."

Her attempts at seduction were clumsy and almost made Zollin laugh, but he didn't want to hurt her feelings.

"Look, you're a pretty girl, but you're too young to be a wench."

"I'm not," she said drawing close to his bed. "I could please you, I know I could."

"That's not what I'm getting at."

"One gold crown and I'll do anything you want," she said, her voice shaking ever so slightly.

"You're worth far more than one gold crown," Zollin said. "But I'm in love with another. I'm sorry."

"No one has to know," the girl said, almost begging. "Please, I'll make you happy. You'll see."

"No," Zollin said firmly. "Why is this so important to you?"

The girl began to cry. Zollin didn't know what to do. He would have comforted her or gotten up so she could at least sit on the bed, but he didn't dare leave the safety of the bed covers.

"Don't cry," Zollin said. "It isn't personal."

"It's not that," the girl said. "My father needs the money."

Relief washed over Zollin. The girl's proposition had made him very uneasy. He loved Brianna and would never think of cheating on her, but the young girl's persistence had struck a chord deep inside Zollin. He didn't like that part of him was enticed, but no matter how hard he tried to discipline himself, he had been tempted.

"This isn't the way to earn money," Zollin said. "Not a young girl like you."

"I'm desperate," she said.

"Here," Zollin said, levitating his coin purse from the table to the bed.

The girl didn't notice the simple bit of magic in the darkness of the room. He pulled out four gold coins. They were the largest in his pouch and heavy. They clinked as he turned his hand over and held them out to her.

"Take these," he said. "Take them to your father tonight."

The girl took the coins. Even in the darkness Zollin could see the girl's eyes grow wide when she felt the weight of the coins.

"Oh, thank you so much," she said.

"It's no trouble," Zollin said. "Now go."

The girl hurried from the room. Zollin lay back, embarrassed, angry, tired, and relieved. Sleep was slower coming this time around. He felt a stab of shame when he thought of how easy it would have been to invite the girl into his bed. And that thought made him wonder what Brianna was doing. He couldn't help but fear that she was being tempted too, and he wondered if she would be faithful. He had no reason to doubt her, but reason played no part in the idle wanderings of his mind as he lay in the dark room. Brianna was beautiful, and Zollin had no doubt she could be with any man she chose. He felt inadequate and afraid; his dreams were troubled the rest of the night.

The next morning, he pulled his dirty clothes back on and went downstairs. The girl must have been waiting for him. She hurried to offer him breakfast. He sat down while she brought out a large tray of food and hot tea.

"My father wanted me to tell you how grateful he is," she said in a quiet voice as she set the tray down.

"I'm glad I could help," Zollin said, trying to keep his sour feeling from being evident in his voice.

"You saved him," she said. "You saved my family."

"I'm happy for you," he said.

The girl fussed over him, but Zollin ate his breakfast and bade her goodbye. Then he went to the market. The sun was up by the time he finished his breakfast and the market in Mountain Wind was brisk with trade. There were venders of all varieties. He had given the girl the last of his gold, but he had plenty of silver marks. He bought new boots with a fur lining, two pairs of pants, and four thick wool shirts. Next, he picked out a heavy, leather vest that was lined with wool on the inside. Then, he bought a thick cloak, which he fastened with a pin made from Elk horn. He also bought a thick blanket, gloves, and a fur-lined cap. Then, he bought a new pack to keep everything in. Finally, he purchased food, three canteens, and a bottle of wine.

His pack was heavy and full when he left the market. He strolled out of town, admiring the rugged mountain peaks in the distance. An hour later, a shadow crossed over him. He looked up and saw Ferno sailing down, the green wings stretched wide. He stopped and watched as Ferno gently landed and turned. The dragon's visage was terrible to behold. The wide face was menacing, with sharp teeth protruding from the immense mouth and smoke puffing from the dragon's ample nostrils.

"It's a beautiful day," Zollin said. "Let's get moving."

He levitated up onto the dragon's back and they took off, flying high into the air and speeding toward the mountains.

Chapter 10

King Felix steepled his fingers and suppressed the smile that was tickling the corners of his mouth. He had sent all of his advisors away except for General Corlis. The two men had become close. King Felix preferred Corlis' bold advice to that of the other generals and counselors who were more conservative and cautious.

"We have more dragons," Corlis said crossly.

"That bothers you?" King Felix asked.

"Yes, as a matter of fact," the young commander was pacing, while King Felix sat in an ornate chair by the fireplace.

"One dragon we can control, three dragons..." he let the thought trail off. "We've both seen what these things can do. If they were to turn on us, our troops could be annihilated."

"The answer isn't less dragons," King Felix explained. "It's more control."

"How are we going to control them? They're animals."

"Perhaps," the King said thoughtfully. "But we have resources."

"We haven't heard back from Ebbson Keep," General Corlis explained. "It will be at least a week before the messengers return."

"Yes, yes, but you see we have more than you think."

Corlis looked at his King doubtfully. Felix sat back, letting his smile show a little. Corlis continued to pace until there was a knock at the door.

"Are you expecting someone?" Corlis asked. He knew that Homan, the King's steward, wouldn't knock and the other advisors had been sent away for the night.

"I am," King Felix said. "Open the door."

When Corlis opened the door he found an aggravated Prince Willam waiting. The Prince wasn't used to being treated like an outsider, but he had felt a cold distance between himself and his father's inner circle ever since he'd returned to Orrock. Seeing the arrogant General Corlis at his father's door did little to reassure the Prince.

"Willam, come in," Felix said, not rising from his chair.

Prince Willam passed Corlis and approached his father. The room they were in held many memories for Willam. He had played in the room as a boy, dueling his younger brother with wooden staves until his father returned from the many duties that kept him busy around the castle. Prince Willam had always loved and admired his father, but as he grew older, a strange wedge had formed between them. Willam guessed that it was difficult for his father to be around someone who would eventually succeed him. Willam had been summoned before his father in the same private chambers they were in now when he'd been sent away to serve in the King's Army at fourteen-years-old. He'd been summoned back to the very same room when he'd been informed that his father was sending him to Osla. Now he was back and there was a feeling of foreboding in Willam as he stood before his father. He couldn't imagine what the King would require him to do now.

"Have a seat... son."

Willam sat on the chair opposite his father's. His body was tense with anticipation, and the heat from the fire made him sweat.

"You've been a good son and a good heir," King Felix said. "You will be king soon and that is good, but a king must have a queen, don't you agree?"

"To be honest, I hadn't given the matter much thought."

"You do like women, don't you?" King Felix said, his voice a barely concealed sneer.

"Of course," Willam said, biting his tongue at the slight to his honor.

"Well then, I want you to woo Brianna. We need her; we need her dragons. I want you to court her and then propose. Can you do that?"

"No," Willam said. "She's betrothed to Zollin."

King Felix laughed and Corlis joined in, although Prince Willam was sure that the general had no idea what was funny.

"I will not besmirch the honor of the man who saved my life," Willam said.

King Felix's laughter stopped abruptly.

"But you will besmirch the honor of my house?" he said angrily. "You will dishonor your father and ignore your King?"

"Father, I didn't mean to give offense," Willam said, shocked by his father's sudden change of mood.

"You have always been so high and mighty," Felix said. "Your mother thought you were noble, but I know better. You've always been spoiled. Well, that ends now. You will court Brianna, and you will marry her."

"Father, I can't do that."

"You can and you will, or by the Maker, I'll have you hanged from the castle walls. You may be the first Prince of Yelsia, but I am still King. We have plans, Willam, and you will not undermine them."

"Perhaps if I knew your plans I could better help fulfill them."

"Why should I share anything with you?" King Felix said, leaning forward in his chair. "You have failed me time and again. You rebel against me even now."

"No father, I want to help."

"Then you must do as you are told, Willam. Put your fanciful notions of chivalry and honor behind you. It's time for you to become a man and do your duty to King and Kingdom."

Willam was speechless. He didn't know what to do. His heart was torn between his ideas and his deep desire to please his father. He had been trained from a young age to revere the King and to always obey. He had never dreamed that his father would ask him to do something so heinous.

"I..." Willam had trouble speaking. "I will do as you wish," Willam said. "But I must say that Brianna and Zollin seemed incredibly close. I am not sure she can be dissuaded from her feelings for him."

"You let me worry about that," King Felix said. "You go to her, give her comfort and companionship. You're the heir to the throne, and there's not a woman in all of Yelsia who hasn't dreamed of winning your favor. And Brianna is beautiful, is she not? She will make a fine queen and give you strong heirs."

"What of her story about Gwendolyn's army? Surely we can't ignore the threat the witch poses."

"No, we cannot ignore any threat to Yelsia. We must ensure that we are strong. That's why I want you to pursue Brianna. She is more than a courtier, and if the conflict she describes is coming, there may not be another chance to ensure our line of succession."

Willam thought about what his father was saying. There was certainly an element of truth in his father's argument, but the idea of stealing Brianna away from Zollin felt wrong. And while his father's argument made sense, Willam knew that he wasn't being told the whole story. He was being manipulated, but he had no idea why? His father cared for him, and certainly understood that Willam would be king one day. There was no gain in forcing him to do something that would undermine Willam's rule or weaken him as a king.

"Fine," Willam said. "I'll court her, but I make no promises, Father."

"There is no need for promises," Felix said, sitting back in his chair again and smiling. "Your word is good enough for me."

"Is there anything else?"

"No, for now, let Brianna be your first and only priority."

"Yes, Father," Willam said.

He left the room wondering why his father didn't include him in his military plans. He couldn't shake the feeling that his father disapproved of him. King Felix knew Willam had commanded Ortis' forces while under the control of Gwendolyn's power, but Willam still felt the sting of that defeat and the shame that he had been broken by King Zorlan's torturer. He had hoped that when the Yelsian army reached the Walheta, he would have the opportunity to confront the king and take his revenge of the man who tortured him. Now he wondered if his father would even allow him to leave Orrock.

Back in the King's chambers, Felix smiled. Corlis looked curiously at his liege. He understood that tying Willam to Brianna and her dragons was practical, but he doubted that Willam, who Corlis considered a ceremonious fool of a Prince, could win the fiery girl.

"Do you think Willam can do it?" Corlis asked.

"I'm sure of it."

"You have a lot of confidence in the Prince."

"He can have the pick of any woman in the kingdom; I don't know why Brianna should be any different."

"She is different," Corlis said. "She rides on dragons and controls fire like a wizard."

"I don't give a damn what she can do. I only care that we ensure her dragons will fight for us. We've worked too hard and endured too much to miss out on this opportunity. My forefathers would have given their right arms to have this chance. We can't let it slip through our fingers."

"And what if she rejects him?"

"I never take anything for granted, general, you should know that about me by now. I won't commit myself to only one course of action. Brianna will accept Willam's proposal; I will see to that."

"You have a devious mind, my liege," Corlis said with a smile.

"I'll take that as a compliment."

* * *

Brianna was outside. The sun was weak and the air was cold, hinting that winter would soon be upon them. Brianna used to love winter. She loved snow and the way it made everything seem new, fresh, and clean. Of course, after being cooped up with her mother and sisters for days on end, she was always ready for spring. Now, of course, the cold air gave her a chill which only made her think of the witch Gwendolyn and the army that Brianna was sure was marching north at that very moment.

King Felix had always seemed a bit aloof to her, but he was a king after all, and she was just a girl from Tranaugh Shire. She was more than that, she knew, but she doubted if King Felix did. She had displayed her powers and told the King and his counselors about the battle in Osla. She told them what she had seen when she had been deep underground, but she sensed that King Felix didn't really believe her.

She walked around the castle to a large area filled with hay. Selix, Tig, and Gyia were curled up together, nestled down in the straw. They didn't like the way the soldiers and servants came to gawk at them. They didn't enjoy being fed either, even if they were given whole cows and sheep. They wanted to fly, to hunt, to be free, but King Felix had asked that for now they stay concealed behind the castle walls. He claimed that he didn't want to attract too much attention, or cause panic in the Kingdom, but Brianna felt trapped. She knew she wasn't trapped, and that she could leave anytime she wanted. She doubted that even the King's Royal Guard could stop her. They were brave men and skilled fighters, but all she would need to do is set the castle on fire, leap from a window and fly away with her pride.

An image of Gyia shaking her head entered her mind.

"I'm not planning to do it," she thought silently. "I just want to be ready for any possibility."

Another image, this time from Tig of the pride flying again, filled her mind. She felt the rush of joy that always accompanied her when she flew. The dragons understood her desires and felt much the same way. They wanted to leave as well, but they honored her wishes and stayed in Orrock.

"We can't just walk away," she said as she neared the stockade where the dragons were kept. "If we do, there won't be a safe place for us anywhere in the Five Kingdoms. This is our chance to prove that dragons and humans can peacefully coexist."

Selix growled and black smoke puffed from the big, golden dragon's nose. Gyia, ever the peacemaker, sent them all a feeling of peace. The long, sinuous, purple dragon moved closer to Brianna. An image of Prince Willam filled her mind.

"I haven't seen him, not for a few days. Everyone seems so busy, but they ignore me." She looked down, kicking at some of the loose hay that had escaped the stockade. "I miss Zollin."

Separate images from each of the dragons came into her mind, all of Ferno, the powerful, green dragon that had joined Zollin in his fight over the Grand City.

"We need to be together," Brianna said. "All of us."

"I hope I'm not interrupting," said a voice from behind Brianna.

She turned just as Gyia hissed, "My liege."

"Prince Willam, were your ears burning? We were just talking about you."

"Only good things, I hope."

"Of course, my lord."

"Please, call me Willam, we are well past pleasantries, wouldn't you agree?"

"If you say so... Willam."

"Good, I was hoping you would accompany me on a ride. I'm having a carriage prepared now."

"Is there news from your father? Is he sending the army to Falxis?"

"No," Willam said sadly. "He is preparing the army, but they are not ready to march south yet."

Brianna frowned.

"It seems frivolous to wait," Brianna said. "We need time to travel and to prepare our defense."

"You're right and I have argued that point myself, but mobilizing an army can take time. We have to make sure that Yelsia is defended, and we have to gather supplies. Preparing to feed an army is no small task."

"I'm sure you're right," Brianna said. "We are just anxious."

"So come for a ride with me," Willam said. "It will help calm your nerves."

"Alright," Brianna said. "I'll be back soon," she told the dragons.

Selix and Tig settled back down into the hay, dozing the afternoon away, but Gyia watched Willam and Brianna. The purple dragon wasn't sure what Willam was up to, but Gyia could see that he was doing his best to charm Brianna. Human relationships were foreign to dragons, who were neither male nor female and did not mate. They were loyal to their pride, but beyond that, they had no deeper attachments.

Willam escorted Brianna to the front of the castle where they found a large carriage with a thick leather canopy. There were two large, white horses harnessed to the carriage and a groom standing near one horse's head. Willam climbed up into the carriage and then extended his hand to Brianna. She took it, and he pulled lightly to help her up. He was amazed how light and graceful she was. She sprang up into the carriage and settled on the bench next to him.

A servant approached carrying a blanket.

"Thank you Hoyle," said Willam, taking the blanket. "We might get chilly," he told Brianna.

She smiled, "That's thoughtful of you."

He nodded and flicked the reins. The carriage rolled out of the Castle's main gate and through the city streets. People all around then bowed and waved, some even tossed flowers into the road and many hailed their prince. Willam was popular, Brianna realized. She was a little embarrassed by all the attention at first, but soon she found that it was intoxicating to be seen with Willam. Fantasies from her childhood flashed in her mind. She, like all little girls, dreamed of being swept off her feet by a handsome prince. She couldn't help but wonder what her mother would think if she saw Brianna now. Just as quickly as these thoughts flashed in her mind, guilt struck and she felt as if being with Willam was somehow unfair to Zollin. She imagined him struggling with his quest to save the Five Kingdoms, while she went on a carriage ride with a Prince.

"I'm not sure this is such a good idea," Brianna said.

Willam was driving the carriage, his eyes focused on the narrow streets that were crowded with rapturous looking people all waving and wishing Willam well.

"What's wrong?" he asked.

"I just think we need to be doing more to prepare for the invasion."

"All of that is being taken care. There is nothing left to do but wait at this stage," Willam said. "When dealing with something this massive, you have to trust the people around you to do their part. You can't control everything."

"I'm not trying to control everything," Brianna said. "But I don't see how carriage rides and feasts in the castle are helping."

"I know what you mean," Willam said. "I'm ready to ride south right now, but I know that if we rush things, it will cost us in the end. If Gwendolyn's forces are marching north, we still have time. We have to make sure we have everything we need and that every soldier is prepared to face mortal danger. That is our responsibility as leaders. If we send men into harm's way that aren't prepared, we have failed them and their sacrifices are tainted."

"You sound so kingly," Brianna said, her guilt easing a little.

"Well, I will be a king one day," he said, "if I live long enough."

"You've been through too much not to wear the crown," Brianna said. "Yelsia needs you."

"You don't think my father is a good king?" Willam said.

Brianna couldn't tell if Willam was asking a question or making a statement.

"I would not judge a king," she said. "I'm just one girl and leading kingdoms isn't something I have any knowledge of."

"You have more than you know. You understand mercy, you care about people, and you feel the responsibility for those who have no idea what dangers threaten them. That is the essence of being a leader."

"I just think your father isn't being as sincere as he pretends."

"That's a serious allegation," Willam said.

"I know, and maybe it's just my impatience, but I can't believe anyone could be so calm and seemingly unconcerned about the monsters that are coming."

"You ride on dragons and yet you worry about monsters?"

"You haven't seen them," Brianna said, her face pinched as she thought about the creatures she had seen pouring from the abyss.

"No, I haven't and that is probably why I can make plans calmly. But that's what Yelsia needs, a well-planned, strategic response to this threat."

Brianna found herself leaning against Willam's shoulder. She did feel a huge burden to protect the people of Yelsia from the army of the witch in Osla, but being with Willam eased the weight of it. He had a way of making her feel like everything would be okay. His self-confidence was like a shield.

She looked over at the Prince. He had thick, brown hair and the traces of a beard on his jaw. His eyes were dark but kind and his finely tailored clothes accentuated his body. The Prince had broad shoulders, and well-muscled arms. He wasn't as big as Mansel, but he was bigger than Zollin and older too. He smiled at her and she felt her face flush.

The carriage had finally reached the open fields beyond the city, and they moved toward a grove of Aspen trees. Brianna couldn't help but feel excited about being so near to Willam. The conflict inside her heart was as ferocious as a pitched battle.

"What are you thinking?" he asked.

"I'm just wondering what I'm doing here," she said.

"You're here because I asked you," he said confidently.

"But I'm no one, just a girl from Tranaugh Shire. Shouldn't you be surrounded by high born ladies?"

"I don't care for high born ladies," Willam said with a smile. "I hope to one day be a good king, but for the most part I think I'm just a soldier. I don't even think I'm much of a commander. The battle with Zorlan's army put that notion to rest. I feel more like myself when I'm with you, Brianna. You make me feel like I can actually be the kind of king I've always dreamed of being."

Brianna gasped; she couldn't believe what she was hearing.

"I know that we haven't known each other long," Willam said. "But I would like to get to know you better."

He slid one arm around Brianna's shoulders. She knew beyond any doubt that she should stop Willam. She knew she should pull away and profess her love for Zollin, but for some reason, she didn't do that. Willam held her close to his side and they watched as the sun sank over the horizon, casting the sky in beautiful shades of pink, punctuated by golden beams that made the clouds look like they were touched with fire.

"It's beautiful," she said, trying to contain her guilt.

"Not at beautiful as you," Willam said.

"Prince Willam, I don't think-"

"No," he said, cutting her off. "We don't need to think about anything. Let's just enjoy this moment."

Brianna, almost against her own will, settled back into the Prince's warm embrace. She let her worries go, just for that moment, and focused on the beauty of the sunset. She felt good, peaceful, and full of hope. In that instant, something inside her cracked her steely resolve and feelings for Willam poured into her heart.

Chapter 11

Zollin and Ferno were finally on the move again. He had finished resupplying in Mountain Wind and met back up with the green dragon. Now they were flying among the southern range of the Northern Highlands. Zollin thought that there was simply no more beautiful place on earth than in the mountains of the Highlands. They flew during the day and Ferno always managed to find a place to make camp each night, usually high up on the side of a mountain. There was little fuel for fires, so Zollin settled for warming the ground he rested on, usually thick granite, with his magic. The air was cold, but the stone held the heat well, so Zollin was comfortable through the long nights. Ferno, on the other hand, used its fiery breath to heat a bed. And if the dragon grew too cold, it would simply turn its long neck and breathe fire back over the brightly scaled body.

Ferno's wounds were slow to heal, but they were little more than shallow cuts and scrapes. It was unusual for anything to sever a dragon's scales, but flying in the sunlight seemed to aid Ferno's recovery.

Zollin wasn't sure where to start his search. He knew he needed to get to the northern range of the Highlands. He wanted to find as many magical creatures as he could. When they crossed over the great valley that separated the northern range from the southern range, he began to let his magic expand out all around them. Ferno, likewise, was able to broadcast its thoughts to any dragons in the vicinity. They had been looking for three days before they found their first magical creature.

Blastom was a black dragon, with massive horns on its square shaped head. It reminded Zollin of Bartoom, the dragon that had ravaged northern Yelsia and eventually was brought under control of the master of the Torr. Blastom wasn't as big as Bartoom, or even Ferno for that matter. The black dragon had a long neck, a short, compact body and a small tail.

The two dragons met in midair, circling each other, before Ferno swooped down. Zollin slid off of Ferno's back and the green dragon moved back, so that Zollin could speak to the smaller, black dragon. Zollin had gotten used to being around Ferno and even the other dragons of Brianna's pride, but approaching a strange dragon was difficult. It made his heart race, even though he knew he could defend himself if the dragon attacked.

"My name is Zollin," he said. "I'm Brianna's mate," he added.

Blastom bowed low and an image of Brianna appeared in Zollin's mind. He felt a little guilty for saying that he was Brianna's mate. That wasn't exactly true; they were promised to one another, but they had decided to wait to get married. Still, Zollin knew that dragons didn't really understand love or marriage.

"We have need of your help," Zollin said.

Ferno flew off in search of food, while Zollin explained the need. Blastom was reluctant to get involved. The black dragon preferred solitude. Zollin finally had to relay the fact that Brianna would be in danger to persuade Blastom to come south with them. They made camp together that night. Ferno returned to the camp with a large mountain goat which was given to Blastom. Zollin lay awake late into the night, staring up at the stars, snuggled close to Ferno for warmth.

The stars were so bright and clear in the highlands that Zollin felt he could reach out and touch them. He was reminded of when he and Brianna had trekked into the mountains to find Bartoom. They had spent many of those nights huddled together, staring up at the stars. He wondered if Brianna was looking at the same stars as he was.

The next morning, the three travelers set off together. Their party grew day by day. They soon had six dragons in total, although most were small dragons. Zollin had also found several giants and sent them to gather their kinsmen and march south. The giants were huge and slow, both in movement and speech, but they were true to their word and eager to help. It took Zollin a long time to find the opening in the mountains where the Dwarves of the Oliad clan lived. They were flying low, looking for the opening when Zollin felt the elusive presence of the strange creature that called itself Aberration.

Zollin knew that the creature would never come close to the pride of dragons. So he sent them in search of food while he levitated down to the steep valley between the towering mountain peaks. Then, he sent his magic out toward the creature, hoping that the beast would come to him. It did, although it moved stealthily and cautiously. Zollin waited patiently and seeing the creature was once again a shock to his senses. Aberration was large, bigger than a Shire horse. It had the body of a great bull with a slick black hide, the legs and split hooves of a goat, and its head was that of an eagle. Aberration also had a long, leathery tail that it could wield like a whip.

"Aberration," Zollin called out when the creature came in sight. "It is me, Zollin. Do you recall me?"

"Wizard," screeched Aberration. The creature could speak, but the voice was high pitched and the beak had trouble conveying words clearly.

"That's right," Zollin said. "I'm a wizard, and I need your help."

Aberration moved closer, the great eagle eyes shifting all around as if it suspected a trap of some kind.

"Aberration does not help wizards."

"I understand," Zollin said. "I know you have been mistreated in the past, but I have no desire to control you or hurt you. I have come to seek the aid of all the free people here in the north. I'm trying to gather a magical army. I'm afraid a very dark sorceress has unleashed an evil army on the land. If we don't stand together, there will be no way to stop them."

"Witches and Wizards don't concern me anymore," Aberration said. "I want only peace and solitude."

"I understand that and respect it," Zollin said. "If you choose to stay here I won't blame you, but alone I can't stop the army of monsters that will make their way here eventually. We must all stand together to stem the tide of evil that is rising against us."

"I am evil. I am a soulless creature, created by your kind, but there are no others of my kind. Why should I help you?"

"I do not think you are evil, Aberration, even if you were created for evil purposes. You threw off the yoke of slavery and came here to find peace. That isn't evil, in fact, that is noble. Come with me, and you will find that not all humans are callous, hateful people."

"It is not my place," the creature said.

"No, it isn't, but I need your help."

"You are not mine to worry over. I cannot help you."

"I disagree and it makes my heart sad that you feel that way. We are marching south, across Yelsia, and the Rejee desert. We will make a stand on the southern side of the Walheta Mountains. If you change your mind, join us there. I would stand with you, unashamed and proud."

Aberration cocked its head to one side, eyeing Zollin warily, then, like a flash it disappeared, its tail snapping behind it and cracking like a whip. Frustration set in and Zollin had difficulty not falling into despair. King Ricard was reluctant to believe Zollin; a handful of small dragons had stepped in to help, but in the end, Zollin feared it wouldn't be enough. He tried to encourage himself; he could look for the giants to come to their aid, but it all felt like too little to make a difference.

He set off on foot, limping through the rocky ravines and levitating over bounders and up steep cliffs. He could have called out for Ferno, but the truth was he wanted to be alone. He didn't want to put on a brave face or pretend everything was okay. To the south, an army of monsters was on the loose. Zollin knew the Five Kingdoms would never be the same, and he couldn't stave off the feelings of guilt that it was all somehow his fault.

Snow began to fall as he trudged along. The scar tissue in his leg ached from the cold and his clothes were soon wet through from the snow. The sky overhead was dark gray and then a harsh wind began to rattle through the canyons. Before Zollin knew what was happening, a winter storm turned the world a dirty white. There was so much snow blowing all around him that Zollin couldn't see further than one arm's length.

He knew he had to find shelter to ride out the storm. Ferno could find him possibly, but the big dragon could also crash into the side of a mountain in the white out conditions. He hoped the big, green dragon would wait until the storm passed to come looking for Zollin.

He stumbled along for a few minutes; fear seemed to take on the voice of the wind which was howling around him. Then he remembered that he didn't have to see; he could let his magic see for him. He made a bubble shield around his body that blocked the wind and snow. Then, he took a moment to collect himself. He hadn't realized how cold he'd gotten or how much the wind had made him lose all sense of time and direction. He took several deep breaths and then let his magic flow out of the bubble to map the terrain around him. It was hard to block out the snow, which was frozen into clumps and was blown in a swirling maelstrom by the wind. But after a few moments of effort, he located what he was looking for. It was small cave, little more than a crack in the rock about thirty feet up the side of a very steep incline. The wind and snow were blocked and at the very least, Zollin knew he would be dry and sheltered from the elements inside the cave.

He closed his eyes and focused his magic. Levitating himself had become almost second nature, but it still required effort, especially with the wind blowing so hard that he could hardly control his ascent. He moved slowly, keeping the magical bubble around him so that the effects of the wind wouldn't wreck his concentration. He landed just on the narrow ledge outside the cave. The rock was already slick with ice and snow. Zollin let the magical bubble collapse and was immediately buffeted so strongly by the wind he feared he would be blown off the side of the mountain.

The cave opening was small and Zollin had to crawl inside. The relief from the wind and snow was so strong that Zollin didn't immediately notice the strong odor inside the cave. It was a musky scent and when Zollin noticed it he felt fear stroking his neck again. The interior of the cave was pitch black, and the howling wind just outside blocked out the sound of the growl from the animal who had already taken shelter in the cave. Zollin tried to ease out of the cave, but the big mountain lion pounced before Zollin could get out.

Chapter 12

All Zollin saw was a flash of tawny hide, and then he was falling, spinning, and crashing down the side of the mountain with the winter storm blocking out even the sound of his own screams. When he finally came to a rolling stop at the bottom of the ravine, he collected himself. Nothing was broken, he was only shaken up. His magical bubble shield had held back the heavy beast, but the ferocious cat's attack had knocked him out of the cave and down the mountain. He was rattled but not seriously hurt. He got slowly back to his feet, and then he was knocked forward again. This time he summersaulted and landed on his stomach. His magic churned like a roaring fire inside him, stoked by his fear and by the incredible weight on top of him. Somehow the shield had held, but the mountain lion was on top of Zollin, biting and clawing in hopes of tearing him to shreds.

Pin pricks of light danced around the edges of Zollin's vision, and he felt the searing pain of his magic breaking through a weakness in his containment. He realized that he was losing control. He let a small shock of blue magical energy jolt the mountain lion, which immediately jumped away with a snarling roar loud enough to be heard over the howling wind.

Zollin rolled over and was just getting to his feet when he saw another blur, and the mountain lion was on him again. The magical bubble was shrinking, and the lion's razor sharp claws and teeth edging nearer and nearer his throat. This time, Zollin lashed out angrily; his magic batting the lion away like a toddler boxing with a toy. Zollin stood up, feeding magic into his shield. There was a roar and another lion pounced on Zollin, but this time he didn't fall. Instead, the shield held, and it was the lion that twisted and fell away. Zollin sent a ball of fire rushing toward the cat. The lion roared again, this time in distress as the fire singed its fur and burned away its wiry whiskers.

Zollin let his magic flow out. There were two cats; the large male was lying sprawled against the rocks, and its back was broken. The female had backed away, but was still looking for an opportunity to strike. Zollin immediately levitated himself back up the mountain, away from the vicious lions. He used his magic to navigate back to the cave. Zollin crawled into the dark space again, breathing heavy and trying to calm the raging storm his magic had become inside him. He took several deep breaths and then lit a small flame to illuminate the cave. The small circle of light didn't reach the recesses of the cave, but in the darkness Zollin could see small eyes glowing.

He fed magic into the flame until the cave was illuminated. The lion clubs began mewling and Zollin sighed. He felt terrible that he had killed the male mountain lion. He knew the big cat wasn't dead yet, but with its back broken it was only a matter of time. The lions had only been protecting their family, doing exactly what Zollin would have done himself. He extinguished the flame and went back out into the raging storm. It took a moment to find the injured lion in the blizzard. The female was gone, probably thinking that Zollin had killed her mate and would soon finish off their cubs as well. There was nothing he could do to bring the female lion back, so he focused his magic on the wounded male lion, letting his healing power mend the lion's severed spinal cord. It took a long time and Zollin was afraid the lion would freeze to death before he finished, but when he was done, the big cat climbed wearily to its feet.

Zollin sat back, his head just under the cave opening, his heart pounding in his ears. Healing the cat from a distance was taxing, and his stamina was almost gone. He let his magic flow out once more, trying to find the female lion, but she was gone. Zollin felt horrible, but there was nothing more he could do. He took a deep breath and slid down the icy mountainside, using his magic to buffer the rough terrain from his backside. He then levitated the terrified mountain lion to the cave. He waited just long enough to ensure that the big cat went inside to the bawling cubs.

He then stumbled on through the storm, looking again for a place to escape the weather. It took almost an hour. Despite his bubble shield, his clothes were covered with ice and snow, and his fingers and toes stung with the early signs of frostbite. He finally found a small shelter; it was little more than an alcove, a depression in the side of the mountain. He was forced to lie down and roll into the small depression. The rock around him was cold but dry. The wind howled and the snow blew, but he was safe in the small hideout. He used magic to heat the rocks, letting his power flow down into the ancient stone until he could feel the tiny bits of matter and their spinning electrical charges. With a little prompting, the mountain's most basic building blocks began to speed up, spinning and shaking, creating heat in the stone until Zollin felt like he was in an oven. Then, warm at last, his clothes steaming from the heat of the rock around him, he fell asleep.

It was dark when Zollin woke up. He was hungry and thirsty and for a long moment he couldn't remember where he was. Then he recalled the snow storm. It must have died out because he couldn't hear the howl of the wind. The stone around him held only the faintest hint of heat, and Zollin guessed he'd been asleep for around six hours. He let his magic flow out of the small cave and as he had guessed, the space was nearly enclosed with snow. He sent out a wave of magic that exploded through the snow, blowing icy chunks far from the cave and letting a wave of cold, fresh air circulate into the small hideout.

Zollin crawled out of the tiny shelter and looked up. The stars were bright overhead, which meant the clouds were gone. The temperature had plummeted and was well below freezing. Zollin knew he needed to build a fire and stay warm until morning, but the cave he'd sheltered in was just too small. He held up a hand and conjured a small flame. The light danced and glistened off the snow all around him. He began trudging through the snow and soon came to a flat area where several small shrubs were struggling to grow in the rocky terrain. Zollin used magic to melt the snow and then pulled his dagger out to cut the shrubs. He didn't need to build a fire, his magic was more than capable of keeping him warm and cooking the food that was in his pack. But

Zollin was beginning to feel lonely, and he craved the cheerful familiarity of a fire.

He used his magic to pull the water out of the wood, and then he arranged the fuel into a small pyramid and used his magic to ignite the fire. Soon, bright yellow flames danced, and he warmed his hands and feet. His pack was full of dried meat, fish, and a few vegetables. He didn't have proper utensils, so he simply warmed some of the meat over the fire and ate it. He drank water from one of the canteens, before filling it with snow. Then he lay down, wrapping his cloak around him and dozing for a few more hours.

The sun came up and woke Zollin. His fire was out, and he was stiff with cold. He stood up and looked around. The mountains all looked the same to him, but he could get the general sense of direction from the sun rising in the east. He moved slowly through the thick snow, neither trying to make good time nor running the risk of exhausting himself. He sucked on some salty meat as he walked, using his magic to help him navigate the steeper terrain. At one point, he let his magic flow out in all directions, including up. He wanted to make contact with Ferno and the other dragons, but there was nothing, not even a mountain goat or the small mice that made their homes under the fallen rocks in the valleys.

Zollin did his best not to let his loneliness turn into depression. He'd been on his own before, in fact, most of his childhood was spent alone. His father had always been busy, and Zollin had few friends in the village where he had grown up. But the last few weeks with Ferno had formed a link between man and dragon. Zollin felt the ache of the big, green beast's absence.

It was almost dark before Zollin felt the hint of a familiar magic. He had been sending out his magic hourly, hoping to find something among the towering mountains. What he found was both surprising and exciting. He couldn't be positive, but he sensed the rhythm of the mountain dwarves. The dwarves used a pounding, pulsing type of music, mostly played on unique drums, to work to. The beat of the drums would be accented by the sounds of chisels on stone and hammers on steel. Zollin couldn't feel the dwarves themselves, but he could feel the vibration of their music in the solid rock of the mountains.

It was almost midnight before Zollin's magic touched on one of the little miners. He followed the elusive vibrations and finally, as the moon set and Zollin's tired feet were starting to stumble on the rough terrain, he found a small opening in the rock face. The opening was sheltered by larger boulders which appeared to have fallen down the mountainside, but in truth, the large rocks were strategically placed.

Zollin trudged to the opening and listened. The sounds of the dwarfish music were faint, but he could hear it. He stuck his head into the cave and shouted.

"Hello!" he bellowed. "Hello down there!"

There was silence for a moment, and then he heard the grunting of a dwarf approaching.

"Who goes?" said the dwarf in a deep voice.

"Zollin, Wizard of Yelsia."

"Never heard of you," said the dwarf.

Zollin could hear the small, booted feet scuttling away from the opening of the cave.

"Wait!" he shouted. "I'm friends with Babaz, chief of the Oliad clan. And also of Jute, head of the Yel clan."

The footsteps returned. Zollin waited, straining his eyes in the darkness. Finally, he saw a shadowy face appear. He couldn't make out the specific details, but he recognized the busy hair and thick beard.

"The Yel clan is far to the south," said the voice, "but I know Babaz. I suppose you're going to tell me that you're the wizard who repaired the Stepping Stones."

"The bridges deep in the mountains," Zollin said. "Yes, I went through with Babaz and repaired what I could. I also stayed with the Jaq clan. Hammert is now my friend."

"Alright, come along, but watch your head," the dwarf said.

Zollin moved toward the hole, and he had to get down on his hands and knees to get inside. The tunnel leading down into the mountain didn't expand for a long distance. Zollin's dwarf guide didn't seem to need any light, but Zollin was forced to kindle a small flame. His hands and knees were skinned and aching by the time he reached the large cavern that served as the dwarf city. There were lanterns hanging on pegs and billowing furnaces casting an orange glow around the cavern. Dwarf children, looking much like their parents, played in small groups. The adults were either working or sitting at low tables drinking ale and smoking pipes. The fragrance of the tobacco smoke gave the dwarf village a distinct fragrance.

"This is the Tradnook clan," said the dwarf who had led Zollin down into the cavern. "I am Avryl."

"I'm Zollin," he said, stretching his back.

"I thought wizards were all old men with long beards and pointy hats," Avryl said with a smirk. "You're just a child by the looks of you."

"I'm sorry to disappoint you," Zollin said.

"Oh, you haven't disappointed me yet. Let me introduce you to Bloc, he'll decide what to do with you."

"Is Bloc your chief?"

"No, I'm the head of the Tradnook clan. Bloc is the descendant of Oglebard, the last king of the dwarves."

"I didn't know the dwarves had a king," Zollin said as he followed Avryl.

"We don't normally. We live in clans and each clan has a chief; there's little need for more than that while we're underground. But sometimes we venture forth from the deep earth, and in those times we need a king to settle disputes and deal with the humans. You tall folk are sometimes hard to endure, if you take my meaning."

Zollin laughed and Avryl looked up at him. Zollin could see the firelight dancing in the dwarf's eyes and for the first time he realized just how old Avryl looked. The dwarf had wrinkles around his eyes and across the round cheeks that were visible under his bushy white beard.

"I understand exactly what you mean," Zollin said. "We are hard to endure."

"Humpf," Avryl responded. "For a minute there, I thought you were poking fun at me, tall one. I might not seem like much to a long strider like you, but believe me I'm still strong of arm and stalwart of heart."

"I've no doubt of that, Avryl; I meant no offense, truly. I am sorry if my lack of manners has vexed you."

"Well, you tall folk take a little getting used to," Avryl said. "No offense was taken. You've manners enough for the Tradnook clan."

Avryl led Zollin back into a richly decorated room. Most of the dwarfish homes, which were carved into the stone around the larger cavern, were sparsely furnished. Most furniture was carved out of solid rock, and there was very little comfort to be had in the small dwellings. The room Avryl led Zollin to was just the opposite. There was a thick rug on the stone floor and wooden chairs with thick, goose down cushions. Paintings in gold frames were mounted on the walls, and there were crystal decanters with rich, red wines set on a table.

Bloc was sitting in one of the chairs. He held a brass goblet in one hand, the other was stretched on the arm of the chair and Zollin noticed a large looking gold ring on the dwarf's middle finger.

"Ho, Avryl, who is your tall friend?" Bloc said.

"This is Zollin, he's a wizard."

"I've heard of Zollin," Bloc said merrily. He had none of the dour traits that Zollin found common in dwarves. "Welcome, Zollin, friend of Babaz and Hammert. Your work on the Stepping Stones has been a benefit to all dwarves."

"It was my pleasure to help," Zollin said.

"What brings you to our beautiful mountain?"

"Dire news, I'm afraid," Zollin said. "I was hoping that the mighty dwarves could help us."

"Mighty dwarves," Bloc said with a laugh. "I like that. Did you hear, Avryl? We are now the mighty dwarves of the Northern Highlands. I confess; I like the sound of that."

"Flattery brings ill tidings," Avryl grumbled.

"Oh, don't be so negative, you old grump," Bloc said.

Zollin was almost shocked by Bloc's teasing. He had never experienced a dwarf that wasn't serious all the time.

"He's right," Zollin said. "The tidings from the southern kingdoms are dire."

"Well, be that as it may, I would like to welcome you to my home, Zollin. A wizard indeed, it's been centuries since my family has had the chance to entertain a worthy guest. Please, you look tired. Have a glass of wine and rest a while. I will send word to the clan leaders to gather, and then you can make your request of us."

"That is very kind," Zollin said.

Bloc waved the thanks away. He hopped up from his seat and began to pour another goblet of wine.

"Avryl, send word to the clan leaders," Bloc said. We shall meet in three days at the dome under the rock."

Avryl nodded, but didn't speak. Instead, he hurried out of the room. Bloc turned to Zollin and handed him a goblet of wine.

"There, that will set things right. Tell me what is happening in the wide world above us."

"It is a long story," Zollin said. "And I'll be glad to share it with you, but the gist of it is that a witch has summoned dark magic. I fought her in Osla, but she fended me off and then she cast a spell that cracked open the earth."

"Yes, I'm aware," Bloc said, his merry expression hardening into a look of severe worry.

"You know?" Zollin asked in surprise.

"There is very little that happens below the earth that we are not aware of, Zollin," he said. "This witch summoned a demon, an immortal spirit lord."

"I saw it," Zollin said.

"They are ancient, even by dwarfish standards," Bloc said. "But this is not new magic the witch wields. I suspected we would hear from the humans at some point. In the dawn of this world, spirit beings called Illuminais worked together creating every living thing. At first our world was a blank canvass and the Illuminai had room to fashion creatures of every kind, but soon the world began filling up and conflict among the creatures spilled over into the Illuminai. Some were killed as they battled one another; others were twisted in their hate and spite. They are powerful beings, but their time in our world passed, and they were banished. They can be summoned back using dark magic, but they cannot work their power directly in our world. Instead they pour their evil into one of us, funneling their hate and fury into destroying what they once created."

Zollin was stunned. He had longed for answers to his questions, and now that he was getting some, he was even more terrified by this new knowledge than he had been when he didn't know what was happening.

"I assume the Leffers have been unleashed?" Bloc asked.

"Leffers?" Zollin asked.

"Winged abominations," Bloc said. "They have the body of a horse, the head and shoulders of a man."

"And a tail like a scorpion," Zollin said. "Yes, we fought these Leffers, but there were too many to stop."

"Yes, they are like a swarm of insects. They aren't intelligent creatures, just mindless monsters intent on carrying out the will of their masters."

"Gwendolyn was the witch who summoned them," Zollin said.

"The person you knew is gone," Bloc said. "The power of the Illuminai will change her forever. She is lost."

"She will not be missed."

"No, I suspect not," Block said before sipping his wine.

"The Leffers are capturing people and flying them back to the great abyss," Zollin explained. "Brianna, my betrothed, believes that Gwendolyn is creating an army."

"Is Brianna the Fire Spirit we have heard tales of?"

"Yes," Zollin said.

"And is it true she has birthed dragons?"

"In a sense, yes," Zollin said.

"These are momentous times," Bloc said, settling back into his seat. "The world is changing. We hang on the balance between the way things have always been, and a cold, merciless new future."

"You think Brianna is part of that future?" Zollin asked, trying to hide his dismay.

"None of us are completely good or evil, Zollin," Bloc said, his merry expression hardening into a look that was both serious and wise. "Surely you know that anyone can be good or bad depending on their choices. This witch in the south had chosen wickedness; you and I have chosen righteousness, or so we hope."

Bloc smiled, but it was not a look of mirth, but rather a glance that seemed to penetrate down deep into Zollin's soul. They stared at one another for a long moment.

"In times like these there are always a few individuals who have the power to truly make a difference. You are such a man. Your betrothed is as well, I suspect. The question before us now is how will you forge the future, Zollin?"

"I will fight," Zollin said. "I will stand against Gwendolyn and whatever evil she unleashes."

"Your race is always quick to choose violence," Bloc said. "Are there no alternatives?"

"I don't know," Zollin said, taken aback by Bloc's statement. "I admit I've never considered any."

"We must consider every possibility," Bloc said. "These decisions cannot be rushed."

"No," Zollin said, "but time is the one luxury we do not have. If Gwendolyn is building an army as we suspect, she will be marching north soon, and probably with three or four times the number of troops we can put in the field against her. That is why I am here. We need the dwarves to join our fight."

"My people will not be quick to join your cause," Bloc said. "The Clan Chieftains rarely agree on anything."

"Then I must persuade them," Zollin said.

Bloc was quiet for a moment and Zollin finished the wine in his goblet. He knew the wine was rare; it was by far the best he'd ever tasted. The warm, soothing feeling of the wine spread through his body and made him feel so relaxed that he was tempted to close his eyes and go to sleep right in the small, dwarfish chair.

"I will go with you, of course, but I cannot aide you in your plea. My family's role for centuries has been to lead our clans when they venture out of our homeland. Few dwarves can communicate with humans effectively. They have a natural distrust for the tall folk, as your kind is known. Only wizards and other magical people have been welcomed in our hallowed halls."

"It is my great honor to have visited your people."

"And our great honor to host you. Please, I can see the fatigue on your face. Come and rest. We can leave for the Dome when you have slept."

"Thank you," Zollin said. "You are very kind."

Bloc waved away the compliment and showed Zollin to a small anti-room. There was no bed, but the floor was covered with thick animal skins, pillows, cushions, blankets, and quilts.

"I hope this will be comfortable enough," Bloc said.

"It is great," Zollin said, remembering that on his last trek through the caverns under the mountains he had slept on solid rock.

"I will wake you when it is time to leave, until then, rest well."

Zollin sat down on the soft pallet and pulled off his boots. It felt good to wiggle his toes. He was warm all over for the first time in days. He pulled off his clothes and lay down. The room was just big enough for Zollin to stretch out. His head was near one wall and his feet near the other, but he was comfortable. He thought of trying to contact Ferno, to let the green dragon know that he was okay, but before he could, he fell sound asleep.

Chapter 13

Quinn was almost through the mountain pass. He was riding a black gaited horse and leading a mule. The journey south from Felson had been uneventful and slow. He had ridden hard, staying close to the coast to avoid the Rejee Desert. The southern portion of Yelsia was sparsely populated, and he was fortunate to have avoided bandits along the way.

Riding through the mountains should have been relaxing, but he had too many worries on his mind to relax. His first concern was for Mansel. He didn't know exactly why he felt so worried about his former apprentice. Mansel had followed them from Tranaugh Shire when Zollin had been attacked by the wizards of the Torr, but that really wasn't surprising to Quinn. Mansel was an adventurous sort. Quinn had taught Mansel to fight with the sword, but it was quickly obvious that Mansel was a natural with a blade. He had the strength and agility needed to be a great swordsman. But the truth was that Mansel and Quinn had not gotten along over the last several months. Mansel had fallen into heavy drinking, and Quinn had left the big warrior on their way south to save Prince Willam. That incident still haunted Quinn; it was a regret that he couldn't forgive himself for.

They had both fallen under the spell of the enchantress, Gwendolyn, and twice Mansel had tried to kill Quinn. The older man knew that those incidents haunted Mansel, even though they were both under the control of the witch at the time. Quinn's only desire was to see Mansel happy and flourishing in life. He couldn't help but wonder if the younger man wouldn't have been better off not learning to fight and instead, applying his skills to a trade.

Quinn was also worried about Miriam. At first, their relationship had been sweet. They were like teenagers, caught up in a whirlwind infatuation, but their personal habits had quickly begun to wear on their romance. For his part, Quinn was used to living alone, to making decisions without input from anyone else or even considering another person's feelings. When he had married Zollin's mother, they had done everything together and he had catered to her every desire. But then she had died and Quinn was forced to make every decision for himself and for their newborn son all on his own. He had tried to include Miriam in his decisions, but she was full of different ideas. She hated all violence and while Quinn always tried to talk his way out of trouble first, with Felson full of refugees, conflict was inevitable. She was quick to take in anyone in need of help, especially children. Quinn was a kind man, but not particularly partial to children.

The biggest conflict between them was Miriam's home. The home, land, and barns had been in Miriam's family for almost a century. It had been well maintained and allowed Miriam to earn a good living as an animal healer in the community, but Quinn felt like an outsider. Everything in the home and around the property was hers. There was never a sense that it was their home and although he knew Miriam had the best intentions, they simply couldn't get along.

He felt guilty for leaving her behind, but he could never sit back and allow Mansel to be in danger. In the past he had enjoyed the solitude and freedom of being on the road, but now that joy was smothered by guilt. One part of him felt like he should be riding to help Mansel and the other part felt as though he should be staying with Miriam, especially if what Brianna had warned them about was coming true. Full scale war was a terrifying thought, especially if the army they were fighting were full of some dark magic that transformed regular people into monsters. Still, if that war was coming, he knew he could never stay safely behind the front lines. It just wasn't in his nature to hide from a fight.

On top of all these concerns, lingering in the back of Quinn's mind was Zollin. His little boy had grown up so fast, and Quinn was incredibly proud of his son. The fact that Zollin was a wizard was still stupefying to Quinn, even though he'd seen his son do the impossible. But it was Zollin's character that impressed Quinn the most. Zollin had his mother's sense of right and wrong coupled with Quinn's own steely discipline. And Zollin also had an independent spirit; he was fiercely loyal, but not beholding to anyone, not even the King of Yelsia. Perhaps that came from running from the Torr who had sought to control him and bend him to their will, or perhaps that trait was already evident and had given him the strength to resist the ancient magical order. Still, Zollin was in almost constant danger, and the thought of losing Zollin haunted Quinn's every waking moment. He knew there was very little he could do for his son, but Quinn still worried about him, as was his right as a father.

The terrain around Quinn was slowly opening up. The valleys were wider and the mountains less steep. The Walheta mountain range was very different from the Northern Highlands which were stark and austere. The Walheta Mountains were covered with lush vegetation, towering pines, and stately fir trees grew thick on the steep mountains. Wildlife was plentiful; in fact, Quinn had managed to kill a young deer not long after he entered the mountain pass. He took a day to smoke the meat and salt as much of the tender venison down with his meager supplies as he could.

There were also people living in the Walheta, hermits mostly, who enjoyed the solitude of the mountains. Quinn had visited with several along his journey. They were friendly folk in their own way. Quinn knew, of course, that the odds of finding Mansel were slim. Still, he asked about the young warrior wherever he went.

Green Glen was a small settlement in a wide valley, just inside the southern edge of the mountains. There was a small inn and Quinn stopped long enough for a meal. He asked everyone he met of news from the south. The rumors coming north were not good. People spoke of monsters, dragons, villages' destroyed, and vile magic unleashed. Quinn always felt a shutter of fear whenever people talked ill of magic. He'd heard such talk all his life, but now he knew better. Still, he hated to think of people judging Zollin because he was a wizard. Quinn knew that his son's power did not come from some wicked sacrifice or allegiance to demonic forces, but many of the people he met were sure that all magic was evil. If the rumors were even partially true, he guessed they had a right to their prejudice.

He learned little of value from most of the people in the village, but one man, a teamster who transported goods through the mountains in heavy wagons, had just returned from a trek to the south. Quinn rode to the man's home. There was a small cottage and a large barn on the property. He tied his horse and mule to a tree and walked toward the barn.

"Hello!" he said loudly.

"Eh? Who's there?"

The door opened and a fat man appeared. He had a large, round gut with thick arms and legs. His head was nearly bald but he grew a long, scraggly beard that was speckled with gray. His eyes were bright and he took in Quinn's appearance and then smiled.

"How can I help you?" the man said.

"Are you Jorgyn the teamster?" Quinn asked.

"I am."

"I'm looking for news from the south," Quinn said. "My name is Quinn."

He stuck out his hand. Jorgyn took it in a firm grasp and shook it briefly. Quinn could see the large draft horses in the barn and the heavy wagons with large wheels that Jorgyn used to haul goods through the mountains.

"Welcome Quinn, are you new to the Glen?"

"Just passing through," Quinn said. "I have a friend in Falxis. He's a young man, big through the chest and shoulders, a swordsman. His name is Mansel. I don't suppose you've run into him?"

"I'm afraid I haven't," Jorgyn said. "I don't usually visit much on my travels. I have to protect the cargo. I don't even stay in the villages to the south."

"That's unfortunate," Quinn said bitterly. "I'm not sure where to start looking for him."

"You don't know where your friend lives?"

"No, he was moving north, but with the rumors I was afraid he might have come to harm."

"I don't know about monsters," Jorgyn said, "but something has the people in frenzy in Falxis. There's a settlement of people not far from the mountains. It's inland from the coast, perhaps a day's ride from the pass. It could be your friend is there or someone there knows of him."

"That is helpful," Quinn said. "Thank you."

"It's no trouble," Jorgyn said. "I hope you find your friend."

"As do I. I won't trouble you further."

"Safe travels," Jorgyn said, as Quinn walked back to his horse.

He rode out of the valley and found another small village where the pass opened up onto the gently rolling plains of Falxis. The sun was just going down when he stopped to rest his horses. He asked for news of the settlement Jorgyn had spoken of. The townspeople weren't happy about the new gathering. They made signs to ward off evil as they spoke of the people there. Night fell and Quinn felt that he could travel safely enough with a half moon and the sky bright with stars, so he pushed on after his brief rest. He felt like he was close to the end of his journey, and he didn't like the idea of stopping now.

The night was quiet, and he grew tired on the long ride. His head was drooping and the gait of his horse was slow as morning approached, but Quinn could smell the stench of the settlement and pushed himself to keep moving. Most permanent villages found ways to deal with trash, human waste, and the smell of animals. The refugee camp, which was clustered around a quickly flowing stream that ran out of the Walheta Mountains, stank worse than a tavern privy.

Quinn's horse neighed in protest the closer they got to the settlement and just as the sun was rising behind Quinn, he could see fires being kindled and people setting about their morning chores in the light of dawn. He rode to the first of the small encampments. There were no buildings, just camps sites. People were either huddled around small fires or around wagons with their meager belongings. Quinn stopped at the first camp and asked about Mansel.

"My name is Quinn," he said. "I'm looking for a friend who may be here. His name is Mansel. He's a big man, carries a sword. Probably has a woman named Nycoll with him."

"Sorry friend," the man said. He looked thin and hungry, his wife and children, all looking terrified huddled behind him. "We don't know many folk except those camped nearby."

"I'll keep looking then, thanks," Quinn said.

He rode to the next group and repeated his questions, getting answers that were much the same from each group. The people in the settlement looked both scared and exhausted. Quinn wondered where they would go. He had gotten used to refugees in Felson, but at least there they had hopes of earning a meal. Here, at the foot of the mountains, unless they could hunt or gather food, there was very little to support such a large gathering, and the natural resources would soon be picked clean.

It took nearly three hours to make his way through the entire settlement, but none of the refugees had seen or knew Mansel. Quinn stopped to rest, frustration making his meal of stale bread and salted meat even more tasteless than usual.

He wasn't sure where to go next. He could go south, but he wondered if he wouldn't be better off to ride west to the coast first. He seemed to recall that Nycoll had lived on the coast of Falxis. Surely she would want to settle near the sea. Brianna had traveled inland without seeing Mansel, so Quinn decided to ride toward the coast. The mountain pass, which started near the coast on the Yelsian side of the mountains, wandered inland and he knew he was still a hard day's ride from the meandering seashore.

He walked his horse through the afternoon and remounted a couple of hours before dark. He knew he would still have half a day's journey once night fell, but he didn't think traveling at night while searching for his friend would be a good idea. He was tired, too. So, just before nightfall, Quinn made camp.

He built a fire bigger than he needed, but the nights were growing cold and he didn't want the fire to die completely, while he slept through the night. He had been asleep a few hours when a strange noise woke him up. At first he heard a deep thrumming sound, but he couldn't make out what the noise was. Then, as he stood with his back to the fire, peering hard into the darkness, while trying to will his eyes to see in the gloom, his horse and mule began to panic. They were hobbled with rope, but they struggled to break free. Something was obviously terrifying them and as Quinn struggled to calm his animals down, fear began to run its icy claw down his back.

He'd heard rumors of monsters and heard Brianna's account of the beasts that had come up out of the abyss in the Grand City. He buckled on his short sword, checked his throwing knives, and strapped his round shield securely to his arm. Then he waited. He decided that even though his mount was terrified and not particularly suited for combat, that he would rather face whatever was coming on horseback. He mounted up and waited to see what would appear.

* * *

Mansel and Nycoll had been on the move all night. At first it seemed that they had made a clean escape, but it wasn't long before they heard the ominous thrum from the centaur-like creatures and Mansel knew they were being followed. They kept moving as night fell. They had yet to see their pursuers, but the sound of the terrifying beasts was growing louder and louder.

Finally, they decided to hide in a small grove of fir trees. They crawled in under the low branches. Nycoll was in a state of shock. Seeing her home destroyed once again, this time by nightmarish monsters added to the unrelenting pace Mansel set for them, had proven more than her fragile psyche could take. She lay curled in a fetal position behind Mansel, silent tears streaking down her face.

Mansel wanted to comfort her, but he had to keep her alive first. For his part, he felt both terror and exhilaration. He couldn't believe what he had seen; monsters roaming the land, and yet he had seen monsters in the sea with Zollin and dragons, too. He had taken Nycoll from their new home with only the clothes on their backs. He hadn't even stopped to pick up the scabbard he had slung from his sword when he fought the terrible centaur-like beasts. And yet, despite their grueling pace and lack of food, he wasn't tired at all. He carried the sword Zollin had given him with the glistening black stone in its pommel, and he felt the same sense of strength and ability he had felt whenever he held the magical weapon. Mansel didn't know what the sword did to him, but he was convinced that Zollin had imparted some type of magical ability to the weapon that somehow filled the wielder with supernatural strength.

Even though he wasn't tired, he still had no desire to fight the monsters. They were big and fast. He could kill them, but they had all the advantages. His sword filled him with an anxiousness to join in battle, but it didn't overtake his senses. Mansel was smart enough to know when the odds weren't in his favor. Perhaps it was his need to take care of Nycoll that kept him from rushing headlong into danger, but he remained cautious. He knew that if something happened to him that she wouldn't be able to help. She would be helpless and alone if he were captured or killed, and he refused to let that happen.

It was scant minutes before the hideous beasts came into view. There were three of them, and they moved more slowly at night. Mansel's heart felt like it would beat out of his chest, as he lay under the spreading branches of the firs, but the creatures moved passed without stopping. Mansel breathed a huge sigh of relief, and then more of the creatures appeared. Four more beasts came toward the group of trees that Mansel hid under; they circled around it once and then moved on.

Mansel decided then that his best bet was to keep moving. If more of the creatures appeared, they could get trapped under the fir trees. And despite his incredible stamina, he knew they needed food and water if they were going to keep up their strength. He decided to find a better hiding place, one that could offer fresh water, at least.

He set out following the group of three creatures. He stayed far enough behind them that they were never in sight, but he could hear them buzzing like giant bees. It was almost midnight when he saw the faint glow of a fire in the distance. Mansel knew instantly that the creatures would be drawn to the light. He increased his pace, never letting go of Nycoll's hand. After a few moments he had closed the distance between himself and the flying beasts. He could see their shadowy forms not far ahead, but they were either oblivious to his presence or too intent on the light ahead to pay him any attention.

Then, to Mansel's horror, he saw a familiar figure near the fire. It was nothing more than a shadow in front of the orange light, but it made his blood run cold. He saw the creatures moving toward the figure and then the man by the fire climbed into the saddle of a skittish looking horse.

"Quinn!" Mansel bellowed.

He saw the figure stand up in the stirrups, but it was obvious that the fire kept his old mentor from seeing what was approaching him in the darkness.

"Get away from the fire!" Mansel shouted again.

Then, he noticed that one of the three flying creatures had turned and was moving back toward him and Nycoll.

"Stay here," he told her, sitting her down in a clump of tall grass. "Stay quiet and still. I'll be back for you."

Nycoll clutched at his hand for a moment, and then she curled up in the grass and lay still. Mansel brandished his sword as he moved away from Nycoll.

"I'm over here, you bastard!" he shouted.

He spared one glance at Quinn and saw his friend ride away from the fire, and then the beast was too close to ignore. Mansel bent his knees, not sure how the creature would attack him. It came forward quickly, the tail held back, ready to strike. Mansel dodged to the side, but the darkness made it difficult to judge distances. He moved too soon, and the creature side stepped out of reach of Mansel's long sword. The tail, however, lashed forward and Mansel was forced to back pedal. He regained his balance, as the creature closed in on him again. The beast's mouth was opening and closing, but no sound came out. The eyes seemed to glow red in the darkness. This time, Mansel waited just slightly too late to dodge the stinger and he was forced to throw his sword up between himself and the creature's tail. The blade hit, but did little damage to the shell like the outer skin of the scorpion tail.

The creature turned in a tight circle, hoping to keep Mansel off guard, but Mansel kicked the beast in the chest, just below the section where the horse body morphed into human-like flesh. The kick did little damage, but it pushed the beast, who was still hovering a foot off the ground, away from him. The creature struck out with its tail again, but this time Mansel brought his sword up point first and impaled the tail, just behind the bulbous stinger.

The creature shrieked in pain and rage, reaching out its long arms, the claws on the end of each finger grasping for Mansel's throat. He stepped back and swung his sword, but the short swing didn't deliver enough force and the thick blade wedged in the beast's arm, just below the elbow. The creature reacted to the pain, jerking its arm back and pulling the sword from Mansel's hand.

Mansel felt like huge weights had suddenly been tied to his arms and legs. He staggered back, fear making his heart flutter in his chest. Fortunately, the creature's reaction to his attack, jerking its arm away from Mansel, ended poorly for the hideous creature. By jerking its arm back, it drove the point of the sword straight into its own throat. It was a fortuitous moment for Mansel, who realized that if the creature hadn't killed itself, it would have surely killed or captured him.

The beast crashed to the ground, almost at Mansel's feet, driving him backward to avoid the flailing tail. He looked up but couldn't see Quinn or the other creatures in the dark. He was panting, his stomach twisting, and his eyes burned with fatigue. He timed the movements of the creature's writhing tail. He recognized the jerky movements, which were simply reflexes convulsing in death. It was like a chicken running hurly-burly around the yard after its head had been cut off.

Mansel darted in, grabbed the sword, and heaved with all his strength. The sword pulled free and as Mansel hurried backward away from the deadly carcass, he felt his own strength returning. He closed his eyes for a minute, letting his heart rate slow while he caught his breath. Then, he heard a scream that was part pain, part outrage, and he was running into the darkness to help his friend.

Chapter 14

It was a full day's journey through the tunnels and caverns under the Northern Highlands to reach the Dome under the Mountain. Most of passageways were like long hallways, barely large enough for Zollin to pass through without stooping. He crossed two of the ancient Stepping Stone bridges he had repaired and came to another that was still in ruins, just after they had stopped to rest and shared a midday meal. The heat from the molten lava at the center of the cavern was so intense that Zollin's thick winter clothes had to be removed and stored in his pack. He spent an hour rebuilding the bridge, and then they pushed on.

There was no sense of day and night inside the tunnels of the dwarves. The hearty folk that lived under the mountains could work for days without stopping for rest. They were masters of the forge, and miners by trade, carving great passages in solid rock as they searched for the elusive ores they coveted.

They reached the Dome and Zollin was shocked to find what seemed like a great void inside the mountain. The ceiling soared overhead, disappearing out of sight into the gloom above. The other dwarves, who had already arrived, had set up small camps, building fires and congregating in small groups. Zollin knew that not all the dwarves had arrived yet, so he wrapped himself in his cloak and lay down. When he awoke, he was shocked to see sunlight streaming into the huge cavern. Shafts of bright light shone down from long tunnels in the cavern's roof. Zollin was dumbfounded.

"It's a sight to see, isn't it?" Bloc said.

"It's unbelievable," Zollin replied.

"This is the birthplace of dragons," Bloc said calmly. "Fire Spirits melt the stone and use gold to form the hearts of the dragons. That's why the beasts crave gold so much and why it acts almost like a medicine to them."

"Gold can heal dragons?" Zollin asked.

"Yes, gold, sunlight, and pure fire. At least that is what the legends say. If your Brianna formed dragons, then there is a similar cavern to this somewhere in the mountains. My people will be anxious to find it. This is a sacred place, my friend."

Zollin could see why. It was easily the largest space he had ever seen in their labyrinth of tunnels and caverns. He had seen crevasses so deep that even a burning torch was lost to sight before it reached the bottom, but very few places so open and bright. The shafts of sunlight all angled down toward a large, round table carved from stone and inlaid with intricate designs of gold.

"It was once believed," Bloc explained, "that in the light of the sun, a dwarf's every thought and motive is exposed. So when our people found the dome they drilled shafts to the surface of the mountain, where sunlight could illuminate our leaders as they made decisions. Sitting at the round table under the dome, no deception or hidden agenda could be kept secret."

"It's a nice sentiment," Zollin said, thinking of the powerful men he'd encountered and their almost constant manipulation.

"Yes, if only it were true," Bloc said.

"You will lead the gathering?" Zollin asked.

"Facilitate is a better word," Bloc said. "My family has led the dwarves for centuries, but only when they venture outside our caverns. Here, I have no power, no influence. I'm little more than a rule keeper."

"But you will present our cause?"

"No, Zollin, Wizard of the World Walkers; that is your burden."

Zollin looked around. He could see that some of the dwarves were watching him with their keen, curious eyes. Others ignored him completely. Avryl approached them and bowed slightly to Zollin.

"We have food and beer," he said. "Better come and have a crack at it before the other dwarves eat it all."

"Aye," said Bloc. "I could use a good meal."

They walked back to the small area where the dwarves from the Tradnook clan had made a small camp. They used coal to cook with, burning small amounts in tiny ovens to roast chickens or pigs, and to bake bread. Zollin never saw the animals, but he had enjoyed the dwarfish feasts before.

Dwarves didn't drink ale, but rather, beer made from potatoes called Shochu. It was stronger than ale and Zollin only sipped at his, but the dwarves drank and ate as if it were their last meal. They sang songs and before long there were contests of strength between different clans. Zollin watched anxiously for the dwarves he knew. Hammert was the first to arrive. Zollin recognized the fat dwarf immediately.

"Ho, Zollin," Hammert cried, as he hurried across the huge expanse of the cavern.

"Hello, Hammert," he replied.

"Back already and causing more trouble I see."

"I guess it's just in my nature."

"Wizards are troublemakers, but don't let me catch anyone else calling you that. How is your Fire Spirit? Rumors are she made dragons."

"That's right," Zollin said. "She is well. She is with her pride to the south in Yelsia."

They spent an hour reminiscing before Babaz arrived. Babaz had a curly beard and unlike most of the other dwarves, his skin was light brown.

"So, you're back," said Babaz. "I knew you couldn't stay away from the beauty of our caverns for long."

"It's good to see you Babaz."

"And you, tall one. Where is your fair lady?"

"She is on another mission. I'm afraid the news from the world of men isn't good," Zollin said.

"It never is," said Babaz.

"The tall folk spend too much time in the sun," Hammert said. "It cooks their brains."

"How would you know anything about brains?" Babaz said.

"I've got a fair deal more than anyone from the Oliad clan," Hammert retorted.

The two dwarves continued to pick at one another, although the joking was lighthearted and playful. Each of the clans had sent a small delegation, so by the end of the day, there was a large crowd of dwarves in the Dome. Bloc sat with Zollin, away from the commotion of drinking, feasting, and feats of strength.

"What about the Jaq clan?" Zollin asked. "Can they really get here in three days?"

"No," Bloc said. "We shall make a decision and then take that decision to the clans in the southern mountains."

"Oh," Zollin said, a little disappointed that he wouldn't see Jute at the gathering. He'd hoped to have as many friends at the conclave as possible.

"What are the chances that the dwarves will join our fight?"

"I'd say fifty, fifty," Bloc said. "Dwarves don't fear a fight, nor are we ignorant of the dangers that have been unleashed from the underworld."

"How do you know so much about it?" Zollin asked.

"News travels through the stone far beneath your feet, my friend," Bloc explained. "And the underworld is a foul place. The beings held in bondage, deep in the earth, have been our natural enemies for centuries, but they dwell in the flat places; we dwell beneath the mountains."

"There is so much about our world that I don't know," Zollin said. "How is it that no one knows about dwarves, and dragons, and giants anymore?"

"Memory is a short thing, especially among men whose lives are fleeting. For the last three centuries, magic has been suppressed in the world. You have seen the decay even among the dwarves. Our Stepping Stones have fallen into disrepair and very few dwarves have seen the light of the sun outside of this great cavern."

"But still, shouldn't at least some people know about magic?"

"Some did," Bloc insisted, "but they hoarded that magic in an effort to control it. You are an example of that effort. You have wondrous power, but very little knowledge. That lack of knowledge is a weakness your enemies can exploit, even if they cannot equal your raw magical power."

"Okay, I guess that makes sense," Zollin said. "But it is hard to believe that people don't even remember what things were like before the Torr came to power."

"Perhaps they don't want to remember," Bloc said. "I'm afraid that many of my kin may wish to stay hidden in our caverns rather than risk open war. It will be a difficult choice."

"Tell me what you know about the underworld," Zollin said.

"It is a dire place," Bloc said. "There are caverns under the flatlands, just as there are under the mountains. Some of those caverns have been filled with creatures better left forgotten."

"So, Gwendolyn just happened to crack open the caverns where the Leffers were banished?"

"In a way," Bloc said. "I don't think her choice of ground was random, any more than a king would randomly choose a field for battle. I cannot say what she knows or even what type of magic she has tapped into, but the underworld is full of dark magic and wicked creatures. I would guess she is calling them to her cause, offering them the chance to roam freely through the world again."

"Can she do that?"

"If no one stops her," Bloc said, his eyes peering deeply into Zollin's, as if he were trying to read the young wizard's thoughts.

"I guess you mean me," he said, trying not to sound as sheepish as he felt at the prospect.

"There are a precious few who can," Block said, raising his mug of beer to his lips.

Zollin sat thinking about what Bloc said. He had no doubt the dwarf spoke the truth. He had known all along that stopping Gwendolyn was up to him, but he felt so inadequate. How could he hope to defeat the evil witch when he had no idea what she was capable of?

"I can't do it alone," he said. "I need your help."

"The question is… can you do it even with our help?"

"What do you mean?"

"I mean that nothing can stand in your way, not fear, not hardship..." Zollin started to interrupt, but Bloc held up a hand. "You have proven yourself in these ways, but you cannot let your feelings for the people around you hold you back."

"What are you talking about?"

"I'm saying that you are a man with great compassion. The clans are all talking about how you risked your life to save the Jaq clan. All dwarves hold you high esteem, Zollin, but if you are to defeat the Witch, people around you will die. The very people you are asking for help will give their lives in that fight. You have to be prepared to see the people you care about die. You have to be willing to sacrifice your own happiness, and that is a great sacrifice for anyone to make."

"Are you willing to do the same?" Zollin asked. "Are you willing to lead the dwarves out of your home beneath the mountains and onto the field of battle?"

"I honestly don't know," Bloc said, taking a long drink of his beer. "That is the ultimate question for any leader. My forebears have made that sacrifice and been lauded in this very hall for their courage and honor. But I care deeply for my brothers and sisters. Leading them into a war we may not win will be difficult."

"So we both must be strong," Zollin said. "I have one advantage over you; I have seen the sorceress's power. I have seen her cruelty and what she is becoming. That gives me a resolve that you perhaps do not have. I will fight her. I will do all I can to stop her and if that means sacrificing my own life to stem her tide of evil, I will make that sacrifice."

Bloc nodded; his gaze steady and unblinking. Neither man nor dwarf spoke for a long minute. Then Bloc, king of the dwarves, spoke.

"Perhaps, you are ready."

Chapter 15

In Orrock, a large wooden wagon rumbled through the cobblestone streets. The exterior of the wagon was plain, heavy wood, forming a large coach, with a driver perched on a narrow bench mounted on top of the carriage. Inside, the wagon was lined with silk cushions and velvet. A lone occupant sat in the wagon with his long, thin hands twisting nervously.

The wagon rolled quickly through the streets and made straight for the castle. It slowed at the massive gate and then rolled to a stop on the servant's side of the castle. Homan, the King's personal steward, met the wagon and escorted the thin, nervous looking man into the huge structure. The servant's quarters, kitchens, and storage rooms were all bustling with activity, but no one paid Homan or this guest any attention. They went up narrow flights of stone, the steps polished from years of constant use; higher and higher into the castle they went, until finally, they came to a long, broad corridor.

Homan led the way down the corridor to a set of heavy wooden doors. The man noticed the horses carved into the doors, and then they were flung open and the man was hurried inside. He noticed the large desk, the thick carpets, and rich furnishings. Then two men stepped out of a side room. One was a soldier, his back straight, his shoulders broad. The other was an older man, his thinning hair gray under the thin circlet of gold that graced his brow.

"Your majesty," Homan said in solemn tones. "May I present Estry, Tailor of Tranaugh Shire."

"My Liege," Estry said, dropping to one knee.

"Ah, it is good to meet you, Master Estry. Thank you for coming so quickly. You may rise."

"Your men made it possible, Sire," the thin man named Estry said, as he got back up on his feet.

"Good, I hope you were well cared for. And your family?"

"They are coming," Estry said. "The escort said they should arrive in a few days."

"Yes, I'm sorry I had to separate you, but we needed you here as soon as possible. Have you heard from your daughter?"

"My daughter?" Estry said, not understanding the question.

"Forgive me; I forget you have four daughters. You are a busy man."

Estry smiled nervously.

"I meant your eldest daughter, Brianna," King Felix said.

"We haven't seen or heard from Brianna for over a year, my Lord. I'm afraid she was killed."

There was a note of profound grief in the tailor's voice as he spoke about his daughter. King Felix smiled.

"She isn't dead, my good man. She's here, with us."

"My daughter is here?"

"She is. She's been through some changes, but she is perfectly safe now. In fact, the reason I brought you here is because I need your help. You see, my son is in love with Brianna."

Felix paused to let the weight of his last statement sink in. He watched as Estry's eyes widened, and he struggled to swallow.

"Unfortunately, these are difficult times, and Brianna needs a little help committing herself to Prince Willam."

"I don't know what to say," Estry said.

"Well, first, let us talk about this arrangement. Is the match suitable to you?"

"Yes, of course, my Liege. It would be the greatest honor to give my daughter to your son."

"Excellent," King Felix said.

"But you must know that she has been married once before. It was in our village last year, just before she disappeared. Her husband was killed the day she disappeared."

"Yes, that is tragic, but it need not concern the future happiness of our children," Felix said. "They are young and both of them need the other. I think it best that we forget the past and do all we can to help them now."

"Yes, of course," Estry said.

"Now, if it would please you, I could bring your family to Orrock on a permanent basis. I will give you enough money to set up a lucrative business for yourself here, so that you can be close to your daughter."

"That is very generous, your highness."

"It is the least I can do. Brianna would bring Prince Willam so much happiness. But there is one other problem that I need your help with."

"Anything," Estry said. "Just name it, my Liege, I stand ready to serve."

"Brianna still has feelings for the Wizard Zollin."

A look came over Estry's face, both fear and hatred. For the last year, Zollin had been blamed for every problem in Tranaugh Shire. The mercenaries who had come into the small village with the wizards of the Torr in search of Zollin had wreaked havoc on the inhabitants. Four had been killed, included Zollin's best friend and Brianna's husband, Todrek. Rumors had trickled in about Zollin, some good, others bad. The black dragon that had run roughshod across Yelsia had been blamed on Zollin. The invasion by the armies of Osla and Falxis had been blamed on Zollin. Everything from failed crops to sickness had been blamed on the boy wizard who had fled the village taking Brianna with him. Estry was torn between a debilitating fear of Zollin and an intense hatred for what Zollin had taken from him.

"Is he here as well?" Estry asked.

"No, but I believe he will return soon. I have treated Zollin like a son," the King said, a sneer slipping past his otherwise controlled demeanor, "but he turned his back on my good will. I will not lie; he has been a help to our Kingdom, but I do not trust him. I am not certain where his true loyalties lie."

"I don't want him anywhere near my daughter," Estry said.

"Then help me convince Brianna to wed Prince Willam. He has not asked for her hand yet, but he will soon. I am not the kind of man who leaves this sort of thing to chance. That is why I felt it was important to bring you here."

"I will do everything in my power to see that she makes the right choice," Estry said.

"That is all I ask," King Felix said. "Homan will show you to your room and make sure that you have everything you need."

"Thank you, my Lord."

"We will soon be family. Please, join me at dinner tonight."

"I would be honored," Estry said.

"The honor is mine."

The King waved to Homan, who hurried to escort Estry out.

"That was shrewd," said General Corlis, who had been in the room but remained silent throughout the King's conversation with Estry.

"Like I told you, I never leave things to chance," King Felix said. "If my son cannot woo Brianna into marrying him, then perhaps her father can convince her."

"And if both fail?" Corlis asked. "She is a powerful person after all; she might not be convinced."

"Then I shall bring the full weight of this kingdom onto her."

"You'll force her to marry him?"

"No, of course I can't do that, but I can be convincing."

"What are you getting at?" Corlis asked.

King Felix whirled around so quickly it caught the haughty, young, commander off guard.

"Who the hell do you think you're talking to?" Felix shouted. "I'll have you flailed alive if you ever have the impudence to question me again."

Corlis paled visibly, but he did not shrink back. His reaction was taken to be fear, because that is what King Felix wanted to believe. He had no idea that the young general was already plotting to topple his sovereign and take Felix's place upon the throne of Yelsia.

"My apologies, O King," said Corlis bowing deeply. "Forgive my lapse of decorum. I was caught up in the moment. I beg your forgiveness."

"You forget yourself at your peril, General," Felix said, his voice still high pitched with anger. "I am sure you have things to do."

"Yes, my Lord," Corlis said. Then he hurried from the room.

King Felix sank into a chair by the fireplace and rang a bell for a servant to come and build up the fire, which had burned down to embers. He steepled his fingers and smiled. His plans were coming together perfectly.

Out in the corridor, General Corlis stalked toward the suite of rooms he'd been given. He was furious, but he kept his feelings in check. He knew that Prince Willam would try to take his father's place once Corlis had dealt with the King and if the Prince was married to Brianna, it would make his task of usurping the throne that much harder. He locked himself into his room and went to the window. He looked down and saw the dragons below.

They couldn't be allowed to subvert his plans. He needed to find a way to stop Brianna from marrying the Prince.

Homan took Estry down one story from the King's domicile and showed the tailor a large suite with three adjoining rooms. He was given hot water and towels. His small trunk of clothes had been carried up and placed in one of the bedrooms. He cleaned himself up and changed clothes. Then he waited nervously for Brianna. Homan showed her in and for a long time both father and daughter stood staring at each other.

For his part, Estry thought his daughter looked more beautiful than ever. Her raven black hair was now streaked with highlights of auburn and her once pale skin was now golden. Her eyes, always his favorite feature of his eldest daughter, sparkled with a light he had never seen in them before.

Brianna couldn't believe what she was seeing. Her father was thinner, his hair turning gray and there were deep lines around his eyes and across his forehead. Tears welled up in her eyes. She had always loved her father so much. She loved sitting on his lap as a little girl and then as she grew older, she loved to watch him work. He had a skill with fabric that was as wondrous to her as Zollin's magic.

"Daddy?" she said softly.

They rushed together, tears spilling down both of their faces.

"I can't believe it," Estry said. "I can't believe you're alive. We feared the worst after Todrek was found."

"I'm well," she said, her voice constricted as she spoke above the soft sobs.

"Better than well," her father said. "Look at you."

He pushed her to arm's length, staring at her.

"You look beautiful," he said.

"Oh, thank you, daddy. I've missed you so much."

"Your mother will be so relieved to see you again," he added, but Brianna doubted that was true. "And to find you here, in the King's castle, it is like a dream come true."

They spent the next three hours talking. Brianna told her father everything that happened to her since she left Tranaugh Shire. He was shocked and amazed. Then she showed him her power over fire, making flames dance and twirl in the air. He looked frightened at first, and then a fierce pride appeared on his face, making him look younger, more like the man she remembered.

They went down to dinner together, and found that the King had seated them at his own table. It was the first time Brianna had been invited to dine at the King's table since she had been in Orrock with Zollin months ago. They ate a lavish feast of roasted rack of lamb with vegetables and fresh baked bread. Rich red wine flowed in abundance and by the time Brianna and her father walked back up to the suite he'd been given, both were tipsy. They leaned on each other as they navigated the long hallways.

Brianna was surprised to find that she had been moved out of the tiny cell down near the servant's quarters and into the suite with her father. They both promptly went to bed, and it was the first time in many days that Brianna didn't lie awake fretting about her feelings for Prince Willam. She had been wracked by guilt at first, but she couldn't deny what she felt in her heart. Willam made her feel like a princess. He was constantly giving her little gifts and taking her for long rides around the countryside.

The impending war seemed farther and farther away. She asked fewer questions about the mobilization of the army and focused more on Prince Willam. He had been a perfect gentleman, although he made his feelings for her clear. She knew she would have to make a choice soon, and she was torn. She had never dreamed that she could have such strong feelings for two men at the same time. Zollin was clever, his power intoxicating, and their adventures had created a bond that was very strong, but he seemed so far away. Prince Willam, on the other hand, was heir to a great kingdom and he offered her the chance to be part of making Yelsia a greater kingdom. He could give her all the things she thought she always wanted as a girl growing up such as: position, acclaim, and riches beyond what she had ever imagined. Zollin offered adventure, Prince Willam stability. She had no idea what she was going to do. Of course, Prince Willam had offered her nothing so far; he had not proposed or even tried to kiss her. His sense of honor was such that he would never soil her good reputation with an illicit affair. If he seduced her now, he would force her to break her vow to Zollin, and Brianna knew he would never do that. Still, she couldn't help but dream of what it would be like to be Queen of Yelsia, and for her children to be princes and princesses.

The next morning, breakfast was brought to their suite and Brianna rose early, but her father was already up. He was pacing in the main room of the suite. Brianna smiled as she thought of all the times she had seen her father pacing outside their modest home in Tranaugh Shire. It hadn't been big enough to pace inside, but he always paced back and forth when he was struggling with difficult decisions.

"What's wrong?" she asked him.

"Nothing is wrong," he said kindly. "Everything is alright; it is better than alright."

"So why are you pacing?"

"I'm trying to decide how to tell you something that is very important."

"Just tell me," Brianna said. "I'm a big girl, daddy. I can handle it."

"I know you are. In fact, you're not my little girl anymore. You've grown into a beautiful woman in your own right. I'm so very proud of you."

"Thank you," she said, blushing a little.

"I spoke to the King yesterday," he said. "He asked me to make a match with you and Prince Willam."

The statement hit Brianna like a physical blow. She couldn't believe what she was hearing. Part of her was thrilled. She had known that Willam liked her, but she had used the fact that no proposal had been made to keep her feelings in check. Now, she knew exactly what the Prince's intentions were; now there was no hiding from the choice she knew she would have to make.

Another part of her was aghast. How could she turn down the Crown Prince of Yelsia? Yet, she was already promised to Zollin. She couldn't turn her back on him; she knew that for certain. And still another part of her was angry that King Felix had summoned her father and tried to strike a deal to arrange a match behind her back. She was a grown woman, a fire spirit, a dragon rider. Yet, here was the king and her father planning her future as if she were still a child.

"And what did you tell him?" she asked, the trepidation in her voice leaching through.

"What do you think I told him? Of course I would give you my blessing to marry the Prince."

"Did he ask for your blessing?" Brianna said.

"Of course," Estry said. "Prince Willam is in love with you. The King told me that himself."

Brianna felt a shiver go through her, but she tried not to show it. She was conflicted, but that didn't stop her heart from leaping at the news that Prince Willam loved her.

"I can't do it, father, I'm promised to Zollin."

Estry's face clouded for the first time since he had seen his daughter. The wrinkles returned, like furrows in freshly tilled soil.

"Zollin has not sought my permission to marry you," Estry said, his voice tense. "Nor has his father. You must know they brought disgrace on the entire village," he said.

"No they didn't, father. I told you what happened. It wasn't Zollin's fault, and he isn't a disgrace. He's a hero."

"He's a sorcerer," Estry said.

188

"No!" Brianna said, raising her voice. "He's a good man. He saved my life, more than once. He saved Yelsia. You don't know him like I do."

"Do you know that four people were killed in Tranaugh Shire last year by the mercenaries chasing him? One was your husband."

"I know that, father. I saw Todrek die. He gave his life trying to protect the people he loved."

"Well, I'm just trying to protect you because I love you. Can't you see that marrying Prince Willam is the greatest thing that could ever happen to you?"

"I can't imagine that it is better than flying with a pride of dragons," she said defiantly.

"I wouldn't know about dragons," he said with a frown, as if his daughter talking about dragons wasn't proper. "But I think a match with the Crown Prince of Yelsia is the right thing. I know what your mother will think and your sisters. Don't throw away this opportunity."

"I don't want to throw anything away, but I don't know what to do. I gave Zollin my word and I love him."

"So you don't love Prince Willam?" Estry asked incredulously.

"I didn't say that," she shot back. "Oh, I don't know what I think anymore, and I don't know what to do."

"Of course you don't," her father said gently, putting his arm around her shoulders. "We never do when we're in the middle of difficult circumstances. You've been through a lot the last year.

You've grown up and changed in ways I didn't think possible. But now you have to make a decision and I think that your heart is pulling you one way and your head is pulling you another way. That's why you should trust my judgment. I only want what's best for you."

"I know that, daddy," she said quietly. "And I did it your way once. I married Todrek, even though I didn't love him. In fact, I hardly knew him, but I did what you told me to do, despite my reservations. But that wasn't the life I was meant to live; I knew that then, but I was too afraid to stand up for what I knew was right for me. This time I have to."

"So you won't marry the Prince?"

"I didn't say that. I just need some time."

"Well, I recommend that you make up your mind before your mother arrives," he said. "After that, there's no telling what will happen."

Chapter 16

Quinn was staring into the darkness, straining to see any sign of movement, his ears attuned to any sound other than the ominous thrumming of whatever was approaching. His heart was pounding, but he braced himself for whatever he might see. He'd seen a huge, black, fire- breathing dragon descend on Brighton's Gate and destroy the city. He'd seen Brianna float down from the backs of dragons as if she were as light as an autumn leaf drifting to the ground from a tall tree. He'd seen Zollin do things that were impossible and even unnatural. He remembered the night in Brighton's Gate when he'd been awakened by his son outside his room in the Valley Inn with a knife in his stomach. He'd thought his son was dead, but Zollin made him pull the blade out slowly as he healed himself from the inside out. Whatever was coming for him in the darkness, he was ready for it. At least, he was as ready as he could be.

"Quinn!"

Hearing his name shouted unnerved him more than he thought was possible. His bowels turned to water and hands began to shake. He didn't know what to do. Should he answer, should he run away?

"Get away from the fire!"

Quinn moved on instinct alone. He dug his heels into the horse's flanks and bent low over the mount's neck. He could feel the horse's mane flapping against his chin, the wind blowing cold against his face, as he raced into the darkness. He had no idea where he was going or what he might run into, but immediately his night vision began to adjust. He could see the huge, looming shadows of the mountains to his right and dark splotches that he took to be trees all around him. Then, just as Quinn was beginning to calm down a little, two horrible beasts reared in front of him.

Quinn's horse bucked, throwing up its front hooves, while the rear hooves dug into the turf as the horse tried to stop its forward progress. Quinn tried his best to hang onto the horse, grabbing a hand full of mane and leaning forward. Time seemed to slow down, and he could feel the horse trembling beneath him. Then something hit the horse in its stomach. The blow was solid, knocking Quinn out of the saddle. He fell, his feet hitting first, then his backside. He rolled, letting his feet come up over his head, and the momentum helped him regain his feet. Just as he looked up he was forced to jump to one side to avoid the writhing, screaming body of the horse.

Quinn felt the splash of hot blood across his face, but he didn't have time to worry about his mount. One of the creatures in front of him had impaled the horse with its long, segmented tail. Quinn's mouth was suddenly dry. He could see the shadowy outline of the creature, but it didn't seem real. He scrambled back, trying to stay out of range of the wicked looking tail which was swaying back and forth over the creature's body. He threw down his sword, so that the blade stabbed into the ground and left the hilt sticking up, quivering from the impact. Quinn kept his shield up in front of him. It was a puny defense against the creature which was larger than a war horse, but he felt better knowing he had at least a little protection.

His free hand found the first of his three throwing knives. In his mind's eye he saw himself as young man, recruited to the King's Royal Guard, the elite soldiers who served as the honored regiment that guarded the King and his family. He had spent hours training with the throwing knives, learning to hit each target with different types of throws. He could bury his knives into a man's chest with an underhand throw that was barely more than a flick of his wrist, but he was afraid that the creature in front of him was perhaps armored somehow, so he drew back his arm and hurled the first knife with all his strength in a massive, overhanded throw. The knife disappeared in the darkness, but the sound of the blade punching into flesh was unmistakable.

The monster roared in pain. Its horse-like hooves flailed in the air as it reared, its wings faltering and dropping the beast's massive weight onto its rear legs. Quinn had no idea where the creature's vital organs were located, so he had no idea if he had mortally wounded the beast, or just made it incredibly angry. He drew another knife and moved to the beast's left. The monster pulled the knife from its chest and flung it onto the ground, but Quinn threw his second knife, again it found its mark. The knife stabbed into the beast's side. It roared again, prancing to its right to get away from Quinn.

He breathed a sigh of relief until he saw the second monster rushing toward him. His fingers fumbled the third knife and by the time he had the blade under control, the monster was almost on top of him. He flicked the knife forward. It sailed up and stuck fast in the human stomach just above the horse body of the creature. It shrieked in agony but kept moving forward. Quinn saw the tail dart forward, and he threw up his shield in a blind act of self-defense. The shield was made of sturdy oak slats, bounded by an iron ring around the edge of the round shield and held in the center by a metal hub. The stinger missed the metal hub and stabbed through the wood. Quinn felt a searing pain in his arm and then the beast jerked its tail, pulling Quinn off the ground. He let go of the shield's handle, but the hoop near his elbow kept his arm from pulling free. The stinger, still stuck fast in the wood, gouged into his forearm again and again as the tail swung.

Finally, the shield broke apart and the stinger was free. It flew up and over the creature, while Quinn collapsed onto the ground. He could feel his left arm going numb and his strength seemed to be melting away, like candle wax before the flame. The beast turned toward him. It was close and seemed huge to Quinn, who was still on his knees. He realized that if he didn't do something he was going to die. He dove for his sword, which was stuck in the ground just a few feet away. The creature lumbered forward, just as Quinn pulled his weapon free. The long arms and clawed hands reached for him, but he slashed with the short, double edged sword, severing two of the creature's fingers.

There was another roar; this one sounding more like anger than pain. Quinn's legs felt almost too weak to hold him, so he stumbled forward, his sword thrust out before him, hoping to impale the beast. Instead, it knocked the sword out of Quinn's hands and then reached to grab him. Quinn felt the sword fly away and then his legs buckled. He fell onto the ground just before the creature could grab him. The beast was backing away, preparing to stab at Quinn with its tail, when out of the darkness, behind the creature, Mansel appeared.

He was running with his big sword held high over his head. He jumped and brought the sword down with all his momentum. The blade sliced through the side of the segmented tail and then carved a bloody wound across the beast's horse-like flank. The beast tried to fly away, but one wing was nicked by Mansel's sword and it crashed to the ground. Mansel dashed forward, running swiftly past the creature and severing its head as he went. The head flew up and the tail lashed wickedly. The horse-like legs kicked in the death throes but it was no longer a threat.

"Quinn!" Mansel shouted again, as he turned back to his mentor.

Quinn was lying in the grass, face down. Mansel rushed to his side and found his former master unconscious. Mansel grabbed his arm and pulled Quinn on the younger man's broad shoulder. Then, he dashed back off into the darkness.

Mansel found Nycoll right where he had left her. She was cowering down, but being quiet. They huddled together, Mansel checking occasionally to see if Quinn was still breathing. In the darkness it was impossible to tell just how wounded the older man was. Mansel ran his hands over Quinn's body and only found the one flesh wound in the older man's arm, but he couldn't be sure that was the only injury. They waited until morning, occasionally hearing another band of monsters in the distance, but none came close enough to be seen. The wounded creatures bellowed through the night, but their cries neither alerted nor summoned the other beasts.

When the sun came up, Nycoll was asleep. Mansel was exhausted, but he kept watch. When the light was enough, he did a visual inspection of his former mentor. There seemed to be no other wounds other than the nasty gash on his forearm. Quinn seemed to be resting comfortably, so Mansel bandaged his arm and let his old friend rest. It was mid-morning before Nycoll woke up. She went to a nearby stream and then ventured to Quinn's campsite. The mule that had carried his supplies was long gone, terrified by the monsters who had come in the night, but Quinn's supplies were still neatly laid out on the ground. There was a blanket, a bag with a change of clothes, a canteen, and some food rations. Nycoll gathered it all up and hurried back to Mansel.

They drank all the water in the canteens, dribbling a little into Quinn's mouth as well. Then they refilled the canteens in a nearby stream. The water was cold and Mansel washed the blood off his face and hands. Nycoll tended Quinn. She seemed happier with someone to take care of. They shared some of the food from Quinn's pack and waited to see if the older man would wake up.

"What if he doesn't wake up?" Nycoll asked.

"I don't know," Mansel said. "I don't think we should stay here once night falls. We need to find a more secure place to get some rest."

"Can we move him?"

"I can carry him," Mansel said.

"Won't that make him worse?" Nycoll asked.

"I don't know. But if we stay out here our odds of being found are high."

The creatures they had fought had died before dawn. And by mid-afternoon their carcasses began to smell.

"Okay, we have to move," Mansel said. "Can you carry the supplies?"

"Yes," she said.

"Good, let's move in closer to the mountains."

Mansel hoisted Quinn onto his shoulder again, and they moved away from the path that ran east and west. They moved over open ground toward the foothills of the Walheta Mountains, keeping a careful watch for more of the creatures that had attacked them. Fortunately, they saw nothing and heard nothing. Mansel had to stop several times and rest. Finally, they found a grove of pine trees with a thick blanket of pine needles that made a soft bed. Nycoll laid out Quinn's blanket and they huddled together as night fell, using their body heat to stay warm. It was a long, miserable night. An hour before dawn it began to mist softly. The rain dripped down through the pine branches above them and by the time the sun came up, they were all soaked.

Quinn began to wake, and Nycoll shook Mansel.

"He's waking up," she said.

"Quinn," Mansel said, patting his mentor's shoulder. "Quinn, how do feel?"

"I'm... I'm okay," he said.

He lay still at first, waiting for something to hurt, but nothing did. Then he slowly sat up. They were all cold and shivering, but Quinn drank some water and flexed his wounded arm.

"It looks like nothing more than flesh wounds," he said as he retied the bandage on his arm. "It sure is good to see you."

"And you," Mansel agreed. "What are you doing here?"

"Looking for you," Quinn said. "Brianna came to Felson and told me she was worried about you. She said you didn't know about these monsters, and she didn't know where you were. So I came looking."

"You shouldn't have risked your life for us," Mansel said, but he couldn't contain the smile that appeared on his face. "But you are welcome with us anytime. Let me introduce someone very special to me. This is Nycoll. She's been nursing you back to health."

Nycoll smiled but didn't speak.

"It is an honor to meet you, Nycoll; I've heard wonderful things about you. Thank you for the help with my arm."

"It was nothing," she said quietly.

"It wasn't nothing to me. I may still need to use this thing," he said, holding up his wounded arm and flexing his fingers. "I don't suppose you collected my weapons?"

"No," Mansel said. "I'm sorry. We didn't want to go near the carcasses."

"I can't blame you, but I won't be much use to you without weapons."

"Surely we can get more somewhere."

"There's a settlement not far from the Western Pass into the mountains. Where are we?"

"Between the mountains and the road. We haven't come to the pass yet. I was thinking we should head into the mountains. We might have a better chance of avoiding those... those... monsters or whatever they are if we aren't out in the open."

"Brianna said there are more than just the monsters to worry about. She said she and Zollin fought the witch in Osla, and that she is using some sort of dark magic to turn people into an evil army. These flying horse things don't kill people; they capture them and carry them back to her lair."

"So there's a war coming," Mansel said.

"Yes, she and Zollin are trying to convince the King to send troops south. King Zorlan plans to make a stand here, along the mountains."

"So, all we have to do is find a safe place to wait," Mansel said.

"For now. I suppose my mule is gone?"

"We gathered your supplies from your camp, but that was all."

"Okay, let's try to find that settlement. We should be able to do that before dark."

Nycoll was shy and didn't talk much, but her spirits seem to revive with Quinn around. Mansel wasn't sure if it was just his old friend's sense of calm and confidence or if it was from having someone else with them after days alone running from the monsters. Either way, Mansel was happy to see her being more herself.

Once again, Quinn smelled the settlement before they actually saw the camps. Unlike before, the smell of garbage and offal was mixed with the sickly sweet smell of rotting flesh.

"Maybe you should stay here with Nycoll," Quinn suggested.

"You think it might be bad?" Mansel asked.

"It wasn't like this when I came through," he confirmed. "I think the monsters have been here."

"I thought you said they don't kill," Nycoll said.

"That's what I was told, but something is dead in that camp."

"Well, I can handle it," she said, trying to sound confident. "Besides, if people are wounded I could help."

"She's a good healer," Mansel said.

"I'm not a healer, but I enjoy helping people. I can't fight like you, but I can do something."

"You're right," Quinn said. "We'll stay together. Come on."

They approached the camp cautiously. They were wet and cold from the sputtering rain which fell intermittently through the day. The settlement was in ruins. Wreckage from wagons and campsites littered the area. There were dead horses and other animals rotting and filling the air with a stench that was difficult to stomach. Despite the rain, clouds of flies buzzed and carrion birds swooped down, cawing at one another and then at Quinn, Mansel, and Nycoll.

"Gather whatever supplies you can find," Quinn suggested. "It won't do anyone any good if we leave it out here."

There was no sign of people anywhere. Quinn feared they had all been carried off by the monsters, but he couldn't focus on that. He had to try and stay positive, even if he was filled with dread.

They found some food, most of it was ruined by the rain, but some was dry and usable. They found a partially destroyed wagon that contained powders and dried herbs. Nycoll was confident she knew what some of the supplies were, and that they had been used by a healer.

"We should take this with us," she insisted. "We may need it."

"There's no way for us to carry it all," Mansel said.

"So, we need to cobble together a wagon that we can pull into the mountains," Quinn said. "You and I can do that easily enough, even without proper tools."

"Okay," Mansel said, "let's do that."

They searched through the camp but found no people. Mansel set up a tent upwind from the camp. It was really little more than a canopy, but it would keep the rain off of them through the night. Nycoll gathered what dry supplies she could find and carried them to their camp. Quinn gathered the unusable wood he found around the camp to use as firewood.

"We can't have a fire," Mansel said. "It will attract the monsters."

"We have to," Quinn said through chattering teeth. "We're all soaked, and the temperature is falling. We won't survive the night in these conditions."

"Well, it has to be hidden," Mansel said, "otherwise those creatures might see it."

"So we dig a hole and burn the wood in the hole. At least that way we can warm ourselves and dry our clothes."

Mansel used a shovel with a broken handle to dig a small pit. Quinn pulled the pieces of several wagons and a few hand carts to their camp. Nycoll used the canvas from some of the ruined tents to cover the wagons with. By night fall they had a small fire and what they felt was a relatively secure camp. Occasionally, they caught a whiff of the stench from the settlement, but once they were dry, warm, and their stomachs full, they didn't mind being so close to the scene of the attack.

"Tomorrow we build a wagon," Quinn said.

"And go where?" Mansel asked.

"There's a town about half a day's ride into the mountains," Quinn said. "We can go there and start preparing for what's coming."

"What if no help comes?" Nycoll asked.

"It will," Quinn said. "It may not be more than Zollin and Brianna, but they'll come."

"The four of us back together again," Mansel said with a smile.

"Five us now," Quinn said.

"It's the way it should be," Mansel said. "No matter what we're facing, we should face it together."

"I agree," Quinn said, squeezing Mansel's shoulder. "I agree."

Chapter 17

"The armies of Falxis and Yelsia will make a stand on the southern side of the Walheta Mountains," Zollin said. He had been pleading his case and explaining to the Dwarves what had happened in Osla. They listened carefully, their faces as inscrutable as the stone they worked. "But we can't win this war alone," Zollin said. "I have come into the highlands to gather as many of the magical folk as I can. It is my hope that the dwarves of the Northern Range join me at the heart of this fight."

When Zollin paused there was some grumbling. He knew his message wasn't being well received and he wasn't surprised. How could anyone hear the horrors of his announcement and be happy about it.

"Why should we join this death march?" asked one of the dwarves. He spoke not directly to Zollin but to the other dwarves gathered around the table.

The round table was lined with headsmen from each of the clans. Their delegations waited several paces behind them, so that there was a ring of dwarves watching the proceedings just outside the direct beams of sunlight that shone through the vents in the mountain. Zollin and Bloc stood side by side at a small gap around the table.

"Would you have us wait here to die?" said another.

"The problems of the tall folk do not concern us dwarves," said a third.

"Do not forget that all the free people of the world are linked," said Babaz. "I do not welcome this news, and despite my friendship with the wizard Zollin, I am not sure I can support his cause, but I will not pretend that the future of the dwarves is not explicably linked to that of the other races."

"I have been guilty of excluding outsiders for too long," Hammert spoke up. "My clan was almost wiped out because I refused to seek help when we needed it. I know what the wizard Zollin is asking will cost us dearly. Many dwarves will give their lives in the fight he is describing, but I, for one, believe it is the right thing to do."

"And I," said another dwarf.

"You are the wizard's puppet, Hammert," shouted a dwarf from the other side of the table. "We all know that."

Several other dwarves jeered in unison, but Hammert slammed his fist down on the stone table with such force that the blow echoed around the massive chamber.

"You know nothing!" shouted Hammert. "You think that because Zollin saved the Jaq clan we would do anything for him, but that is not the case. Did you not travel here across the Stepping Stones that Zollin repaired? Did you not benefit from the knowledge he gave us about the disease that nearly annihilated my clan and would surely have spread to the other clans? For three hundred years we have hidden here, our power declining, our clans withering. Now illness such as we have never seen threatened to wipe out not only the Jaq clan but perhaps all the clans. What would have stopped the spread of the disease? How many of us would have survived if not for the wizard's intervention? Zollin did not just arrive at the Jaq clan by chance. Now is the time for all magical folk to stand together and stem the tide of darkness that threatens to overrun the world."

Zollin guessed that about half of the dwarves present shouted in agreement with Hammert. He was silently thankful that his rotund little friend had spoken so passionately in favor of helping.

"If we go to war with you, Wizard," came the voice of an elderly dwarf across the table from Zollin. "Who will lead us? You? Your king?"

"I cannot yet speak for King Felix," Zollin said. "Brianna and her pride of dragons have gone to Orrock to seek his help. King Zorlan has pledged to join us at the Walheta, but his army has been overrun and there is no telling how much help he will actually be in the fight to come. For my part, I would leave leadership of the dwarves in your own hands. Your pledge will be to help as you see fit. I, nor any other person or beast, will command you against your will."

"And will you lead us, Bloc?" asked another dwarf. "Will you take up the mantel of your forefathers? Will you heft the hammer of leadership and be our advocate with the tall folk beyond the mountains?"

Zollin turned to Bloc, but the dwarf beside him did not answer at once. He stood looking down at the table, his hands flat on the smooth stone surface. The other dwarves fell silent, waiting for Bloc to speak.

"I do not know what I fear most," Bloc said finally. "It is not the battle before us or the witch in the south. I fear the fate of my forefathers. I fear that I cannot spend your lives in a fight that is not our own. I fear making the wrong decisions. The weight of the Dwarfish people rests heavy on my shoulders. But I will not run from my place among our people. For over eight thousand years my forebears have shouldered the weight of Kingship when it was needed. I will not break that line now. I shall lead our people from the great caverns we love if you so desire. I will stand between the tall folk and all dwarves. I will give my life, if I must, to protect all that we hold sacred. Yes, I will lead us, if you will follow."

There was another moment of absolute silence, and then one by one the dwarves around the table stood and cast their votes. Only three voted not to join Zollin's quest, including Babaz. Zollin felt a huge weight lift from his shoulders, and when the votes were all in, Bloc brought the conclave to a close.

"It is decided then," he said. "Zollin, Hammert, and I will meet with the dwarves of the Southern Range. Then we will meet together in the caverns of the Yel clan in one week."

He slapped his hand palm down on the stone table and the cavern erupted in shouts and cries of excitement. The dwarves watching from beyond the sunlight who had been silent up until that moment joined in the exuberant outburst.

Hammert waddled over to where Zollin stood, taking in the raucous scene.

"Do not look so relieved, tall one. We march to war, and dwarfish battle is terrible to behold."

A few hours later the dwarves had all returned to their clans. Bloc and Zollin traveled with Hammert back through the tunnels to the Jaq clan. Zollin soon realized that Babaz had taken him on a circuitous route when they passed through the tunnels under the mountains before. He guessed that Babaz had wanted Zollin to repair as many of the Stepping Stone bridges as possible before he left the mountains. They were able to travel the distance to the Jaq Clan cavern easily in just under a day.

In the Jaq clan they rested, and Hammert saw that his clan was ready to march south with the other clans. His son, Pounder, would lead the dwarves in Hammert's absence. Zollin, Bloc, and Hammert set out early the next day. Zollin was worried about Ferno and the other dragons, but he hoped he would be able to make contact with them once they came out of the caves to cross the great valley.

They traveled a full day, and Zollin expect that they would head for the surface at any time, but the second day their tunnels went down rather than up.

"When will we go up and cross the Great Valley?" he finally asked Bloc.

"We won't," said the smiling dwarf. "This path goes under the valley and links the two mountain ranges together."

"But it is a dangerous path," Hammert said crossly. "The Luggarts have been especially active."

Zollin remembered the huge, fiery worm that seemed to be made of molten rock. He remembered mostly the red eye that appeared when the Luggart opened its mouth. *It was the stuff of nightmares*, he thought, but he had defeated the creature once. He guessed he could do it again, but he wasn't looking forward to the challenge. Not to mention the fact that he might be out of the Northern Highlands before he was able to reach out to Ferno. He didn't like being separated from the green dragon, but he would have to trust his friend to find his way south.

On the third day of their journey, the tunnels began to change. The walls became rough and uneven. The temperature steadily began to rise, and the moisture in the tunnels increased so that Zollin was soon sweating profusely. It wasn't long until a mist could be seen hovering in the dark corridors and then patches of phosphorescent moss appeared along the rough tunnel walls. At the lowest point, they passed through a section of the tunnel where water dripped. It was so hot in the tunnel that the water sizzled when it touched the stone floor. Large cracks in the tunnel glowed from the molten rock that lay like an ocean beneath them. Zollin's strength seemed to wane in the deep tunnel, and they were forced to make frequent stops to rest. At one point they heard the screeching roar of a Luggart, but they kept moving and the sounds of the fiery worm diminished. Finally, after several hours, they began climbing out from the deep tunnels. The cooler air was refreshing to Zollin. His clothes were drenched in sweat, and he had consumed all the water in his canteen.

Bloc assured Zollin that they were close to the caverns of the Molar clan, but when they came to the opening of the tunnel into a larger cave, they were shocked by what they saw. The fires of the forges were all out and the lanterns dark.

"What is happening here?" Hammert asked.

"The Molar clan," Bloc said. "They are gone."

"Something is here," Zollin said, letting his magic flow out into the cavern.

He could feel the small homes and shops where the dwarves had lived and worked. Most were empty, but some had life in them. They were large creatures, curled up in sleep. He pushed his magic further and found a large dwelling where dozens of dwarves were stacked up like firewood. He probed the dwarves and found them to be sleeping too, and encased in silky cocoons.

"The Molar clan was attacked by something," he whispered to the others. "Big creatures that wrap their victims in cocoons."

"The Anacrids have returned," Hammert said in horror.

"They were wiped out," Bloc argued. "There are no more Anacrids."

"What other creature wraps its victims in cocoons?" Hammert argued.

"What are Anacrids?" Zollin asked.

"Giant spiders," Bloc explained. "They lived in the caves thousands of years ago, just below the surface where they could come out to hunt. When the dwarves made the mountain roots our home, the Anacrids came down. They attacked small groups or individuals. There is only one other instance where an entire clan was attacked. When that happened, my great, great, grandfather rallied the clans and attacked the hairy beasts. We killed them all."

"Not all," Hammert said. "Obviously some survived."

"What should we do?" Zollin asked.

"We should wait," Hammert said. "In a few more days the other clans will start coming through, and we can attack them together."

"If we wait," Block warned, "we won't have time to rally the clans of the Southern Range."

"There may not be any more clans in the Southern Range," Hammert argued. "The Molar clan is the deepest of all the clans this side of the valley. If the Anacrids have worked their way down this far, what are the chances that the other clans survived?"

"Are you saying that the other dwarf clans could be dead?" Zollin asked.

"Yes," Hammert hissed.

"Then we must push on," Zollin said. "I'll not sit idly by while more dwarves are killed. Not when I can do something about it."

"Wait," Hammert said, grabbing Zollin's arm. "We have a way of fighting the Anacrid, but we need more dwarves. They're big creatures, terribly fast and strong. They can climb the walls and drop down on you from above. They'll cut off our escape if we move forward. They'll overwhelm us and kill us."

"You stay here," Zollin said. "I'll do this myself."

"Don't be foolhardy," Bloc said. "This is no time for heroics."

Zollin wasn't sure what to think. The dwarves were hardy folk. Babaz and his clansmen had faced the massive Luggart without fear or shrinking back. He couldn't believe that Hammert and Bloc were afraid to face the Anacrid.

"They're spiders," Zollin said. "We'll crush them, save the Molar clan and move on."

"These aren't just spiders," Hammert said. "They're bigger than you can imagine."

"What are their weaknesses?" Zollin asked.

"We take out their legs," Bloc said. "But they have eight; that's why we need more help. Hammert and I can't do it alone."

"And after you take out their legs?"

"They can still bite you. Even a little nick is poisonous. We have to very carefully bludgeon them to death. Then we burn the bodies just to be sure they're dead."

"Alright, you two stay here."

Before Bloc or Hammert could object, Zollin walked boldly into the large cavern. It was completely dark inside the common area of the Molar clan village. Zollin let his magic flow out in all directions, so that he could feel the spiders as they moved. The huge Anacrids didn't stir at first. Zollin got the impression that they had feasted and were now resting. The temptation of a single person moving through their new home didn't interest them enough to rouse them from their slumber.

Zollin held up one hand and a small flame appeared over his palm. He began to move his arm in circles around his head, as if he were twirling a lasso. The flame grew and changed color, from orange-yellow, to blue, and then to white. Then, the flame transformed into magical energy that looked like molten rock. It glowed white, was hot, thick and long. It stretched out, waving around Zollin like a long whip. He swung and twirled the energy, waiting for the spiders, which he could feel stirring.

Light from the magical molten energy flashed around the cavern which was in shambles. The goods of the dwarves in the Molar clan had been destroyed, even many of the stone tables and benches. There were blood stains on the stone floor and walls too. A few dried husks that had once been Anacrids lay curled in upon themselves. The dwarves of the Molar clan had not gone quietly, it appeared.

Then the first of the giant spiders came out into the cavern. Zollin felt it before he saw the beast. His magical senses filled the cavern, which was large, but nowhere near as massive as the Dome under the mountain. Zollin waited as the spider slowly approached. He could sense a very basic sort of magic from the Anacrids. They were magical creatures but possessed no power of their own outside their natural abilities.

Soon, there were nearly a dozen spiders all creeping toward Zollin. He could also feel Bloc and Hammert, both watching from behind a large Stalagmite, both huddled fearfully together.

Zollin lashed out at the nearest spider, extending his arm as if he were cracking his fiery whip. The molten energy lashed forward, rolling like an ocean wave, and then popping back with a crack like thunder that echoed around the cavern. A handful sized blob of the magical energy shot forward, as if it had snapped off the end of the whip. It splashed onto the spider, sizzling and burning. The coarse hair that covered the spider's body vanished, and the black flesh erupted into flame. The spider jumped back, sailing over the other Anacrids and slamming into the wall of the cavern. Its screams echoed around the room as it thrashed around uncontrollably. The magical energy burned its way into the spider's body until the huge beast finally died.

The other spiders began to move forward more cautiously. Some moving side to side directly in front of Zollin, others creeping around behind him. Zollin felt them all, even those watching from inside the houses and workshops of the dwarves. He let his restraint go as anger fueled the magic inside him into a roaring inferno. He cracked the magical whip over and over, first one way, then another, his body in constant movement. The spiders tried to dodge the magical energy blobs that were flying at them, but they were frightened, both by the sight of Zollin and by the ear splitting cracking sound of the magical energy. Almost every shot found its target. A few were hit on one of their long, spindly legs. The energy burned through the leg then fell to the floor. The Anacrids were adept at overcoming lost or broken limbs, so the shots to their legs didn't stop them. Still, the blobs that landed or splashed onto their bodies were devastating.

Zollin worked his magic without hesitation, letting his magic pour into the molten whip. He could feel the heat of it causing him to sweat, but he focused on the spiders. At one point, a spider jumped from behind several of its companions. It sailed into the air and then shot down straight at Zollin. He swung his whip up and the magical energy wrapped around the spider's body, which burst into flame. Zollin then swung the spider as if it weighed nothing. The burning spider was like a hurtling bonfire. When it crashed into the group of spiders, the body split apart sending burning shards everywhere.

Only the most cunning of spiders survived by hiding either behind the bodies of their fallen or in the inner rooms of the dwarf village. Zollin, panting and sweating, let the magical energy burn down until it was just a little flame dancing over his right shoulder, casting light in small circle around him like a torch.

"Are they all dead?" Hammert asked.

"No," Zollin said.

"That was unbelievable," Bloc said in awe.

"I never doubted him," Hammert boasted.

Zollin didn't respond. He stalked toward the remaining Anacrids. The first spider didn't move; it just stood waiting until Zollin got close. Then it scurried forward, the light reflecting from two rows of glossy, black eyes and glinting off the large mandibles at its mouth. Zollin levitated the huge spider and hurled it across the cavern. It slammed into the floor, bouncing and rolling before coming up on its feet and rushing back toward Zollin. He silently cursed himself for his foolishness. Of course the spiders weren't hurt by falling; all his life he'd seen little spiders fall great distances without being hurt. Zollin turned and sent a blast of blue magic toward the spider. The Anacrid tried to veer out of the way, but it wasn't fast enough. The shock of the lightning-type magic knocked the beast back. It landed on its back, its legs curling in death, while smoke rose from the scorch marks across its body.

Zollin took his time, cornering and killing each of the huge spiders. An hour later he was exhausted, but there were no more of the giant spiders still alive. He sank down onto the floor, his back against a stone tabletop that had been overturned. Bloc and Hammert came out slowly, still fearful of the huge spider carcasses.

"Are they all dead?" Bloc asked.

"Yes," Zollin said. "Although I can't be sure that a few didn't escape."

"That was the greatest display of magic I've ever seen," Bloc said.

"Have you seen a lot of magic?" Hammert asked sarcastically.

"I was a boy when Ingmar last visited our people," Bloc shot back.

"Ingmar the cowardly," Hammert laughed. "He was no wizard."

"He was the last of the wizards to resist the Torr," Bloc shot back angrily. "He was friends with my father."

"Don't fight," Zollin said. "Let's find some water."

"We can do better than water, I'll wager," Hammert said.

Zollin lit the torches the dwarves had carried with them into the deep tunnels. Hammert hurried off to find food and drink, but Bloc looked around the cavern in horror. It wasn't the huge bodies of the Anacrids that shocked him; it was the loss of the Molar clan.

"They're all dead," he said sadly. "A whole clan, lost forever."

"Not all of them," Zollin said.

"What do you mean?"

"I mean that there are a lot that have been poisoned and bound up by the spiders, but they're alive. The Anacrids didn't kill them or the food would spoil."

"You mean they're alive?"

"Yes," Zollin said. "In that storeroom over there," he said pointing.

Bloc ran with his torch toward the storeroom. Inside he found a mountain of small, dwarf sized cocoons. Silky spider webs had been spun around each of the survivors, wrapping them until they were completely covered. Bloc settled his torch into a wall sconce and reached for the nearest cocoon. His hands stuck to the silky threads. He pulled and pulled but couldn't break free. He put his knee against the cocoon and then his other knee, still trying to pull his arms free of the threads.

"Help!" he shouted, just as Hammert reappeared with a small cask of Shochu beer.

"What's he on about?" Hammert asked.

"He's stuck to the cocoons," Zollin said.

He couldn't hold back a mischievous smile. Hammert giggled as he poured them both a mug of beer. They drank their entire contents down and Zollin held his mug out for more.

"You can free him, right?" Hammert asked.

"Yes."

"And the dwarves inside the cocoons?"

"We can free them, too," Zollin said. "I should even be able to counter the effects of the poison."

"Excellent," Hammert said. "It won't hurt to knock the good king down a few notches."

He waddled off toward the storeroom.

"What is it now, your Highness?" Hammert said in a mocking tone. "Have you lost your slippers?"

"I'm stuck," Bloc cried out. "Help me, you old fool."

"Hey, who are you calling old?" Hammert said. "We're almost the same age."

"Get in here, Hammert. Get me off this thing."

Zollin laughed and drank three more mugs of beer. He was tired and hot. The walls of the dwarfish cave dwellings were beginning to feel like they were squeezing him. He wanted to be out in the open air, and it was hard to shake the claustrophobic feelings of panic that made it hard to breathe. He closed his eyes and concentrated on the task ahead. He needed to free the dwarves, and then they could move on. He knew they couldn't be more than a few days away from Jute's Yel clan. Then, he could go outside again.

He went to the store room and found Hammert pulling on Bloc, trying to free the dwarf from the spidery cocoon he was stuck to.

"You're going to pull my arms off," Bloc said between clenched teeth.

"I'm doing my best," Hammert said.

218

"It's not working."

"I know that."

"Well try something different."

"I'll bet I could chisel you free," Hammert said, suddenly producing a mallet and chisel.

"Don't even think about it, you fool," Bloc said.

"Let me have a go at it," Zollin said.

Hammert backed away, smiling broadly. Zollin let his magic flow into the silky threads. He heated the sections around Bloc's hands and the little dwarf pulled his hands free, although they were covered in a gluey substance. After another minute, Bloc was completely free of the cocoon and working to get the sticky goo off his hands and legs.

Zollin then focused deeper into the cocoon. The silky strands by themselves weren't hard to break, but all together they were very strong. Zollin had to delve deep into the strands, and pull them apart. It was tedious work, but the cocoons split open, and Hammert helped the sleeping dwarves out of their bonds. The dwarves were covered in the goo that had been on Bloc, but they had found that water and sand could scrub the goo away. Bloc and Hammert's clothes, and that of the poisoned dwarves, were ruined though.

It was late when the dwarves were all free. None had woken, but they were alive. Zollin slept while Hammert and Bloc kept watch. After a few hours, Zollin roused himself, ate and began healing the dwarves. The poison, which rendered the dwarves unconscious, was not difficult to deal with. He flushed it though their systems and the dwarves began to come around.

"They'll be thirsty," he said. "They need water first, then beer."

"Water first," Bloc said hurrying off.

Hammert busied himself reassuring the dwarves who were waking up. Zollin stayed at his task until the dwarves of the Molar clan, slightly more than four dozen of them, were all awake. They were in shock, but they were alive. Zollin slept again, while Hammert and Bloc helped the others to take stock of what they still had in the Molar clan cavern. The huge carcasses of the Anacrids had to be disposed of. Fortunately, the dead spiders seemed to dry up and their bodies were easy to move. The dwarves piled the dead spiders in a corner of the cavern and burned them. The smell was overpowering and woke Zollin.

"We must move on," Bloc said. "We still have a day's travel to meet with the other clans."

"I've sent messengers," said Hammert. "Although I doubt they're moving very fast. They're still regaining their strength."

"Well, let's move," Zollin said. "I want to get away from this smell."

Most of the Molar clan went with them. Only a few of the oldest dwarves stayed behind to rebuild the clan cavern and spread the news of what had happened. The rest insisted on going with Zollin. He was their rescuer, and the story of his battle with Anacrids was told by Hammert and Bloc over and over again.

Chapter 18

All Brianna wanted was to be left alone. She felt like the whole world was on her shoulders. Things had been difficult with her father in Orrock, but when her mother arrived three days later with her sisters in tow, her situation became impossible.

Brianna's mother was shown into their suite as Brianna and her father sat discussing her situation. Brianna still felt torn. She had spent the last several days with Willam. She felt the exhilaration of new love whenever she was with him. He took her places around the city she had never been, sampling the best food and wine. He showed her his plans for Yelsia, and they talked about what it would be like when he was King. His mother had passed away, so Brianna had no real example what life would be like as a queen. She tried her best to imagine it, but she never openly discussed it with Willam. The proposal was like a secret they shared; they hinted at it, but never actually talked about it.

Brianna wanted to spend time with her pride, but there were so many demands on her time. Her father wanted as much time with her as possible. He took her to visit many of the tailors in the city. She was fitted for dresses, which felt odd after so many months wearing pants on adventures with Zollin. She took him to meet her pride once, but the dragons were growing restless at being forced to stay inside the castle. Brianna tried to get the King to allow them to hunt at night when they wouldn't be seen, but he forbade it. The dragons growled when she brought her father around, even Gyia seemed angry. They were intimidating beasts under the best of circumstances, but their throaty growls and the smoke rising from their nostrils made them even more fearsome. Her father was uncomfortable around the dragons and couldn't understand his daughter's connection with them.

All her circumstances worked together to make her feel like everything she knew and loved was slipping away from her. Prince Willam reassured her constantly and made her feel like anything was possible, but in the back of her mind she still longed to be with Zollin.

"Can you believe it?" her mother said to Brianna's sisters when they were shown into the room.

At first, Brianna's sisters seemed happy to see her, but her mother seemed indifferent. She was, as Brianna had suspected, infatuated by the luxury of the castle.

"Priam," her father said. "We were just discussing Brianna's options? Girls," he said to her sisters. "Please settle into your room and give us some privacy."

The girls, laughing and giggling, went into the third bedroom, which they would share. Brianna's mother, Priam, smoothed her dress, and Brianna noticed it was her finest. Her father always made her mother beautiful gowns, but she had saved her finest clothes to show off in Orrock. Brianna wasn't surprised at all; she knew how her mother felt about being noticed and admired, although she doubted that her mother's finest would stand out in the royal court.

"Why are we here?" Priam asked.

"To see Brianna of course," her father said, trying not to sound disappointed that Brianna's mother had ignored her completely.

"Oh, yes, it is good to see you again," Priam said to Brianna.

"And you as well, Mother," Brianna said, trying to hide the iciness in her tone.

"We have good news," Estry said.

"It's not news yet," Brianna said. "I still haven't made my decision."

Her father ignored her. "The King has asked to make a match with Brianna and Prince Willam."

Brianna's mother brought her fist to her lips and tears glistened in her eyes.

"What is the bride price?" she asked.

"Mother," Brianna said. "I'm not cattle for you to sell. I'm a woman, and you don't own me. I make my own decisions."

"You've made a mess of your decisions," Priam snapped. "Your husband was killed; do you know that? Do you even care? Did you mourn him? Did you consider what people would think of us when you ran away with a sorcerer? Or how your father would make a living when people refused to do business with him because of you?"

"Father," Brianna said. "Is that true?"

"Or how people would react to a dragon being set loose on the countryside by your friend? Do you think we haven't heard of his exploits as he gallivanted around the countryside?"

"We haven't heard anything about Brianna, Priam," Estry said. "I won't have the two of you fighting."

"It's time she learned to respect us," Priam said. "We spoiled her and this is the thanks we get for all our sacrifices."

"You sacrificed nothing!" Brianna shouted. "We were your slaves, Mother. You sat preening, while my sisters and I did all the work."

"Brianna, that's uncalled for," her father said.

"But it's true."

"You ungrateful, little bitch," her mother said.

That was the last straw for Brianna. Flames erupted from her hands, burning up the long sleeved gown she wore. Her eyes shone in the heat, and her mother and father were sent stumbling back from her.

"Ah, ah, a demon!" her mother cried out.

"Shut her up, Father, or I'll not be held back," Brianna warned. "You will speak only when spoken to, Mother," she said the last word with such bitterness that the flames on her body flared brightly. "I will not hear another word of your lies. You do not know me. You do not know Zollin."

"Estry, save us," Priam cried.

Brianna's father got to his feet, his voice shaking as much as the hands he held up before Brianna.

"Control yourself, Brianna," he said. "Please, before someone gets hurt."

Brianna tamped down the rage that she felt and stormed out of the suite, ignoring the fact that her dress was burned to the shoulders and singed down each side. She went out to the pen where the dragons were kept. They howled and growled, but they didn't move.

"I can't do this," she said. "My mother is such a haughty, arrogant, witch."

Selix growled and an image of Gwendolyn flashed in Brianna's mind.

"No, she isn't a real witch, she's just mean."

"Who is mean?"

Prince Willam had come up silently behind her. He put a hand on her shoulder, and she turned into his embrace.

"It's my mother," Brianna said. "She's awful."

"At least you have one," he said.

"I know it's hard for you to understand," she said as tears rolled down her cheeks. "But my mother is hateful and cruel. She cares only about herself, and she thinks I'm her prize cow to be auctioned off to the highest bidder."

"I somehow doubt that it is as bad as all that."

"She is," Brianna cried. "I swear she is."

"Well, I want to make sure you are at dinner tonight and looking your best. The entire court will be there, and I want to ask you something," he said.

She pulled back, looking at him through her tears. He was handsome, dressed in the finest silk and wearing a gleaming sword. His hair was curly and thick, a neatly trimmed beard framed his square jaw, and his eyes were like gemstones. She felt weak whenever she looked at him. He was more handsome than she had imagined as a child, and she felt awkward and plain next to him. It was hard to believe he wanted to be with her, but the fact that he did made her feel incredibly special.

"You are too good to me," she said. "I don't deserve your attention."

"That's not true," he said. "I love you Brianna. I know you are promised to another, and I owe Zollin my life. But I need you here with me. I can do anything if you stay at my side."

"Oh, Willam," she said, starting to cry again.

"Please," he said. "You will be the greatest Queen Yelsia has ever known. Don't let your mother ruin this night. I promise I can make you happy."

Selix growled, menacingly, but Gyia growled back.

"Clean yourself up," he told her. "Make things right with your family. I will see that they have a good place in the city. They won't bother you after tonight. Just..." he let his thought trail off. "Well, I hope that you will make me the happiest man in Yelsia this night."

He kissed her cheek. It was their custom. He never pressed himself on her; no matter how much being close to one another made the two of them burn with passion. His kisses always seemed to calm her down.

He squeezed her shoulders and then he left her. It was late in the afternoon, and she wasn't sure what to do. She knew that if she went to dinner with her family, the pressure to say yes to Prince Willam's wedding proposal would be so great she would have to say yes. She wanted to say yes, but she was afraid. She still loved Zollin, but he felt so far away. She didn't want to break her promise, but she also wanted to be a Queen. She wanted to live in the castle with Willam and have children and see them have bright futures.

Selix growled and an image of her flying on his back, jubilant with the pride of dragons all around her, flashed into her mind. She smiled and reached out for Selix.

"I could never leave you," she told them.

She patted Selix on the huge dragon's golden snout, rubbing softly between the smoking nostrils.

"If Willam were King you would be the pride of Yelsia," she said. "You would always be safe here, no matter what."

Tig growled menacingly, and Brianna felt the emotional pull of the little dragon. She knew that being safe wasn't what the dragons wanted. They wanted to be fierce and free, not pets to a king.

"Willam is an honorable man," Gyia hissed.

"He is. More than that, he is a good man and my feelings for him run deep."

An image flashed in Brianna's mind of sitting alone, looking lonely with a golden crown on her head.

"I won't be lonely," she told Selix. "I could help a lot of people as Queen."

Then an image came of the pride leaving, flying up into the sky, as Brianna watched from the ground, waving.

"You wouldn't have to leave," she said. "You won't have to stay pinned up here much longer. I promise."

A servant hurried up to Brianna, but was careful not to get too close to the dragon pen. He made sure Brianna stayed between himself and the dragons.

"Lady Brianna," he said. "The King requests your presence in his private chambers."

"Now?" Brianna asked, conscious for the first time at the state of her clothes.

"Yes, my lady. It is urgent."

"Alright," Brianna said.

She bade her dragons' goodbye and followed the servant up to the suite where the King stayed. She had been in the room with Zollin before. She remembered that clearly, but Zollin seemed to be fading from her memory.

"Your family has arrived," King Felix said, not getting up from the padded chair he sat in near the fire.

"Yes," Brianna said.

"Good," the King said. "Willam will ask for your hand in marriage this evening. What will your answer be?"

"I'm not sure, your Highness."

"Of course you are," King Felix snapped. "You know your own heart. Now tell me."

"I..., I'm not sure what to do," she said, looking fearful. "I need more time."

"There is no more time," King Felix said. "As you have said yourself many times, the enemy from Osla will be upon us soon. We must move quickly if we are to be ready."

"It would be better if we waited until the conflict is over," Brianna said. "Then I could give my answer."

The King's eyes narrowed. "That is unacceptable," he said. "We have given you every courtesy. I will not bandy words with you, Brianna. Accept Prince Willam, or the consequences will be dire."

"Are you threatening me?" she asked in surprise.

It was the one thing she had not expected, and it made her angry. She knew that King Felix had been holding back his plans from Prince Willam, which she thought was foolish, but she had no idea he could be so cruel and arrogant as to threaten her. It hardened her resolve and while she managed to keep her anger under control, she made up her mind in that instant.

"The answer is no. I'm promised to Zollin."

"That is unfortunate," Felix said. "I'm afraid your refusal has forced my hand. Our forces will not march to Falxis."

"What? You can't mean that?"

"But I do," he said, his voice dripping with condescension. "If you want the army of Yelsia to help your wizard, then you must marry Prince Willam."

"He would never agree to this."

"He will never know."

"I'll tell him."

"If you do I'll have your family killed," King Felix said matter-of-factly. "I really won't take no for an answer."

"I'll kill you," she said angrily, the flames appearing on her hands.

Royal Guards appeared, all armed with crossbows which were loaded and ready to fire. They appeared from every room, too many to stop.

"You may," King Felix said. "And you may even be able to kill some of my guards, but not all of them. Can you survive multiple shots from a crossbow at close range? I really doubt that. I'm not a cruel man, Brianna, but I will do anything for Yelsia. You should know as well as I that this threat from Osla must be dealt with. I cannot afford to take chances. Your dragons give us an edge we wouldn't have otherwise. I really must insist on controlling them."

"Forcing me to marry Willam won't give you control of the pride."

"I never leave things to chance, my dear," he said. "Surely you should know that by now. But I won't have you interfering with my plans. Marry my son, or live with the consequences of your actions."

"I cannot."

"You can and you will. You will never speak of this moment. You will never tell Willam anything other than your undying love. You will bring your dragons under my control, and you will not put yourself in danger. Those are my conditions."

"Fine," Brianna said, tears stinging her eyes again. "You leave me no choice."

"I know," he said, and began to laugh.

Brianna ran from the room. She started to run down to the dragon pen but then she realized that if she did she couldn't keep her thoughts from the dragons. She couldn't take that chance. The dragons would tear the castle to pieces, and her family would be killed. Willam's words came back to her mind. A true leader puts the welfare of his people first, he had said. Brianna realized that she really had no choice. It wasn't about her, or her family, it was about the people of Yelsia and about Zollin. They needed her to do the hard thing.

She ran up to the top of one of the watch towers. She couldn't stop the sobs that wracked her body. She cried for nearly an hour, and then she calmly went down to her rooms and got dressed for the feast. Her father was there, and he helped her into the finest gown. They didn't speak, but he could see the unhappiness in her eyes. He did his best to comfort her but he, too, was on the verge of breaking down.

She waited in her room until the others had gone down to the feast. Then, realizing that this was probably the last time she would truly have to herself, she walked slowly down to the great hall. She spent those precious few moments remembering Zollin. She wondered what he would think of her. She knew if he were there he could rescue her from the craziness of King Felix, but he wasn't there. He was far away in the north, and she was all alone.

Chapter 19

Meeting with the dwarves of the Southern Range was much different from the conclave in the north. They met in a small cavern near an underground lake. There was no time for festivities. The dwarves had heard of the Anacrids attack on the Molar clan, although no one knew where the giant spiders had come from. The dwarves of the Molar clan shamed any of the dwarves who didn't support Zollin, and after an hour of debate, the issue was settled.

Jute had kept his distance from Zollin until after the conclave. Once the meeting broke up, Jute ambled over and gazed at the Wizard intently.

"It's no surprise to me that you're back, Wizard," Jute said. "You tall folk aren't hardy enough to win a fight on your own."

"I'm glad to have you as an ally," Zollin said.

"Did you bring more ale?"

"Not this trip," Zollin said. "But I'll see that you are well supplied once we head south."

"Well, I can't stay and visit. With all the clans passing through the Yel Clan cavern, I need to get back and prepare."

"I'll see you soon," Zollin said.

"Aye, I suppose that can't be helped," Jute said playfully.

The next day, Zollin and his entourage made their way to the home of the Yel Clan. Zollin was amazed at how quickly they could travel under the mountains. The tunnels certainly didn't seem straight, yet what took three or four days through the mountain passes above ground, could be accomplished in one or two days in the tunnels underneath.

The Yel Clan cavern was a hive of activity. Food and drink were being prepared to feed the other clans as they gathered. Most of the dwarves carried war hammers, with heavy steel heads, but some carried battle axes and others knives. There were grinding wheels setting edges on blades and forges roaring as last minute weapons were crafted. Zollin was respectful, but he hurried to the surface as quickly as possible.

His heart raced as he climbed up the tunnel that led to the little clearing where he'd first met Jute and where Mansel had arm wrestled the stout dwarf. He felt as though he couldn't catch his breath until he was finally out of the cave. He stood, his face pointed up toward the sky, sucking in great breaths of fresh air. It was nearing winter, and the air was cold, but Zollin didn't mind. He felt a huge relief to be out of the caves, even if it was just for a little while.

"Well, don't act so relieved, Southlander," Jute said.

"I'm sorry," Zollin said. "I was starting to get claustrophobic."

"We get the opposite feeling after being away from the caverns too long. We weren't meant to walk around on the skin of the world."

"Well, I'm glad you will, even if the cause isn't pleasant," Zollin said. "I am in your debt."

"No more than we are in yours," Jute said. "You repaired the Stepping Stones in the north. You saved the Molar clan. This witch you will fight would come after us in the end. Stopping her now only makes sense, but you are right, it is not pleasant."

"You've been a good friend, Jute," Zollin said. "You have helped me, and I am very grateful. But I must try to find the dragons."

"Dwarves and dragons fighting together, it is truly a wondrous time, Southlander. We are both born of the mountain, but the dwarves rule under the mountains, the dragons above them. I cannot remember a time when we were allies."

"You are now," Zollin said. "Dwarves and Dragons, Giants and Men, all fighting together. And, if we are successful, perhaps it will be the beginning of a new era of peace and trade among our races."

"Perhaps, but I will wait and see. We dwarves are patient people, we will wait and see."

Jute turned and went back down into the caves. Zollin turned and made his way out of the forest. Telford Pass was nearby, and the road running south toward Felson. The area opened up and Zollin stood in the weak, autumn sunshine for several minutes, just letting the light bathe his body. Then he sent his magic out. The heat of his magic blew through him, long, hot blasts as he called out to Ferno. There was no reply. Zollin gathered firewood and built a small campfire. He sat down on the soft turf, watching the crackling flames and occasionally sending out another magical call to the north.

Zollin could only hope that given time, Ferno or one of the other dragons would hear his magical plea. Ferno knew that Zollin was headed south; eventually the green dragon would come for him.

It wasn't long before Bloc appeared. He was thin for a dwarf, but that only made the powerful muscles in his arms and shoulders more prominent. He settled in beside Zollin, his feet near the fire, face turned up to gaze at the sky. For a long time, neither man nor dwarf spoke. They were comfortable with each other, and to Zollin's surprise, Bloc seemed comfortable outside of the caves.

"The sky is a wonder to me," Bloc said at last.

"You aren't afraid of it?" Zollin asked.

"I don't suppose we dwarves are afraid of anything. But we are small folk and being outdoors makes us feel even smaller I suppose."

"I can understand that," Zollin said. "I felt much the same way on the sea."

"You've been to sea?" Bloc asked incredulously.

"Yes."

"And you survived?"

"Of course," Zollin said.

"But wizards can't go to sea. Everyone knows that."

"I didn't know that."

"The knowledge of men is no reflection of their stature. We dwarves may be smaller than humans, but at least we know a thing or two.   You really went to sea, as in a ship out on the water?"

"Yes, but it wasn't without disaster," Zollin said.   "I accidentally summoned a huge sea creature that destroyed my first ship. And I was attacked by Mermen another time."

"It's a wonder that you have lived this long, Zollin," Bloc said with a chuckle.

Zollin laughed too, but he knew that what Bloc said was true. He only hoped that his luck would hold.

Two days later, the dwarves were all assembled.   They marched out of Peddinggar Forest and down the southern road. They were a sight to see, row after row of grey bearded dwarves, both men and women, it was impossible to tell them apart. Zollin walked at the head of their host, with Bloc, Jute, and Hammert. Babaz remained with his clan and the survivors of the Molar clan took on the role of Zollin's servants. They took care of his every need on the march, even when he insisted on doing things himself.

The dwarves carried their own rations and gleaned food from abandoned fields along the way. The north was still mostly abandoned; the towns empty and the farms deserted. Zollin didn't mind. He had planned to fly ahead with Ferno and prepare the way for the dwarfish army, but he still hadn't made contact with Ferno. It was worrisome and part of Zollin wanted to turn back and find the green dragon, but he knew he didn't have the time. Ferno and the other dragons would have to catch up on their own time.

The dwarves' short legs made their progress slow, but they had great endurance. They marched from first light until well after dark, with no breaks. Zollin was exhausted after just three days. And he guessed that another week would bring them to Felson. Occasionally, they met people along the road. No human had seen a dwarf other than Zollin and Brianna in over three centuries. Some people simply stood and stared, but others cheered, even if they had no idea where the dwarves were headed or why they were marching.

Zollin heard rumors of the King conscripting soldiers. No one was surprised by the military buildup, given that the armies of Osla and Falxis had recently invaded. The fact that those armies had been beaten back filled most of the people Zollin met with a sense of pride in their king and kingdom. Zollin guessed that the buildup meant that Brianna was having success in convincing King Felix to mobilize the army. His heart ached when he thought of Brianna. He missed her so terribly and while he knew that they had done the right thing by splitting up, he still felt the ache of her absence, like a part of his soul was missing.

* * *

The feast in Orrock had been grand. It seemed that everyone knew of the pending proposal and had shown up in droves to the feast. There was food of every kind: wine, ale, cider, and even hot beverages. The mood was festive, and everyone seemed to be enjoying themselves, except for Prince Willam and Brianna.

Willam was nervous. He still wasn't sure he was doing the right thing. He didn't like the fact that his father was manipulating him. If not for his personal feelings for Brianna, he wouldn't have gone along with it. But the truth was he had been smitten with Brianna from the first time they met. She was beautiful, smart, passionate, and strong. There was no pretentiousness to her, and she had no sense of entitlement, unlike most of the women in the royal court. He wanted Brianna to be his wife, to love him and share his throne, but he wasn't entirely sure that she wanted him. He knew that she had feelings for him, but he didn't know if they were stronger than the feelings she still had for Zollin.

Brianna, on the other hand, was sure that she didn't want to marry Prince Willam. The temptation to become Queen of Yelsia had been a fantasy, but now that it was being forced upon her, she realized that it wasn't the future she wanted. She wanted to be with Zollin. The Prince was handsome and charming, and the future he offered was enticing but safe. She wanted to fly with dragons and experience new things. She wanted to live life out in the open, where things were different each day. And she wanted to be with Zollin. He wasn't as handsome or charming as the prince, but he was powerful and compassionate, quick to laugh even at himself. And most of all, he made her feel like an equal, not just a mate. She missed that. She had been so focused on her mission and then dealing with new feelings, that she had forgotten how Zollin made her feel. She wanted to see him again more than anything. She silently hoped he would arrive suddenly, burst into the grand hall, and put an end to the madness she found herself in. But he didn't come, and before she knew it, Prince Willam was calling for silence.

"Please, pardon my interruption of the night's festivities," he said. "As most of you know, these are tumultuous times in the Five Kingdoms. I, for one, know personally how quickly life can change, and not always for the better. But tonight I am hoping to usher in a new era of good tidings here in Yelsia."

He turned to Brianna who was trying her best not to let the horror she felt show on her face.

"Brianna, you have helped me see what kind of man I want to be. You have brought hope to me when none else could. And your dragons have revealed the future of our kingdom. I can't imagine even one day without you by my side. I love you. Will you do me the great honor of becoming my wife and Princess of Yelsia?"

The room was as silent as a tomb, and Brianna felt as if her future were just as bleak. Internally she was screaming *no, no, no.* But outwardly, she did her best to look happy. She had considered every possibility, but King Felix had ensured that she had no other options. She had to agree.

"Yes," she said quietly.

The crowd erupted in cheers and applause. Trumpets sounded and drums beat out the cadence of the King's Army. Prince Willam pulled Brianna close and for the first time kissed her lips. Brianna kissed him back not wanting anyone to see her hesitation, but Prince Willam felt it and when he pulled away, looking deep into her eyes, he knew the truth. She had said yes, but her heart wasn't in it.

He kept up the appearance of a happy groom to be, but Brianna could feel the tension in him. Entertainers appeared: singers, acrobats, and jesters. More food was brought out and spirits consumed. Brianna drank her wine slowly; she was afraid of what she might say or do if she let the strong drink go to her head. Prince Willam didn't touch anything, not food, not wine, only Brianna's hand. He smiled and acted happy, but Brianna knew he wasn't.

When the night finally wound down, her father escorted them back to their suite of rooms. Her mother and sisters were on cloud nine, but her father knew that Brianna wasn't happy. He held her back when the others went in to bed. There was fire in the fireplace and a decanter of wine on the table across the room. Estry poured them both a goblet of wine, and then joined his eldest daughter near the fire.

"You aren't happy," he said.

"No," Brianna admitted.

"So, why did you say yes? Not because I wanted it, I hope."

"No Father, I didn't do it for you, or for Mother, or even for all of Yelsia."

"So?" he asked.

"It isn't important," Brianna said. "All that matters now is that I keep my commitment."

"Sweetheart, is marrying the Crown Prince of Yelsia really so bad?"

"It is when you love another," Brianna said.

"But you love Prince Willam, too."

"No," Brianna said. "I care for Willam; he is a good man and I believe he will be a great king, but I am not in love with him."

"Love is like a flower. It starts off as a seed, small and simple, but in time it grows and becomes a beautiful flower. You have the seed of love for Prince Willam. He will make you happy. The more you get to know him, the greater that love will grow."

"Father, I love Zollin. He is the man I was meant to be with. I cannot deny it. And yet, fate has seen fit to rob me of him. I shall never be happy. If I am lucky, perhaps I will one day be able to deny the resentment that has risen up in me. All I want is to be free of this place... to fly with the dragons of my pride... to feel that the whole world is before me again."

"Surely if the world is before anyone, it would be a queen."

"But it isn't," Brianna said. "Don't you see that? If I marry Prince Willam my whole life will be dictated to me. Where I shall live, what I shall do, who I shall see and not see. That isn't what I want."

"What about helping people," he said, grasping for anything that might make her feel better about the match with Prince Willam. "You said yourself that a queen can make a difference in many lives. Think of all the good you can do."

"Yes," Brianna said. "I can make everyone happy but myself."

She cried quietly, and Estry held her close. He didn't know what else to do or how else to help her. He loved his daughter, but she was beyond his influence now. So he held her, crying with her, and telling her he would always love her.

Chapter 20

It took a full day's work to make it to the village of Green Glen. Mansel and Quinn pushed and pulled the wagon they had cobbled together. It was loaded with supplies, but mostly the herbs and powders that Nycoll had discovered. They passed the small village that guarded the western pass into the mountains, but it was deserted, so they traveled on. The hills that led into the mountains were not steep but the long, gentle slopes exhausted both men as they pushed the wagon up and then did their best to control it as they went back down.

In the village of Green Glen, they found the survivors of the settlement attack. The people there were in shock, many were wounded and the people of the village were completely overwhelmed. They were met at the edge of the village by the same teamster that Quinn had gotten information from on his way through the mountains. But this time the burly man named Jorgyn wasn't alone. There were four other men with him, all armed, and although they didn't look confident with their weapons, they did seem intent on their task.

"We'll be asking you to move along," the teamster said. "We can't take in any more refugees."

"We're not refugees," Mansel said.

"Surely you remember me," Quinn said. "We spoke just days ago."

"I remember," the big man said, "but the town's full. There are no more rooms to be had. We'll be lucky to make it through the winter without half the town starving."

"We aren't looking for a room or for food. We can take care of ourselves," Quinn said. "But we'd like to wait here for King Zorlan and the armies from the north."

"What are you on about?" Jorgyn asked.

"You've heard of the monsters no doubt," Quinn said. "They're just the beginning. King Zorlan's army was defeated by these monsters, but there is an army coming north now, and the kings have given their word to make a stand at the Walheta together."

"King Zorlan is coming here?"

"He's coming to the mountains," Quinn said. "I can't be sure where he'll make camp. Let us stay and help. We've got supplies."

"Medicines," Nycoll said.

"We can hunt," Quinn continued.

"And help keep the peace," Mansel said.

"We'll even help patrol for the King's forces," Quinn said. "And if the monsters make it this far, you'll want every able bodied man you can get."

"Well," the teamster said, thinking things through. "I guess you could make camp at my place; that's if you don't mind sharing a barn with my horses."

"That's very generous," Quinn said. "We won't get in your way."

"The town's in need of a healer," the Teamster said, introducing himself to Nycoll. "I'm Jorgyn."

"I'm not a healer," Nycoll said. "But I can help."

"My name is Quinn, and this is Mansel."

They all shook hands.

"That's quite a sword you're wearing," Jorgyn said to Mansel. "And from the looks of things, you know how to use it."

Mansel nodded, but didn't speak.

"The healer is your woman?" Jorgyn asked.

"We're together, yes," Mansel said.

"I'm not trained," Nycoll said. "But I've some knowledge and we've got supplies in the wagon."

"You pulled that rickety thing up the mountain path?" Jorgyn asked.

"It's from the settlement you told me about," Quinn said. "We had to cobble it together from various pieces and without tools."

"You are industrious, aren't you?"

"We aren't shirkers," Quinn said.

"Well, there's a community meal in the village. Let's go down and see what you can do to help."

The men with Jorgyn continued to patrol the edge of the village. Green Glen was little more than a few shops and a dozen or so homes. There was an inn and a common area in the middle of town.

"The sick are laid up in the Cloverleaf Inn," Jorgyn explained. That's where the community meal is being prepared as well. Everyone has donated whatever they can to the cause."

"That's generous," Quinn said. "We've got extra supplies we salvaged from the settlement. We'll be glad to contribute."

They spent the next four hours helping with the wounded. Mansel kept several pots of water boiling, and Quinn helped Nycoll clean wounds and prepare poultices. The locals had supplied cloth for clean bandages, but there was no healer in the village. Nycoll had a rudimentary understanding of what was needed and gave precise instructions on how the sick were to be treated.

They ate a supper of stew and hard crusted bread. There was ale, but it was rationed. It was well past dark when the three of them returned with Jorgyn to set up their own little shelter in the teamster's barn. There was one unused horse stall; it was swept clean and Mansel helped situate it for Nycoll, so that she could have a little privacy. There was plenty of room and even an old wood stove in one corner, which they used to heat the barn at night.

The next day, Mansel took a bow and went hunting. Quinn spent the morning helping Nycoll in the village, then spent several hours chopping wood. By the time Mansel returned, carrying a young stag over his broad shoulder, everyone was tired. Mansel handed his trophy over to the Inn Keeper who immediately began to butcher the meat. Some was used in that night's meal, the rest hung to be used in the days ahead.

The nights in the mountain village were cold. The stars were bright in the sky, but most of the village kept indoors. Quinn had arranged straw for their beds, and blankets from the inn had been borrowed. They built up a warm fire in the stove and rested well in the barn.

The days went on in a similar fashion for a week. Quinn helped the locals plan and implement a strategy to keep watch over the village. He also trained the villagers in how to use their weapons in combat. The villagers had a wide array of weapons, some clubs, a few rusty swords and spears.

More people drifted into the village and while there was no more shelter to be had, Quinn and Mansel built frames that the locals could cover with canvass, creating pavilions that kept the worst of the weather off of those forced to take shelter out of doors.

On the seventh day, a rider came galloping into the village. He wore the uniform of the Falxis Royal Army, but it was covered with dirt and grime. He looked weary, but excited.

"The King is coming," he said in a hoarse voice. "Make room for the King."

The news sent the village into a tizzy of excitement and work. Most of the sick and injured were recovered enough to be moved. Jorgyn moved his horses out into his corral, and the barn was cleaned out so that those who still needed care could be sheltered in the barn with Nycoll. The next day, the army of Falxis arrived.

To everyone in the village's dismay, the army consisted of around two hundred soldiers and nearly a thousand refugees. The broad valley was soon filled with people, tents, and animals. The valley, once beautiful and idyllic, was soon rendered into a crowded, smelling ghetto.

Quinn and Mansel did their best to stay busy without drawing undue attention to themselves. It didn't take long before tensions arose as homes were broken into and fights erupted between locals and refugees, civilians and soldiers. King Zorlan, looking gaunt and exhausted, took over the Cloverleaf Inn and wasn't seen again outside the small establishment. Food, which had been a concern before, now became the number one priority. Quinn and Mansel took turns hunting, but the game was soon scared away by the numbers of people roaming through the mountains searching for any wild creature they might kill and eat. And neither man trusted that Nycoll would be safe unguarded. She stayed in Jorgyn's barn, which was now a makeshift hospital. The King brought two healers in his refugee army, but one was a drunk who always managed to find enough spirits to stay inebriated.

The king's soldiers made a halfhearted attempt to train the men that had fled into the mountains, but the refugees were either surly or scared, and the soldiers were too tired to give the effort much time or energy. Scouts were sent south and many reported on a daily basis, but while the flying, centaur monsters still roamed the now deserted countryside, there was no sign of the Yelsian forces.

Occasionally, small bands of the flying monsters appeared in the mountains and tried unsuccessfully to attack the village. The bands were always small, never more than five of the wretched creatures, and the soldiers beat them back easily.

The valley had been occupied for over a week before Quinn was summoned to the Cloverleaf Inn. Two soldiers appeared at Jorgyn's barn calling for Quinn to accompany them back to the inn to meet with King Zorlan.

"What the hell does he want?" Mansel asked sourly. His mood had not improved with the arrival of the King. What had once been a source of hope, had become a bitter disappointment.

"I don't know," Quinn said. "You better stay here until I get back."

Mansel had been preparing to go hunting. He had always been a fairly good archer and could move through the forest quietly, although his tracking skills were below average. He could usually find game if he stuck to it long enough, and of late, if he ventured far enough from the camp.

"I'll be here," Mansel said, testing the draw of his bow.

Quinn followed the soldiers through the crowded, muddy streets of the village to the Cloverleaf Inn. He went inside and found that the common room was now a war room. The long tables were covered with maps, and the king's officers were busy trying to plan a strategy to protect the village if a larger attack was launched against them.

King Zorlan was seated in a small chair near the fireplace. He looked sick, his skin pale and sagging, and his hair limp and greasy. His eyes were half closed, but they opened up when Quinn was announced.

"The man from Yelsia," one of the soldiers said. "His name is Quinn."

The King gazed at Quinn for a few seconds before speaking.

"You were in Yelsia recently?" he asked.

"It's been a few weeks now," Quinn said.

"And is Felix mobilizing his forces to join us here?"

"I know that Brianna and my son Zollin are trying to arrange that," Quinn said.

"Zollin the Wizard is your son?" King Felix asked.

"He is."

"And will he bring an army to make a stand with us here?"

"If he said that he would, he will," Quinn said. "Unless he's dead."

"Do you think he might be dead?"

"No, I have no reason to think that he might be dead. I'm just saying that death is the only thing that would keep him from fulfilling his word."

"Good. I hope that King Felix comes soon. We have to set up some sort of supply chain. I don't suppose there is much in the way of food and supplies north of the mountains?"

"Not really, Sire, the area between the Rejee desert and the coast is sparsely populated. The best hope would be to sail supplies from western Yelsia down here."

"That was my guess as well," Zorlan said, "which is why I chose the western pass through the mountains to make my base of operations. I have soldiers to the east, but not many, Scouts mainly. The rumors around the village are that you served in Felix's royal guard."

"I did, Sire, but that was long ago."

"You look like you're in good shape to me."

"I can hold my own, Sire, but the problem isn't so much physical as it is logistical. I don't have good weapons anymore. I lost my short sword and throwing knives fighting the monsters."

"Tell me why you came here?" King Zorlan asked.

"I came to find a friend and help him if I could."

"Did you find your friend?"

"Yes," Quinn said.

"Good, then your task is done. I will give you a new one. I want you to move in here with me. I need advisors. I doubt that King Felix will be happy to see me."

"No, I don't suppose he will," Quinn said.

"I will need you to vouch for me. Can you do that?"

"I'm just a simple carpenter, Sire. I wouldn't dare speak for a king."

"I'm ordering you to do that. You will have time to get to know our plans. You will be given every luxury that can be provided within our limited means. No one can ask for more than that."

"I do not wish to impose, Sire," Quinn said. "I will speak on your behalf, but I do not wish to move into the Inn. All I ask is that whatever assistance you would have given me be given instead to the hospital."

"You are a noble and generous man, Quinn. I do not trust that in a man. I prefer to work with people who are in my debt."

Quinn's jaw tightened, but he didn't respond.

"You will stay here, and your friend as well. Please do not think that I am a fool. Your friends will not be safe here or anywhere else unless you do as I say. Is that clear enough for you? Surely even a washed up soldier from Yelsia can understand that."

"Your threats are unnecessary, Sire," Quinn said, tension making his voice more gruff than usual. "I will do as you ask."

"Yes," Zorlan said, his eyes narrowing. "I know you will."

Chapter 21

Prince Willam was angry. He didn't know what to do with such strong feelings, since he knew the only person he could blame for his uncomfortable situation was his father. As a son, he had no problem confronting his father, but as the Crown Prince of Yelsia, he loathed the idea of challenging his King. Still, he knew he couldn't stay in Orrock. The time had come to move the army south, and he was determined not to be left behind.

He stalked to his father's domicile. The richly carved doors were standing open, Prince William could hear the chatter of his father's advisors. The fact that he was always left out of the King's plans made him even angrier. He strode into the room, ignoring the advisors who oversaw the administration of the kingdom. Felix was surrounded by his generals, and Willam broke into the tight group.

"Father, it is time the army moved south," he stated bluntly. "I will be going with them."

"Of course you won't," King Felix countered, "you have a wedding to plan."

"No," Willam's voice was almost menacing. "The marriage will take place once we return to Orrock."

"Don't be a fool," King Felix said. "You must not risk the royal line by rushing off to war, especially since this fight is not even our own. Stay here, marry Brianna, and make babies. That's the best part of marriage anyway."

"Father, I will not be left behind. I am the Crown Prince of Yelsia, and I have trained all my life for battle. I am going south, and nothing you can say will stop me."

General Corlis leaned over and whispered in King Felix's ear. The King frowned as he looked up from his seat and stared at Prince Willam. When he spoke it was slowly and with an angry growl.

"You may go to Felson, and take the cavalry south through the Western Pass."

"Fine," Prince Willam said.

He was just turning to leave, when his father spoke again.

"You will serve under Commander Hausey."

Willam froze. He couldn't believe he was being placed under another officer's command, but he decided not to argue. He needed space from his father and the stifling expectations of the royal court.

He returned to his lavish quarters and packed a small bag. He had one thing to do before he left the capital, and he was dreading it almost as much as seeing his father. He slung his pack over his shoulder and walked down the winding stone staircase. He needed to see Brianna, and he expected to find her in the suite of rooms she was sharing with her family. He was surprised to find her sitting alone in the stairwell.

"What are you doing out here, my lady?" he asked her.

She looked up, her eyes red and puffy.

"Are you okay?" he asked.

"I couldn't stand another minute with my mother," she said. "She thinks because you proposed that she is now Queen of all Five Kingdoms and the rest of the world combined."

"She is a demanding woman," Willam agreed.

"No, she is a selfish, hateful, unhappy woman. And she takes it all out on her daughters. She thinks that because we are getting married, she is the most important person at court. She has no idea that everyone is just humoring her and that behind her back she is the laughing stock of the city."

"It can't be that bad," Willam said.

"It is, and because I'm not jumping for joy making wedding plans, she is making my life miserable."

"You don't want to get married, do you?" he said sadly. "At least not to me."

"Oh no," she said quickly. "I love you, Willam, honestly. But there is a war coming. A war I'm not sure we can win. It is difficult to think beyond that at the moment."

"Yes, well..." he hesitated, not sure how to say what he needed to say. "I'm leaving for Felson. Gyia and I will fly there and help move the cavalry south."

"You're leaving?"

"The army is ready to move," he said. "Isn't that what you wanted?"

"Of course it is; I guess I just thought we would leave together."

"There is no reason why we shouldn't," he said. "Let your mother stay and plan the wedding. We can leave as soon as you're ready."

"Alright," Brianna said, brightening at the prospect of leaving Orrock and escaping her mother's constant demands.

She hurried to her room and Willam went down to the kitchen. He gathered enough rations for the two of them and then went outside to meet Brianna.

* * *

"Are they ready?" King Felix asked, still angry from his son's confrontation.

"Yes, my Lord," said the goldsmith. "I've engraved the names you requested into the crown, just as you ordered."

"Good," King Felix said, taking his crown from the goldsmith. "You may go."

"Yes, my Liege."

"What now?" Corlis asked. He was the only advisor still in the king's domicile.

"We go up to the watchtower and see if this really works."

"The scholars said it would," Corlis said. "But it certainly seems too easy."

"We shall know soon enough," King Felix said.

They made their way up the long set of winding stairs that led to the top of the watchtower. Corlis threw open the trap door, and they made their way onto the roof. There were four men standing watch and Corlis sent them away.

King Felix sat the crown on his head and closed his eyes. He didn't feel any differently. He tried not to let the foolish feeling he suddenly felt keep him from giving his best effort.

"Selix, Tig, Gyia... come up here!" he ordered under his breath.

Then he stepped back from the edge of the rooftop and waited.

"Did you do it?" Corlis asked.

Felix ignored him. It had been a week since his messengers returned from Ebbson Keep. They had brought all the translated scrolls from the recently discovered library in the ruins of Ornak and two of the scholars who had been working on the difficult translations. The scrolls told of kings who controlled dragons by writing the names of the huge beasts inside their crowns. It seemed strange, but King Felix was willing to try anything to gain control of the dragons. He wouldn't leave anything to chance.

For a long moment it seemed that the plan had failed, but then they heard the unmistakable sound of the dragons' wings beating against the wind as the terrible beasts soared up from the pen down in the courtyard. Selix was the first to appear; the great golden dragon snarled furiously, but landed gracefully on the watchtower roof. Tig and Gyia quickly followed, all three roaring angrily.

"Bow before me," King Felix shouted.

Flames billowed out of the dragon's mouths, but they lowered their long necks before the king. He smiled in triumph. The plan had worked.

"Return to your pen," he said, "And speak of this to no one."

The dragons turned and glided down to the timber corral filled with hay where the dragons were kept in the castle courtyard.

"My Liege," Corlis said in awe. "You did it."

"Yes," King Felix said, holding in the glee he felt. "Now everything will be as it should. Yelsia will overthrow the other kingdoms, and I shall rule them all."

* * *

Brianna hurried down to the courtyard of the castle. She felt better than she had in days. Her father had tried to help her see all the good that could come from marrying Prince Willam, but her mother had nearly driven her insane. Brianna couldn't believe that her mother could be so arrogant. *She was just a tailor's wife from a small village*, Brianna thought, and yet she acted so high and mighty, looking down on Brianna for not wanting to forget everything else and focus all her attention on wedding details.

Brianna had been anxious to rejoin her pride and take to the skies once again. She knew the dragons would be excited to leave the confines of the castle pen as well. She was shocked when she saw them, and the dragons weren't lying down as they usually were. Instead, she found them on their feet stalking around the confines of the pen, smoke billowing from their mouths and low, menacing growls rumbling from deep in their chests at anyone who ventured too close to the pen.

"What is going on?" she asked, as she hurried up to the wooden railing.

The dragons refused to look at her.

"Selix!" Brianna said. "What has happened?"

The great golden dragon roared so loudly it shook the ground and reverberated all around the castle. Brianna saw an image of chains in her mind, but she didn't know what it meant, and the dragons would explain no further.

"I don't know what has gotten into you but calm down," she told them. "We're leaving."

The news that they would be leaving the castle was the only thing that seemed to sooth the beasts. They sent images of returning to the castle.

"No," she told them. "We are leaving with Prince Willam and flying to Felson. From there, we'll fly south back to the Walheta Mountains to prepare for the fight."

The dragons bellowed in what Brianna took for happiness. When Prince Willam appeared, they bound their packs that contained their clothing and food together and gave the heavy bags to Tig. The small dragon couldn't carry a person, but it could fly with their belongings in its big, blue talons.

Brianna jumped up, summersaulting and then landing lightly on Selix's broad back. The golden dragon roared again and took to the air. Tig followed close behind. It took Willam longer to climb up onto Gyia's narrow back and get a good grip. Once he did, the purple dragon reared onto its more powerful hind legs, then jumped into the air. The wide wings flapped hard, propelling them both up into the sky behind Selix and Tig.

The countryside flew by beneath him. There was traffic on the Weaver's Road that ran east and west through the heart of Yelsia from Ebbson Keep through Felson, Orrock, and all the way to the trading city of Tragoon Bay on the western coast. The sun was shining and both man and dragon felt a sense of freedom that they had sorely missed.

Brianna forgot about the strange behavior of the dragons. They stopped at midday a few miles south of the Weaver's Road. They took shelter beneath a large oak tree that grew beside a swiftly flowing stream. Brianna and Willam ate while the dragons rested from the long flight. Gyia was exhausted after carrying Prince Willam so far, but after a couple of hours they continued their journey.

Night fell before they reached Felson, and they made camp for the night near a homestead that sheltered them from view of anyone on the road. Prince Willam introduced himself to the farmer and his family, and assured them that their animals were safe from the dragons. Brianna built a fire and unfurled the blankets that were in their packs. They ate toasted bread and cheese for dinner, while the dragons hunted.

Brianna was reminded of camping with Zollin in much the same way. The thought made her sad and quiet.

"You haven't said more than two words all evening," Willam said. "What's troubling you? I'm sure the dragons are fine."

"No, it isn't the dragons," she assured him. "I'm just remembering happier times."

"Most women would think that being betrothed to the Crown Prince of Yelsia would make these happy times."

"They are, in a fashion," she said. "But it's hard to think about marriage and settling down when we're about to fight a war."

"Perhaps we won't," Willam said. "Perhaps this is all for nothing. Maybe the monsters went away or perhaps they have no interest in Yelsia."

"You know that's wishful thinking."

"Of course it is," Willam said. "I think we have to plan for the worst and hope for the best. It does us no good to dwell on the bad things that might happen. For instance, I'm not dwelling on the fact that you don't want to marry me."

"What?" she asked suddenly shocked out of her revelry.

"I knew the night I proposed that you didn't really want to marry me. I suppose I shouldn't be surprised, but I admit that I am. I thought that you felt the same way for me that I feel for you."

"Why do you think I don't want to marry you?" she asked, trying desperately to sound convincing. "I wouldn't have said yes if I didn't want to marry you."

"We've spent a lot of time together," Willam said. "I feel like I know you pretty well. We've had some intimate moments. But when we kissed at the feast I could tell that everything had changed."

"I really don't know what you're talking about."

"Then tell me that you love me," he said, moving closer, his face highlighted by the dancing flames of their campfire.

"You know I love you," she said, not meeting his eye.

"I think you do love me, but you're not in love with me."

"I have said yes, what more do you want from me."

"I want everything," Willam said. "I want your heart and soul, every bit of your happiness, excitement, and passion. I want to know deep inside that I am the man you want to be with, not Zollin."

"I love you both; I can't just stop caring for him."

"Yes, I understand that, but it's more than just care. I won't venture a guess at how you feel for Zollin, but I do know that you care enough to be deeply conflicted."

"Is that wrong? I was promised to him. Breaking that promise did not come easily."

"So, why did you do it? You can tell me."

"I wanted to," she lied.

"Please, you are not a good liar, Brianna. Tell me the truth."

"That is the truth."

"What did my father threaten you with?" he asked, his voice softer and this time it was Willam who couldn't look Brianna in the eye.

"What? Why would you think that?"

"Because I know him and because something has changed him. I always idolized my father, despite the fact that he rarely had time for me or Simmeron growing up. I worked so hard to win his approval, always doing whatever he told me to do. He was always so focused on being a good king and seeing Yelsia prosper, but now, his ambitions have grown. I don't believe there is anything he wouldn't do to further his plans. I don't know why my marrying you was part of his plans; he excluded me completely when I returned to Orrock. But I have no doubt he pressured you somehow to accept my proposal."

"He and my father worked out an arrangement," Brianna said. "The King didn't want me to do anything that would embarrass my family, but he didn't pressure me."

"I don't believe that. I hope someday you will tell me the truth."

"I wish you would just believe me," Brianna said, trying her best to sound hurt.

"I wish I could."

"How can I prove it?" she asked.

Willam thought for a moment and then he leaned closer.

"Your virtue is safe with me," he said. "But if you really want to marry me, kiss me now. Kiss me with the same passion and selfless abandon I see on your face when you fly with your dragons. Then I will believe you."

Brianna hesitated for a second, both scared and excited. Willam was handsome and kissing him was appealing, but she had lost the thrill of a romance with the Prince when King Felix forced her to accept the wedding proposal. She wasn't sure if she could get that thrill back, or if she could fake it convincingly enough.

Still, she closed her eyes and leaned toward the prince, her lips seeking his. The kiss was long and passionate. She fought to keep from thinking of Zollin, trying instead to focus just on Willam. Her hands went around his neck, and he pulled her body close to his. She could feel him trembling slightly, and she wondered why he would tremble for her.

When they pulled apart there were tears in his eyes.

"Oh, what I wouldn't give to have you kiss me like that every day of my life," he said.

"Why won't you believe me?" she asked.

He didn't respond, instead he wrapped himself in his cloak and lay down with his back to the fire. Brianna didn't push him. She didn't want him to keep questioning her. She had done all she could to convince him of her feelings, but he was right and she doubted she could keep up the rouse.

She lay down, her head resting on her pack of clothes, her body wrapped in a long, fur lined cape. She closed her eyes and saw Zollin in her mind's eye, but she couldn't keep the tears from rolling down her face. She knew that sooner or later he would learn of her betrayal, and then she would have to face the reality of her decision to marry Prince Willam. She wasn't sure if her heart would survive.

Chapter 22

It was late on the fifth day of their march when Zollin felt Ferno and the other dragons approaching. He stopped, letting the long column of dwarves march past him. He was tired at any rate and appreciated the rest. It took almost ten minutes for the dragons to come into view. The dwarves were focused only on the dwarf in front of them, and paid no attention to Zollin or to the sky above. The entire army of dwarves had marched past Zollin when the dragon arrived.

Ferno and the rest of the dragons circled, and then Ferno swooped down. An image of Zollin disappearing into the snow storm flashed in Zollin's mind.

"I know," he said. "I got lost in the storm and then I couldn't find you. I did find the dwarves though."

Ferno growled, but it was obvious the dragon was happy to see Zollin.

"I'm just glad you brought the other dragons south without me."

Another mental image appeared in Zollin's mind. It was a picture of a group of giants marching through Peddinggar Forest.

"I hope they avoid the cities," Zollin said.

A sense of slowness came over Zollin.

"We can't wait for them," he explained. "They'll arrive when they can, and we'll be glad to have them, I'm sure. For now, we need to introduce you to the dwarves. Fly back up until I call you down."

Ferno took to the sky and Zollin, using his magic, levitated himself up off the ground and sped himself forward. He glided easily over the dwarves and then came down twenty yards in front of the army. He stood catching his breath as they approached.

"That's a handy trick," Hammert called out. "But don't try it on me; I'll keep my feet firmly on the ground thank you."

"The skin of the world is as high as I care to venture," Jute added. "No need to go floating up in the clouds like a fairy."

The dwarves chuckled, but Zollin ignored their jesting. He just smiled.

"Are you ready to meet your reinforcements?" he asked.

"We're dwarves," Jute said loudly. "We don't need reinforcements."

"The dragons are here," he said. "I thought it best if you and your fellows meet them now. It takes you hardheaded runts time to accept change."

"Dragons, eh?" Jute said.

"No one likes change, Southlander," Hammert said testily.

"I would like that very much," said Bloc, out of all of the dwarves he looked excited at the prospect.

"I guess it wouldn't hurt," Jute said. "But you might as well remind them that we won't take lightly to being stepped on."

"Or eaten," Hammert said.

"Or burned to a crisp," Jute added.

"You've got it," Zollin said with a chuckle.

He sent a mental image of the dragons landing in front of the head of the column as a message to Ferno. His mental capacity could be enhanced with his magic, but he still preferred using words to communicate. The dragons swooped down and landed several hundred paces from the dwarves. There was a murmur down the long column of dwarves. They marched five abreast and nearly ninety dwarves deep, almost 450 dwarves all told. They didn't try to move closer.

Ferno left the other dragons and moved closer to Zollin, who was followed by Hammert, Jute, Bloc, and Yagger, who was the new headman for the Molar clan. Ferno was the largest of the new group of dragons. The beast was dark green, its scales glistening in the sunlight. It dropped its massive head when it was close to Zollin, who stroked the dragon's forehead affectionately.

"My friends," Zollin said, speaking to the dwarves. "May I introduce you to Ferno. We have had many adventures together, and I owe this magnificent creature my life. He would be a friend to the dwarves."

"Well met, Ferno," said Bloc. "You are a wonder to behold. It is good to see the dragon kind back in the skies of our world. You are truly kings of the air."

Ferno growled and shook slightly. Then, in the dragon's hissing speech, spoke to the dwarves.

"My thanks, friends."

"He talks!" shouted Jute, stumbling back.

The other dwarves chuckled at his surprise.

"Go ahead and laugh," Jute said. "I've never heard of a talking dragon and neither have you."

Bloc raised a hand.

"That's not true," he said. "I've heard that dragons and kings were once friends. I hope that they will be again."

"Spoken like a true king if ever I heard one," said Hammert.

"Are all your dragons as noble as you?" Bloc asked Ferno.

The dragon shook its head and an image of the dragons far away from the dwarves entered Zollin's mind.

"The other dragons are not used to humans or dwarves for that matter," Zollin said. "They prefer to keep some distance."

"Well, that is understandable," said Bloc.

"And not unwelcome," added Jute.

"Behave yourself," Bloc said. "Don't shame the Yel clan."

"I'm just saying... we wouldn't want to make them uncomfortable."

The other dwarves chuckled.

"I think it best if I go on ahead with Ferno. You should reach Felson tomorrow, and there will be troops stationed there. I can get some news and warn them of your approach. Then, we can make our way down to the mountains."

"That sounds wise," Bloc said.

"That's right," Jute added. "Make sure the tall folk have plenty of ale and meat on the table when we arrive."

"Is drinking all you think about?" Hammert asked.

"I said meat too," Jute argued.

"These two need their heads knocked together," Yagger said.

"I'll leave it to you to keep them in line," Zollin said.

Then he levitated up and onto Ferno's back. The green dragon shook its head and flames shot out of its mouth. It wasn't a dangerous act or one of anger, but an expression of the beast's jubilation at being reunited with its friend. Ferno then jumped into the air with its great, leathery wings flapping hard and billowing up dust and dirt around the dwarves.

Ferno soared in the sky; the late autumn air was cold, and Zollin hunched down close to the big dragon's neck. The other dragons fell into formation behind Ferno. Zollin was bombarded with mental images and feelings of happiness at having found him. They flew south toward Felson throughout the afternoon, and Zollin was happy for the respite from the long marches. He thought of himself as fit, but the dwarves' stamina was unrivaled.

Night fell and the dragons flew on. It wasn't long until the lights of the city appeared below them. The dragons landed in an empty field a mile from the city. Zollin continued on foot, stretching his tired legs as he walked. He missed his staff and wondered briefly what had become of the bow he'd fashioned out of the staff in the Northern Highlands. Brianna had loved the bow, but she had left it behind when she went off with the big, black dragon, Bartoom.

Zollin made his way straight for the army camp which was on the north side of the city. He wanted to find whoever was in charge and discover what was being planned. He noticed the horses in the corrals and saw soldiers working in and around the big barns that the cavalry troops used to keep their tack, weapons, and sometimes their horses. He didn't like that there appeared to be no sense of urgency in the camp. The barracks were in use, and the big mess hall was a hive of activity.

Zollin couldn't help but wonder why the cavalry wasn't moving south already, or at the least, why they weren't preparing to move south. He doubted that it would take the legion of mounted soldiers long to mobilize, but he expected that a good bit of supplies would need to be loaded up onto wagons to feed the soldiers and bring medical supplies for the wounded.

Zollin remembered the command center where Hausey, the acting commander of the light cavalry, preferred to operate from. The main officer's quarters were in the city proper, inside the fort that housed the men assigned to watchtower duty. The huge, stone, watchtower that stood like a silent sentential over Felson was a very distinct landmark. From the top of the watchtower a man could see for miles in every direction. Zollin had no doubt that if it hadn't been dark when they approached Felson, the pride of dragons would have been spotted. The cavalry's history with Bartoom, the huge, black dragon they had fought, probably would have sent them into a panic at the sight of eight dragons flying together. That was one of the reasons Zollin had come into the city alone.

The door to the officer's quarters was open, and light was spilling out into the small yard. Zollin peered inside and was pleased to see Commander Hausey staring down at a map on his workbench.

"Hello," Zollin said.   "It's good to see you again, Commander."

Hausey's head tilted up, and then his eyes opened wide in recognition.

"Zollin, is that you?"

"Yes, Commander. How are you?"

"I am well, and you?"

"Tired," Zollin said.   "Hungry and a little worried.   I thought the King's cavalry would have mobilized by now.   Did Brianna not make it to Orrock?"

"She did," Hausey said.   "The army is mobilizing, but we await word to move out.   We can be on the move in just a few hours. I have been studying the routes south."

"Why is King Felix taking so long?" Zollin asked, as he dropped into a wooden chair opposite from Commander Hausey.

The Commander's brows furrowed and he didn't respond for a second.   It was enough of a pause to let Zollin know that Hausey wasn't happy about something.

"I don't pretend to know the mind of a king," he said, as he walked to the open door and pulled it closed. He then uncorked a bottle of wine and poured two small cups of the dark red liquid.

"You aren't telling me everything," Zollin said.   "Are you commanding here?"

"I am," Hausey said.

"Then you must be privy to the King's plans."

"I know some of them, but things have changed in Orrock since the invasion."

Zollin took a drink of the wine that Hausey offered him. The wine was harsh and hot as it flowed down Zollin's throat. He tried not to grimace at the taste.

"How so?"

"General Corlis," Hausey said quietly, "has inserted himself into the King's council, diminishing the roll of all the other advisors. The other generals are scared to oppose him. The King made Corlis high commander of the King's Army."

"And Corlis doesn't want to join the Falxis forces to oppose Gwendolyn's army?"

"The only thing I know for sure is that Corlis only wants what will benefit him. The King isn't open to reason. Prince Willam has been excluded from the King's plans. I doubt that Brianna is being taken seriously."

"But you said the army is being mobilized?" Zollin said. "Surely she must have convinced King Felix of the danger."

"I cannot say," Hausey said. "I'm afraid that with the peace treaty between the Five Kingdoms broken that the King's true intentions are more nefarious than we know."

Zollin couldn't believe what he was hearing. King Felix had at first been extremely kind and accommodating to him, but then his attitude had changed. During the siege of Orrock, the King had wanted first to control Zollin and then, when that failed, he had attempted to hand Zollin over to Offendorl, the master of the Torr. Now, Commander Hausey was convinced that the King's ambitions were driving him more than the need to protect Yelsia from the army that Gwendolyn was sending north.

"Well," Zollin said, his exasperation bleeding into his voice, "we'll have to deal with all that later. All we can concern ourselves with now is preparing for the defense of Yelsia."

Hausey's head bowed, as if to say he agreed.

"I have a small pride of dragons with me," Zollin said.

He watched Hausey's face twitch, but the commander didn't say anything.

"Don't worry, they won't be here come morning. I'm sending them on ahead of us. There is also an army of dwarves on the march. They number a little over four hundred all told. They're hearty creatures, so don't underestimate them. I was hoping to have ale and food ready for them when they arrive tomorrow evening."

"They are coming here?" Hausey asked a little flabbergasted at the idea of dwarves marching into Felson.

"They'll stop here and make camp nearby. They won't be interested in going into the city, at least not all of them. Their leader is a dwarf named Bloc. He will be easy to deal with. The others will most likely keep their distance."

"I will see that their needs are met," Hausey said.

"Thank you," said Zollin. "I am glad you are still in command."

Hausey nodded, but didn't smile.

"I sometimes wish I wasn't."

* * *

Zollin had eaten a quick meal with Commander Hausey and then set off into the city to find his father. He wound through the crowded streets. Despite the late hour, people moved everywhere. The refugees wandered the streets while groups of self-appointed peace keepers herded the refugees like cattle. In the few months since the black dragon had begun ravaging the northern villages, the population in Felson had quadrupled. News that the dragon had been driven out of Yelsia hadn't motivated the people to return to their abandoned homes, villages, and farms.

Zollin was surprised to find out that he remembered the way to Miriam's home. He had found navigating the winding streets of Felson difficult in the past, but he made good time and came to the small home with its wide yard, corral and large barn, easily this time. He went to the door and knocked, excited to see his father again.

Miriam opened the door. She looked as if she had doubled in age since Zollin last saw her. She was in her forties but still trim and fit. Zollin had thought she was attractive despite the fact that she was twice his age, now she just looked tired. Her eyes were bloodshot, deep lines creased her forehead, her hair was disheveled, and her clothes were wrinkled.

"Oh, Zollin," she said in surprise. "What on earth are you doing here?"

"I came to see Quinn," he said.

She stepped back and waved for him to come inside. Miriam was an animal healer, and her magical gift had been awakened when she met Zollin. Being near him always stirred the faint echoes of magic that resided inside of her. She did her best to smile at the young wizard but failed despite her efforts.

"What's happened?" Zollin said, feeling a cold void of fear opening in his stomach.

"Your father left me," Miriam said. "I did my best to dissuade him, but he was adamant."

"He left you?" Zollin asked, not believing what he heard. "What happened?"

"Here, sit down," Miriam said. She already had a bottle of wine open and poured him a goblet.

Her home was warm and cozy. Three rocking chairs sat near the stone fireplace where a merry looking blaze popped and crackled. A hanging lamp cast a soft glow around the room. There were books in a nice looking set of shelves that Zollin recognized immediately as his father's handiwork. The smooth wood flooring was covered by an expensive rug. Zollin sat down, taking the wine and waiting to hear an explanation.

"Brianna came here. I guess you expected that."

Zollin nodded. He hadn't known that she would pass through Felson, but he wasn't surprised by the news.

"She was worried about your friend Mansel."

"Did she think he would be here?" Zollin asked.

"No," Miriam explained. "But she knew your father would be concerned. She told us of the evil creatures you fought in the south and how Mansel was unprepared. So, of course your father had to set out in hopes of finding him," she said with a hint of bitterness.

"Quinn went south to find Mansel?" Zollin asked in surprise.

"Yes," Miriam said, her voice thick with worry.

"Why? I thought he was through with fighting? That's what he told us when we left Orrock."

"Perhaps he thought he was," Miriam said. "He came here and we were happy for a while, but he grew restless. With all the refugees in the city it was hard not to have conflict. We argued because I didn't want him to use force with people. He insisted that it was the only thing some people understood. Our relationship grew tense. I don't know if he was really worried about Mansel or if going in search of your friend was the escape he needed from me."

"I'm sorry," Zollin said.

He could tell by looking that Miriam's heart was broken. Zollin knew from years of experience that living with his father wasn't easy. Quinn liked things done a certain way, and he could be quick to anger. Quinn had never raised his hand in anger to Zollin, but he was not a peaceful man, not the type to take an offense and look the other way.

"When did he leave?" Zollin asked.

"A few weeks ago," she said. "He took one of the horses and a mule."

"He went south, to the Walheta Mountains?"

"Yes," she said.

"Miriam, I am so sorry things haven't worked out the way you hoped, but I am grateful for the news. I'll do my best to find him and bring him back to you."

Miriam looked up; hope glimmering in her eyes for the first time that evening.

"He may not want to come back," she said.

"Of course he will," Zollin said, trying to sooth Miriam.

"No, I'm not easy to live with, Zollin. He doesn't have to come back to me. I just want to know he's safe. That's all."

"I'll send word as soon as I can," Zollin said as he stood up.

He drained the last of the wine in his cup, letting the warm feeling of the strong drink flow down his chest and out through his arms and legs.

"You'll stay the night, won't you?" she asked. "I've room. You could use a night in a bed for a change."

"That would be nice, but no," Zollin said. "I need to leave before sunup. I'm taking a group of dragons south, and it wouldn't do for them to be seen. The last thing we want is to start a panic here in the city."

"Oh, you have dragons, too?" Miriam said.

Zollin could tell that Miriam was surprised and excited.

"It's the dragons that Brianna left in the Highlands. They're solitary beasts, not as friendly as the dragons in her pride."

"It's incredible," she said. "Who would have thought we would see dragons roaming the kingdom."

"They're amazing creatures," Zollin agreed. "I would ask one favor of you. Could you take a message to Commander Hausey for me?"

"Of course," Miriam said.

"Let him know I left tonight, heading south. Tell him I'll look for him in Falxis."

"Alright," Miriam said.

She stepped close and hugged Zollin.

"Be careful," she said softly.

Zollin was stiff. He wasn't used to maternal affection and although he liked it, he wasn't sure how to respond.

"Tell your father I still love him," she added, her voice cracking. "Tell him I'll always love him."

"I will," Zollin said.

He stepped back, gave Miriam what he hoped was a reassuring smile, and then he slipped out the door and into the cold night.

Chapter 23

When Brianna woke up, the sun was just turning the sky a pearlescent pink. She lay wrapped in her long cape, Selix beside her, the dragon's long tail wrapped around her and keeping her warm. There was frost on the grass and trees, giving everything a silvery outline. She knew they would be moving on soon, and while she welcomed the distraction that staying busy would give her, at that moment, she laid still; guilt and misery combining and nearly choking her. She felt terrible for kissing Willam and even worse for enjoying it. She was angry that she was being forced to marry Willam and even angrier that she couldn't talk to anyone about it. In fact, she had to keep her thoughts and feelings pressed down deep inside of her. If Selix or Tig picked up on her feelings, they would press her until they got the truth. There would be no way to keep it from Willam if that happened. Brianna was positive that the Prince and Gyia had bonded so close that Gyia wouldn't be able to keep a secret from him.

And Brianna felt bad for Prince Willam as well. He deserved a wife that would love him unconditionally, not one that was forced into a marriage she didn't really want to be in. Still, no matter how hard she tried, she couldn't imagine an outcome that didn't end badly for her. Perhaps if Zollin knew what King Felix had threatened her with he could keep her family safe, but there were no guarantees short of assassinating the King, and that would leave her family as exiles, at best. There simply were no good options.

"You ready to get moving?" Willam said as he stood up, stretching his back and shoulders.

"Sure," she lied.

"It shouldn't take us long to reach Felson; then we can make plans to move south."

"That sounds good," Brianna said, as she climbed slowly to her feet.

Selix growled at her, wanting to know what was wrong.

"I'm tired, that's all," she lied again, hoping that the dragons couldn't sense her trepidation.

The day before she had exalted in being free of the capital and beyond the reach of the King, she had focused on the thrill of flying with the pride, letting the tension that had built up from her mother's demands melt away. But now, the realization of what lay before her made her time in Orrock seem like child's play. They were going to Felson, and sooner or later they would join up with Zollin. When that happened, she would have to tell him she was breaking their engagement to marry Willam. She would have to convince him that this was what she wanted in her heart of hearts, and she had no idea how she would pull that off.

"You want breakfast?" Willam asked.

"Sure," Brianna said, taking the small loaf of bread he offered.

"There's some fruit preserves in my pack," he said, "I'll get it for you."

They spread the fruit on the bread and ate it quickly. The bread had been baked the day before and was still soft. The preserves were sweet and normally Brianna would have enjoyed her breakfast, but guilt was so strong that she tasted nothing.

"You seem preoccupied," Willam said. "Is something wrong?"

"We're going to war," Brianna said. "I can't shake the feeling that we're in over our heads."

"The witch Gwendolyn is powerful," Willam admitted. "Do you think she'll lead the army she's assembled?"

"No," Brianna said. "I don't think she will. She's not the same person you knew."

"I wouldn't say I knew her," Willam said frowning. "I was under her spell and I'll admit I was closer to her than most anyone else, but she never shared her thoughts or plans with me. I was less to her than a dog, just a tool."

"It's nothing to be ashamed of," Brianna said tenderly. "But her days of beauty and enchantment are past. She's deep into the dark magic she unleashed, and it has twisted her physically. I only saw a glimpse of her when I was underground. She's a monster now."

"So if she doesn't leave her unground lair, is it possible that her army is just to protect her, not for conquest?"

"If I hadn't seen her work and felt the evil intent that radiated from her, I would say that was possible. But she isn't interested in simply surviving. She wants to kill everyone, especially every man. I've never felt such hate. As long as she is alive no one in the Five Kingdoms is safe."

"Well, we should get moving then. The cavalry will need time to mobilize and get on the road."

They mounted their respective dragons and took to the air. Brianna tried to let her worries fall away, but they would not leave her mind. The air was cold, and there were dark clouds looming to the south. The sun seemed weak, and there was no warmth from its rays. Brianna would normally have let Selix cover her with flames, but she couldn't undress or let the fire burn away her clothes. Instead, she stretched out on Selix's back, laying her face just to the side of the dragon's long neck. She watched the countryside pass beneath them, flowing like a green and brown river. She saw small farms, villages, tiny camps where refugees huddled together near the Weaver's road.

Soon they could make out the watchtower that loomed over Felson. They turned north and approached the large cavalry base slowly. They had circled the area several times from high above, the dragons taking in every detail with their enhanced vision and sharing what they saw with mental images to Brianna and Prince Willam. They were just circling down toward an open field outside the base when Brianna spotted the column of dwarves in the distance.

"What is that?" she shouted to Selix.

The golden dragon growled in reply and then peeled away to the north. Tig, the smaller and faster dragon, shot ahead, flying swiftly but staying high in the air. Then, after a moment, a mental image of the dwarves appeared in Brianna's mind. She was surprised by the number of dwarves. They marched slowly, their small legs moving in unison, their long beards swaying in the cold wind. She recognized Hammert, and she thought that Jute looked familiar, although she didn't remember him exactly. They all looked so tiny in the wide open world, their skin and beards dull gray.

"Take me down to them," Brianna told Selix.

An image of Gyia and Willam landing near the army base below flashed in Brianna's mind, and she sent out an affirmative response to Gyia. She knew that Willam would want to make contact with the commander of the King's cavalry as soon as possible and ensure that the soldiers were making themselves ready to move south. After flying with dragons, marching with soldiers, even ones on horseback, would seem incredibly slow.

"You stay in the air until I call you down," Brianna told Selix. The dragon growled but she remained firm. "No," she said. "I'll be fine. We don't want to scare them."

Brianna waited until they were a few hundred yards in front of the dwarves, and then she jumped high into the air from Selix's back, flipping head over heels behind the dragon, her body stretched out and rigid, and her long cape flapping around her. Then she let gravity take over. It pulled her down and she began to hop from one thermal updraft to the next, like a child hoping from stone to stone across a shallow stream.

With one final summersault she dropped to the ground, landing gracefully less than a hundred feet from the dwarves. She saw the surprise on their faces. They had never thought to look up, most of the dwarves didn't like the wide open sky; it made them feel too small, too insecure. None of the dwarves had known she was dropping down from the back of the great, golden dragon until she landed in front of them.

"What is that?" cried one.

"Halt!" bellowed Bloc.

"It is the Fire Spirit," Hammert said in a loud voice. "I gave her the fire stone," he said proudly.

"You are Zollin's companion?" asked Jute.

"I am," Brianna said softly. She was walking slowly toward the dwarves; her hands open in front of her. "I would be friends with the noble dwarves."

"You already are," Hammert said.

"I am Bloc, King of the dwarves living under the Northern Highlands," he said bowing. "It is a pleasure to meet you. We have heard of your great works."

"And I am pleased to meet you," Brianna replied to Bloc before turning to Hammert. "Have you seen Zollin then?" she asked.

"Of course we have," he said. "He was marching with us until just yesterday, and then his dragons showed up and carried him away."

"You are the dragon maker?" Bloc asked.

"I am dragon kind," Brianna said.

"But you created the dragons?"

"Many dragons," she answered. "Just look up."

Bloc and the others tilted the heads back and saw Selix and Tig for the first time.

"The dragons are pleased to meet the kings under the mountain," Brianna said. "Would you mind if they landed nearby?"

"No," Bloc said. "They are welcome. My people are cautious, but we are honored to meet you and your dragons."

Brianna sent a mental image of Selix and Tig landing behind her. A moment later, the two dragons swooped down and landed less than a hundred yards from the dwarves.

"Magnificent," said Bloc.

"They don't eat dwarves, do they?" Jute asked.

"No," Brianna said.

"That's good," he replied. "I would hate to have to bust their teeth."

"What? On your hard head?" Hammert teased.

"With my hammer, you fool."

"Please pardon their jesting," Bloc said.

"It is nothing to pardon," Brianna said. "Come, let me introduce you."

The next hour was spent with the dwarves slowly inching closer and closer to the dragons. The dwarves were both awed and terrified. They didn't like anything that was as huge as Selix, yet they were fascinated by the beasts that were formed from living stone.

Bloc peppered Brianna with questions about where she had formed the dragons and how she had done it. She answered as honestly as possible. Selix was patient and calm, even lowering the dragon's massive head down so that the dwarves could touch its scaly neck. Tig, on the other hand, took flight, preferring to perform aerial tricks to impress the dwarf army.

Once Bloc and Brianna decided it was time to move on, Tig sent word that a contingent of soldiers were on their way north. He sent mental images to Brianna of a group of six officers in armor and riding horses.

"The soldiers from the city are coming," she told Bloc.

"Is Zollin among them?" he asked.

"No," Brianna said. "But he will have made sure that you are welcome."

Selix and Brianna moved to one side of the road, and the dwarves reformed their long column beside them. They waited for the soldiers and Brianna. Using her enhanced vision she looked to see Prince Willam, but he wasn't with the officers. She did recognize Commander Hausey, though, which made her breathe a little easier.

The horsemen rode to within a hundred feet of the dwarves and then they dismounted. Commander Hausey left the horses with one of the other officers, while he and three other men walked forward, their helmets under their left arms.

"Ho, Bloc, leader of the dwarves," Commander Hausey said, as they approached.

"I am Bloc," said the little dwarf, stepping forward.

"I am Commander Hausey, the officer in charge of his majesty's light cavalry stationed in Felson. I want to welcome you to our camp."

"Thank you, Commander," said Bloc.

"We have food and ale ready for your people. I'm afraid my orders to move south have just arrived today. Your people can make camp near our base and rest, and then we will move south in the morning."

"The dwarves don't need much rest," Bloc said.

"But ale would be welcome," Jute spoke up.

"And food," Hammert added.

"All of that is being arranged," Commander Hausey said. "Zollin told us you would be arriving. I've had our people preparing for your arrival since sun up."

"That is most gracious of you," Bloc said.

"We are honored to be allied with the dwarves," Hausey said. "May I have the honor of marching back to our camp with you?"

"Of course," Bloc said.

The other officers remounted their horses and rode slowly on the right side of the long column of dwarves. General Hausey and Brianna walked on the left. Selix and Tig flew in circles over the parade. When they reached the base, they found row after row of mounted soldiers, all at rigid attention with flags flying in honor of the dwarves. Trumpets blew as Commander Hausey led the dwarves to a pavilion where long tables of food, ale, and wine had been laid out. There were also bonfires burning. Selix and Tig joined Gyia who was curled next to one of the fires a short way from the pavilion.

"Eat, drink, rest," Commander Hausey said. "I shall join you shortly with Prince Willam."

Brianna went with Hausey back to the low-roofed building that he used for officers' quarters. Hausey was a practical man, and Brianna could tell by the look on his face that he wasn't happy.

"Now," he said, as he burst through the door to his quarters. "What's this nonsense about me retaining command?"

"The King has ordered it," Willam said. "I shall serve under you."

"That is absurd," Hausey said.

"What's he talking about?" Brianna asked.

"When my father sent me here, he was very specific that I was to serve under Commander Hausey."

"Which is clearly improper," Hausey said.

"Perhaps not," Willam said. "I was defeated by King Zorlan's forces in Osla. It is clear that my father has no faith in my abilities to lead."

"Don't be so hard on yourself," Brianna said.

"It really doesn't matter," Willam said. "For now, my father is king and his word is law. Whether I like it or not, whether it makes sense or not, makes no difference."

"Fine, but I am lodging an official complaint," Commander Hausey said. "Now, if you'll excuse me, I must see to the mobilization of the cavalry."

"Your orders, commander?" Willam asked.

"I could use your help with the dwarves, your highness."

"Of course, I'll make sure they have what they need."

Brianna followed Willam back to the dwarfish camp. The tables and benches were too tall for the dwarves to sit at, but they didn't seem to mind at all. Instead of sitting, they stood on the benches and made short work of the food and ale. The cavalry's mess officers were constantly on the run, bringing more food and a lot more ale.

Most of the dwarves ignored them, intent only on the food before them and their own company. Brianna introduced Bloc to Willam, and they sat down at the table with the dwarves. After a few minutes of polite questions, Brianna finally asked what was on her mind.

"Why did Zollin leave?" she asked.

"I'm not sure," Bloc said. He, alone of all the dwarves, wasn't stuffing himself with food and ale. He sat calmly sipping wine and talking with Brianna and Prince Willam.

"He went to prepare this feast for us, but did not return," he explained.

"Did he mention any other magical folk that would be helping us?" Willam asked.

"Giants," Bloc said. "I'm not sure how many or when they'll actually arrive, but they are coming."

"Giants?" Willam asked.

"They're shy creatures," Bloc said. "I doubt you'll see them at all until they arrive in the mountains."

"This is truly a historic hour," Willam said. "Our races coming together in friendship and mutual aid. I, for one, am honored to stand with you during this dark hour."

Brianna had to bite her tongue to keep from laughing. The Prince was sounding so formal that he seemed almost like a different person.

"I know that if my father were here he would be deeply honored," Willam continued.

"Your father won't be joining us in the battle?" Bloc asked.

"Yes, of course he will," Willam said. "He and the other generals will be bringing the body of our army south by sea."

"Oh, that makes sense," Bloc said. "Although, I, for one, would not enjoy bobbing along in a ship so far from solid ground."

"Nor I," said Hammert.

"I'll keep my feet firmly on the ground, thank you very much," said Jute. "Or under it would be even better."

"I would like to visit your home in the mountains one day," said Willam.

"The dwarves would be honored to host the Crown Prince of Yelsia," said Bloc.

Brianna excused herself and went to check on the dragons. The huge beasts were napping by the bonfire. She felt all alone. Willam was in his element hosting the dwarves. The soldiers were all busy preparing to leave Felson. The dragons were asleep, and Brianna's only company was the fears that circled in her mind like bats in a cave. She couldn't help but wonder if Zollin had somehow discovered that she had broken her promise to him and was now engaged to Prince Willam. The very thought of causing Zollin pain made her want to weep, but she forced herself to stay calm and composed. It wouldn't help her cause to break down. She simply had convinced everyone that she was doing what she wanted to do; there was too much at stake to risk even one person discovering her secret.

Brianna feared for Zollin's life. She knew the King would do anything, even have Zollin killed. He could just as easily withdraw his troops from battle or betray them all by not showing up at the rendezvous on the southern side of the Walheta.

Then, out of the blue, Brianna realized that Zollin was probably with his father in the city. She couldn't believe she had actually forgotten that Quinn and Miriam were living in Felson. She left the camp and hurried into the city. The streets were crowded with people. There were many more women and children than men. Brianna guessed that most of the able-bodied men had been recruited into the King's Army. The refugees still looked hungry and frightened. She wished she could do something to help them, but there was nothing to be done until the war was over. The best way to help the refugees now was to turn back the invading army and bring peace to Yelsia. Not every husband would return home, she knew that, but those that did could start rebuilding their lives.

She found Miriam's home after an hour of searching. She had been forced to stop and ask directions, but she had finally found her way through the narrow streets to the familiar house she recognized so easily from the air. She knocked on the door to the house but got no reply and so, after a few minutes, she went around to the barn. There were several animals in the corral, two horses and some goats. None looked healthy; in fact, one of the goats had lost most of its hairy fur.

She went to the large door of the barn, which was open, and peered inside. There were more animals, most in stalls, but one horse was being brushed by a small girl who had to stand on a milking stool to reach the horse's back.

"Hello," Brianna said to the girl. "I'm looking for Quinn or Miriam."

"Miriam is in that stall," the girl said pointing.

"Thank you," Brianna said.

She walked over to the stall and saw Miriam feeding a sickly looking colt. The colt's mother was lying on her side, struggling to breathe. Miriam had a large bottle with a thick cloth stuffed into the opening. The colt was sucking the milk from the fabric, as it soaked through from the bottle.

"That's inventive," Brianna said.

"Oh, Brianna, I wasn't expecting to see you again so soon," Miriam said with her voice strained just slightly. It was obvious she wasn't happy to see Brianna.

"I'm sorry for dropping in unannounced," Brianna said. "I was hoping to find Zollin. Has he been here?"

"He was here last night," Miriam explained, as she struggled to hold the colt's head steady and keep it from pulling the fabric out of the bottle top. "He left in search of his father."

"Quinn isn't here?" Brianna asked.

"You know he isn't," Miriam said coldly. "He went south in search of Mansel, just as you knew he would."

Brianna nodded. "I'm sorry to trouble you," she said. "But if you don't mind, did Zollin leave this morning?"

"No, he left in the middle of night," Miriam said. "I tried to get him to stay but he wouldn't."

"Thank you," Brianna said.

She walked out of the barn, her mind spinning. So, Zollin had gone south to find Quinn. He would be halfway to the Walheta Mountains by now; she was certain of that. Still, she didn't like the idea of waiting around with the cavalry. She would push on with Selix and Tig; she only hoped that Prince Willam would understand.

Chapter 24

Zollin and the dragons had flown hard through the night, and by midday, they could see the ocean spreading out to their right. The dragons that had come south with Ferno marveled at the sight, but Zollin only shivered. He couldn't help but think of the huge sea monster the sailors had called the Kracken or the look of the angry mermen who had hurled their brass tridents at Zollin.

An hour before sunset, Zollin had Ferno land. He sent the dragons into the desert to search for food, while Zollin hiked into a small village to spend the night. He was exhausted, but walking felt good after clinging to Ferno's back for so long. The dragons had stopped periodically to rest. Ferno was strong, but flying with Zollin was taxing, even to the powerful dragon. Still, Zollin had done little during their breaks, staying close to the dragons and eating a little of his dried rations. Now, he took long strides and stretched the muscles in his legs and back.

The village didn't have an inn, but he was able to find a widow who was only too happy to fix him a warm meal and prepare a bed for him by her fire. He paid her in silver and bought a small keg of sour ale from a local man who brewed ale in the village. The food was hot and there was plenty of ale to wash it down. Zollin hardly tasted anything. He stretched out on the floor by the fire with a full stomach and was asleep almost instantly.

The kick that woke Zollin was hard, bruising his ribs. Zollin coughed and rolled over, not sure what had happened. He felt as though he'd just closed his eyes, but it was late in the night. The widow woman was held by another man in the corner of the room. Zollin heard her weeping, and the men in the room were all chuckling at Zollin's discomfort.

"No time for sleeping stranger," said a man with a thick accent. "You've not paid your taxes."

"What?" Zollin managed to say.

"This is my town, stranger," said the man. "My name's Otho and strangers aren't welcome here. You should know that."

"Look," Zollin said. "I don't know who you are, but I'm sure this is just a misunderstanding."

"No it ain't," said the man. "You're tresspassin' and I'll be damned if I'll let that slide."

"I didn't mean any offense," Zollin said. He had gotten onto his knees and was holding one hand to his side.

"Well, it's too late now. You'll have to pay. Word around this dump is that you've a purse of silver on you. I'll take half."

The other men laughed, but Zollin frowned.

"I don't give my money to outlaws," Zollin said.

"Boy, I ain't askin' for charity," Otho said. "Now give me your damn purse before I kick your teeth out."

"No," Zollin said.

He was starting to get to his feet when the big man named Otho lunged at him. Otho and the men with him were big, dirty, their hair long and greasy, and their clothes tattered. Zollin saw that most of them had teeth so dirty and rotten that he was surprised they could chew anything other than gruel. He didn't want to do anything that might damage the widow's house, so instead of hurting the outlaw, he held him in a magical grip, his inner power blossoming to a hot glow. Zollin shook the last of the sleep from his mind and stood up.

"Why don't we take this outside?" he said.

"What the bloody hell is going on?" screamed Otho.

Zollin opened the door with a mental push. The wind was blowing in off the sea, whistling through the eaves of the small cottage. Zollin levitated the outlaw a few inches off the floor and then out into the darkness.

"I'm taking back this town," Zollin said. "You and your thugs aren't welcome anymore."

Zollin sent the man flying across the yard. He screamed just before he crashed to the ground, rolling and flopping to a bone snapping halt in the dirt.

"Okay," Zollin said, "who's next?"

There were four other men in the room. Three had been spectators, and the fourth still held the frightened widow. Zollin let his magic race up and down his body in the form of crackling, blue energy. The outlaws' eyes grew round with fear. Then they moved slowly toward the door.

"Don't stop," Zollin said. "Leave this town and never come back; is that understood?"

The men nodded, and then hurried out of the house. Zollin turned to the man who was holding the widow. He had one beefy arm around her neck and the other had wrenched her left arm behind her back. The poor woman looked terrified, and Zollin felt sorry for her.

"Let her go, and I'll let you live," he said.

"No," the outlaw said with a crazy look in his eyes. "You get out or I'll kill her."

"No you won't," Zollin said.

He let his magic flow into the man and slowly began to squeeze the outlaw's lungs.

"What..." the man said. "What are you...?"

He couldn't get enough air into his constricting chest to keep speaking.

"Let her go," Zollin said.

The look of crazed fear in the outlaw's eyes turned one of hateful determination. Zollin knew, in that instant, that the man was going to kill his hostage. Zollin sent a jolt of power through the man's body that ripped the outlaw's heart to shreds. He fell to the floor, dead.

The widow cried out and scurried away. Zollin levitated the body and sent it flying out the open door before the release of the man's internal muscles fouled the widow's home with the outlaw's excrement.

"I'm sorry about that," Zollin said. "But they won't bother you anymore."

"What did you do?" the woman asked.

"I'm a wizard," Zollin said.

Fear washed over the widow once more.

"I won't hurt you," Zollin said. "I'm not evil."

The woman settled herself into one of the wooden chairs by her table. It was the only furniture in the cottage besides an old rocking chair that had been pushed into the corner to make room for Zollin's pallet on the floor.

"Here," Zollin said, as he poured up a cup of ale from the keg he had bought. "This will help settle your nerves."

The woman took a drink and grimaced at the taste.

"Luc should be ashamed for selling you this," she said.

"It's not the best ale I've tasted," Zollin said with a smirk.

"He's not a greater brewer, but he makes better than this," she said, taking another drink. "What is a wizard doing here?"

"I'm headed south," Zollin said.

"Are you demon born?" she asked.

"No," Zollin said, chuckling a little. "Just a regular man. In fact, I'm searching for my father. He might have passed this way. His name is Quinn. He was riding a horse, leading a mule."

"I don't remember him," the woman said. "But most people don't stop here if they can help it. We don't have an inn or a tavern, or apparently even any decent ale."

She held up the cup, squinting at its contents before drinking it down.

"Well, I'm not looking for trouble, just a place to rest for the night. I was planning to move on in the morning, but I can go now, if you prefer?"

The widow frowned, thinking for a minute before she answered.

"No," she said. "You can stay. I don't suppose you'll be any more trouble tonight."

"Good," Zollin said. "Please, help yourself to the ale. I won't be taking it with me."

He stretched back out in front of the fire. It was an hour before the mob arrived. The three outlaws Zollin hadn't killed had stirred up the town. Zollin was asleep again and this time the widow woke him.

"I'm sorry," she said.

"What?"

"The town heard about the fight," she said. "They want you to leave."

Zollin had trouble keeping his temper in check. He was so tired his joints hurt, and his stomach felt like he might be sick. He got slowly to his feet and was just about to go to the door of the cottage when torches started falling on the roof and porch. Smoke immediately rose from the torches as the wooden shingles caught fire.

The widow screamed in fright, but Zollin let his magic flow out. He snuffed the fires one by one, and then walked slowly to the door.

"What is the meaning of this?" he shouted.

"There he is," shouted one of the outlaws. "That's the sorcerer that killed Otho."

"I'm no sorcerer," Zollin shouted. "My name is Zollin, Wizard of the Five Kingdoms. I'll hold anyone who tried to harm this house to account."

"We don't want your kind around here," said an old man. "You're not welcome."

"I'm not staying," Zollin shouted back. "I was simply resting for the night. I'll be gone in the morning, but until then, I suggest you all go home."

"He's a devil," one the outlaws shouted. "We have to kill him."

"I wouldn't recommend that," Zollin said.

"You should leave now," said another person. "We don't want you here."

"You wanted my silver," Zollin said angrily. "When trouble comes you'll want my help. Now go home."

He slammed the door shut. His magic was swirling inside, stoked by his anger. He paced for a few minutes, letting his magic flow out to the crowd so that he would know what they were doing. Some left, others stood talking. None moved toward the cottage.

"It looks like the danger is past," Zollin said. "Your roof is scorched, but it's not damaged."

"That's okay," the widow said.

"I'm afraid I've made you an outcast among your people."

"Nonsense, there are things a lot worse than being the talk of the town at my age," she flashed him a smile.

"I could leave," he suggested.

"They could come back and burn my house down," the widow said. "I'd sleep better knowing you were here tonight."

"Alright," Zollin said. "I'll stay."

The rest of the night passed uneventfully. Zollin had planned to walk out of the village at daybreak and then rendezvous with the dragons when he was far enough away that the huge beasts wouldn't attract attention. But, he feared that leaving the village quietly would put the widow in more danger after the entire town knew she had sheltered him the night before. So, he ate the breakfast she prepared and then sent a silent, magical call to Ferno.

Zollin walked from the widow's small cottage to the center of the village. He knew people were watching him, which was exactly what he wanted. It was only a moment before a shadow passed over Zollin. People began to come out of their homes and shops. Men on the pier stopped what they were doing and looked up.

Ferno's growl was so loud it echoed out across the water and all around the town. The huge, green dragon dove straight for Zollin, flaring its wings at the last second to slow its descent. The fearsome beast landed right beside the wizard bellowing a gout of flame that transformed into oily black smoke that smudged the air.

"I am Zollin, Wizard of the Five Kingdoms!" he shouted. "The widow Ula is under my protection. If any harm comes to her or her home, I shall know of it and no one in this village will be safe until she has justice."

Ferno bellowed again, and Zollin levitated himself up onto the dragon's back. Then Ferno jumped up, beating its mighty wings and flying up into the pride of dragons' overhead, before soaring away from the village.

Zollin couldn't help but laugh as Ferno sent him image after image of the frightened looking villagers. The green dragon thought the show was great fun, and Zollin was relieved that Ferno didn't mind being used to frighten the villagers. He made a mental note to stop at the village on his way back through to check on the widow. She had been kind to him, and he didn't take that sort of thing lightly. In a world that was quickly turning against him, every little kindness counted. He only hoped he would be alive long enough to ensure that Ula wasn't harassed on his account.

Chapter 25

Late that afternoon they saw the Walheta Mountains in the distance. The dragons didn't often communicate with one another. Their curiosity had kept them content as they traveled across Yelsia. But the sight of the mountains was exciting to them. The dragons loved high places and the Walheta, while not as tall as the Northern Highlands, were still several thousand feet above sea level. Snow coated the tops of most of the mountains and stood in stark contrast to the dark browns and greens of the fir trees that lined the mountaintops. The dragons began to growl happily, and after finding a suitable place for Zollin to camp, they set off into the twilight in search of food.

Zollin gathered as much dry wood as he could. He was just below the snow line and had a comfortable place to make his camp. He used the fronds of the abundant ferns that grew around the base of the towering Lodgepole pines to make himself a soft bed. He built a fire between two large boulders, which reflected the fire's heat. Zollin stretched himself out on the bed of ferns and watched the sky fade to black and the stars appear overhead.

It was a peaceful night and Zollin lay warm and comfortable, dreaming about seeing Brianna again. Commander Hausey had assured Zollin that Brianna had made it safely to Orrock, and he was confident that she would bring King Felix and the army of Yelsia south soon. The dwarves were on the march, and he was bringing dragons. With a little luck and some sound strategy, they should be able to turn back whatever army Gwendolyn threw against them. So he was able to relax, even though he had no idea how he would find his father. Still, everything else seemed to be going his way; he had no reason to believe searching for his father would be any different.

He had eaten a satisfying stew for his supper, using snow to boil in a little pot and adding dried meat, old vegetables, and a little salt that he kept in his pack. After his stomach was full of warm food, he lay back staring up at the stars, his mind dreaming of his reunion with Brianna. He didn't notice the clouds that were scuttling across the sky at first, but soon the clouds became thick and blocked out the stars. A strong wind began to blow through the pines and Zollin could smell rain. The temperature was falling, and Zollin thought that a snow storm might be coming. He began gathering fallen branches to make a shelter to keep him dry when the sleet began to fall. At first it was little more than stinging beads of ice, pelting down on him, but then the wind picked up and the sleet was hurtled sideways.

Then lightning began to crackle through the clouds. At first it was little more than flashes of light inside the thick clouds, and the gentle rumble of distant thunder, but then a bolt of white energy split the clouds and shot down onto the mountainside. The resulting crack made the mountains quake, and the thunder was so loud that Zollin ducked his head to ward off the sound.

Then Zollin was inundated with terrified images of the lightning from several of the dragons at once. He remembered that lightning was the one thing the dragons feared. It was dark and

Zollin couldn't see anything outside of the frail light of his hissing fire, which was being smothered by the falling sleet.

He closed his eyes, struggling to concentrate with the barrage of mental images the dragons were sending him. He let his magic flow out, searching down the mountainside and across the valley. He needed to find shelter that was big enough for the entire pride of dragons. None of the dragons who had followed Ferno out of the Northern Highlands were as big as the green dragon that had bonded with Zollin, but they were all larger than horses.

Zollin found nothing at first and was forced to expand his search, but over the next ridge, he found a cave. The mouth of the cave was small, but the interior was like a wide tunnel that ran along the edge of the mountain, just feet beneath the surface. Still, it was the best place Zollin could find.

He levitated himself up over the towering trees, as Ferno came hurdling toward him. He sent mental images of the cave and settled onto Ferno's wide back, as the green dragon flew past. The sleet was growing larger, becoming hailstones that were the size of walnuts. Zollin used his magic to create an arching barrier over himself and Ferno that blocked most of the hail, but the wind was tossing Ferno around like a rowboat on an angry sea. Zollin was nearly tossed off several times, even though the trip to the cave was relatively short.

Ferno swooped down and then blasted the trees around the cave with dragon breath. The trees were wet, but they burst into flame just the same, until the mouth of the cave was a ring of fire, illuminating the way for the other dragons to find safety.

Another bolt of lightning struck, this time tearing through the wing of one of the dragons. Zollin saw the poor creature clearly in the glare from the lightning, but then the wounded dragon was lost in the darkness of the storm. Zollin sent his magical awareness out and felt the beast crashing into the trees. It was alive but terrified and unable to fly.

"You go inside with the others," Zollin shouted to Ferno. "I'll go after Embyr."

Zollin slid off Ferno's back, as the green dragon dove for the cave. The heat from the burning trees felt odd but welcoming among the flying rain and hail of the storm. The wind was blowing so strongly now that the trees around Zollin swayed back and forth. Limbs cracked and fell some hitting Zollin's magical shield so hard he was knocked off his feet.

The terrain was steep, and Zollin had to move slowly toward the injured dragon. Behind and above him, flames shot from the mouth of the cave as the dragons bellowed their fiery breath both in fear and to warm the wide crack in the mountain. Zollin ignored it, just as he ignored the storm. The steep mountainside was becoming treacherous, as the hail built up into an icy layer that made the rocky slope even more slippery.

Zollin was resolute in his task and began using his magic to speed his progress. Like the dragons, levitating himself above the trees where he would be exposed to the storm and the lightning was not something Zollin wanted to do. Instead, he slid down the mountain, bouncing from tree to boulder, using his magic to keep himself moving at a steady pace. It took nearly ten minutes to reach Embyr; the dark red dragon lay on its side, moaning in pain.

Every dragon that Brianna had made was different. Ferno was a big bull of a dragon, thick and strong, with a powerful tail and spikes that ran up its neck ending in large horns that adorned the green dragon's head like a crown. Embyr was smaller, with thick hind legs and tiny forelegs. Most of the dragons had long necks, but Embyr's neck was only a few feet long and almost as thick as the dragon's chest. Its head was wide and long, like a horse, with large eyes and a small mouth. Embyr's tail was thicker and less flexible than the other dragons, but its wings were long and wide. The dragon could fly all day and night without the need to stop for rest. Like an eagle, it could lock its wide wings into position and glide for hours on the thermal updrafts that Brianna danced on.

The wings were made of leathery skin that stretched over flexible bones that could be folded up neatly on the dragon's back. Zollin found Embyr lying on its side, one wing folded tight against its body, the wounded wing stretched out with a gaping hole in the leathery skin. All around the wound the red wing was charred black, and the dragon's big eyes looked terrified as Zollin approached.

"Hold on," he shouted over the wind. "Everything is going to be okay."

He slid down beside Embyr's head and placed one hand on the dragon's jaw. He formed a canopy of magic over them that blocked the wind and hail. They both sat breathing heavily as they waited for the raging storm to pass.

For the next hour, Zollin did his best to keep Embyr calm. It wasn't an easy task. His magic didn't work to heal the dragons, only Brianna could do that. And the storm raged on and on, the lightning shattering the dark sky above with flashes of brilliant light and crashes of thunder so loud it shook the ground beneath them.

Finally the storm passed, the hail turned to rain, and then to snow that drifted down in the darkness around them. Embyr moaned from the pain in its ruined wing, creating a mournful sound.

"Don't worry," Zollin said. "Everything will be okay."

An image flashed in his mind of the pride leaving Embyr behind, and a feeling of loneliness washed over Zollin.

"Tonight we have enough to worry about without thinking about that," he said. "I don't know how, but we'll figure something out. Tonight, we need to keep you warm."

* * *

Brianna, Selix, and Tig had been flying nonstop since learning that Zollin had gone on ahead of her. She had reached the edge of the Walheta shortly after dark and had finally decided that they should all rest. They could see the storm ahead of them, the lightning flashing far away, like fireflies glowing on a summer night. They settled onto the side of a mountain and slept. Brianna doubted that there were any enemies in the mountains, nor any predators that would dare attack a creature as large as Selix. They were all exhausted and immediately fell asleep.

The next morning, Brianna was up before dawn. She washed her face with water from her canteen, ate some stale bread, and woke the dragons. They flew south, with Tig forging ahead and hunting for both dragons. Tig killed a deer before they had been in the air half an hour. Tig could normally eat a whole deer, but it saved a little of the venison for Selix. Tig next killed a wild boar. It caught the animal in a clearing, swooping in and snatching the three hundred pound animal in its powerful talons. Tig couldn't carry the animal far, but with a strong twist of its talons it broke the hog's back. Then it landed in another clearing and waited for Selix to catch up. This time, the big, golden dragon ate the entire animal. Devouring it in seconds and then roaring with pleasure.

They were just about to move on when Brianna went rigid. The dragons watched her closely at first, and then looked to the sky. Two other dragons were circling.

"Zollin," Brianna said, her voice trembling.

She jumped into the air, summersaulting onto Selix's back. The golden dragon launched itself into the air, and Tig followed closely behind. They turned east and flew quickly toward the dragons they saw. Images flashed in Brianna's mind of the storm, only this time it wasn't far away and safe. This time the images were horrifyingly close, with thick bolts of lightning flashing down all around. She saw images of the cave, its craggy walls wet with moisture and filled with dragons. She felt the concern for Embyr, and she saw the dragon was hit with lightning. She also saw Zollin fearlessly plunging down the mountainside, in the midst of the storm, looking for the fallen dragon.

Then she saw images of Zollin and Embyr from the air. There was a large fire burning to keep them warm, but the dragon's wing was ruined. Brianna knew from that single mental image that unless she healed Embyr, the red dragon would never fly again. She saw more images, some from the air that revealed other dragons in the clearing with Zollin and Embyr and some from the ground.

It took only moments to reach the mountain where Zollin and Embyr were waiting, but to Brianna it felt like an eternity. Her worry about facing Zollin was replaced with worry over the wounded dragon and gratitude for Zollin's selfless actions.

Selix swooped over the clearing, and Brianna leaped from the beast's golden back. She tumbled and flipped, bouncing from current to current, before landing softly near Zollin. He turned and looked at her, a smile on his face.

"Oh Brianna, are you a sight for sore eyes," he said.

"Zollin," was all she managed to say before she was running into his arms.

It was a long, exquisite moment before Brianna regained her composure. Then she turned to Embyr. The dragon looked at her with its big eyes, the pain making them dull and glassy.

"I'll need to clear the area before I heal Embyr," she said.

"But you can do it?" Zollin asked.

"Yes," Brianna said, her voice suddenly stiff from the realization that she would soon have to tell Zollin that she could not marry him. Her body was tense, but Zollin seemed not to notice.

"Okay, we'll give you the room you need," he said.

He patted Embyr on the neck before speaking softly.

"See, I told you. Everything is going to be okay."

He levitated up into the air and Ferno swooped in beneath him. Ferno then rejoined Selix and Tig. Brianna looked up and could tell that the big, green dragon was thrilled to be back with the pride. She was surprised to see half a dozen other dragons circling in the sky above. She thought it was a beautiful sight and couldn't help but smile. At that moment, she wished more than anything that she could just forget the world and stay in the mountains with Zollin and the dragons. She forced herself to look away and focus all her attention on healing Embyr.

Fire billowed out of Brianna's hands. It was pure flame, not a consuming fire that fed on combustible materials and left ash in its wake. There was no smoke, just flame. The ground, saturated from the rain and snow that had fallen the night before, steamed from the heat of her fire. The flames washed over Embyr's wing. The dragon moaned, but Brianna knew the fire would heal the beast.

She mentally focused on visualizing the wing repairing itself, the red, leathery skin re-growing, the charred edges healing. It took over an hour to repair the damage, but by midday, the work was done. Embyr roared when Brianna finished. It nuzzled her with its long snout for a moment and then it took to the air, climbing high before diving down, spinning and turning loops. It was like a child full of glee in the freedom of being whole once more.

Brianna sat down and Zollin came floating down beside her. He had her pack, which Tig had been carrying. He handed her the canteen.

"Nothing but water to drink, huh?" he asked.

"It's all I want," she replied. "I'm thirsty."

"You should eat too," he told her, holding out some bread and cheese.

They sat down on the soggy ground, both eating and enjoying the silence. Brianna had so many questions but she couldn't speak, her voice was choked by the realization that soon she would shatter Zollin's heart.

"So, how did things go in Orrock?" Zollin asked.

"Not as well as I hoped," she said.

"Didn't Prince Willam back you up?"

"He did," Brianna said, suddenly unable to look Zollin in the eye. "But King Felix is acting strange. He was cold to me at first."

"But he's mobilizing the army, right?"

"Yes, he is."

"Thank goodness, for minute there you had me worried."

Brianna tried to smile.

"It's probably my fault he wasn't more cordial," Zollin said around a mouthful of food. "He's probably still mad at me for calling him to account for his actions."

"I don't know," Brianna said. "He's gotten close to a general named Corlis."

"Yes, I know him. He's younger than most of the other officers. I'm surprised he's a general."

"He's not just a general," Brianna said. "He's the High Commander of the King's Army."

"Really?"

"Yes, and the King listens to him."

"Well that's strange, but is it a bad thing?"

"I can't say for sure," Brianna said. "Willam says the other officers are afraid of him."

"Willam?" Zollin said smiling. "Listen to you, on a first name basis with the Crown Prince."

Brianna's heart nearly stopped beating, but Zollin just laughed. He was teasing her, she realized. He had no idea just how close she had become with the Prince.

"It took the King forever to get things ready, but he's moving his army south and will take them across the sea to avoid the long march."

"Well," Zollin said, considering the news. "That makes sense. Commander Hausey told me as much. Are they on the move?"

"I think so. The Prince was sent to serve with the cavalry."

Zollin nodded.

"But Zollin, he wasn't given command of the cavalry. He's to serve under Commander Hausey."

"Wow," Zollin said. "That seems odd. Is this coming from General Corlis?"

"No," Brianna said. "From the King, I think."

"Well, we can't worry about all that now. The dwarves are on their way, and some of the giants too. We need to keep moving south and scout out the situation. I want to try and find my father as well. He went in search of Mansel."

"Yes, Miriam told me," Brianna said.

"I can't believe they're having problems," he confessed. "It's not like my dad to leave someone like that."

"I'm sure he had his reasons," she said.

"I can't image anything being bad enough between them for him to leave her. He was so smitten. He told me he was giving up adventuring and settling down. He looked so happy the last time I saw him."

"Sometimes things happen that just can't be avoided," Brianna said, her throat so tight that her voice was strained.

"What?" Zollin asked looking at her. "Are you okay?"

"I'm fine," she lied. "We should get moving."

Chapter 26

King Felix stood on the command deck of the huge flagship Frostbite. The ship was the first of a large armada that included supply ships, troop transports, and even ships filled with the large battle horses the King's officers rode on in battle.

The weather was brisk on the open sea. King Felix could see for miles. They were sailing southeast and looking through the long, brass telescope, and the King could just make out the Walheta Mountains. He smiled grimly as he studied the dark clouds that were building over the mountains. He hoped the storm front wouldn't turn out to sea. If he lost even one ship on their voyage, it would be a severe setback for his plans. Of course a heavy storm in the mountains would dump rain, perhaps even snow on King Zorlan. Felix couldn't wait to see the look on his contemporary's face when the King of Falxis learned that he'd lost his kingdom to Yelsia.

Then King Felix turned his attention further south. It would take a few more days to make Luxing Bay, and only if the weather held. A storm could blow them off course, or a shift in the wind could make the journey take much longer. Still, King Felix was hopeful. He doubted that his son or Brianna understood the possibility that was ahead of them. Three Kingdoms were ripe for the taking, and the only thing that stood in his way was a woman's army. He couldn't believe his good fortune. His hope was that he would bypass the witch's army, allowing it to march north and be defeated by Zollin's dwarves and the remnant of King Zorlan's army. Whoever survived that conflict would be no match for Felix's forces, which should already be entrenched in the capitals of Falxis, Osla, and Ortis.

Of course he might lose his son in the process, but Felix didn't consider that a great loss. He'd had hope that Willam would become a good leader of men, but the boy's naive notions of honor and chivalry had rendered the Crown Prince impotent. If Willam were being honest about what had happened in Osla, then he'd proven himself an incompetent military commander as well. King Felix wouldn't mourn the loss of his son, the loser. He'd already banished Simmeron and if Prince Willam fell in battle, King Felix would have no surviving heirs. But a young wife would change that; King Felix was certain he could father more children.

He wrapped his heavy cloak more tightly around his shoulders and took a long drink of the mulled wine that sat in the weighted mug on the rail before him. The hot liquid filled the King with a comfortable sensation of warmth that spread slowly through his body.

The ship's captain approached and cleared his throat. King Felix turned and nodded at the man. Captain Alswyth was a serious man. His stoic nature suited King Felix, who had decided he like the seamen's efficiency.

"You've seen the storm?" Alswyth asked.

"Yes," King Felix replied. "Will it turn out to sea?"

"It's hard to say," the Captain explained. "Normally the weather around the mountains stays inland, but occasionally it will blow out to sea. I doubt we'll be bothered by it."

"Good, I want nothing to hold up our progress."

King Felix stayed on the command deck until it became too dark to see. The storm in the mountains had grown stronger and the wind had shifted, kicking up large waves that made the ship rock up and down so strongly that it is was impossible to ignore. King Felix went to his cabin, which was spacious as ship cabins go, large enough for a plush bed behind a screen and a large table where Felix hosted nightly dinners.

The officers all attended the evening meal in the King's cabin with the exception of General Corlis, who was so seasick he couldn't leave his own small room. The other officers seemed to enjoy the respite from the young High Commander and spent as much time as possible ingratiating themselves with King Felix.

They dined on pheasant, with a mix of stewed vegetables, cheese, and wine. Normally the talk around the king's table was upbeat, but the rough seas made dinning a chore. The men were forced to hold onto their plates and drink their wine from the wide bottom, weighted mugs the sea officers used to keep their drinks from spilling.

"Will the storm knock us off course?" asked General Griggs.

The sea captain, Alswyth, also attended the nightly feast. He normally refrained from the conversations which almost always either concerned their invasion strategy or matters of court. The storm, though, made all other topics seem inconsequential.

"Captain?" the King said.

"It's hard to say," Alswyth replied. "It's possible, I suppose."

"How will the fleet stay together in such foul weather?" asked General Tolis.

"This isn't foul," said Alswyth. "This is nothing more than a slight blow. I've seen storms at sea that would turn your bowels to water. I've seen forty foot waves and winds so strong it rolled ships and split masts. All the King's ships are sailing with lanterns hung in the rigging. As long as the ships keep in sight of one another, we'll stay together alright."

"You don't think the weather will get worse?" King Felix asked.

"It could, but I doubt it," Alswyth persisted.

He was wrong. The storm that began in the Walheta Mountains turned out to sea and churned the waves into towering swells. Fortunately for the king's ships, the winds were favorable. The captain soon left the dinner to supervise the sailors handling the ship in the storm. Most of the sails were furled, but still the ship sped along through the night, rising and falling on the tumultuous waves until half the crew was laid low with sea sickness.

When morning finally broke, the sea was an angry gray and the waves were still nearly eight feet high, but the Walheta

Mountains were behind them and King Felix was pleased. He couldn't wait to make land fall so his conquest could begin.

* * *

Willam looked up wistfully. Gyia was circling lazily overhead, while Willam rode along on a lightly armored stallion. The horse didn't like the slow pace any more than Willam, but Commander Hausey had assigned the Prince to be the liaison to the Dwarves. Willam guessed that it was easier for a Commander to move the Crown Prince to an independent assignment rather than have the King's son second guessing every decision the commander made. Willam didn't blame Hausey for reassigning him. Being a liaison to the dwarf army was really the perfect situation for a prince. It was a duty that kept him out of harm's way but was of significance at the same time. The only problem for Willam was that he was a fighter. He'd learned his lesson in Osla, he didn't mind commanding, but he would do it from the front from now on. Being assigned to escort the dwarves on the march south was honorable, but it wasn't what Willam wanted.

Commander Hausey had given Willam a staff of three junior officers. Most of the supply train was traveling with the Dwarves as well. Hausey had wanted to assign a century of cavalry soldiers to help protect the supply train, but Willam had insisted he refrain. The dwarves were a proud people; Prince Willam had learned that very early on. He felt that sending a squad of soldiers to protect the supply train would have been perceived as an insult. The dwarves were hardy folk. They marched nonstop from sunup until dark. They would have pushed on long into the night; the darkness was more comfortable to them than the bright sunlight, but they stayed with the supply train. Perhaps it was out of a sense of duty, or simply being near so much food and ale, Willam wasn't sure, but the dwarves had attached themselves to the soldiers driving the heavy wagons.

With so much free time on his hands, Willam couldn't help but think about the future. For him, Brianna was that future. He still worried constantly that she had agreed to marry him out of some sort of obligation, but he didn't like to dwell on that thought. Instead, he wiled the hours away dreaming of their return to Orrock, the wedding, their children, his coronation, and all the good things he would do as king.

"So?" asked Bloc one night as they sat around a small fire. "What is being a prince of Yelsia like?"

"Not as glamorous as you might think," Willam said. "I had a happy childhood and went into service for my father when I was fourteen."

"It's hard to imagine how brief human lives are," Bloc said. "We dwarves can live five times as long as a human, but at fourteen we are already two years into our apprenticeships."

"Really?" Willam asked.

"Oh, yes, usually with our fathers, but sometimes with other members of the clan, if a need arises."

"You live in clans?" Willam asked.

"Yes, our clans are not much different from your cities. Each clan has its own space under the mountains and each is independent of the others."

"But you are the king of the dwarves, aren't you? Do you have a capital or a castle somewhere in the mountains?"

"No," Bloc said, with a smile on his lips. "My family has served as the kings of the dwarves for thousands of years, but we do not rule under the mountains. Our role has been to lead the clans when we leave our wonderful homes. My forebears have worked with the humans and other races to make sure the dwarves are treated fairly. In truth, I am little more than a liaison, much like yourself."

"How do the clans settle disputes without a king?" Willam asked.

"Disputes are rare under the mountains," Bloc said. "But we have traditions that dictate how clans treat one another. If a complaint cannot be settled without help, they may call on me, but in that role I am a facilitator, not a judge."

"That is fascinating," Willam said.

"In some ways it is, but my family has no clan, no permanent home. I move from clan to clan, with no real wealth or place of my own. The other dwarves gain honor through their craft and prestige within their clan, but I am more like a beggar, reliant on the hospitality of the clans I stay with."

Willam considered how different being a king was like in his world. His father was the wealthiest man in the entire kingdom, even though he earned none of the money in the royal treasury. He was treated with deference wherever he went, and had absolute power among the citizens of Yelsia, as well as a place of honor in the Royal Court in Osla with the other rulers of the neighboring kingdoms.

Willam couldn't help but wonder how different his own life would be if he could see himself as dependent on the people of Yelsia, instead of above them. His father had taught him that a king ruling his people provided them with a better life, but the truth was they provided the King with everything. People treated Willam as if he was different, but he was just a man. He had the best education and opportunities to prove himself as he grew up, but the truth was, he was no different than any other person in the kingdom.

"I think there is merit to your way," he told Bloc. "I think I have much to learn from your people."

"The dwarves and humans can always learn from one another," Bloc said, "If we are willing. It is unfortunate that so much time has passed without contact between us."

"Why is that?" Willam asked. "Why don't the dwarves come out of their caves more often?"

"For the same reason you do not come down into the caverns under the mountains," Bloc said. "For most dwarves, venturing out of their homes is not an enjoyable experience. In our caverns the world fits us, on the surface, we feel out of place. Everything is so large, so open, and so infernally bright."

"I would like to ensure that our people benefit from one another," Willam said. "When all this is over, when we have peace once more, I would like to come and visit your home under the mountains."

"And you would be welcome," Bloc said. "We will have feasts like you have never experienced. But as you say, we must first survive the coming battle."

"It gives me confidence to know that we will fight side by side," Willam said.

"Yes, we will fight, but even all together we may not be able to stem the tide of darkness that rolls toward us. I feel deep in my bones that our world is on the cusp of a new era."

"One of new friendships and prosperity, I hope," Willam said, trying to sound confident.

"Yes," Bloc said, a shadow crossing his face. "I hope so as well."

But there was no hope in his voice.

Chapter 27

Zollin felt the tension from Brianna and the dragons with her. The pride, now larger than ever, was flying again and talking wasn't really a possibility, even though Zollin really wanted to talk. He told himself that the tension didn't have anything to do with him, but he was having trouble believing it. He realized that he just wanted to talk so that he could be reassured that he wasn't the reason for her tension. So, he did his best to rise above his personal feelings and put himself in Brianna's place.

When he thought back to their time together in Osla, he realized she had been tense then, too. She had just lost Torc, the small, blue, twin dragon that looked almost identical to Tig. Then they had fought Gwendolyn together, and both of them had seen horrors beyond belief. He remembered just how shaken up Brianna had been after diving down into the ground, using her unbelievable fiery powers to melt the ground underneath the behemoth that Gwendolyn had sent to kill them. She had seen the witch's work down in the depths of the underworld. Zollin couldn't imagine how that would affect a person. Now, she was going back to face the very army she'd seen Gwendolyn creating. He chastised himself for worrying about his own happiness instead of realizing what a difficult task going south must be for Brianna.

They flew all through the afternoon, and Zollin began to send out waves of magic in search of King Zorlan's forces. The sun was setting when he sensed the large settlement with his magic. He redirected the dragons, and they flew toward the village of Glen Green.

They were a little over a mile from the valley where the village was located, which was now filled with refugees and soldiers. Zollin directed the dragons to land on a mountaintop. In the distance they could see the glow from the settlement's many fires.

"It's probably better if we don't go flying into the middle of the settlement with a pride of dragons," Zollin said. "I can only image what state King Zorlan's army is in."

"I doubt they could hurt the dragons, but if they tried, it could send the wrong message to the dragons you brought with you."

"They are a little shy," Zollin said with a smile.

"I'm surprised they came with you at all," Brianna admitted.

"They were worried about you, I think," Zollin said. "At any rate, they are most welcome. I'll go into the settlement and find out what's what. Do you want to come?"

"No," Brianna said quickly. "I'll stay here with the pride for tonight."

"Alright," Zollin said, tamping down his feelings of insecurity. "I'll miss you. It's hard to separate again after finally reuniting."

Brianna didn't speak, rather she just nodded, but didn't meet Zollin's gaze. Ferno's rumbling growl was likewise ignored. Zollin suppressed a sigh, and then nodded at the big, green dragon.

"Good hunting," he told the pride. "I'll be back tomorrow."

There were growls and barks from the dragons. Zollin smiled, still finding it hard to believe he was in the middle of a pride of living, breathing dragons. He started off down the steep mountainside. He slid down the loose soil, letting gravity do the work as he sprang from tree to tree to keep himself from tumbling down the steep incline.

It was impossible to see in the dark with the tall evergreen trees blocking the light from the moon and stars above. Zollin let his magic flow out around him, sensing more than seeing the path he needed to take. The distance to the village was little more than a mile, but it took him nearly an hour to travel the distance. By the time he was walking down the final hill leading into the valley, he was sweating, despite the cold weather. His clothes were snagged and torn from the tree branches he'd been forced to cling to, as he made his way down the mountainside.

He walked into the settlement, which was little more than a huge campsite. Many of the refugees huddled around fires with no other place to go. There were large pots hung over fires with what looked and smelled like gruel of the worst sort. Still, the people eyed the pots hungrily, many with bowls and spoons in their hands as they waited to get a small helping for their supper. There were tents, but not enough to shelter the multitudes of people, most of which looked shocked and frightened. There were large, wooden frame pavilions with canvass stretched over the frames to give the refugees a place to escape the weather.

Zollin could only guess how miserable the storm had been on the settlement. Zollin wound through the small groups of people and made his way to the village. There were so many strangers in the valley that no one seemed to notice him. Zollin wasn't sure where to go, but then he saw soldiers standing guard around what appeared to be a small inn. Zollin made his way to the building and was stopped by the guards.

"No one is allowed inside after dark," said one of the men. "If you have a problem, it'll have to wait until morning."

"I'm here to see King Zorlan," Zollin said. "He's expecting me."

"No one is allowed inside," the man repeated. "You'll have to wait until morning."

"Tell the King that Zollin, Wizard of the Five Kingdoms is here."

"Sorry, I'm not a servant," the soldier said. "Now beat it or I'll give you a taste of my boot leather."

"There's no need to be rude," Zollin said.

He stepped forward toward the door of the inn. The soldiers on either side of the door tried to move forward and block his way, but they found themselves rooted to the spot. Zollin couldn't help but give the soldier a quick glance. The man's eyes were bulging with shock. He was straining to move or speak, but Zollin's magic held him and his partner in place.

"I'll release you in a moment," Zollin said softly.

The door to the inn was bolted from the inside, but a quick burst of magic levitated the thick cross beam up and out of the rough wooden slots. The beam fell with a thud as Zollin swung the door open. Light spilled out, along with the smell of roasting meat. Zollin's stomach growled at the smell, but he didn't notice. He was riveted by the sight of a man sitting against the far wall.

Quinn sprang to his feet, and Zollin rushed forward. They embraced, both men laughing and slapping each other on the back.

"What is the meaning of this," thundered King Zorlan, who sat in a large chair by the fireplace. Zollin and Quinn both ignored him.

"Guards!" the King thundered.

Soldiers came rushing into the inn's common room.

"What is happening?" Zorlan shouted. "Why are you letting people into the inn?"

"That was my doing," Zollin said. "I'm sorry, but I didn't see the point in waiting."

He released his hold on the two soldiers' right outside the door. The two men rushed inside, but didn't speak, although Zollin saw their angry glances and tried not to smile.

"Who are you?" the King asked angrily.

"You don't recognize me?" Zollin asked.

"You look like a beggar."

"It's been a long time since I last slept in an inn," Zollin said. "I daresay I need a good washing and fresh clothes, but my mission hasn't provided the luxury of those things."

"Are you the wizard?" King Zorlan asked.

"Aye, he is," Quinn said. "This is my son, Zollin."

"I didn't recognize you," the King said.

"That's quite alright," Zollin said. "I have good news from Yelsia and the magical people from the Northern Highlands."

"They are coming to help?" Zorlan asked.

"They are, indeed. King Felix is sailing most of his army down, but the King's Cavalry are moving south through the mountains. The dwarf army from the Northern Highlands is coming south as well. Even some of the mountain giants, but I'm not sure when we'll see them."

"And the dragons?" King Zorlan asked.

"I have a pride of dragons with me. They are spending the night in the surrounding mountains, hunting and resting after our long journey."

"They'll have to venture far afield to find game," Quinn said. "The surrounding area is barren. We've been forced to exhaust the game hereabouts in an effort to feed all the people."

"The dragons can probably help with that," Zollin said. "They're excellent hunters."

"When will King Felix's force arrive?" King Zorlan asked.

"I'm not sure," Zollin said. "Brianna may have a better estimate on their arrival. She was with them, I wasn't."

"Where is this Brianna?"

"She's in the mountains with the pride of dragons," Zollin explained. "She'll come down tomorrow."

"Fine," the King said. "You'll dine with us, of course. But you'll have to sleep in your father's room."

"I wouldn't have it any other way," Zollin said.

Zollin and Quinn talked late into the evening. Unlike the King, they limited themselves to just one mug of ale each, and Zollin gave the remaining food in his pack to the innkeeper's wife to add to the supplies she was using to feed the refugees.

Zollin was happy to learn that Mansel was safe. Quinn had not seen or heard from Mansel or Nycoll since he'd been sequestered with the King in the village's tiny inn. Zollin assured his father that he would check on them the following day.

"So, you're a prisoner here?" Zollin asked.

"As good as a prisoner," Quinn said. "The King," he added with a nod of his head in Zorlan's direction, keeping his voice low, "is desperate. He thinks I'll have some sway with King Felix."

Zollin snorted.

"He snubbed Brianna," Zollin explained. "I'm sure the King is still angry with me."

"Well, perhaps now that you're here we can get out of this inn and actually help."

"We need to make contact with King Zorlan's forces along the coast."

"That won't be easy," Quinn said. "The King's soldiers have taken all the horses, even the draft horses and farm animals. Those that can't be ridden have been butchered for their meat."

"Are things really that dire?" Zollin asked. "Didn't King Zorlan bring supplies?"

"No," Quinn said. "I think he came running up here just as fast as he could and left a trail of bodies behind him. Anyone who can't take care of themselves won't make it here."

"Okay," Zollin said. "I can get to the coast with one of the dragons. What about the defenses?"

"There are none to speak of," Quinn said. "Zorlan's forces are spread thin. He has about two hundred men here in the valley, the rest are scouting along the line of mountains. And to be honest, I'm not sure how many trained soldiers. I think Zorlan has put a sword in the hand of every man he could."

"I'm not sure that's a bad idea," Zollin said. "We need everyone we can find to hold the line."

"What do you know of this army that is coming against us?"

"Very little, actually."

"Will it be more of the flying horse people?"

"They're called Leffers and no, they won't be part of her army, at least not the army she is building. The Leffers carried innocents to her realm in the underworld, and she used dark magic to transform them into her minions."

"But we don't know what we're facing? There's no way to prepare then."

"We'll send scouts," Zollin said. "The dragons can scout from the air and cover long distances much faster than we can."

"Good," Quinn said. "I'd hate to face anyone now, as we're simply unprepared."

"Shouldn't King Zorlan be working on that?" Zollin asked.

"The good King sits moping day and night. I don't know whether he mourns for the people he has lost or his own ambitions that were dashed. Either way, he hasn't been much good around here."

"We'll have to change that," Zollin said.

"You can't change the mind of a king," Quinn said bitterly. "I've reasoned with the man until I was blue in the face. He's afraid of King Felix."

"I suppose he should be," Zollin said. "He did invade Yelsia and now his army is lost while Felix moves his army south. He really is at the mercy of the King."

"Well, you can't let that happen," Quinn said. "As much as I'd like to see Zorlan dethroned and made to do something useful, we can't have the kings fighting each other if they're going to stop an invasion."

"I don't see how I can stop them," Zollin said.

"You're a wizard," Quinn said. "I've seen you do the impossible over and over again. You've led armies to this valley. Not just the King's Army, but dwarves and dragons. Everyone will be looking to you, son. We have to make sure that no one person or one group, is taken advantage of."

"You're right," Zollin said. "I hadn't really thought of that before."

"You need to set up your own base of operations, and impose your will on the kings."

They spent the rest of the evening discussing what needed to be done. Zollin slept on the floor in his father's room, insisting that Quinn take the narrow bed. Zollin could hardly sleep anyway; his mind was buzzing with things that needed to be done. He was up before dawn and he made his way to the teamster Jorgyn's home. He found Mansel standing watch outside the big barn.

"Ho there, Mansel," Zollin called out. "You look as fit as ever."

Mansel stood with his massive sword propped on one shoulder. His hair was shaggy, and his clothes worn, but his thick chest and round shoulders were unmistakable.

"Zollin," Mansel said, his face splitting into a smile. "You old trickster, how are you?"

"I am well," Zollin said. "I hear Nycoll has sick patients."

"She does, she's busy night and day inside. It's all I can do to get her to stop long enough to eat a few bites."

"I'll see what I can do to help if you'll do me a favor."

"Name it," Mansel said.

"Brianna is camped on the top of that mountain," Zollin said, pointing to a nearby summit. "She has a pride of dragons with her. Can you go and have her meet me at noon?"

"Sure," Mansel said. "It will be a pleasant change to get out of the stench of this valley."

"Great. Have her meet us here. I'm going to take charge of this rabble. I'll need you by my side. Can I count on you?"

"Always," Mansel said, slapping Zollin on the back. "It's good to see you."

"You too. We'll get Quinn out of Zorlan's custody today and be setting up our own camp a short ways south of here."

"That will suit me," Mansel said, "but Nycoll won't leave her patients."

"She won't have to," Zollin said with a smile. "I think we can fix them up and send them back to their places in the camp soon."

Mansel showed Zollin inside. Nycoll looked exhausted. Zollin was tempted to use his magic to put her to sleep, but he realized that using his magic in such a way was wrong. He couldn't force his powers on people without their knowing it. Nycoll smiled, but she wasn't sure how Zollin could help her.

"Most of them are sick," she explained. "The water here is getting contaminated and making people ill, especially the children. I do have a few wounded though."

"Take me to the worst ones first," he said. "Do you have helpers?"

"No, it's just me, really. Mansel tried to help, but he didn't have the patience."

"I understand."

She led Zollin to a small girl who lay sleeping. Her skin was pale, with a bluish cast to it. Her bedclothes were soiled with sweat and sickness. She looked to be little more than skin and bones to Zollin and her breathing was ragged. He let his magic flow into the girl and found the cause of the sickness rather quickly. It didn't take him long to get the girl's body to fight the sickness, but that did little to help her at that moment. Her lungs were slowly filling with mucus, and her heart was weak.

Zollin first used his magic to remove the fluid from her lungs, and then he massaged the girl's heart. Soon, her eyes fluttered open and she looked around. Zollin heard a quiet gasp from Nycoll, who was watching from behind him.

"I'm hungry," the girl said.

"Good," Zollin said with a smile. "We'll get you some food."

He stood up and turned to see Nycoll with tears in her eyes.

"What did you do?"

"I can heal people with magic," Zollin said. "In a few hours, your patients will all be well. I imagine we'll need some food, though, and wine if we can find any."

"We don't have any food," Nycoll said. "Mansel always finds enough for us, but never more than a day at a time."

"I'll get food here," Zollin said. "Stay with her, and give her some water until I get back. It will take a few hours for her body to be strong enough to fight the sickness on its own, but the worst is over."

"I can't thank you enough," Nycoll said.

"You don't have to thank me," Zollin said, realizing that he'd talked more to Nycoll in the last hour than he had in all the time he'd known her.

He left the barn and went back to the Inn. There were still soldiers surrounding the small building, although who or what they were guarding was a mystery to Zollin. Perhaps they were there to keep the refugees from taking the choice foods from the King's larder, but that was exactly what Zollin planned to do.

"I need food for the sick," Zollin announced as soon as he walked inside.

King Zorlan barely stirred in his seat by the fire.

"Who is in charge here?" Zollin shouted.

"I am," said the innkeeper, scurrying out of the back room. "I am, sir. What can I do for you?"

"I need food for the sick," Zollin said, "Wine, bread, broth, and fresh water."

"I have all of that, sir, but the King's orders were that no food or supplies were to be taken from the inn."

"I don't care what the King said!" Zollin said loudly. "Get me that food."

"You don't care what I say," said King Zorlan with a sneer. He was slowly getting to his feet. "I am the sovereign ruler of this kingdom, wizard. Tread lightly or I'll have your head on a pike."

"Is that so," Zollin said, turning to face Zorlan.

"Zollin, stay calm," Quinn said, appearing from the small room he occupied.

"I'm very calm," Zollin said.

"Your father stays here at my command," King Zorlan said.

"Not anymore," Zollin said. "Quinn leaves here with me now. And you will see that the food is sent to the hospital. It's about time you got up and made yourself useful around here."

"How dare you speak to me like that," King Zorlan sputtered.

"How dare you do nothing while the people around you suffer," Zollin said. "I have been here less than a day, and yet I've seen people starving. There is a barn full of sick children just down the street. Where are the defenses you should have put in place? Why aren't these people preparing for war? Why do you do nothing when it is in your power to help?"

"Guards!" screamed the King. He was in a rage now, fumbling with his own weapons.

"Wait, calm down, both of you," Quinn said.

"I'll not sit idly by and be insulted," the King shouted.

"But you'll sit idly by and watch your people die?"

"How dare you," the King said.

"How dare you? You are a spineless, selfish, cruel man."

"Guards!" King Zorlan shouted. "Take this man and throw him into the stocks!"

"Don't!" Quinn said, throwing up his hands to stop the soldiers who had rushed into the common room with weapons drawn.

"It's too late," King Zorlan said with wicked glee. "Your son shall be tried and executed, if it's the last thing I do."

Chapter 28

Brianna enjoyed her time alone, even though she knew it was the calm before the storm. She would have to tell Zollin the truth very soon, at least part of the truth. He couldn't know the whole the truth, no one could. She had gotten herself into a mess, and only she could get herself out of it. And there was no way to keep the people she loved from being hurt.

She had been completely unprepared for how painful it was to see Zollin again. Just being near him made her feel weak. She had no doubts about her feelings, not after seeing Zollin again. She knew only the crisis at hand had kept him from pushing her on what was holding her back, and she also knew that sooner or later she wouldn't be able to hide the truth any longer.

The night had passed quickly. She had set her clothes aside and transformed herself into a living bonfire, reveling in the freedom of her power and the heat of living flames. When the dragons returned from their hunting, they gathered around her and curled up on the ground. Eventually, she let the flames die down. She dressed and found a place among the dragons. They slept until almost noon, and then Brianna got up and went looking for fresh water. She heard Mansel huffing and puffing as he made his way up the mountain, long before she saw him. She sat by a stream and waited on the big warrior to make his way to her.

"Finally," he said panting.

"You're out of shape," Brianna said with a smile.

"It's been hard to get enough to eat around here."

"I'm not surprised. The dragons were gone most of the night hunting."

"I hope they had more luck than I have lately."

"They ate well, but they had to hunt far a field. What brings you up onto the mountain?"

"Zollin," Mansel said with a smile. "He wants you to meet him at noon."

"Where?"

"In the teamster's barn. Nycoll has turned it into a place for the sick."

"I don't know where that is," she said. "You'll have to come with us."

"I can't," he said. "There's no way I can make that trek again and be there by noon."

"So, you'll have to fly with us."

"I prefer to keep my feet on the ground," he said frowning.

"There really isn't any other way," she said, smiling broadly at his discomfort.

"I remember you being nicer," he said.

"I remember you being braver."

She led him up the mountainside where the dragons lay basking in the early winter sunlight. The temperature on the mountaintop was cold, but the sun gave a little warmth. Mansel swallowed nervously. He had gotten used to Brianna's pride when he had traveled with her in Osla, but the dragons were intimidating just the same. Even the smallest of the dragons was larger than a horse; their eyes were intense and their forked tongues slipping in and out of their mouths reminded Mansel of snakes. There were even more dragons now than before, many staring at Mansel so intently that he felt uncomfortable.

"Ferno," Brianna said. "Would you mind to carry Mansel back down to the valley? We need to meet Zollin soon."

Ferno roared and shook its great, green head. It moved forward and puffed black smoke from the huge nostrils above the rows of razor sharp teeth.

"Great," Brianna said. "That's settled."

She patted Mansel on the shoulder and gave him a wicked smile. He gave her a withering look and moved to Ferno's side. He could see the scars that the gargoyles had left on the dragon's scaly skin, and he wondered briefly what kind of creature could harm a dragon. Then he focused on the task of getting up onto the green dragon's back. Zollin could just magically levitate up and settle into place. Mansel, on the other hand, would have to climb up.

"Can you squat any lower?" he asked the dragon.

Ferno's head whipped around and glared at Mansel with a hiss, but the green body lowered onto the ground. The dragon's elbow joint on its front leg was as high as Mansel's waist, but he put his hands on the wide leg and levered himself up. Mansel had to stand on the leg and reach up to grasp the horns that ran down the dragon's neck and ended at the bony intersection between the dragon's wings. The scales were hard, but rough, and Mansel was able to get enough traction to pull himself up and used his knees and feet to clamor into place.

"Are we ready?" Brianna called out from the back of the golden dragon.

Mansel grasped the small horns at the base of Ferno's neck before nodding.

"Alright then," Brianna sang out. "Let's fly!"

The dragons all took to the air except for Ferno. The downdraft from the pride of dragons beat down on Mansel like a storm's winds. He felt a moment of panic, wondering if he needed to do something to make Ferno fly like the rest of the dragons, but the big beast growled and slowly stretched its wings out.

"Don't let me fall," Mansel said quietly.

Ferno shook its head and growled again, and then it reared onto its hind legs slowly. Mansel squeezed the dragon with his knees, wishing he had a saddle or at least a strap to tie himself on with. Then Ferno jumped, but it wasn't the dragon's normal leap into the air. It was more of a hop, combined with a mighty flap of the huge wings. The result was that the dragon flew up slowly, just above the height of the surrounding trees, and then, with wings extended, Ferno shifted its weight so that the dragon glided down the mountain, just above the treetops. Mansel held on tight, the cold wind stinging his face and making his eyes water. He realized that the dragon could have flown up high into the air like the other dragons, but instead, Ferno seemed content to stay as close to the ground as possible.

They glided down toward the valley with Ferno doing as little as possible, as they flew so that the ride was as smooth as it could be. Mansel was afraid, but he was also thrilled. He had never moved so fast in all his life. The trip back down to the valley that would have taken him so long on foot was now completed in less than a minute. He felt a shout of joy and exhilaration building up inside him and finally he let it out. Ferno replied with a roar that shook the trees and got the attention of the entire valley. Ferno flew over the campsites straight toward the center of the little village.

"There," Mansel shouted. He was pointing toward the teamster's barn. "Land over there; next to the big barn."

Ferno had to turn its long neck so that the dragon could see where its rider was pointing. Most of the homes and shops in the village were small, so finding the teamster's barn was easy enough. Finding a clearing large enough for the massive dragon to land was another matter entirely. Ferno circled once, and then settled onto the ground. Mansel was a little disappointed that the flight was over so quickly. He slid to the ground and turned to the massive beast.

"I'm sorry I was afraid," he said. "I misjudged you."

Ferno growled and bobbed its mighty head. Then it hissed a word that sounded like *friends*.

"Yes, I would like that," Mansel said, holding his hand out to the dragon.

Ferno nuzzled the hand and then turned as Nycoll came rushing out of the barn.

"Mansel!" she said, clearly shocked to see him with Ferno.

"It's okay," he said. "This is Ferno, remember?"

"I, I, think so," she said.

"Where's Zollin."

"I don't know," she said. "He went for food and water, but that was over an hour ago and he hasn't returned."

Just then Brianna dropped down lightly beside Mansel, causing Nycoll to jump in fright.

"Sorry," Brianna said. "I didn't mean to startle you."

"We aren't used to people falling out of the sky," Mansel said sourly.

"Oh, don't be such a worrywart. Nycoll must be a strong woman; she puts up with you."

Brianna flashed Nycoll a smile and was surprised to see a smile in return.

"Zollin's not back," Mansel said. "He's been gone awhile."

"What's he doing?"

"He went to get food for the sick," Nycoll explained. "I thought he would have been back long ago."

"You think he's run into trouble?" Brianna asked.

"King Zorlan has held Quinn in the local inn for over a week now," Mansel said.

"Why? What did Quinn do?"

"Nothing," Mansel said. "I think he wanted leverage over Zollin or at least over King Felix."

"We better find out what's going on," Brianna said. "Ferno, you should join the pride."

There was crowd gathering around the front of the teamster's barn, looking in awe at Ferno and pointing up at the flight of dragons circling in the sky above.

"Yes, that's a good idea," Mansel said, and then he turned to Ferno. "Thank you again for the ride."

Ferno growled, and then jumped into the air. The people watching all cried out, some in alarm, others in fascination.

"Let's go," Brianna said.

They walked down through the town toward the inn. Mansel slowed, nudging Brianna with his elbow and speaking in low tones.

"There are twice as many soldiers around the inn as normal," he said.

"Well, I guess that answers our question about where Zollin is," Brianna said.

"What should we do?"

"I don't know; are the soldiers jumpy?"

"They aren't kind. Most of the people here avoid them whenever possible."

"If we hurt the soldiers, they won't be able to fight when we need them," she said. "And if Zollin is working something out, I don't want to ruin that by starting a fight."

"So we wait?" Mansel suggested.

"We wait and we watch."

"We don't exactly blend in," he said.

"That's okay," Brianna said. "I don't want us to blend in. I'm hoping for an invitation to Zollin's party."

* * *

"Zollin," Quinn said quietly. "What you do now will define how you lead these people. Think before you act."

Zollin was reminded of what Bloc, king of the dwarves, had said to him - *Your race is always quick to fight.* The words reverberated in Zollin's mind, and he felt the weight of truth in those words. He was quick to fight, to use his magical power to force his way. He needed time to calm down and think. Luckily, he had thrown up a magical barrier around himself, Quinn, and King Zorlan. The soldiers had crashed into the barrier and cried out in alarm. They hacked at the barrier with their swords, but the weapons bounced off harmlessly. Now they stood, pressing against the barrier in an effort to knock it down.

"What devilry is this?" King Zorlan shouted.

"I'm not here to bandy words with you, King Zorlan," Zollin said. "And I'm not going to let you throw me in the stocks. We need to work together."

"I am a king!" Zorlan shouted. His eyes were bulging, and his face was red and sweaty. "Who are you to dictate terms to me? I'll have your head for this, boy. Mark my words-"

"Enough!" Zollin shouted back. "I will not listen to your vain threats. Now sit down, Zorlan. I'm not here to fight with you. I will take the food I need and leave you to govern this valley, but you must take care of these people."

"With what?" Zorlan cried. "We have no food, no weapons, and no money."

"But you do have hope," Zollin said. "I will help with everything else you need, but you must manage what I give you and take care of your own people."

"How can I care for them if you are stealing the very food I need to feed them?"

"Don't try to turn yourself into a martyr," Zollin said. "You haven't been feeding anyone but yourself with the food here in the inn. Now, I suggest you go and clean yourself up. We can speak to the people of the valley together and make sure that they know you will help them, but they must be ready for the fight ahead."

Zorlan looked like he might pass out. He was sitting on the edge of his seat, leaning forward, sweat dripping from his forehead and nose.

"I... I can't," he said, and then he fell forward.

"What did you do, sorcerer?" screamed one of the soldiers.

And then they were all screaming and beating their fists against the barrier.

"What happened?" Quinn asked, as he and Zollin rushed to the King's side.

"I don't know," Zollin said.

Quinn rolled Zorlan onto his back, and Zollin thrust his magic down into the King's body. He could feel the pressure in the King's blood vessels and the lack of blood flow. The vessels were constricted, and the heart was straining to beat.

"It's something with his heart," Zollin said

"Can you save him?" Quinn asked in a strained voice.

"I'm trying."

The soldiers who were outside the inn came crowding into the common room. They joined the other soldiers who were beating on the magical barrier with their swords and shoulders. Zollin felt the pressure on his magic shield and realized he couldn't concentrate on saving King Zorlan and keeping the barrier intact.

"Back off!" Zollin shouted. "I can't save him like this."

The soldiers, thinking that victory was close to hand, doubled their efforts. Zollin wasn't at risk of being overwhelmed by the soldiers, but he couldn't focus on the minute causes of the King's illness while they shouted and pressed on his magical shield.

"He'll die if they don't stop," Zollin said.

"Please," Quinn shouted. "Let Zollin work. He'll save the King."

But Quinn's protests went unheeded. Then, suddenly there was a popping sound overhead. The wood of the roof creaked and snapped as two huge talons tore the roof of the inn away. Everyone inside covered their heads to protect themselves from the falling debris. And then a roar shook the inn. Some of the soldiers fell to the floor in fear.

"Don't hurt them!" Zollin shouted.

"Everyone out, or the dragons will tear this place apart," Brianna shouted.

She and Mansel had followed the soldiers inside and had seen what was happening. She had sent a message to Ferno, who swooped down and tore the roof off the inn with its massive, green talons. The soldiers nearest the door ran outside. People were gathering around the inn. Some of the soldiers stayed at the magical barrier, but they no longer pushed in on it.

"Zollin will heal the King," Quinn told them. "Go out and wait with the others. If he doesn't live, we can't escape. Go now, and let him work."

Zollin focused on the King again, while doing his best to block out the distractions around him. The king's heart was in distress and as Zollin spread his magic through the King's body, he found one of the major arteries blocked. He focused on the blockage and slowly broke the impediment up. Blood began to flow again, but the vessels were still constricted, and Zollin knew the blockage could happen again. He focused on getting the heart beating regularly again and then relaxing the vessels.

King Zorlan's eyes fluttered open. He looked pale and weak.

"Don't try to speak just yet," Zollin said. "You're out of danger, but you need to rest. Dad, can you get him some wine?"

"Sure," Quinn said.

Zollin dropped his magical barrier, and Quinn walked past the stunned soldiers. Zollin levitated the ailing King back up into his chair. It took a moment before one of the soldiers had the courage to venture past where the magical barrier had been. He approached King Zorlan slowly.

"Sire, do you still want the wizard locked up?"

"He needs rest," Zollin said. "He's out of danger, but his body has been through a difficult shock. Send someone to help him bathe and sleep. Who is the ranking officer here?"

"I am," said an older looking soldier, his voice gruff.

"Good, you're in charge now. See to it that the valley is protected and what little food there is gets shared with everyone. I'm going back to the hospital with food for the sick. The people there will be well by this evening. Tomorrow, I will be moving the headquarters of this combined army to the village at the head of this pass. Once King Zorlan has fully recovered and has seen that things are well managed here, he may join me."

"Aye," said the officer.

Zollin nodded at Quinn as he brought out a goblet of wine.

"The food for the children is ready," Quinn whispered as he passed Zollin.

"Mansel, will you help me with the supplies for the hospital?"

Zollin and Mansel went to the kitchen and found three bags of food, most of it bread. There were also two bottles of wine and a small cask of chicken broth.

"I can make more broth if it's needed," the innkeeper's wife said.

"I don't think it will be, not for the sick children anyway," Zollin told her. "Thank you for your help."

"Of course, of course," the woman said.

Mansel hefted the cask of broth and carried the sacks of food, while Zollin carried the wine. When they left the inn, followed by Quinn, and Brianna, the gruff-voiced officer was barking orders that could be heard outside the inn.

"Sounds like he'll get them all in line," Mansel said with a smile.

"Why do you always end up in trouble?" Brianna said to Zollin.

"What?" Zollin argued. "I was just trying to help."

"This whole situation is bound to be a disaster," Quinn said. "Zorlan is terrified of King Felix and so he should be. There's really no telling what will happen when the army from Yelsia arrives."

"We can't fight each other and the army Gwendolyn is sending against us," Zollin said.

"Speaking of that army," Brianna said. "Has anyone heard news of it yet?"

"No, just the flying horse monsters," Mansel said.

"They're called Leffers," Zollin added.

"We need to send out scouts then," Brianna said.

"I think so too," said Zollin. "Any of the dragons up for the task?"

"Yes, most of them I would think," she said.

"Good," Zollin said. "Here is what we need. First, we send the fastest dragons to scout to the south and another to search the coast for King Felix's forces. They should be in sight any day now. We also need the dragons to hunt for us. Food is in short supply here in the valley, and we need to help if we can."

"Alright," Brianna said. "I can see to that."

"Quinn, Mansel, I need you both to go and see that some sort of camp is established in the village at the mouth of the pass."

"That place was abandoned," Mansel said. "The Leffer monsters probably destroyed it."

"That's why I need the two of you to build something useful there. We need a central headquarters where the decision-makers from the different armies can meet and plan."

"We can do that," Quinn said, "If Mansel doesn't mind leaving Nycoll here."

"Are you staying?" Mansel asked Zollin.

"Yes, I'm going to help Nycoll with the sick, and then help her distribute some of the herbs she has and make sure the water here is clean. We'll follow you all in the morning."

"Alright," Mansel said. "We can do it."

"Good, we've all got a lot of work to do," Zollin said, looking at Brianna wistfully. "Perhaps soon we will find some time to rest and catch up."

"That would be nice," Brianna said, though she looked tense again.

"We'll have a suitable place prepared when you arrive," Quinn said. "But I don't have weapons or tools. Can you do something about that?"

"Sure," Zollin said. "Find me some spare iron; that will make the work faster."

An hour later, after Zollin had shown Nycoll what herbs to mix for the children and fashioned new weapons for Quinn, he focused his powers on creating tools. He made hammers, saws, and a canvas sack full of nails.

"I hope that's enough," Zollin said, after taking a long drink of wine. His magic was churning hotly inside him, but he wasn't overtaxed and exercising his power felt good.

"It will do," Quinn said.

"I've sent dragons south to scout and more of them back into the mountains to hunt," Brianna said. "Ferno thinks flying the two of you south to the town is possible. It's not too far, is it?"

"No, we could walk there before dark," Quinn said.

"Alright, Ferno will take you and then stay to help you keep watch, just in case you run into trouble."

"There's really no need," Quinn said. "The walk will do us good."

"Quinn, we'll need the daylight just to inspect the place and make a plan," Mansel said. "Why do you want to walk?"

"I don't want to walk," Quinn said. "But surely the dragons are needed elsewhere. You and I can take care of ourselves."

"You're afraid to fly, aren't you?" Mansel teased.

"It takes some getting used to," Zollin said. "But once you get the hang of it, it's like riding a horse."

"Well, there's really no need," Quinn maintained. "There's no reason we can't walk."

Mansel clucked like a chicken and Quinn threw a friendly punch at the big warrior, but Mansel was expecting it and dodged back out of the way.

"Well, I don't care how you get there," Zollin said. "Just get something set up that we can use."

"Consider it done," Quinn said.

"I've got to help Nycoll with some of children," Zollin said.

"We'll meet again in the morning," Quinn said.

"If we survive the flight," Mansel teased.

Chapter 29

Brianna was happy to be away from Zollin, although she felt guilty that once again she had not told him the truth. They had been too busy to discuss their personal lives and although she felt bad, Brianna was happy for the distraction.

She was riding high above the clouds with Selix. The air was icy cold, but for once Brianna didn't mind the discomfort. It was a fit penance for her unfaithfulness to Zollin. She could see the coast in the distance, her enhanced vision barely able to make out a thin strip of ocean blue ahead.

"Lower," she ordered Selix.

The big, golden dragon obeyed. They dropped below the clouds and raced over the open countryside. There were a few farms and homesteads nestled at the foot of the Walheta Mountains, but they were all abandoned now. They saw cattle occasionally, never more than one or two animals, most wandering aimlessly across empty fields. Brianna could feel Selix grumbling with hunger, but they ignored the easy prey and kept flying. It would be nightfall before long and although that wouldn't hinder Brianna, whose night vision was almost as good as the dragons; she wanted to speak with the soldiers who had been stationed along the coast as lookouts.

They passed over the small seaside village that had been Mansel's home for a short time. The devastation there was heart-wrenching. They saw campfires where the soldiers sheltered in the ruins of the homes and shops that had made up the small town. There was no sign of any ships. Selix turned up the coast and flew north for another hour, well past dark, but there were still no ships to be seen. As the big dragon landed to rest, Brianna walked along the rocky shoreline, pondering the absence of the King's Army. She guessed it might be possible that Felix had never left Yelsia, although there had been more than enough time for the army to mobilize and set sail for Falxis. She should have been able to spot the group of ships by now, she reasoned.

They set out again, flying out to sea, due west. Brianna had shed her clothes, which Selix now held in one giant talon. Brianna covered herself with fire, so that she and the golden dragon looked like a falling star, streaking slowly over the waves, only there was no one to see them. They searched for three hours over the seemingly endless expanse of the sea. There was still no sign of the King's ships.

Brianna and Selix turned back and followed the coastline to the edge of the Walheta Mountains where King Zorlan's soldiers were stationed. The sun was just coming up as Brianna and Selix landed near the village. They found the soldiers gathered together with weapons ready to fend of the golden dragon.

"Ho there," Brianna shouted. "We come in peace. We seek news of the Yelsian army for King Zorlan."

"How do we know who you are?" shouted one of the soldiers.

Brianna sighed, wondering why everything had to be so difficult.

"We have orders from the king's headquarters in the village of Green Glen. He holds court in the town's small inn. We have come from the Northern Highlands to help you fight."

"I suppose telling you we ain't got no news from Yelsia wouldn't hurt," the soldier said.

They were lowering their weapons and looking slightly more relaxed, even though they never took their eyes off of Selix, who stood silent behind Brianna.

"You haven't seen any ships?" Brianna asked.

"Sure, we've seen ships," the soldier said. "We saw a big group of ships. Thought they were your King and his army, but they sailed south, didn't even slow down."

"You saw ships?" Brianna asked again.

"At least a dozen," said another soldier.

"More than that, I'd say," said the first.

"They were sailing together?" Brianna asked.

"In one big group," the soldier explained. "Haven't seen any ships before or since, but saw those."

"And they were sailing south? When was this?"

"Days ago," the man explained. "The day of the storm."

Brianna thought back. The storm was several days past now. The King should have landed his troops and marched inland to the mountains, but if he had, the dragons she had sent out as scouts would have reported back within hours. In fact, the King's Army would have had time to reach the western pass and Green Glen. She knew instinctively that something was wrong, but she didn't know what.

"Did the ships seem damaged by the storm?" she asked.

"No, they were sailing south as fast as they could," the soldier said. "They had their sails all out, and the ships were dashing across the waves."

"You could see the white from the ship prows all the way out here," said another.

"They're fools for sailing south," said the first. "There's nothing but death that way."

Brianna thanked the soldiers and sprang up onto Selix's back. The golden dragon took to the air, and they raced back toward the rendezvous with the others. Brianna knew that King Felix had double crossed them, and she guessed that the greedy king was planning to take over Falxis. She didn't know why he disregarded her warning about the witch's army, but what truly troubled her was why the King had forced her hand into marriage with Willam. He had wanted the dragons of her pride; that was his reason for forcing her hand at least that was what he said. So why did he leave the dragons behind now? It didn't make sense.

She felt ill. She was tired, hungry, and scared, but she knew she couldn't hide the truth any longer. She would have to tell Zollin what had happened in Orrock. She laid her head on Selix's long neck and wept.

* * *

Zollin had spent the entire afternoon and part of the evening healing the sick in Nycoll's makeshift hospital. It was rewarding work, but after hours of healing, he was tired and hungry. The next morning, even the sickest of the patients was so improved they wanted to return to their families. Zollin had sensed the magic in the supply of herbs that Nycoll was using. He showed her and several of the refugee families how to mix the herbs together to fight the sickness which arose from the contaminated water supply in the valley.

Then Zollin went out with a group of soldiers and found places for wells. Zollin even used his magic to dig the first pit down to the water. When the fresh, clean water bubbled up, the soldiers were convinced and after marking places for several more wells to be dug, Zollin rejoined Nycoll for breakfast.

"I have everything packed," she said. "I'm only taking a small supply of the herbs and leaving the rest here."

"That's a good idea; we may need them, but not all of them. So you're ready to go?"

"Yes," Nycoll said.

They set out, walking from the village. After weeks of flying with Ferno the pace seemed terribly slow to Zollin, but he enjoyed spending time with Nycoll. She was shy, but with no one else around she opened up to the young wizard. He let her take her time, thinking before she spoke, and he found that trait admirable.

They talked about Mansel, about Zollin's memories of apprenticing with the big warrior. He confided how he had been jealous of Mansel, but how their struggles since leaving Tranaugh Shire had forged a strong bond of friendship. Nycoll shared selective pieces of her own past. How her husband had died at sea and how the village they had lived in treated her differently after that. Everyone had expected that she would remarry, but until she met Mansel, she simply hadn't thought it was possible to love anyone other than her late husband.

"Most people don't think love plays an important part of marriage," Zollin said, "At least not in my experience."

"No," Nycoll had said. "My neighbors didn't understand why I choose to live alone. They thought there must be something wrong with me, or some secret I was hiding. Rumors sprang up which only made my pain worse."

"I'm sorry," Zollin said. "I know what that is like. Most people are afraid of wizards. Even my best friend back in Tranaugh Shire didn't want to have anything to do with me once he learned that I was a wizard. He thought I was controlled by the devil."

Nycoll smiled, the look was empathetic. She had a tenderness in her eyes that was in stark contrast to the no nonsense practicality of her physical appearance.

"Do you really think that you can defeat this witch and her army?" she asked, after they had walked along in silence for a while.

"I know I have to try," Zollin said. "I don't know why I was given this magical power, but I would never turn my back on a chance to help people when I can."

"But can you defeat her? Wouldn't we be better off to go north and let her have the southern kingdoms?"

"If only she would be content with those kingdoms," Zollin said.

"But how do you know she won't?"

"I don't know," he said, "but common sense tells me that if we allow her to settle into the southern kingdoms and grow strong, we will never be able to defeat her."

"But do we have to defeat her? Do we have to fight at all?"

"I know two things for certain," Zollin said. "First, she is evil. I saw her slay her sister to solidify her new dark powers. Secondly, she hates men. Mansel and Quinn can attest to that. Prince Willam confirmed it. She cares nothing for the life of her fellow man; they are resources to be used and discarded. That's not the kind of neighbor I want to live next to. I believe with all my heart that even if she didn't invade Yelsia now, she would soon. If we can make her think twice about attacking Yelsia, we can save thousands of lives."

"Aren't you terrified?" she asked.

"Yes," Zollin said. "But I'm more afraid of what will happen if I don't act, than what may happen if I do. My dad always told me when you're afraid to focus on what's right in front of you, on what you know to be true. Fear comes from what we *think* might happen, but courage comes from what we *know*. I know that I can fight Gwendolyn."

"But you don't know that you can defeat her."

"No, I don't know that. But I do know that I have the best chance of anyone. I also know that all my friends and the people I care about are with me. They will be here for me no matter what happens. That gives me courage."

"I don't have many friends," Nycoll said.

"That's not true."

"It is true," she argued. "Everyone I've ever known was lost to the monsters. I don't know anyone but Mansel now, and I know he'll fight. If he dies, I'll be alone again."

"You won't be alone," Zollin said. "Quinn, Brianna, and I all care about you. And you've made friends in the valley. All the parents of the children you saved would give anything to help you."

"You saved their children," she said. "Not me."

"That's not true," Zollin said. "I swept in at the last moment and did the finishing work. You were the one who spent night after night with the sick, taking care of them and making them as comfortable as possible. You made a place for them when there was no place for them to go. You gave them hope when all seemed lost. You are a very special person, Nycoll."

"I'm not a healer," she said, looking down at the ground. "I like helping, but I don't have the gift that you have."

"No, but you have other gifts that are just as important. Very few people have the capacity to care for the sick and helpless the way you do."

"It's nothing," she said.

"No it isn't, and I think you know that. We have a hard fight ahead of us, but we must face it together. None of us can afford to be on our own right now. We need each other. I need you. Mansel needs you. We all need you."

He glanced over and saw tears in Nycoll's eyes. She was ten years his senior, with twice as much pain and heartache as he had endured. Still, he caught a glimpse of what Mansel saw in her.

A tender heart and a vulnerability that made him want to protect her.

They walked in silence for a long while; each content with their own thoughts. Finally, Nycoll spoke.

"Thank you for what you said."

"I meant every word," Zollin said. "I'm happy that Mansel has you. He deserves good things in life, and I can't imagine someone more suited to make him happy than you."

They were almost to the village. A roughhewn sign said Walheta's Gate, one mile. With their destination so close, they increased their pace. When they came over the last hill and saw the village below them, they were both excited and depressed at the same time. The big central building of the village, part inn, part feasting hall, was intact and they could see Quinn and Mansel still working on the building. The homes and shops around the big building were nearly all destroyed. A bonfire was burning outside the feasting hall; Quinn and Mansel had been throwing useless scraps of wood and trash on it all night. Zollin and Nycoll hurried down to join them.

"Hello!" Zollin shouted as they came near.

Quinn and Mansel looked up and lowered their tools.

"It's about time you got here," growled Quinn good-naturedly. "I thought you were leaving at sunup."

"I had to help dig a few wells this morning," Zollin explained. "I thought you would be finished by now."

"We're just making improvements," Mansel said.

"Show us what you've got."

They went inside. The room was large and open; the tables which Zollin guessed had once been in the room were now gone, but thick wooden shutters hung beside each of the high windows and small platforms stood under each so that archers could stand on the platforms and fire arrows. There was a large fireplace at the far end of the room and work spaces behind it.

"That's the kitchen and storeroom," Quinn said. "Empty of course, but it's all intact. We had to rehang the doors and touch up a few things, but the place was pretty much untouched."

"It's better than I hoped for," Zollin said.

"There are rooms upstairs, nothing fancy, but they have beds and blankets."

Two stair cases ran up to a second floor that lined both sides of the long hall. The central part of the room was open to the rafters, high above and the rooms were simple squares that looked out over the feasting space.

"It's perfect," Zollin said.

"The rest of the town is in ruins," Quinn explained. "There are maybe one or two structures that can still be used. The rest is scrap."

"All we need is a place to strategize and meet with the other leaders," Zollin said.

"It's as neutral as we could make it," Mansel said.

"You've both done well. Where is Ferno?" Zollin asked.

"I think he went hunting this morning," Mansel said. "It's kind of hard to understand a dragon."

"Alright, so we wait for Brianna and then we make a plan."

They didn't have to wait long. Ferno returned first with a small portion of a freshly slaughtered sheep. Mansel cut what little meat the dragon hadn't consumed into long strips. Zollin cooked it with his magic in only a few seconds. They didn't have anything to go with the meat, but Nycoll had some spices which they sprinkled on the hot mutton strips. They drank water and ate while Quinn talked about building some tables from the scrap wood in the village.

Then there was the unmistakable *whosh, whoosh, whoosh,* of dragon wings. Ferno growled and sent Zollin a mental image of Selix flying toward them. They all went outside to meet Brianna. The golden dragon landed and skidded to halt. Brianna summersaulted off the high back of Selix, landing gracefully just a few feet away from where Mansel and Zollin stood.

"I'll never get used to that," Mansel said.

"It's impressive," Zollin agreed.

"We have a problem," Brianna said. "A very big problem."

Chapter 30

Brianna drank almost a whole canteen of water and then scarfed down what remained of the mutton before telling her story. The others had questions, but she made them wait. She knew if she didn't tell about her engagement to Prince Willam that she wouldn't be able to go through with it.

"So, the King is sailing south," Zollin said. "I should have expected it."

"There's more," Brianna said, holding her hand up. "I should have told you sooner, Zollin. I'm so sorry. I never meant for anything like this to happen."

"What?" he said, looking scared.

"When I was in Orrock..." she had trouble forming the words. Tears sprang up in her eyes. "The King sent for my father."

"Estry?" Quinn asked. "Is everything okay in Tranaugh Shire?"

Brianna nodded, but tears rolled down her cheeks as she finished her story. "He wanted to make a match with me and Prince Willam."

Zollin's chest tightened, and he suddenly couldn't breathe. He knew instantly what Brianna was about to say, and he didn't know if he could face it. He started to turn away, but she grabbed his arm.

"I never meant for this to happen," she said.

"You're marrying Prince Willam?" he asked, his throat suddenly so dry all he could do was whisper.

She nodded and he felt his world crumble around him. Pain as he had never felt erupted like a poorly stitched wound inside him. Outside the feasting hall Ferno roared and Selix roared back. Zollin started to back away from the group but then his legs gave out from beneath him, and he fell hard on his back side.

"Son!" Quinn said.

"Zollin!" Mansel echoed.

They both rushed to his side and Zollin struggled just to breathe. When he had given Brianna the White Alzerstone ring in their village, he had felt the bond between them, but she had been promised to his best friend Todrek and Zollin would never have done anything to stand between them. When Todrek had been slain, Zollin mourned his friend and pushed Brianna away, feeling as if he were betraying Todrek by having feelings for Brianna. When he had finally gotten over his grief and accepted that he loved Brianna and she loved him, he longed to spend every moment of his life with her. He had followed her to Orrock when Brannock the evil wizard of the Torr had kidnapped her. He had held onto hope even when Brianna had been afraid of her feelings for him. He had felt that they were meant to be together when Brianna had come into magical powers of her own in the caverns of the dwarves under the Northern Highlands. And he had grieved for her when Bartoom, the giant black dragon, had taken her away. He had thought that Brianna was dead and the pain of that loss was the greatest of his life, until now.

His grief at the thought of Brianna's death paled in comparison to the crushing anguish of her rejection of him. Had it been anyone else he would have doubted her, but Prince Willam could not be denied. He was the Crown Prince of Yelsia, wealthy, handsome; he was everything that Zollin was not.

"Just breathe, Zollin," Quinn said. "It's going to be okay."

Brianna stood with tears streaking down her face.

"Why tell him this?" Mansel said. "Why now?"

"Because the King doesn't care about me or his son," she said through her sobs.

Nycoll held Brianna's shoulders, her eyes mirroring the heartbreak on Brianna's face.

"He only wanted control of the dragons," Brianna said.

"So?" Mansel said.

"So, why did he go south without them?" Quinn said. "If you agreed to marry Prince Willam, why did he let you leave with the dragons?"

"I don't know," she sobbed.

Zollin wanted to curl up into a ball on the smooth stone floor of the feasting hall and die. But even in the darkness of his greatest fear, he realized he knew the answer.

"He knows how to control them without you," he whispered.

"What?" Mansel asked.

"The dragons," Zollin said, as tears ran down his face. "The King has found a way to control them."

"How?" Quinn asked.

"I don't know," Zollin said. "But Offendorl did it and it wasn't magic."

"No," Brianna said. "He can't."

"We know where he's going," Quinn said. "He'll be marching for Luxing City."

"So, what do we do?" Mansel said.

"We have to warn him," Quinn said. "The witch's army will destroy him on open ground and then there won't be anything to stop her from taking Yelsia."

"Help me up," Zollin said.

His legs were shaky and he was still having trouble breathing, but he wanted to get outside. He needed to talk to the dragons.

"Zollin, I'm sorry," Brianna cried. "I love you. I'm sorry."

He ignored her, but her words seared his heart like acid. Quinn felt so helpless. He loved Brianna like a daughter, but he couldn't believe she would hurt Zollin like this. He followed his son outside.

"There has to be a reason, Zollin," he whispered in his son's ear. "She wouldn't betray you without a very good purpose."

"How could she say no?" Zollin asked. "He's the Crown Prince."

"The Prince you saved, if I remember correctly."

"Do you think that really matters to him? He sees what he wants and takes it. That's the way all rulers are," Zollin said bitterly.

"Don't let this ruin you, son. Talk to her, and find out what happened."

"I can't even look at her," Zollin said.

"Wait, Zollin!"

But he was already levitating up onto Ferno's back.

"Fly," he whispered to the green dragon. "Take me away from here."

Ferno jumped into the air, roared, and flew away.

"Damn!" Quinn said.

"What now?" Mansel asked.

"Beats the hell out of me," Quinn said. "That boy is our only hope. But heartbreak like this can ruin a man. I've seen it."

"She had to have a reason, Quinn."

"I know," he said. "Let's go find out what it was."

They went back inside the hall. Brianna was slumped on the floor. Nycoll knelt beside her, holding Brianna as she cried. Quinn's anger softened. He knew that Brianna didn't want to hurt Zollin, and he had to be careful how he asked the next few questions.

"Brianna," he said softly. "Tell us what happened."

"I've told you," she said. "King Felix brought my family to Orrock. They made an arrangement for me to marry Prince Willam."

"You could have said no," Mansel said.

"I said yes," she said, suddenly stiffening. "I fell in love the Prince. He asked me to marry him and I said yes. That's all there is to it."

"You said King Felix wanted to control the dragons," Quinn said.

"He does, that's why he approved the match… I think. He brought my family to the capital to convince me to marry Willam."

"So they pressured you," Mansel said, his voice curt.

"No, well, yes, but that's not why I said yes."

"Why did you say yes?" Quinn asked, the pain he felt evident in his voice.

"Because I love Prince Willam," she said. "I need you all to understand that. I did it freely, and I hope you can support me in my decision."

"We can't blame you for wanting to become Queen of Yelsia," Quinn said.

"That's not why I did it," she said hotly. "I don't care if I become queen or not. I did this for love and for no other reason."

"Okay," Quinn said. "I'm sorry. It's a little shocking, that's all."

"I know, and I'm sorry too. I've hurt you, and I've hurt Zollin. I don't expect you to ever forgive me, but this is what I have to do."

"It doesn't seem like you," Mansel said.

"Well, it is," she said, wiping the tears from her eyes. "I made this decision, and I'm sticking with it."

"Then you have our support," Quinn said. "We love you, and we only want you to be happy."

"Thank you," Brianna said, fighting fresh tears.

"But we still don't know what King Felix is doing," Mansel said.

"I'll go south. I have to try and convince him to join us here," she said.

"That may be exactly what he wants you to do," Quinn said. "If you take the dragons south, he can control them through you."

"No, I won't let him."

"He's not the kind of man to leave things to chance," Quinn said. "We should wait for Zollin to return and make a plan together."

"Okay," Brianna said softly.

The huge feasting hall suddenly seemed too small. Quinn and Mansel returned to their labor. Quinn began gathering wood for tables, while Mansel made sure that Nycoll had blankets and water for the night. Brianna went out to be with Selix, while Nycoll swept the feasting hall with a broom she found in the store room.

An hour passed and then another. Brianna was growing restless and feeling more and more out of place. She had always felt more at home with Quinn and Mansel than she did with her own family, but now she felt completely alone. She was sad, but her resolve to say nothing about the King's threat hardened. If she confided in any of them, they would tell Zollin. She even hid the truth from Selix.

Finally, Ferno returned. Zollin looked terrible; his eyes were swollen and skin was pale. He slid off the big, green dragon's back and patted the beast on the neck.

"You're a good friend," he told the dragon, who growled in return.

"You're back," Quinn said, as he hurried to Zollin. "Are you okay?"

"No, but I think I may have an answer to the riddle."

"What do you mean?" Mansel asked.

"When Brianna and I were fighting the black dragon and we went to the ruins of Ornak with Commander Hausey, we discovered a hidden library. Kelvich took the scrolls to Ebbson Keep. He was hoping he might learn something about dragons that we could use to defeat the beast."

"Did he?" Quinn asked.

"In a way, yes," Zollin said. "Dragons are impervious to fire, but not to lightning. I was able to conjure lightning when the dragon attacked Orrock and drive the beast away."

"Okay, but what does that have to do with controlling the dragons?" Quinn asked.

"Nothing," Zollin said. "But Kelvich was only there a short time. He was only able to work through a portion of the scrolls. What if the scholars at Ebbson Keep discovered the way to control the dragons the same way that Offendorl controlled the black one?"

"Bartoom couldn't resist the call of the wizard," Brianna said. "I remember being with Bartoom and trying to convince the ancient dragon not to give in."

"So maybe King Felix can now control the dragons without you," Zollin said. "Maybe that's why he sent you away. He knew you wouldn't agree to his plan to take over Falxis, so once he had a way to control the dragons he didn't need you anymore."

"That can't be true," Brianna said.

"I would have said the same thing about you marrying someone else," Zollin said, letting the verbal barb sink in.

"So, what do we do about it?" Mansel asked. "We have to get King Felix back up here or we're done for."

"We have to go after him," Zollin said. "There's no other choice."

"We'll both go," Brianna said.

"I don't think that's a good idea," Zollin said.

"No, if King Felix can control the dragons, she may be the only other person who can break that hold," Quinn said. "She has a connection to the dragons that not even you have Zollin."

"He's right," Mansel said.

"Fine," Zollin said. "Let's get our things together."

Zollin went back into the feasting hall to get his pack.

"The other dragons will be returning soon," Brianna said. "I've sent word to Embyr to bring its catch here, instead of to the valley. That should give you enough food for several days."

"Thanks," Quinn said.

"You be careful," Mansel said.

"I will be."

Quinn was just turning to have a final word with his son when Selix roared loudly and sent a gout of flame toward one of the broken down workshops near the feasting hall.

"What the hell?" Mansel shouted.

"Selix, what are you doing?" Brianna shouted.

The big, golden dragon swung its head from side to side and roared again. Then, it jumped into the air and sped away south. Ferno roared too, but didn't fly away.

"What's happening?" Zollin said as he and Nycoll ran out of the feasting hall.

"Selix just left," Brianna said in shock.

"Quick, we have to put out that fire before it spreads to the feasting hall," Quinn shouted.

Zollin raised his hand and sent his magic shooting into the fire. He could feel the flames consuming the wood and straw, as well as the air around it. He pulled the air away and the flames sputtered and died, almost instantly. Holding the air back was difficult and he fashioned a magical bubble around the structure, sucking the air out and suffocating the fire.

"Get water," he told the others. "It may flare up again."

Quinn found buckets, and they filled them with water from the town well. When they returned, Zollin let the magical bubble collapse and the air rushed back in. The wood was still so hot that in places it ignited again, but it only took a little water to control the fire and soon it was safely put out.

Brianna stood frozen, her face a mask of shock and pain. Zollin approached her, swallowing down his own pain.

"What happened?" he asked.

"I don't know," she said, tears once again streaking down her cheeks.

"Something had to set Selix off."

Ferno, the green dragon, was shaking all over. It moaned pitifully and growled like a frightened dog.

"What is it, Ferno?" Zollin called out.

An image of Selix being pulled away, a great chain about the golden dragon's neck, flashed into Zollin's mind.

"Did you see that?" he asked Brianna.

"Yes," she said, her lips trembling.

"Isn't that like the black dragon?"

"Yes," she said again.

"We have to stop King Felix. At the very least we have to free Selix."

"If he is controlling Selix, he may be controlling Tig and Gyia as well," Brianna explained. "They were all at the capital together."

"So we go south," Zollin said.

"Is this madness?" Quinn asked. "I mean, isn't it possible the witch called the dragon south? You said that Offendorl controlled the black dragon. Perhaps it is the witch now controlling Selix."

"I felt no magic at work," Zollin said.

"You said that Offendorl didn't use magic either," Mansel chimed in. "If we lose you two, we won't stand much of a chance against the army Gwendolyn is sending north."

"Well, we can't sit here and do nothing," Zollin said.

Ferno growled again, this time a mental image of Embyr, still miles away and high in the sky, flashed into Zollin's mind. The red dragon carried the half-eaten carcass of a moose in its talons.

"Embyr is almost here," Zollin said.

"Then we go as soon as the dragons are ready," Brianna said.

"You're sure," Zollin asked her. "Are you sure you can do this?"

"Just try and stop me," she said.

Chapter 31

Prince Willam was actually starting to enjoy the long march south. For weeks he had been wooing Brianna and being with her filled him with an inexplicable joy, but after days on the road with the men of his staff and spending time each night with the dwarves, he was once again enjoying the camaraderie of men pursuing a common purpose. The dwarves were stoic during the day, marching south with a tireless pace, oblivious to the weather or obstacles, but at night they became animated and loud, especially when drinking ale.

Prince Willam stayed busy during the day, moving from the front of the supply chain to the rear, fixing problems. When things were slow, he would walk his stallion beside the cheerful Bloc. Hammert and Jute were constantly trading barbs, which Willam found vastly entertaining. The young men of Willam's staff were eager to please the Crown Prince. They were each from noble families, although none would inherit their father's titles. At first Willam had worried that the officers, none of them much older than Zollin, were simply interested in getting on the future king's good graces. But over time, he had come to respect their abilities and they, in turn, had relaxed in his presence and learned that Prince Willam valued honesty and hard work.

At night, when the vast company made camp, Willam made sure everyone had what they needed to pass the night in safety. Bloc set a rotating watch, with dwarves lining the perimeter of the camp, their sharp eyes seeing more than any human soldier could see. Then, Willam and the dwarfish headmen dined together around a roaring fire. The dwarves told stories and made jokes, often at one another's expense. It was very ordinary, almost mundane, but Willam respected what they accomplished each day, and how they spent time together each night.

They had been on the road south of Felson nearly a week when Gyia suddenly disappeared. The purple dragon had gone off usually at night to hunt. During the day, the long, serpentine dragon had flown slowly overhead. Occasionally Willam would ride up with Gyia to get a lay of the land around them, but the dragon could send mental images of what it saw to Willam, which was usually greater than Willam could see for himself. The dragon had become a kind of mascot to the men and dwarves, but Gyia rarely spent time among them preferring to keep a distance between dragon and humans. Willam had noticed that Gyia seemed more leery of everyone since they had left Orrock, but he chalked it up to nerves and the dragon's desire not to frighten people or make his work harder than it had to be. But all that time Gyia had been mentally connected to Willam, the dragon might be high in the air, but Willam could always communicate with the great purple beast.

Suddenly, Gyia was simply gone.

"What's wrong?" Bloc asked. They were walking side by side at the head of the long column of dwarves.

"Gyia," Willam said. "I can't feel Gyia anymore."

"Probably off hunting," Bloc said.

"I've never lost touch with the dragon before," he said, frowning.

"I'm sure all is well," Bloc said.

They marched the rest of the afternoon but Willam was distracted, constantly looking up into the sky in search of the dragon.

"We'll be in the mountains soon," Bloc told him. "The dragon is probably just ranging ahead. There's more game in the mountains. The Walheta are old and full of mystery."

"Are there dwarves under the Walheta Mountains?" Willam asked.

"Not anymore," Bloc said. "Once, long ago, the dwarves of the Walheta were a mighty race. Your people stamped them out though."

The Walheta were not friendly folk," Hammert said. "They didn't like the humans passing through their mountains."

"It was said they were stalwart warriors," Bloc said. "If they were alive today, they would be a great boon in the battle before us."

"If you could get them to fight," Jute said. "They were stubborn."

"Did you know them?" Willam asked. "How long do dwarves live?"

"The average life span of a dwarf is 350 years," Bloc explained. "But the Walheta Dwarves died out long ago. All that's left of them are the stories our people tell."

"And their caverns," Hammert added, "If you're brave enough to find them."

"They're filled with all kinds of nasty creatures now," Jute said. "It's not a pleasant place."

"Perhaps we could reoccupy the caverns," Bloc said. "Drive out the monsters."

"That would take a hundred years," Hammert scolded.

"We've the time," Bloc said. "It wouldn't hurt us to broaden our horizons."

"This war is about as broad as I plan to get," Jute asked. "I'm only here for the ale."

Willam's attention began to wander. He felt naked somehow without Gyia. He knew his feelings were just phantom pains, but he swore his wounds from King Zorlan's torturer had begun to ache.

* * *

The first day back on land had been difficult. King Zorlan had waited impatiently for his army to disembark. They set up a perimeter and then they unloaded ship after ship of supplies. Wagons were carried to shore, piece by piece, reassembled, and loaded with goods. The horses had to be blindfolded and helped off the ships, and of course, weapons and armor unloaded. It was late on the second day before they could begin the march toward Luxing City. The ships had made excellent time, and they landed on a long stretch of beach that was uninhabited. King Felix had little doubt that news of their arrival would reach the city before his troops did, but he was confident that in the two days it would take to march to Luxing City that he could still catch his adversary unaware.

His first item of business once the army was on the move was to summon the dragons he now controlled with his golden crown. He placed the circlet on his head and focused his mind on the dragons, calling them one at a time.

"Selix," he said out loud, envisioning the huge, golden dragon in his mind. "Come to me, Selix, king of dragons."

Then it was time for Gyia. He called the purple dragon south and then Tig. It was less than an hour later when Tig responded to the King's summons. It was warm in Falxis, despite the fact that it was early winter. The King's head was covered in sweat around the heavy crown, and his neck ached from the weight of it. Still, he didn't want to risk breaking his control over the dragons, so he left it on.

He saw an image in his mind of Tig; the small blue dragon was fast and racing toward him. He stood up in his stirrups and looked north, but after seeing nothing in the bright sky, he turned his attention south. At first all he could see was a dot in the sky. He couldn't make out the shape of what he could see. Another image flashed in King Felix's mind; this time of the army marching. The image was from much closer than the dot in the sky, causing Felix to look around in vain for the blue dragon.

When he looked back at the dot in the distance, he could see that it was closer. He turned to Corlis and smiled.

"What is it, my liege?" the commander asked.

"The first of our pets draws near," Felix said.

"Where?" Corlis asked.

"There." Felix pointed out the tiny blue dot in the distance.

"What? How can you tell that is anything at all?"

"I am your king," Felix snapped. "Do not question me!"

"Forgive me, your grace. I only meant my eyes can barely see the creature; it is so far away."

"I am connected to the dragons," Felix said. "They make me powerful."

Corlis had to hold back a snort of disgust. He watched the King out of the corner of his eye. Felix was growing fat; his skin was loose and wrinkled. Corlis thought the King looked more like an old man every day, and he wondered why he tolerated the bloated old fool. Still, he thought it wiser to let Felix lay claim to Falxis and then, when both kingdoms were firmly in the King's grasp, Corlis would slay him and take the throne.

Prince Willam had been a concern, but the Prince had run away, making Corlis' task of usurping the throne that much easier. He had command of the army, and they were loyal to him now. The other generals feared him; they would submit or be executed. *It would be soon,* he thought to himself. Then, he could stop feigning loyalty to King Felix and bring the entire kingdom under his control.

Corlis couldn't help but think of his childhood. His whole life he had been treated as second best. His older brother would inherit their father's titles, even though his older brother was a fool with no ambition what-so-ever. When Corlis becomes king, he looked forward to stripping his brother of the title, their lands, and any treasures they still had. He would put his brother out on the streets and then see how noble he was.

It was nearly ten minutes before Tig came fully into view. The blue dragon flew by in a streak of fire, black smoke, and blue dragon scales.

"Magnificent," King Felix shouted as the dragon raced by. "Now, return to me and keep pace with us."

Tig circled in a long, lazy curve, then flew over the marching army, slowing until the blue dragon was moving as slowly as the army. They marched through the afternoon and made camp just before dark. Tig circled over the army the entire time. When night fell, King Felix sent the little, blue dragon to scout out the city.

It was morning before Tig returned and by that time Selix had arrived too. The huge, golden dragon was tired from flying nonstop to obey the King, but Felix didn't care. He was ready to move and intent on reaching Luxing City by nightfall.

Tig relayed mental images of the capital city of Falxis to King Felix. The images were stark. The city seemed abandoned and in disarray. Many of the homes and buildings were smashed. Black scorch marks showed where buildings had burned down. There was no sign of any people, but of course it was the middle of the night when Tig had scouted the city and King Felix chocked the lack of people up to the late hour.

They marched on and only stopped to rest at noon. Corlis was surly, and the temperature which would have been pleasant under normal circumstances, was driven up by the blazing sunshine and the choking dust.

"Ready your men, General," King Felix said imperiously.

"Yes, my King," Corlis said with a short bow.

By late afternoon they were less than an hour from Luxing City. Selix and Tig were still circling overhead, their heads sagging from fatigue, their wings beating tiredly. Just before the army resumed its march, two more images popped into King Felix's mind. He saw two more dragons approaching; there was a huge, bull of a dragon with forest green scales and a male rider. The other was a smaller dragon with a short neck and short tail, red scales and a female rider.

"Blast," said King Felix.

"What is wrong, my liege?" Corlis said lazily from the saddle beside him.

"We're being pursued," Felix said.

"Where? By who?" Corlis asked, standing in his stirrups and looking behind the long column of soldiers.

"Dragons," King Felix said. "I suspect Brianna and the wizard are with them."

"Form up around the King!" bellowed Corlis.

The King's Royal Guard surrounded King Felix and Corlis. Then a full squad of one hundred mounted soldiers surrounded the Royal Guard.

"Send the dragons to fight them," Corlis urged.

"No, let us hear what they want."

The two approaching dragons landed, although Ferno roared defiantly. The riders talked for a moment, and then the man slid off the green dragon and began walking toward the army. The woman, her red dragon and the green dragon, took to the air again.

An image of the lone man approaching filled King Felix's mind. He saw the young man, tall and lanky, walking with a slight limp. He wore tattered clothes, his hair was long, his chin clean shaven. He had no discernible weapons, but that gave Felix no confidence.

"That's close enough," King Felix shouted when Zollin was still a hundred paces away from him. "What do you want?"

"King Felix," Zollin shouted back. "Why are you marching to Luxing City? Didn't Brianna warn you of the army marching north as we speak?"

"I see no army but my own," Felix cried. "I do not jump when you speak because you are a wizard, boy."

"Please, my lord, don't do this. Turn your army north and join us at the Walheta Mountains so that we might have a chance of success against the army that pursues us."

"I've heard enough of your fear mongering speeches, lad. From now on, I'll hold my own council about what is good for Yelsia."

"Send the dragons south; let them scout the approaching danger for you."

"Nay," Felix responded. "First, I will lay claim to the throne of Falxis," he said with a smile. "Then I will turn my attention to Osla."

"Sire, let me accompany you," Zollin said. "Let us reason together before it is too late."

"Fall in at the rear of my forces, and do not try to interfere with my plans. I have designs set in motion to ensure that no harm befalls me or those you care most about will die with me."

"My Lord, I will not harm you in any way, I swear it."

"Fall in then, we have ground to cover."

Zollin walked to the rear of the army, while Brianna and the two dragons with her circled the entire force. Selix and Tig flew slowly, doing their best to stay directly over King Felix. It was almost twilight when another dragon approached. Brianna, Embyr, and Ferno flew to the smaller dragon. It was one of the pride members that had joined Zollin in the Northern Highlands. Brianna had sent the dragon south to scout out the army they expected was marching north. The dragon was just now returning from its mission.

The dragon slowed and circled with Ferno and Embyr, and then it flew on to the north. Zollin was hit with image after image of what he could only consider to be a nightmare. As far as the amazing sight of the dragon could see, was a vast army. The front rows were Leffers, but behind them came a ragtag army of grotesque deformities. They walked upright and had the distorted features of men and women, but they stood much taller, their muscles bulging at unnatural angles. They dragged weapons, swords mostly, with thick metal blades that were more like axe blades than thin, sword blades.

Zollin used his magic to leap high into the air, and then levitate toward King Felix.

"My Lord," he shouted as he approached. "We must turn north, immediately."

"Hold your tongue, boy," Corlis shouted. "Or I'll cut it out."

Zollin ignored the General.

"King Felix, please. Listen to me. A scout has just returned. The army of the witch is only a day away from here. Open your dragons' minds and let them tell you what the scout that just passed by us saw."

Felix was about to dismiss the claim, but there was something in Zollin's eyes that made him hesitate. He knew that it could be a trick, but he was still worried about the fact that he hadn't seen a living soul across the vast plains of Falxis. The image of the abandoned city still played in Felix's head, so he nodded at Zollin and whispered to Tig to open up to the other dragons.

It only took a moment for the blood to drain from King Felix's face.

"Stop the army," he said to Corlis.

"What? Tell me you aren't buying this fool's lies."

"Do as I say Commander, or you'll find yourself mucking the stables in Felson," King Felix roared.

Corlis looked angry, no longer trying to hide his disgust.

"Make way," the King said, as he steered his high stepping destrier toward Zollin, who had come down to the side of the long column of soldiers.

"Is what I saw the truth?" he asked.

"I'm afraid it is, your majesty," Zollin said. "It is as we feared. Gwendolyn has created a horrible army from the innocents she captured with the Leffers."

"Leffers?" the King asked.

"The flying horses with the scorpion tales. Did you see them?"

"Yes," Felix said.

"They captured people and carried them back to the witch's lair in the underworld. Everything Brianna told you is true. If you will come back to the Walheta Mountains, King Zorlan will confirm our story. He was at the battle of Osla."

"Fine," Felix said. He looked visibly shaken. "We shall turn north and return to the mountains with you."

"Thank you," my liege. "Thank you," Zollin said.

He immediately communicated their success with Ferno, so that the dragon could relay the message to Brianna. He watched as the dragons turned and flew back toward Zollin.

King Felix rode back to Corlis and ordered the general to turn the army north.

"My Lord," Corlis said, "we are less than an hour from Luxing City. Your conquest is within your grasp."

"You didn't see what is coming," Felix said patiently. "I did. We march north, immediately."

"You can't be serious," Corlis said, his face pinched in anger.

"I am," the King said, turning his horse around. "Give the order."

Instead, Corlis drew his sword and stabbed King Felix through the back. The King arched, his muscles in spasm and hard in pain, and then he toppled backward off his horse.

Zollin saw the assassination, his mind refusing to believe what he saw. Finally, as Corlis reached out for the royal crown of Yelsia, Zollin shouted.

"The King is under attack!"

But the Royal Guard didn't move. The soldiers in the army looked around dumbly as Corlis placed the crown on his own head. Zollin saw the general's lips move, and then Selix and Tig roared in unison and dove straight for Zollin, bellowing fire as they came.

Chapter 32

Zollin and Brianna had flown through the night trying to catch up with Selix. They caught sight of the army late the next day. Zollin knew that trying to persuade the King was a long shot at best, but he wanted to distract Felix from Brianna's efforts to find out what had caused Selix to leave her and join the King. When they saw Tig flying with Selix, Brianna had been crushed. They had spoken little through their long flight. Ferno seemed strong, but Embyr was struggling to carry Brianna on the red dragon's back.

They landed and Zollin took the opportunity to say what he really felt to Brianna, before approaching King Felix.

"I know you love me," he said.

"Zollin, now isn't the time-" she tried to say, but he interrupted her.

"It may be the only chance I have," he said. "I will always love you. I don't know what made you change your mind, but I will always be here for you. I will always love you, no matter what. Be safe."

Then he slid off of Ferno's back and started walking toward the King's Army. Brianna looked down from Embyr's back as they flew back up into the air. She noticed for the first time since they had reunited in the Walheta Mountains that Zollin was still limping. She thought he was so selfless, always helping others but not himself. He needed someone to love him and take care of him.

She longed to be that person, but she was still afraid that King Felix would have her family killed. So she pushed the feelings down, closed her eyes, and tried to talk to Selix.

The great golden dragon would not respond to her. She could see, even at a distance, that both Selix and Tig watched her as she flew. She thought she could see them pleading with their eyes, but she didn't know what had happened to them, or why they wouldn't respond to her. She had never asserted herself as head of the pride, now she wished she had.

All afternoon they circled the huge army. Thousands of troops marched slowly across the grassy plains of Falxis. Some were on horseback; others led a long line of wagons filled with supplies for the army. Most marched on foot, wearing ill-fitting armor and carrying weapons they probably had no confidence using. She had to leap onto Ferno's back to let Embyr rest. The red dragon had great stamina, but the added weight was just too much for the smaller dragon to carry anymore. She tried over and over to reach out to Selix and Tig, but they rebuffed her every effort.

An hour before sunset she saw another dragon in the distance. She called to it mentally, and the beast changed its course. She waited impatiently to learn what the dragon had seen. She had sent it south to scout out the witch's army and now it was returning. Before she could even ask her mind was flooded with images. She was horrified at the creatures she saw, the grotesque figures lumbering along behind the Leffers. There were so many that her heart sank. She couldn't imagine how they could ever turn back such a tide of evil.

"Ferno, send those images to Zollin," she told the green dragon.

Ferno rumbled and then she saw Zollin, who was meekly marching at the rear of the army come flying forward, his power seeming to radiate off of him now with the urgency of their mission.

She watched as Zollin communicated with the King, then finally, Selix reached out to her. She saw an image of chains around the dragon's long, graceful neck. It was a cry for help; a message that conveyed that the great golden dragon was a prisoner somehow. Another image flashed of the King and his lackey general on the rooftop of the castle in Orrock, while commanding Selix, Tig, and Gyia. Brianna's blood boiled, but she knew she had to put those feelings away and help Zollin.

She sent Selix the images that she had seen in her mind. And then she saw the King ride out to Zollin. She and the other dragons were circling wide. It would be several minutes before they were back on the same side of the massive army as Zollin. They were too far away to hear what Zollin shouted. They were all watching the wizard when the King was slain. Ferno had just turned toward Zollin, instinct ringing in all their ears that something was wrong when Selix and Tig dove. Brianna couldn't believe her eyes; the dragons she had created and that she loved, were attacking Zollin.

Zollin immediately raised a shield around himself that protected him from the fiery breath of the dragons. He knew that someone or something was controlling the great beasts. He had spent time with Selix and with Tig. They were not the type of creatures that would turn on someone. He dropped down onto his stomach as the flames roared around him. His magic was churning inside him even hotter than the flames outside his shield. He felt the bump as Selix tried to snatch up his body with the golden talons, but his shield held.

Immediately, he rolled to his back where he could see. Tig and Selix had passed; both were climbing back up into the sky before turning for another pass at him. Zollin looked back and saw Ferno roaring as the huge green dragon sped to the wizard's aid. Brianna was standing up on Ferno's back, although how she kept her balance or kept from being blown backward by the screaming wind was a mystery to Zollin. He pointed at Selix and Tig and mentally pushed the thought, *keep them busy.*

Zollin ran forward, straight toward the army. There was only a squad of light cavalry in front of the King's Royal Guard. The rest of the army was spaced out behind the King and his generals. Felix had fallen onto the ground and the horses around the king's body were prancing nervously. Zollin wasn't sure who he needed to fight, but he knew that Corlis had killed the King and there was no way that Zollin would let the arrogant knight get away with it.

The Royal Guard, however, formed up around General Corlis as if he were the King. The general shouted an order and the light cavalry wheeled in formation, coming around the column to attack Zollin from the side. He didn't want to kill them, or even hurt them. He couldn't understand why the soldiers were obeying Corlis when the traitor had just murdered their king. Perhaps it was discipline to obey orders, or maybe a grand conspiracy, but Zollin didn't care. He didn't have the time to work out who was right and who was wrong. He needed to stop General Corlis and he needed to do it quickly.

Brianna was spending all her mental energy trying to break the hold that had come over Selix and Tig. It wasn't working. The smaller blue dragon sped past them not bothering to engage but trusting that its speed would see it past Embyr and Ferno.

"Stay together," Brianna shouted, sensing that Embyr wanted to turn and chase Tig.

Selix flared its huge golden wings, billowing fire and raising the massive talons. Ferno, not bothered by the flames, dove directly in front of Selix, drawing its own green wings in to keep them from being slashed to ribbons by Selix's talons.

Brianna waited until the last possible moment, and then she leaped into the air with her back arched, her arms and legs spread wide. The hot air from Selix's fiery blast blew her upward and she flipped, guiding her decent and landing lightly on Selix's back. The golden tail whipped up and crashed into the dragon's back, but Brianna had already swung around on the dragon's neck, as agile as a spider on a web.

Ferno and Embyr looped back up, forcing Selix to dive forward. Brianna turned and saw Tig diving for Zollin. The wizard, trying to avoid the horsemen, had levitated up, but he was now an easy target for the blue dragon. Brianna screamed Zollin's name, but Ferno had already warned Zollin of the danger.

Zollin let his magic pour out as he propelled himself up. He didn't want to be caught off guard and was thankful when Ferno flashed an image in his mind of Tig diving for him. The image was there and gone in less than a second, but it was enough of a warning. Zollin felt the dragon entering his field of magic. He clamped down on the dragon's wings while simultaneously sliding himself out of the way. Tig couldn't fly, and came hurdling down toward the group of guards who were massed in front of General Corlis. Zollin knew, at a glance, that Tig's crash would kill most of the Royal Guard, but Zollin didn't want the men dead. He strained to lift the falling dragon and released his hold on the beast's wings. It gave Tig just enough boost to keep the dragon from crashing, but the men all hit the deck in anticipation.

Zollin threw himself forward, thinking that he could attack Corlis while the guards were off balance. He was almost close enough to hit the general with a blast of his magical energy when he felt the huge dragon behind him. He threw up a hasty magical bubble around his body, just as Selix's teeth clamped down on him. Zollin wasn't hurt, but Selix carried him away from the army, flying higher and higher, the golden dragon's teeth grinding against the invisible bubble of Zollin's shields.

Brianna saw what was happening and for a moment she was frozen in terror. When Selix snatched Zollin out of the air, she expected to see blood and gore, but there was nothing. She could see Zollin's legs sticking out of Selix's mouth, and she could only hope that he was okay. She knew as Selix climbed higher and higher that she needed to do something, even though she was loath to hurt the dragon that had been her constant companion for so long. She let her hands heat up and placed them on Selix's neck. The dragon's scaly hide was impervious to fire, but Brianna's heat could melt solid rock. She quickly made the dragon so uncomfortable that it released Zollin and swatted at her with its tail again.

Brianna jumped away from the dragon, flipping and spinning. She saw Ferno flash past, catching Zollin on its broad back. Then Embyr was streaking under her, and Brianna touched down on the red dragon's back. The small dragon tucked into a tight curve and hurtled back toward the action.

"Wait!" she shouted. "Turn back."

She sent a mental image of Embyr and Ferno landing well away from the soldiers. They both agreed and turned wide, arcing turns that kept them and their riders well away from Selix who was hovering over the army.

"What's our plan?" Zollin shouted, as they came down on the grassy plain over a mile away from the army.

"I don't know," Brianna said. "But if we keep this up someone is going to get hurt."

"How do you fight dragons without hurting them?" Zollin asked.

"I'm not sure, but however they are being controlled, I can't get through to them."

"I can scare them," Zollin said. "At least I think I can. I scared the black dragon away from Orrock."

"How?" Brianna asked.

"Lightning."

Both dragons growled at Zollin.

"I won't hit them with it," he said.

"If the person controlling them doesn't allow them to leave, it could ruin them," Brianna said.

"So what can we do?"

"You have to attack the army."

"We need the army alive."

"So don't kill them," Brianna said. "Whoever is controlling Selix and Tig is in that group of soldiers. We have to take them out."

"And General Corlis too; he killed King Felix."

"Alright, so those are our targets."

"How do we know who is controlling the dragons?" Zollin asked.

"I have no idea."

"Great," Zollin said.

* * *

Tig would have been vulnerable going after the others alone and General Corlis refused to let the huge golden dragon leave the station directly above them unless they were under attack. He could see the wizard and the other dragons waiting and plotting their next move, so he decided to go on the offensive.

He called up the cavalry. Most of the King's horse soldiers had marched south from Felson, but General Corlis had one hundred light horse soldiers and two hundred heavily armed knights on horseback. He ordered the light horse soldiers to attack. The riders had helmets and shields, but no other armor. They carried lances, but the horses were not armored and were bred for speed.

"Attack them," he told the commander. "Move straight toward them and drive them away."

"Won't their dragons burn us up?" the commander asked.

"No, I don't think they will," Corlis said. His eyes grew narrow as he saw the commander looking at the body of King Felix lying crumpled on the ground. "You can obey me, Commander, or join him."

"Yes, Sire," the commander said.

Corlis smiled. He knew that if he could convince the Royal Guard to side with him, the rest of the King's Army would follow. Once he had the crown and control of the dragons, no one could stop him from taking the throne in Orrock, perhaps not in any kingdom.

"I don't think they want to harm the army, so charge straight at them," Corlis instructed. "If they land again, charge again. Don't let them rest. Understood."

"Yes, Sire," the commander said.

Corlis stood in his stirrups and watched as the cavalry galloped forward, kicking up dust in the fading daylight. He watched as the dragons took flight again and then an idea struck him. *If the wizard and dragon lady could ride on the huge creatures, why not him.*

Down! He ordered Selix.

The huge, golden dragon landed next to the column of troops. Corlis swung down off of his horse and was about to walk over to the dragon when General Grigg drew his sword and attacked. Grigg had once been a formidable warrior, but years of command had slowed his reactions and weakened his sword arm. He kicked his horse which leapt forward, but Corlis had been expecting resistance from the other generals. He jumped clear of his horse and drew his own sword, but it was an unnecessary reaction. Three Royal Guardsmen attacked the general with their throwing knives. One glanced off the general's polished breastplate, but the other two found their mark. General Grigg toppled out of his saddle and lay moaning as his life's blood leaked out on the ground.

Corlis smiled cruelly and then walked confidently toward the massive, golden beast. Selix growled angrily, but Corlis was confident in his control over the dragon.

On your belly! He commanded. He preferred to use mental commands over spoken ones. He thought it made him look more powerful to his troops. Selix lowered the massive body to the ground and extended one leg. Corlis climbed carefully up onto the golden dragon's back. Then, the huge dragon took to the air. Corlis held on tightly, forcing himself to stay calm as the ground receded below him. He needed time to get used to flying on the big dragon; there were no stirrups or reins to hold onto, not even a saddle horn or blanket. He sat just behind Selix's long neck, using his legs as well as his hands to hold onto the rough scales. He leaned forward and watched as the other dragons circled even farther away than before.

* * *

"We should wait until dark," Zollin said. Then I could sneak into their camp and take them out."

"Do we have time for that?" Brianna asked.

"Not really."

He considered his options again. The renegade general had sent the cavalry against them, causing them to fly up and further away. It was clear that he wouldn't make the mistake of letting Brianna draw the dragons away from the army so that Zollin could attack him.

"There's only one way to do this," Zollin said after having considered his options.

"And what's that?"

"We go straight at them," he said.

"Wait," Brianna said. "The general is getting on Selix."

"You mean he's going to ride the dragon?"

"It looks that way."

Zollin couldn't see as well as Brianna and the dragons, but they watched as Selix rose back up into the air. Ferno sent Zollin a mental image of General Corlis on Selix's back.

"How do you think he's planning to protect himself from a fiery attack?" Zollin asked.

"I don't think he is," Brianna said.

"Let's do it."

The dragons flew forward, separating so that they could come toward Selix from different directions. Tig shot toward Ferno. The smaller blue dragon was fast and instead of making a strafing run, the dragon barreled straight into the bigger, green dragon. Ferno rose up at the last second to protect Zollin. Tig crashed into Ferno's stomach with such force that it knocked the bigger dragon backward in the air, snapping ribs in the process. Tig fell, and the smaller dragon had broken its leg and one wing. It spiraled down and crashed hard on the ground, breaking more bones.

Zollin was thrown by the impact. It took him a moment to regain his senses. As his magic slowed his fall, he was almost on the ground. It took a huge effort on his part to reverse his own momentum, but he managed to land without hurting himself. Ferno, on the other hand, was barely able to stay in the air.

Zollin let Ferno know he was okay and they both turned to see Embyr and Brianna's attack. Selix was waiting to swat Embyr out of the sky with its huge tail, but Embyr stayed out of range. Brianna produced huge balls of orange fire, which she hurdled across the distance at the golden dragon and its rider. Selix twisted, so that the fire hit the golden scales, not its human rider. Brianna didn't stop, as Embyr flew around the larger dragon, she hurled fire bombs as fast as she could. It seemed like Selix was forced onto the defensive, but then suddenly the bigger dragon darted forward, the long neck stretching out, the huge mouth gaping open.

Zollin saw Brianna perform a rear flip, summersaulting off of Embyr's back. The smaller, red dragon tried to twist away in midair, but Selix was too fast. The golden dragon's razor sharp teeth snapped down, tearing into Embyr's neck and swinging back and forth before tossing the lifeless body of the smaller dragon away, like a dog attacking a squirrel.

Ferno roared in anger, and Zollin dropped to his knees. The dragon he'd spent the night with in the storm, the same dragon he'd bonded with over countless miles, was now gone. He felt the loss deep in his gut, and he sent his magic up into the sky. He could feel the tiny particles there, floating harmlessly. He began to swirl them, letting the particles clash and rub together, letting the energy and heat build.

Brianna flipped and twirled quickly down to the ground. She knew that Embyr was dead, but she didn't have time to be sad. She knew Selix was coming for her next, and the fire balls wouldn't hold the big, golden dragon back. She needed a way to move out of the dragon's reach, but she couldn't fly on her own.

As soon as her feet hit the ground she was running and looking up over her shoulder. Selix was diving, but the human on its back was having trouble hanging on, so the dragon was forced into a slower, shallower dive. It only gave Brianna a few seconds, but it was enough time for her to escape. She let her heat build and build as she ran, then she stopped and sent all of her fire into the ground. The intense heat melted the soil and then the bedrock underneath. She slipped into the molten hole that opened beneath her and disappeared.

Chapter 33

Zollin was terrified for Brianna. He knew she could handle the fall, but he wasn't sure how she would survive after that. Still, he knew his best chance for saving her lay in his power and the spell he was casting now. It was really the only hope he could think of. He felt the heat from his magic blowing through him and up into the sky. Billions of tiny particles swirled and clashed. He was so intent on his spell that he almost didn't hear the thunder of one hundred horses charging toward him. In fact, he felt the ground rumbling before he realized what he was hearing.

He didn't know how close the horses were, or if he would even survive, he only knew that if he didn't complete the spell he was working on, Brianna would have no chance. He sent a quick mental message to Ferno asking for help, then returned his attention to the spell.

Ferno had wanted to fly to Brianna's aid, but the pain in the big dragon's side made fast movement impossible. The huge, green dragon was able to stay in the air, but just barely. When it got Zollin's message, a quick glance revealed the danger. Ferno dove, roaring in pain as it flared its wings to land. The wings fluttered under the pressure and Ferno dropped the last ten feet, landing with an earth shaking crash between Zollin and the cavalry that was almost upon him.

The horses reared and Ferno roared again, blowing fire up into the sky in an angry display that spooked the horses. Several of the riders were thrown from the saddle and a few were even injured in the fall, but the charge failed and the cavalry commander called his troops back.

Zollin just needed a few more seconds; the energy was building. He felt the little flashes as the lightning charged from the friction of the swirling particles. Then, at last, he released the energy and a dazzling bolt of lightning arced across the sky. The resulting crackle and boom of thunder caught Selix's attention. The big dragon, which had just seen Brianna disappear into the earth, swerved away from the army and started flying south.

Then, just as suddenly, it turned back, roaring in fury as it flew back toward the army. Zollin released another bolt of lightning; this one slammed down to the ground and the pop was so loud that it even startled Zollin. Ferno moaned like a scared puppy. Tig, still on the ground from its injuries, lay flat against the earth. Selix, who was closest to the lightning, swerved suddenly, and General Corlis nearly lost his hold on the dragon. The crown slipped from his head and for an instant, Selix and Tig were free. They both cried out to Brianna for help, but she was nowhere to be found and Corlis risked his life to move the golden circlet back in place.

Selix swooped to the ground and Corlis climbed down. Zollin was focused on his magic, but Ferno was sending him mental images of what was happening. The cavalry was trying to flank Ferno and charge at Zollin again, while the army commanders were having trouble keeping the foot soldiers from breaking and running. Chaos seemed to be everywhere, but General Corlis sent Selix after Zollin.

The wizard saw the dragon launch itself into the air and fly toward him. Ferno roared, and Zollin knew the green dragon would sacrifice itself to save him. Zollin had to risk something. He couldn't let Ferno get hurt any worse, but he couldn't take out Selix without at least some risk to the golden dragon. He made up his mind and hoped that Brianna would forgive him, and then he dropped a lightning bolt directly into Selix's path. The energy was growing, and the lightning was hard to control. Zollin tried his best not to hurt the big, golden dragon, but the lightning struck too closely to the dragon's face. The light blinded the dragon, and the energy singed the golden scales. Selix tried to swerve away, but the tip of its wing was caught in the bolt and burned away. Selix crashed to the ground, gouging a long crater in the soft, grassy earth.

Zollin felt bad that he had hurt Selix, but now he had to act, to stop Corlis from usurping the throne and getting the King's Army killed. He ended the lightning spell and levitated himself forward. The Royal Guardsmen were forming up in front of Corlis who had remounted his charger. Zollin lowered himself to the ground barely a hundred paces from the mass of guards around Corlis just as the sun cast it's last scarlet rays across the sky. There was still enough light to see by, but it was fading fast.

Zollin raised a magical shield between himself and the guards, several of which hurled their famed throwing knives at him, but the weapons merely bounced off the invisible barrier.

"Stop this madness, Corlis," Zollin shouted. "Your dragons are beaten; release these men before anyone else gets hurt."

"Never!" Corlis cried. "I am King of Yelsia now, and no one will stop me."

"You're mad," Zollin shouted again.

Suddenly, Corlis' horse began to jump and buck. Heat rose from the ground in a massive wave, and the horse's hooves sank into the red hot soil. The horse screamed and jumped, trying to get away, throwing Corlis to the ground and sending the royal crown inscribed with the names of the dragons flying. In that instant when the royal guards looked back at their General, Zollin sent his magical barrier rushing toward them. It hit and knocked the first row of men backward. The magical push hadn't been strong enough to kill, and Zollin only hoped none of the elite soldiers would be injured. The first row of men were knocked back into the others, and chaos erupted.

General Corlis screamed in pain, his hair singeing from the heat as he scrambled to his knees, which sank into the turf as his trousers caught fire. Then Brianna, covered in molten flame, rose up behind Corlis like a fiery god of the underworld. The entire army froze, every eye turned toward Brianna. Corlis turned too, screaming as Brianna wrapped her fiery arms around his chest and pulled him down into the ground, which was glowing now and starting to bubble like molten lava. Corlis screamed until he disappeared under the ground.

Zollin knew that he had only a moment before the entire army broke and ran in panic. If that happened, Yelsia would be lost, along with the other kingdoms. He magically amplified his voice so that everyone in the army could hear him.

"Wait!" he shouted. "Don't flee. Listen to me. I am Zollin, Wizard of the Five Kingdoms. General Corlis' treachery has been witnessed by you all, and so has his punishment. Now is not the time for panic. We must work together."

General Tolis rode toward Zollin. He was an older man, proud and strong, yet he had been cowed by General Corlis and now his king was dead. His only thought was to get the army to safety.

"What would you have us do?" he shouted.

"We must return to the ships," Zollin said. "An evil army is marching north. We must join the other forces massing at the Walheta to stop them."

There was a murmuring across the army, but Zollin, his voice returned to normal, stepped toward General Tolis.

"You must lead them back," he urged General Tolis. "Sailing north is the only way to get to the mountains before the army of the witch overtakes us."

"And what will you do?" the General asked. "Are you taking up the crown of Yelsia?"

"No," Zollin said, the pain of what he knew he had to say sent pain straight through him. "Yelsia has a king," he said, "Prince Willam. The Prince will be in the mountains. He leads the cavalry from Felson."

The general nodded, satisfied with that answer. He turned his horse, and Zollin amplified his voice again.

"King Felix has fallen. We will honor him. Prince Willam is with the King's Cavalry in the Walheta Mountains. We will go to him."

There was more murmuring, and then someone shouted, *long live King Willam!* Others took up the chant, and General Tolis gave orders to the commanders. The Royal Guard picked up King Felix's body and carried it on their shoulders while the rest of the army began to slowly turn back toward the coast. The light cavalry picked up their wounded and moved back toward the long column of soldiers and wagons.

Zollin, exhausted, fell to his knees. Tears spilled from between his eyes. He was so tired of fighting, so tired of death. He mourned for Embyr and even for King Felix, but more for what the King could have been than what the man was in life.

"You give a good speech," Brianna said from behind Zollin.

He turned and his heart nearly skipped a beat. She was clothed in dancing flames, her hair blown back by the heat and her face radiant. She was so beautiful that he thought he could sit and stare at her forever.

"What?" she said, self-consciously.

"You're so beautiful," he said.

"Zollin!"

"I'm sorry," he said. "I guess I shouldn't say that but I can't help it. You were amazing."

"As were you," she said, her gaze so penetrating that Zollin thought his heart was heating up in his chest.

"I hurt Selix," he said sadly. "I didn't mean to."

"It couldn't be helped," Brianna said. "I can heal the dragons."

"Even Embyr?" Zollin asked.

"No," Brianna said sadly. "Embyr is gone forever."

"Damn," Zollin said softly.

"It was a noble sacrifice. We don't have time to mourn now."

"You're right," Zollin said. "Is there any chance the army can make it back to the coast before Gwendolyn's forces overtake them?"

"I don't think so," Brianna said.

"Then we have to slow them down. You get started healing the dragons. I'll get us some supplies and make sure that the army moves as quickly as possible."

Zollin went first to a supply wagon. He hurt all over as the adrenaline from the battle wore off. He was so tired he thought he could lie down on the ground and sleep for a week, but that simply wasn't an option. He got food, water, and a change of clothes for Brianna. Then, he levitated himself to where General Tolis was meeting with the commanders of the army.

"Zollin," the commander said deferentially.

"General, I'm sorry to interrupt but I must press on you the urgency of our situation."

"What exactly are we facing?" asked one of the commanders.

"An army of magically enhanced people," Zollin said. "I don't know how they will fight or how hard they will be to kill, but the witch that has transformed them into her army is deadly. I would expect nothing less than ruthless efficiency from her minions."

"How much time do we have?" Tolis asked.

"They don't sleep," Zollin said. "They don't need rest, and probably don't even eat. They were less than a day away a couple of hours ago."

"There's no way we can make it back to the coast before they reach us," said one of the commanders. "We have no choice but to form up in a defensive position and make a stand."

"No," Zollin said. "We have to get you to the Walheta Mountains. That's where we will make our stand. It's the only chance we have of defeating her army."

"But there isn't enough time," the commander argued.

"So I'll buy us some time," Zollin said. "The dragons and I will delay the evil army as long as we can. If we fail, we will send word to prepare your defense. But you must march through the night. Don't stop until you reach the coast. Get your men and your supplies loaded as fast as possible. You can rest on the voyage north."

"How long should we wait for you?" Tolis asked.

"You shouldn't. Brianna and I will move north with the dragons once you all are safely on the ships and sailing north."

"You're sure this plan will work?" asked one of the commanders.

"I'm not sure of anything, except that if we fail now, all is lost."

"Alright," General Tolis said. "You heard the man. Our King is in the mountains. We will go to him with all haste. Get your troops moving as quickly as possible."

"General," Zollin said as the other commanders turned away. "I have to know who was controlling the dragons and how they did it."

"I have no idea," Tolis said.

"Don't lie to me now," Zollin said. "We can't go into battle and have the dragons pulled away by some unseen force."

"I know the King sent someone to Ebbson keep to find out how to control the dragons. But I was never included in the discussions when the scholars were brought back."

"Who was?"

"General Corlis for sure, but I don't know who else."

"Was the King close to anyone else besides the general?"

"Not that I'm aware of," Tolis said.

"Okay, well we'll just have to hope for the best."

Zollin started to leave, but Tolis grabbed his arm.

"Thank you," he whispered. "Thank you for doing what we should have done."

"There's no need to thank me," Zollin said. "I only want to ensure that Yelsia has a bright future."

"You be careful," Tolis said. "We need you."

"Thank you, General, but the truth is we need each other. I can't do this alone."

"You won't have to, Zollin of the Five Kingdoms. I'll get these bastards to the Walheta Range if it's the last thing I do."

Zollin smiled and General Tolis snapped him a perfect salute before turning back to his troops. Then, Zollin began the long walk back to Brianna. She had moved to Ferno first and after a few minutes, she was covering the thick, muscular dragon with pure white flames. Zollin went first to Selix, but the golden dragon closed its eyes and would not look at Zollin.

"I'm sorry," he told the huge beast. "I didn't mean to hurt you."

The mental image of Selix killing Embyr flashed in his mind and the dragon moaned mournfully.

"It wasn't your fault," Zollin said.

The dragon couldn't be consoled, and he moved on to Tig. Along the way he found the king's crown. It was a simple gold circle, thin along the bottom edge and thicker at the top so that it would rest securely on a person's head. He picked it up and slipped it into the pack of supplies without looking at it, and then he turned his attention back to Tig. The smaller blue dragon lay panting for breath, the pain evident with each wheezing breath.

"I'm sorry I can't help you," Zollin told the blue dragon. "Brianna will be here soon."

He sat with the dragon who suffered in silence. Zollin guessed that their shame at having been controlled and forced to turn on Brianna and their fellow dragons was hard to deal with. He hoped in time that the shame would diminish. He remembered how difficult it was for Mansel to live with his actions while he was under the influence of Gwendolyn's enchantment.

Zollin ate quietly, watching Brianna work. Healing a dragon was much different than Zollin's power to heal. What he did in quiet concentration, Brianna did with bright, billowing fire. He wanted to sleep, but he knew there was no time to rest. Once Brianna finished healing Ferno, Zollin and the massive green dragon took to the air, flying southwest to meet Gwendolyn's army.

Zollin could see very little of the dark landscape far below them, but Ferno could see almost as well at night as in the daylight. They flew for two hours before catching sight of Gwendolyn's army. There was no torchlight, no camps, just a sea of lumbering flesh.

Ferno sent Zollin mental images, and he was horrified. It would be difficult to kill people he knew were no longer in control of their actions. They had been physically and mentally altered by Gwendolyn's evil power. Zollin guessed that at the rate they were moving, they would reach the King's Army shortly after dawn.

Chapter 34

Brianna put her hands on Tig's face. The blue dragon's body was broken, the right front leg was shattered, the thin bones of the dragon's wing were snapped in several places, but most disturbing were the broken ribs which were causing the dragon to bleed inside. Blood was slowly filling the dragon's lungs.

Brianna had no idea how she could know so much about the dragon just by touching it, but somehow she knew. She also knew that her fire could heal the dragon; the only question for her was how long it would take to heal the little blue dragon. She knew that she didn't have much time and if the witch's army overtook the dragons before they were well enough to fly, they would be killed. Brianna simply wasn't sure she had enough time to heal both Tig and Selix.

"I'll be right back," she told the blue dragon. She hurried to where Selix lay prone on the ground, the soft soil piled up around the huge body where the impact had carved a massive crater in the ground. She put her hands on Selix's head and the dragon moaned. Selix was blind; many of the dragon's iron-like scales were marred by the lightning and were now brittle as clay. The tip of the dragon's left wing was burned away, and most of the leathery wing was scorched and burned; there was no way it support the huge dragon in flight. Worst of all, the dragon's eyes were ruined.

"Damn," Brianna said.

She was so angry that the dragons had been under someone's control and that whoever it was had so little regard for the life of her pride mates. She made a quick decision, even though she felt guilty about it. Tig needed her help more than Selix, but the bigger dragon was more of an asset than the little blue dragon. If she only had time to heal one, she decided it had to be Selix.

"Hold on," she told the dragon.

Then she stepped back and let her fire rage. She didn't have time to do things slowly. She needed to heal the dragons as quickly as possible. Selix moaned as the fire washed over the golden scales. Brianna couldn't see through the white flames, they billowed out and over the Dragon's body, but she could feel the subtle magic of her kind. There was a feeling of mending happening to the dragon, and she trusted it was exactly what Selix needed. The only question now was *would it happen fast enough?*

* * *

Zollin knew he didn't have a lot of time to waste. Still, he decided he needed to know more about the massive army below him before he attacked. Even with his limited eyesight in the darkness, he knew that the army was too big for the combined forces in Walheta to stop. If the evil army didn't split up and go around both sides of the Great Sea of Kings, Gwendolyn's wicked army would eventually overrun the Yelsian forces.

There were more Leffers than he wanted to see. The big, horse-like monsters with their insect wings, scorpion tails, and human upper bodies were a horrific sight. They led the army, which meant the first casualties would eventually be the very monsters the survivors would have to fight. Zollin knew that the Leffers were vulnerable to fire and his electric magical energy. He could hurt them; he knew that, but what about the others? And did they know he was there, high above them, circling and studying them?

Finally, he decided that there was nothing more to be learned from observation alone. He let his magic flow down, but his magic was rebuffed by the dark magic that animated the army. The Leffers were evil creatures that acted as if they were controlled by a single consciousness or hive mind. But the army was actually supported by Gwendolyn's magic. The witch had to empower her monsters, and Zollin couldn't imagine the strain. Either Gwendolyn was stretched to her breaking point, or she had become immeasurably powerful. It made Zollin shudder to even contemplate what facing her in battle would be like. In the pit of his stomach, he felt the inevitability of that conflict. If they were to stop Gwendolyn, at some point he would have to face her and defeat her.

"Well, Ferno, we have a job to do," he said, rubbing the dragon's neck affectionately. "We better get to it."

Ferno roared, the sound seemed to make the very air quiver with fear. Then the dragon dove. They went straight down, Zollin using his magic to hold him tight to the dragon's back. Ferno unleashed a torrent of fire on the army below. The fire ignited the grass around them, and the rags that were what remained of the peoples' clothes before they were transformed by the witch's dark magic. Their skin shriveled, and the monstrous beings screamed in agony. Those consumed by the flames fell; their bodies burning up. Those on the fringe of the attack were burned, but they kept moving, as if they didn't even feel the pain.

"Not bad," Zollin shouted.

They could see that the army had stopped marching and were glaring up at them.

"Looks like we slowed them down," he added.

Ferno sent an image of the Leffers flying up toward them.

"Well, here we go," Zollin said.

Ferno turned in a tight loop and then charged at the Leffers who were flying upward slowly to engage him. The Leffers had powerful wings, but their bodies were so heavy and ill-suited for flight that they were neither fast nor agile. Ferno blew fire at the Leffers and then swooped away, never getting close enough for the creatures to engage him. For the next hour they flew hard, Zollin blasting any of the creatures that came close with molten magical energy. He didn't want to use his electrical magic, since the dragons were so frightened of lightning.

They fought hard, but there were so many Leffers that after a couple of passes, they were forced to flee the horde of monsters. Once they were far enough away, the Leffers would fly back down to their position at the front of the army and resume their trek north. Then Zollin and Ferno would begin the attack again.

It was a slow, tiresome process, and hardly efficient, even though the number of creatures that were slain grew with every pass. They seemed to be in limitless supply, and Zollin found it hard not to become discouraged. He could tell they were being pushed further and further north. He focused on the western flank of the evil army and had successfully slowed the monsters on that side, but he couldn't stop the entire line.

They landed near a stream a couple of miles from the horde of monsters moving north. They drank and rested for just a few minutes. Zollin couldn't shake the feeling that Brianna was in danger. He kept expecting to see her with Selix and Tig flying up to them at any minute, but they were nowhere to be found. He had flown southwest, knowing that the King's Army was marching west and so he didn't need to stop the entire body of the marching monsters, only the western flank. But did that leave Brianna in danger? He wasn't sure. He had thought she would join him as soon as she healed the dragons, but she had yet to arrive and he couldn't help but worry.

They attacked again; this time trying a new tactic. Zollin moved on the ground, waiting until the Leffers rose up to fight Ferno. Then he rushed forward and blasted the grotesque army with his powerful magic. Dozens fell, never to rise again, but the others just stepped over the fallen and kept moving. Zollin blasted them again and again, but was forced to move back as the horde drew near and the Leffers began returning to the ground.

The sun was starting to lighten the sky, and Zollin's only relief was that they hadn't yet caught up to the King's Army. Zollin and Ferno were both exhausted. Zollin's magic was almost too hot to wield, and he was lightheaded and shaky. They landed once more and Zollin ate. There wasn't enough food in his pack to curb Ferno's hunger. The dragon drank his fill from a swiftly running stream but then they took to the air again.

An image of Brianna on Selix flashed in Zollin's mind, and he was filled with a questioning wonder.

"I don't know where they are," Zollin said. "I only hope they're alright."

* * *

Brianna finished healing Selix an hour before dawn. Her head was spinning from the exertion, and she wondered how she had worked for days in the mountains creating dragons with no food or rest. Now all she wanted was something cool to drink and a chance to close her eyes. She found the supplies that Zollin had left for her as Selix took to the sky. She gulped lukewarm water from the canteen, and then poured some over her head. The water felt cool on her scalp. She scrubbed her face and carried the supplies over to where Tig was waiting. The blue dragon was unconscious and barely breathing. Brianna felt a wave of guilt for taking a moment to herself while Tig lay on death's doorstep.

She immediately began work on the blue dragon, but the long process was soon interrupted. Brianna saw an image of the monster army coming toward her. She cursed herself for being so slow and doubled her efforts, but Tig was simply too wounded to heal quickly. The sun rose and the warm rays added their strength to Brianna's efforts, but soon she could hear the heavy footsteps of the horrific army that was approaching. Selix was worried, but Brianna refused to stop working on Tig.

The smaller dragon was coming around, but was far from being able to fly. At Selix's urging, Brianna glanced over her shoulder and saw the monsters less than a mile away.

"Tig, can you hear me?" Brianna shouted over the flames. "I don't have time to finish. We're in danger. We've got to move you, I'm sorry."

Brianna let her flames die. Then she stepped forward and put her hand on Tig's head. The dragon's internal bleeding had stopped and most of the blood had drained from the dragon's lungs, but its leg was still shattered and the wing ruined. There was no way for Tig to escape the evil horde that was approaching without help.

Brianna quickly pulled on the clothes that Zollin had left her and pulled the strap of the pack of supplies over her shoulder. Selix swooped down just as the Leffers moved forward to attack Brianna. She sent a wall of fire blazing toward the monsters, and then she jumped into the air, flipping over backward and landing on Selix's back, just as the golden dragon snatched up Tig with its huge talons.

Tig had been asleep, but the jolt from being snatched by Selix woke the poor beast, as waves of pain from its leg and wing rolled over the dragon's consciousness. Tig roared, but it was more of a high-pitched wail of agony. Brianna had to put the thought out of her mind as she watched the Leffers rise up after them. She threw balls of fire at the monsters. It reminded her of throwing snowballs with her sisters when she was just a child, only this time the effects were horrific. The balls of fire would burst much like a snowball when they hit, only they spread the fire to whatever they touched. The Leffers' screams made her blood run cold. A hit to the head of one of the creatures would kill them, but a hit to the body only wounded them. The sight of the hideous creatures following her, their bodies blackened, blood and puss oozing from the hideous wounds, was enough to almost paralyze her with fear.

As each monster drew near she found the courage and the strength to drive it away. Finally, Selix turned and spewed a gout of flame that drove the horde of flying horse-like creatures back to the ground. Then Selix swooped forward, locking its wide, leathery wings and rising up on the air currents.

"We must go west," Brianna said. "We have to find Zollin and see that the army escapes."

Selix turned and flew. After an hour of flight, the monster army started to thin. Brianna could tell that Zollin was being effective, her only question was how effective? It took another hour to reach the army. They were not in danger yet, but they still had half a day's journey just to make the coast. Brianna and Selix dove down and gently laid Tig in one of the wagons. Brianna jumped off of Selix's broad back and landed near the officers.

"I must ask your help," she said.

"What is it?" General Tolis said, turning his horse to face her.

"The monsters are close," she told him. "You need to move faster."

"We're marching as fast as we can, ma'am," said one of the other officers.

"Then you're all going to die," she said savagely. "This is not a request. Move faster or die. Do you understand?"

The men nodded.

"I can't promise that wagon will support the weight of your dragon," Tolis said.

"It will have to do. We can't fight and carry Tig. The dragon is much wounded. Just keep that wagon moving, and I'll do the rest when I can."

"Alright," Tolis said. "We'll push our men to their limits."

"I'm sorry, but it's the only way."

Brianna ran and jumped as Selix swooped low again. This time she landed on the dragon's tail, and the big, golden beast flipped her up and forward. The soldiers watched as she twirled through the air and then dropped lightly onto Selix's back.

* * *

Zollin and Ferno were at yet another stream, this one barely a trickle, but it was in a deep ditch. He scooped up water with his hands and slurped the cool liquid down between gasps for breath. He had no more strength to fight with. He didn't know how Ferno was able to keep moving. Then he remembered how he had joined with the dragon's unique magic in the forests of Baskla after the gargoyle attack. The dragon magic had been a strong, steady anchor to his own reserves. After drinking, he climbed onto Ferno's back and let his magic mingle with the dragon's. Ferno rumbled appreciatively, and Zollin felt his inner defenses strengthening. The heat from his own power cooled, and he felt a little better.

Then an idea struck him. He thought it might work to really slow down the lumbering monsters, but he could only do it with Brianna's help. He and Ferno had fought through the night and most of the morning, and now they rose up to do it again. Their strategy had not changed and although they had slain hundreds of monsters and Leffers, it hadn't seemed to make a dent in the huge army. Zollin's only real comfort was that he had managed to slow the massive army, at least a little.

They made pass after pass at the monsters. Each fiery blast that reached the transformed human army caused them to swirl and move in different directions. It was like kicking over an ant hill and watching the tiny ants running around in confusion. Unfortunately, the Leffers were always there to drive them away, so they could only slow the army once for every three or four attack runs they made.

They were in the middle of a hard fight when Ferno sent a mental image of Brianna and Selix flying toward them. This time the image was combined with a sense of relief and excitement. Zollin sent two more blobs of molten magic at the Leffers behind them and then turned to look for Brianna.

"Did you see Tig?" he shouted.

Ferno shook its mighty head, and they dove down to draw more Leffers away from the evil army. This time as they rose up, Selix came charging below them, blowing through the Leffers with a powerful blast of fire.

Ferno and Selix had obviously communicated because Selix then dove down and attacked the monsters. Brianna and Selix made pass after pass while Zollin and Ferno drove off the Leffers who tried to stop them. It was an effective strategy, but Zollin knew that he and Ferno couldn't keep it up much longer. When they rose back up into the air to regroup, Zollin shouted at Brianna.

"Follow me, I have an idea!"

They flew north, passing the edge of the monster army and continued moving until they could see the King's Army in the distance. The troops were jogging, and Zollin guessed they must be even more exhausted than he was. Ferno swooped down, and they landed hard. The gracefulness of the dragon had long been replaced by utter fatigue.

Selix and Brianna swooped in beside Zollin.

"They aren't going to make it," Brianna said.

"They might, they're only a few miles from the beach."

"How long will it take them to load everyone and everything onto the ships?"

"I don't know, but I think I can buy them some time. What if we were able to make a molten river around the landing site?"

"You mean turn the ground to lava?" Brianna said.

"Yes, almost like a moat around a castle. Could you do that?"

"I could," Brianna said. "But the size of the army would make it difficult. I wouldn't be good for much of anything else."

"I think we have to try it. We won't be able to hold the monsters back, but if we can give them a barrier they can't cross, they may even just go around us without attacking."

"What about the Leffers? They could just fly over the ground."

"We'll have to fight them," Zollin said. "But maybe the army could help. They have archers."

"It's worth a try," Brianna said.

They flew back to the army, which was only two miles from the coast. Zollin outlined his plan, while Brianna started carving a huge arc around the beachhead were the army's ships were gathered. Turning the soil into lava was extremely difficult, so instead she decided to heat the soil until anything crossing it would burst into flames.

Zollin began to levitate the supply wagons onto the beach and then unloaded the contents onto the boats. By the time the army arrived, Brianna had finished half of the arc, and Zollin had eight boats ready to return to the ships and be unloaded. The soldiers went immediately to work. There wasn't time to take the wagons apart, so they were left behind. The supplies and horses were loaded first, then the troops.

Zollin and Tolis arranged the archers so that they could defend the army as the monsters approached. Selix had flown high in the air, sending mental images to Brianna and Zollin to keep them updated on the approaching horde. The army was halfway through getting all the soldiers ferried out to the ships when the Leffers appeared.

"Archers ready!" Zollin shouted.

He knew his own magic and the fire of the dragons would be more effective, but he was curious to find out how the Leffers would respond to more conventional warfare. The archers drew back their bows and as the Leffers crossed the barrier; they released their first volley. The archers had already been given the opportunity to fire several test shots so that they had a good idea of how to aim to cover the distance from their firing positions to the edge of Brianna's fiery barrier.

The wagons had also been moved to create a wall of cover for the archers to stand behind. The arrows arced into the sky, tilted then fell like a deadly rain on the exposed Leffers. Arrows that hit the horse portion of the creatures only wounded, but arrows that found the human chest or head were deadly. Arrows bounced harmlessly off of the hardened segments of the scorpion tail, but they tore through the insectile wings and several of the Leffers dropped onto Brianna's fire line and burst into flames.

"At least we know your boundary works," Zollin said.

Brianna nodded, but was busy feeding continual heat into the ground. Zollin moved forward to confront the Leffers who had escaped the arrow barrage. He began to blast away with his magic. Blue energy crackled up and down his body, as he sent wave after wave of magical power into the creatures. The dragons joined in, diving and blasting the Leffers with gouts of fire. The soldiers moving onto the ships were exhausted, but seeing the Leffers scared them into an increased pace.

Occasionally, Zollin would glance over his shoulder to see how many more soldiers waited to be rowed out to the ships. It was dishearteningly slow. When the monsters started trying to cross Brianna's boundary, the scene became a nightmare. The wails of the grotesque creatures, as they burned alive, had been terrifying; as was seeing their bodies falling in the flames.

"It's working," Zollin said to Brianna. And he was right for about ten minutes. Unfortunately, the monsters kept coming, despite the obvious danger. Before long, the boundary was covered with bodies, so that the lumbering soldiers could walk across the barrier on the backs of their fallen comrades without being hurt.

"What now?" Brianna asked, panting.

"We take our positions and stand our ground until the last possible minute," Zollin shouted.

He and Brianna took up stations on either side of the killing ground that stretched in front of the archers. Selix and Ferno circled overhead. As the monstrous warriors came through the barrier, the archers began to fire careful shots. The hideous fighters never increased their pace and did not react to wounds. Only a shot to the heart or brain stopped the creatures. Zollin, unable to magically alter the poor creatures, was forced to use his magic against them physically. He waited until the brutes were nearly on top of him, and then he lashed out with a magical barrier that crashed into the monsters with supernatural strength. The blast would send the creatures flying back, their bones shattered.

More and more of the soldiers escaped to the ships, but it was a slow process. Brianna and the dragons poured fire onto the creatures, until heaping piles of charred carcasses littered the beachhead. Beyond the area where the soldiers sought to escape to the safety of the sea, the army of evil creatures marched on with single-minded purpose. They were like a swarm of insects that devoured everything in their path but paid no attention to what was happening all around them.

The work of holding the monsters back became harder and harder, until at last the archers were forced to retreat back to the waterline. Zollin and Brianna were picked up by the dragons. Everyone was exhausted, but they continued to fight. The piles of dead monsters made crossing the battle field difficult for them, but they climbed over their fallen companions, and went around the heaped up bodies. The dragons made pass after pass, spewing flame onto the mindless warriors. A few made it out to the waterline, and the soldiers were forced to fight them in close combat.

The monsters were enormously strong, hacking with their heavy swords. Shields were of little value, since the heavy blows of the creatures' swords shattered most shields. Nor was a sword able to parry the heavy weapons of the hideous warriors. But spears were especially effective, since they could stab at the creatures from a distance and the warriors seemed not to care if they lived or died. They offered no defense of their own, nor did they seem to learn from the mistakes of their companions. Their strategy didn't change. They came straight forward, killing anything within reach until they were killed themselves.

Finally, a last group of boats picked up nearly all the remaining warriors. Selix was carrying Tig again, taking the poor dragon out to one of the ships while Zollin levitated the remaining soldiers out to their ships. The monstrous army kept moving forward, no longer concerned with the Yelsia forces that had successfully evaded them. Ferno and Selix circled over the ships. The dragons were too big to land on the vessels and had no love of the water. Zollin and Brianna jumped from the dragons and landed on the massive flagship that had carried King Felix and his officers. General Tolis had taken charge and was doing a good job of organizing things. The ships' crews were already unfurling the sails and getting the armada moving north.

They placed King Felix's body on one of the smallest jolly boats. The King looked small in death, his skin waxy and his eyes dull. The crew on the big ship stood at attention, although most of the men were so tired they could hardly stand up.

"He was a noble ruler," General Tolis said. "His reign was not without hardship and his death was tragic, but he left an example of steadfast loyalty and determination that we can all admire and do our best to emulate. May the Gods carry him swiftly to the rest of kings."

The men cheered, and the boat was released. At a signal from Brianna, Selix spiraled down and incinerated the small boat. It floated for a time, the flames leaping high into the air, before it sank beneath the waves. Then Tolis met with Zollin and Brianna.

"What now?" he asked them.

"We have to prepare for the battle in the north," Zollin said. "You must do your best to make it there with all speed."

"We will," he said. "The captain assures me we can outrun the devils."

"Good," Zollin said. He pulled the King's crown out of his pack. "I picked this up on the battlefield," he said to Brianna. "You should take it to Prince Willam. It's his now."

"You should do it," she said, having trouble meeting his eye.

Part of Brianna wanted to celebrate. King Felix was dead and surely her parents were safe now, but she couldn't be certain of that. She didn't know what to say to Zollin, she was so tired and scared.

"No, you are his betrothed," Zollin said, trying not to sound bitter. "Besides, I'm not going north with you."

"What?" Brianna said in shock.

"You must," General Tolis said. "We cannot hold back this tide of evil creatures without you."

"You can, if you plan things well. The dwarves will be there. Prince Willam is a fine strategist, and Commander Hausey will be a great help. You will have Brianna and the dragons. That is more than you need. Ferno and I must go south to confront the witch."

"Not alone," Brianna said. "I'll go with you."

"No," Zollin said, his voice sounding angry. "You made your choice in Orrock, so now you must honor it."

"But Zollin, you don't understand," she tried to explain, tears springing up in her eyes.

"I understand the only thing that is important right now," he said. "And that is that I must stop Gwendolyn."

"But not alone," Brianna was saying. "I can't lose you."

"You'll never lose me," he assured her. "You must do what you can do. My fate lies south of here. No matter what happens, you know my feelings for you."

"You will be sorely missed," General Tolis said, holding out his hand.

Zollin shook it. "You have acquitted yourself well, General. Get these troops to the mountains, and you will be a hero."

"I don't care about any of that. Maybe I did once," he admitted, "but not anymore. I've seen too much. I only want to survive and to see my men survive."

"Good," Zollin said. "I wish you all luck."

"Zollin," Brianna said, putting her hand on his arm.

"I must go," he said stiffly. "I will miss you."

"Don't go," she whispered, but he was already levitating himself up into the air.

Selix dove down after Ferno and Brianna jumped high, landing on the golden dragon's back. They flew after Ferno, south down the beach. The horde stretched on as far as Zollin could see, but he assured the exhausted dragon that they could rest soon.

"I won't leave you," Brianna shouted at Zollin.

"You must," he said. "Take the crown and return to Willam."

"I don't love him, I love you."

Zollin wanted to believe her, but he didn't. How could she reject the Crown Prince for him? She deserved the very best in life, and Willam could give it to her. He was headed for a fate he could only guess at, and he was almost certain he would not return. It made him sad, but if he could ensure the safety of others it would be worth it. And, if he was being honest with himself, he wasn't sure he could watch Brianna be happy with someone else.

He kept his head down, trying hard to think, which was becoming difficult because he was so tired. There was a wide strip of sandy beach several dozen yards from the coast. It was a sandbar, little more than a temporary strip of sand that rose out of the water, but secure enough to let them shelter for the night. The dragons circled down. The sand was soft and warm. The two beasts nestled together and fell asleep almost instantly. Zollin walked to the water's edge, staring across the calm waters to the shore. The monstrous army had thinned but was still moving north in the darkness. Zollin guessed that Gwendolyn would keep sending the people she transformed north until she ran out of people to bewitch.

He sat down on the sand and hugged his knees. Brianna put her hand on his back. They were tired, filthy, and exhausted. They stayed that way for a long time, neither speaking. Finally, Brianna broke the silence.

"I wavered," she said softly. "Willam was so sweet and part of me liked the attention. I spent more time with him than I should have, even after I knew his intentions. I had to make sure of what I wanted."

"And you wanted him," Zollin said, his voice shaking just a little. "I don't blame you."

"No, Zollin. I chose you, but then King Felix threatened my family. He said if I told you or anyone else he would kill my parents and my sisters. He threatened to withhold the army if I didn't agree to marry Willam. I didn't know what to do. I wracked my brain trying to find a solution, but the only thing I could do was go along with things. But now King Felix is dead, and I don't have to marry Willam."

"Yes you do," Zollin said, trying not to sound coldhearted. "You gave your promise."

"I gave you my promise first. He had no right to ask me to break it."

"A promise to me is just words. A promise to a king..." he let the thought trail off. "Willam is a good man; he would not punish you for rejecting him, but you would have no place in Yelsia if you did. Neither would your family. The truth is that if we are somehow successful in this fight, there's no guarantee that we'll get the other kingdoms back. If Yelsia is all there is, you can't break your promise. Besides, we both know the chances of me coming back are almost nonexistent. I release you from your promise, Brianna."

"I don't want to be released," she said sadly.

"Willam needs you. Yelsia needs you. You'll be a great queen. The Five Kingdoms need you and your dragons, but not me. Perhaps I am the last wizard left in the world. Maybe that is the way it was meant to be. I don't know. But if I am to die fighting Gwendolyn, I will rest in death easier knowing that you are safe and that you are loved."

"No Zollin, I won't let you go alone."

"Okay," he said. "Okay. Let's rest then we'll decide."

Then he did something he had promised Brianna he would never do to her. He used his magic to make her drowsy. It wasn't difficult, as she was exhausted. He carried her in his arms, trying to memorize exactly how she felt. Her skin was so soft, and she was light, almost like a child. She smelled of smoke, but underneath that was a sweetness he burned into his memory. Then he laid her beside Selix. The massive golden tail came around instinctively, cradling her against the softer scales along the huge dragon's stomach.

He sat down and pulled the tattered sleeve from his tunic. With a little concentration the fabric began to shake, then blur, and finally transform into parchment. He had made three sheets, and he laid them on the sand. Then he found a small piece of driftwood and used his magic to burn it into charcoal. He let it cool while he thought of what he wanted to say. Then, he wrote a note, first to his father, then to Mansel, and finally to Brianna. He told them all he loved them and wrote personal things to each about how they had made his life better and what he hoped for their future. Then he said good-bye. In Brianna's note he asked her to deliver the others. He also asked her not to follow him. Then he rolled them up and tucked them into her pack.

"Ferno," Zollin said, nudging the green dragon. "We must leave."

The dragon grumbled but got to its feet. Zollin levitated up onto the huge dragon's back. Then they were off, flying south again, following the coast. The mutated army thinned until only the occasional straggler remained. Zollin looked at the countryside; it seemed so peaceful, as if nothing dark or scary was happening anywhere in the world. Ferno, despite the dragon's weariness, flew through most of the night. They finally settled in a thick grove of trees and slept just before dawn. Zollin was thankful that he was too tired to dream.

Epilogue

When Brianna woke up it was almost noon. She woke with a start and looked for Zollin, but not seeing Ferno she knew he had left. She cried and Selix, still heartsick over killing Embyr, cried with her. The dragon's tears fell and splashed onto the sand, turning it to glass wherever the tears fell.

As soon as Brianna could get control of herself, she stopped crying. She was so thirsty that she found her pack and pulled out the canteen. Zollin's letters fell out as well. She read them all, but read and reread her own, over and over. Then she packed everything away and wiped the tears from her face.

"It is time to go home, Selix," she said.

The dragon growled. She jumped up onto the dragon's back, and Selix jumped high into the air. They flew fast north, sailing up in the clouds. Brianna lay stretched out on the golden dragon's back, thinking about what Zollin had written, and doing her best to remember everything she could about him. The way he smiled, his thick brown hair that fell across his eyes, his strong arms and long fingers. She remembered the way he held her, the way his embrace felt strong, and safe, and tender, all at the same time. She remembered how he had looked battling Bartoom to keep her safe in Brighton's Gate. She remembered how she felt seeing him in Orrock when he had come to rescue her. She remembered their time in the Northern Highlands, working together, staring up at the stars each night, resting in one another's arms so warm.

That was how she would remember him, she vowed. No matter what happened, she would always remember Zollin. She would always love him, even if she couldn't be with him.

* * *

Dearest Brianna,

How can I express my love for you? I remember you as a girl in Tranaugh Shire, always so beautiful, fierce, and full of life. I remember you in the caverns of the dwarves, becoming the woman you were meant to be. Your memory is my strength, always.

I have many hopes for you. I hope above all that you will live a long, happy life. Marry Willam, he will make you happy and give you a future we could never dream of. Deliver these letters to Quinn and Mansel for me. And don't try to follow me. Your fate lies with the pride of dragons in the Walheta Mountains.

Comfort my father; I fear he will take my death hard. And remember me, my beloved. I hope that I won't be forgotten. I have gone to ensure that your future is good. Make the most of it, for both of us.

Zollin

About The Author

Toby Neighbors is the author of twenty novels who has fully embraced the digital age of publishing. Since 2012 Toby has written the best selling Five Kingdoms series, Lorik trilogy, and Avondale series. He lives in the mountains of north Idaho with his family and plans to write many more books including the Kingdoms in Chaos series which picks up where the Five Kingdoms series left off and includes characters from the Lorik trilogy.

Made in the USA
Middletown, DE
23 August 2020

16080967R00260